Dream OF HER Heart

Hearts of the War Book 3
by
USA Today Bestselling Author

SHANNA HATFIELD

Dream of Her Heart
Hearts of the War Book 3

Copyright © 2018 by Shanna Hatfield

ISBN: 9781723882319

For permission requests, please contact the author, with a subject line of "permission request" at the e-mail address below or through her website.

Shanna Hatfield
shanna@shannahatfield.com
shannahatfield.com

This is a work of fiction. Names, characters, businesses, places, events, and incidents either are the product of the author's imagination or are used in a fictitious manner. Any resemblance to actual persons, living or dead, business establishments, or actual events is purely coincidental.

Cover Design by Shanna Hatfield

To those who give their all...

Books by Shanna Hatfield

FICTION

CONTEMPORARY

Blown Into Romance
Love at the 20-Yard Line
Learnin' the Ropes
QR Code Killer
Rose
Saving Mistletoe
Taste of Tara

Rodeo Romance
The Christmas Cowboy
Wrestlin' Christmas
Capturing Christmas
Barreling Through Christmas
Chasing Christmas
Racing Christmas

Grass Valley Cowboys
The Cowboy's Christmas Plan
The Cowboy's Spring Romance
The Cowboy's Summer Love
The Cowboy's Autumn Fall
The Cowboy's New Heart
The Cowboy's Last Goodbye

Silverton Sweethearts
The Coffee Girl
The Christmas Crusade
Untangling Christmas

Women of Tenacity
A Prelude
Heart of Clay
Country Boy vs. City Girl
Not His Type

HISTORICAL

The Dove

Hardman Holidays
The Christmas Bargain
The Christmas Token
The Christmas Calamity
The Christmas Vow
The Christmas Quandary
The Christmas Confection

Pendleton Petticoats
Dacey
Aundy
Caterina
Ilsa
Marnie
Lacy
Bertie
Millie
Dally
Quinn

Baker City Brides
Tad's Treasure
Crumpets and Cowpies
Thimbles and Thistles
Corsets and Cuffs
Bobbins and Boots
Lightning and Lawmen

Hearts of the War
Garden of Her Heart
Home of Her Heart
Dream of Her Heart

···★ *Chapter One* ★★··

Portland, Oregon
May 1942

"Do they have wonders of nature like that where you're from, Lieutenant?" A gnarled finger entwined with soft blue yarn pointed out the train window in the direction of a massive waterfall.

Zane West stared at the cascade of silvery liquid as it tumbled and flowed over a rocky hillside, surrounded by lush greenery. The splendor of it was quite unexpected.

Then again, so was his traveling companion. Zane had dashed onto the train in Pendleton to find the only seat left was next to a tiny old woman who looked like a strong breeze would fell her. She'd given him a perfunctory glance, closed her eyes and napped the first part of the trip. About an hour ago, she'd awakened and kept him entertained with details about the areas through which they traveled.

He turned his gaze from the picturesque scene outside the window to the elderly woman who'd introduced herself as widow Esther Wilkerson. "No, ma'am, they sure don't. About the closest I've seen to a waterfall like that at home is the one time the east end of our ranch flooded with spring rains and the run-off washed out a section of fence."

The old woman's blue eyes twinkled with amusement then she turned her attention back to the knitting on her lap. "I can hear a bit of a drawl in your voice. Texas, perhaps?"

He nodded. "I grew up about forty miles from Amarillo."

One white eyebrow lifted. "What in the world are you doing on a train headed to Portland, then? How did you end up in Pendleton?"

Zane considered her question. His youthful adventures in Texas seemed like a lifetime ago. So much had changed since the day he left the ranch. "Well, the short version of that story is my best friend crashed his plane and is in the veteran's hospital in Portland. I've got four days of leave and want to make sure he's doing better than how I think he's probably faring."

Mrs. Wilkerson shot a concerned glance his way. "Oh, gracious. I'm so sorry, Lieutenant. Is he in a bad way?"

"Can't rightly say, ma'am. The last letter I had from Rock was more than a month ago and he wasn't doing well then. I just have to make sure he's not knocking on death's door before I ship out next week."

"Where are you stationed?"

Zane watched the woman's knitting needles flash in the afternoon sunlight streaming in the window. The sight of something so simple, so domestic, loosened one of the coils of tension tightly wrapped around his midsection. "I've been in Hawaii for more than a year, but a little accident left me with time to kill until the powers that be let me get back in a plane, so I've been training pilots in Pendleton."

Mrs. Wilkerson's needles stilled and her eyes widened. "Were you at Pearl Harbor?" she asked in a hushed voice.

"I was, ma'am." Zane didn't like to think about that day, about the screams and the horror, the explosions and death. He'd jumped in a plane and chased after the enemy in such a hurry, it wasn't until he'd returned to the ground that he'd realized he wore only a pair of pajama bottoms with his boots.

The old woman jammed her knitting needles into the blanket she was making and reached over to him, placing her hands on top of his. With a strong, comforting squeeze that belied her frail outer shell, she offered him a look of gratitude. "Thank you, dear boy, for whatever you did that day and each day since."

Emotion threatened to claw up Zane's throat, so he swallowed it down and forced a charming smile, one that displayed his dimples and gave him a boyish appearance. "It's my honor to serve our country, just like the next fella."

Mrs. Wilkerson scoffed and picked up her needles again. "Don't feed that bosh to me. Why, my granddaughter's husband said he watched one of his coworkers run his trigger finger through a buzz saw just so he wouldn't have to go to war."

Zane didn't know what to say in polite

company about such blatant displays of cowardice. It irked him that some people failed to stand up like real men and do what was right, especially when the country needed every able-bodied man to join the fight. He'd seen too many good, brave men die to be able to fathom such a spineless act. Yet, he easily pictured his lone sibling doing something that cowardly to get out of serving.

Unwilling to dwell on thoughts of his brother, he looked to Mrs. Wilkerson again. "You said your granddaughter's husband just left for training at Fort Lewis. Is that right?"

The woman nodded. "Yes. He waited until Jenny had the baby before he left, but little Miller is only four weeks old. The poor girl is nearly beside herself what with a newborn to care for and her husband heading off to war."

"You're going to stay with her a while?" Zane asked, reaching out and fingering the edge of the blanket. The yarn was so soft it almost felt like fuzz from a cattail.

Mrs. Wilkerson gave him a knowing smile as he rubbed his fingers over the yarn. "I plan to stay as long as she'll have me. I might be getting a little long in the tooth, but I can still cook and clean, and rock a baby to sleep." She released a sigh full of longing. "I can hardly wait to see Jenny and Miller."

"She's probably anxious to see you, too." Zane smiled at her then gave the waterfall one more glance before it disappeared from his line of vision.

"The natives tell stories about that waterfall," Mrs. Wilkerson said, eying him as she added more stitches to the blanket. "One legend, my favorite, says it was created by a handsome brave to give a young maiden, his true love, a private place to bathe."

Zane smirked. "I reckon I can see why that one might be a favored story, especially among women. What's the other legend?"

The old woman's brow wrinkled into a frown. "It's not a very happy story. You see, the chief had several sons and one daughter. The sons all died in battle, so he cherished his beautiful girl. Only the best would do when it was time for her to take a husband, so he chose a young chief from a neighboring tribe. The two tribes gathered together to celebrate the wedding, but people began to fall ill. Many suggested a sacrifice was needed, but the chief dismissed the idea. His daughter, who was caring for the ill, decided to offer herself as a sacrifice in hopes of saving her people. She made her way to the cliff and jumped to her death on the rocks below. The sickness immediately departed from those gathered, but the young chief frantically searched for his love. He found her broken body at the base of the cliff. The tribe descended the rocks below the cliff to bury her. When the deed was done, her father called to the spirits for a sign that they'd welcomed his daughter's spirit. The sound of water reached them just before it cascaded over the cliff and it has run without stopping since."

"You're right. I like the first one better," he said, thinking of the sad story.

Before he could delve into a new topic of conversation, Mrs. Wilkinson gave him another

SHANNA HATFIELD

studying glance. "You said you were injured. Have you fully recovered?"

"Yes, ma'am. My plane was shot down back in March. Took a chunk of metal through my thigh and I've been out of commission while it healed. I figured I could be doing something useful instead of sitting around, so that's how I ended up in Pendleton, training new pilots. From Portland, I'll be returning to my previous post in Hawaii."

"Have you seen many of the islands there?" she asked, looking at him inquisitively.

"I have. It sure is a pretty place, but about as different from our Texas ranch as a thoroughbred from a flat-footed mule."

The old woman laughed. "I suppose so."

Zane had no desire to answer questions about his brother, the ranch, or the war. "Now, tell me more about you. Didn't you mention some other grandchildren?"

By the time the train rocked to a stop at the depot in Portland, he'd learned all about her family, how long she'd been a widow, and her hopes of staying in Portland because the winters in Pendleton were too cold for her old bones, or so she said.

Zane reached out to steady Mrs. Wilkerson as she got to her feet. He slipped his duffle bag over his shoulder then took her suitcase and carried it while keeping one hand beneath her elbow. Slowly, they made their way off the train, across the platform, and into the jostling crowd.

"Do you see your granddaughter?" he asked, lifting his head and searching the sea of faces, having no idea what the granddaughter looked like other than the brief description the old woman had given him.

"There! That's her over there." Mrs. Wilkerson flapped her now-gloved fingers in the direction of a young woman holding a wailing baby.

Zane stepped forward with a determined look on his face and unyielding set to his broad shoulders. His commanding presence parted the crowd just enough he could guide Mrs. Wilkerson to her granddaughter.

"Jenny! Oh, it's so good to see you, my darling," Mrs. Wilkerson said, wrapping her arms around an attractive young woman with brown hair pinned in the popular Victory roll style. She appeared fashionably attired, yet weary. Tears welled in her brown eyes as she and her grandmother embraced.

Zane figured he'd carry Mrs. Wilkerson's suitcase to the car for her then see about finding transportation to the hospital. After he checked on Rock and spent a few days ensuring his buddy was well, he'd make his way to California where he'd fly back to Hawaii and report for duty.

"Who is this, Grandma?" the young woman asked, dabbing her tears on the edge of a yellow flannel baby blanket. The tiny baby in her arms continued to fuss.

Mrs. Wilkerson shoved the big handbag she carried at Zane then took her great-grandson in her arms, cuddling him close. The baby stopped crying almost immediately and the old woman released a pleased sigh.

"That's better," she said, then smiled at Zane.

"Lieutenant Zane West, this is my granddaughter Jenny Matthews."

Zane tipped his head to the young woman. "It's nice to meet you, Mrs. Matthews."

Jenny smiled and kissed her grandmother's cheek. "Still picking up strays, Grandma?"

"Not at all, my dear. The lieutenant kept me entertained on the train ride and gallantly escorted me through this ridiculous crowd. Now, let's get Miller out of all this noise. Goodness only knows what germs are floating around."

Jenny offered her grandmother an indulgent look and took the handbag from Zane. "My car is parked over there. I managed to get a good spot, but it meant arriving a little early. That's why Miller is fussing."

"Oh, he'll be just fine until we get home." Mrs. Wilkerson glanced back to make sure Zane followed them.

"Here's your suitcase, Mrs. Wilkerson," he said, setting it inside the trunk Jenny had opened. "It was a pleasure to meet you, ma'am."

The old woman refused to let him leave. "Now, don't you go running off, young man. Do you have a ride to the hospital?"

Zane took a step back. "I don't, but it's easy enough to hire a car to take me there."

"I won't hear of it." She turned to her granddaughter. "Jenny, we must give Lieutenant West a ride to the veteran's hospital."

"Sure, Grandma. It's no trouble, but I'll warn you, the baby may get a little loud before we get there." Jenny offered Zane a friendly smile and motioned for him to climb in the car.

"I don't want to be an imposition." Zane took another step back. "You should head home and take care of the baby."

"Nonsense," Mrs. Wilkerson said, somehow managing to hold the baby, tug on Zane's sleeve, and open the car door. "Miller will be perfectly fine. Besides, Jenny doesn't live that far out of the way from the hospital, do you, dear?"

Zane had an idea Jenny lived a long way from the hospital, but she merely nodded in agreement.

"Please, sir, allow us to give you a ride." Jenny's eyes filled with tears again. "I'd like to think someone somewhere will pay a kindness to my husband. This is my small way of returning the favor. You wouldn't want to deprive me of that, would you?"

"Well," Zane rubbed the back of his neck, knowing he had no choice but to ride with them. "If you're sure it's not going to put you out and upset the little buckaroo, the ride would be most appreciated."

Jenny smiled and helped her grandmother onto the front seat as Zane opened the back door of her sedan and tossed his bag onto the floor on the other side. He waited until Jenny was settled behind the wheel before he slid onto the backseat.

On the drive to the hospital, he asked Jenny about her husband, where he'd worked, how long they'd been married, and how she liked living in Portland. Twenty minutes later, she pulled up at the curb outside the hospital. The baby had fallen asleep and remained quiet as Zane got out of the car and retrieved his bag. He bent down and leaned in the window, rubbing a gentle finger over Miller's plump cheek.

"You take care of this guy. His daddy has plenty of reasons to fight hard to come back home and watch him grow up to be a good man."

Jenny sniffled and dabbed at her eyes with a handkerchief while Mrs. Wilkerson reached out and patted Zane's hand. "Be careful, Lieutenant, and take good care of yourself. If you're ever back in Portland, I hope you'll come visit us."

"I might just do that," he said with a grin. He slipped a piece of paper with Jenny's phone number and address into his shirt pocket. With one long stride backward, he lifted a hand and waved at the two women as they left.

Zane removed his hat and ran a hand through his hair before settling it back on his head. He straightened his tie, brushed the front of his shirt, then swung his bag onto his shoulder and headed up the hospital steps.

It took him ten minutes of inquiries to locate the floor where someone thought he'd find Rock. The prevailing stench of sickness, fear, and desperation mingled with the pungent odors of chemicals used to sanitize and sterilize, making him want to wrinkle his nose and rush outside for fresh air.

Regardless of the location, it seemed hospitals all smelled the same. He'd spent a few weeks in one when he'd injured his leg and couldn't wait to get out. Considering the months Rock had been a patient, he couldn't even begin to think about how much his friend must want to leave.

He walked up to the nurse's station and waited. The nurse had her back to him, jotting down notes on a chart. The woman was short in stature, but plenty of curves were evident beneath her uniform. Hair the color of summer wheat coiled into curls at the back of her head and around the edges of her nurse's cap.

A slight whiff of perfume, one he recognized as a popular choice among the females he'd been around the last few years, tickled his nose. On this woman, though, it held a deeper, richer fragrance of spices flirting with citrus-infused bouquets. If he had plans to be in town more than a few days, he might even ask the woman on a date. As it was, he tried to keep from being distracted by females. Married to his career and dedicated to serving in the war, he didn't have time left over for courting.

Impatient to see Rock, Zane cleared his throat. The woman spun around, stealing his breath as his gaze collided with hers. Big green eyes the color of moss glimmered behind thick lashes. A pert little nose and pink lips added to the flawlessness of her face. She might not be any bigger than a minute, but the nurse was stunning. If she hadn't been wearing a crisp, white uniform, he might have taken her for a pin-up girl.

When she smiled at him, he felt his mouth stretch into a broad grin. "Howdy, miss."

"Howdy yourself," she said, cocking an eyebrow. "May I help you?"

A dozen various lines guaranteed to earn him a smack across the face floated through his mind, but he merely snatched the hat off his head and nodded. "I sure hope you can. I'm here to see a good friend, Captain Rock Laroux. Would you please point me in the direction of his room?"

The color drained from the woman's face and she reached behind her toward a file-strewn desk, seeking a means of support.

"What's wrong?" Zane asked, unsettled by the growing sense of alarm rapidly rising in his chest. "Where's Rock?"

"I'm sorry, sir, but Captain Laroux is…" She pressed a hand to her throat and blinked back tears. "He's gone."

Zane slumped against the counter in front of him, unable to accept the fact a man who was closer to him than his own brother was dead. He couldn't be. Wouldn't he know if that was true? Wouldn't he have felt something at Rock's passing?

A soft hand touching his arm drew his attention back to the nurse. "We were all so shocked when he left like that."

"Left? What in blazes are you saying?" Zane snapped upright, pinning the nurse with a cool glare. "Is Rock dead or alive?"

The woman dropped her hand and bumped into the desk behind her, as though she wanted to put distance between them. "Alive, I think, sir. At least he was the last time I saw him."

"But you said he's gone. If you didn't mean…" The look he shot her held confusion and a bit of irritation. The woman wasn't making a lick of sense. For all her beauty, he began to wonder if she was a bit shy in the brain department.

"Let's try this again," she said, smiling at him in a way he found both disarming and invigorating. "I'm Nurse Brighton. Who might you be?"

"Lieutenant Zane West. Rock and I have been best friends…"

"Since the first day you met at West Point," the nurse said, offering him a knowing look. "He spoke of you often. It's nice to meet you."

Zane had no idea who the nurse was even if she seemed to have an inkling of his friendship with Rock. "Where is he? What happened to him?"

The nurse crossed her arms over her full bosom and sighed. "I was on duty three evenings ago and left Captain Laroux in his room eating his supper. He hasn't been doing well the past several weeks so I was happy to see him take an interest in the meal. When I went back to check on him, he was not in his room. He left a note that said something about dying at home, but he was nowhere to be found. Of course, we called the police and searched the entire hospital. We even had someone go out to the farm he owns, but the man who rents it hasn't seen him either. It's as though he's disappeared into thin air."

Zane dropped his duffle bag to the floor and swiped a hand over his face. "You're telling me a man who was practically on his deathbed got up and walked out of here, and no one noticed?"

The woman chewed her lip, drawing Zane's attention to its rose petal-hued perfection. Most women had taken to wearing what they called Victory red, but it was refreshing to see a kissable pair of lips in a lighter, much more natural shade.

Nurse Brighton frowned as he continued to

glare at her. "That's exactly what happened. If you have any suggestions on where or how to find him, I'm all ears."

"Hardly," Zane muttered without thinking.

The nurse straightened her spine and glared at him. "If you'd like, you could speak with Captain Laroux's attending physician."

"That'd be dandy. Just point the way." Zane grabbed his duffle and moved to the end of the counter.

Nurse Brighton pushed away from the desk. "If you'll wait here a moment, I'll see if he's available."

Zane watched her hurry down the hallway. The slight sway in her step made him think it wasn't intentional, which he liked. There was nothing more off-putting than a girl who tried too hard to snag a fellow's interest.

Nurse Brighton soon returned then showed him to a tidy office where a middle-aged man sat behind a large desk. The man rose to his feet and held out a hand. "I'm Dr. Ridley. Nurse Brighton said you're here to see Rock Laroux."

"Yes, sir. I have a few days of leave and wanted to check on him. Looks like I should have made the trip a week earlier," Zane said, sinking into the chair the doctor indicated. Nurse Brighton gave him one more glance then rushed out the door. He shifted his attention back to the doctor as the man regained his seat. "Can you tell me what led to Rock's escape?"

The doctor shook his head. "I really shouldn't discuss this with you, but from what Rock said, you're the closest thing he has to family. Isn't that right?"

"That's right. He has no siblings. His folks are gone. Rock's been... well, he's been my rock more times than I can count, sir." Zane refused to think about the possibility that Rock had left the hospital and died. It just wasn't an option as far as he was concerned. "The nurse said someone went out to the farm to see if he was there."

"Yes. We've checked with the man who rents the place. He hasn't seen or heard from Rock, but he promised to let us know if Rock shows up there." The doctor released a weary sigh and leaned back in his chair. "As you know, Rock was injured in a plane crash back at the beginning of the year. Those wounds were healing, albeit slowly, but Rock's health declined by the day. We truly have no idea what made him so weak and ill. I've read every textbook I can lay my hands on. I've consulted doctors from Seattle to Chicago and no one can figure out why he's dying a little day by day in front of our very eyes. I hate that a robust young man like him can barely hold up his head some days or drag his feet half a dozen steps across the room. There's no reasonable explanation for his declining health. It's as though some unseen foe continually attacks him."

"But that still doesn't explain how he left the hospital," Zane said, growing frustrated. "How could a man in Rock's condition, as you've described it, get up and walk out of here?"

"That's the question we've been wracking our brains to answer." The doctor sighed again. "Three days ago, Rock asked me to give him the unvarnished truth, and I did. I respect him enough not to give false hope where none exists. He was having a fairly good day, at least for him, and Nurse Brighton had cajoled him into going for a walk down the hall. Another nurse needed help with a patient, so Nurse Brighton left Rock to get himself to his room, which he did. After she brought him his dinner tray, she left him for about an hour, but when she came back, he was gone. His uniform and bag were missing, so it was easy to assume he'd gotten dressed and left. We searched the hospital from top to bottom and back up again, but he'd already gone. No one outside had seen him, or at least hadn't noticed him. A soldier who limps or acts a little weak getting down the steps outside isn't uncommon and people don't think anything of it."

"The assumption is that Rock didn't like the idea of spending his last days on earth here in the hospital and took himself elsewhere. If he isn't at the farm, where in the dickens would he have gone?"

The doctor opened a drawer and took out a file, handing Zane a slip of paper. "Your guess is as good as mine. That's the note Rock left us."

Zane read a hastily scribbled message about Rock dying where there was fresh air and blue sky at home. It was easy to understand why everyone would assume he'd headed to the farm his father had left to him. But if he wasn't there, then where could he be?

"Do you think he was too sick to make it there? Is it possible someone took him in? Have you checked other hospitals in the area?"

The doctor nodded. "That was one of the first things we did. No one matching his description has been admitted to any of the area hospitals. We've notified all the authorities. Short of combing every inch of the entire region from here to his farm, I don't know what else to do other than wait and pray that Rock will turn up.

"He will. He's too stubborn and mule-headed to die. At least like this." Zane handed the note back to the doctor. "I appreciate you speaking with me. If anyone hears from Rock, would you please let me know?"

"Of course," the doctor said. He pushed a tablet and pen toward Zane. "I'll put your address in Rock's file."

Zane wrote down his information then shook the doctor's hand. "Thank you, sir. I'm sure you did the best you could for Rock and I appreciate it."

"I'm just sorry you came all this way to find him gone."

"Me, too."

The doctor walked with him to the office door then Zane made his way back down the hall to the nurse's station. The beautiful blonde was there speaking to two other nurses. All three of them looked at him as he approached the counter.

He tipped his head to the one who'd answered his many questions. "Thank you for your help, Nurse Brighton."

She nodded. "Oh, it was nothing, Lieutenant West. I'm just sorry Captain Laroux isn't here."

Zane's stomach chose that moment to rumble

loudly. Heat seared up his neck and burned his ears when the three women grinned at him.

"Come on. You might as well get something to eat while you're here. I'll show you where to find the cafeteria." Nurse Brighton stepped around the desk and started walking toward an elevator across from the nurse's station.

In spite of his plans to leave, his feet revolted against his head and followed her to the cafeteria.

"The chicken pot pie is always good or the hot turkey sandwich," she said, as they moved into the short line. She got herself a cup of coffee and a banana while Zane chose the chicken pot pie, a green salad, a cup of coffee, and a slice of lemon cake.

She led the way to a table in front of a sunny window overlooking a courtyard filled with plants and a wide, paved path.

Zane watched as a few patients made their way along the path, several using canes or crutches.

He bowed his head and offered a brief word of thanks for his meal then dug into the food. Nurse Brighton was correct, the pot pie was delicious.

"I'm sure you have better things to do than sit with me, but I appreciate you keeping me company. It's no fun to eat alone."

"No, it isn't," she said, leaning back as she sipped her coffee and nibbled the banana. She eyed him a moment then offered him an inquisitive look. "What will you do now?"

"I don't have to report for duty until Monday, so I'll spend the next two days doing my best to locate Rock. Someone, somewhere had to have seen him." Zane took another bite of his meal then wiped his mouth on a napkin. "I can't leave without at least trying to find him."

Nurse Brighton studied him several moments then set her coffee cup on the table. "If you have no objection, I'd like to help you. I have tomorrow afternoon and the following day off."

Zane felt a smile stretch across his lips. He couldn't think of anything he'd like better, short of Rock walking through the nearest door, than the pretty nurse accompanying him. "Are you sure? I bet you don't get much time off just to enjoy yourself."

"We're all fond of Captain Laroux." She leaned toward him and dropped her voice to a conspiratorial whisper. "Well, maybe not Nurse Homer, but she detests everyone."

Zane grinned.

She reached across the table and placed her hand on his arm again. "Please. I'd like to go with you, if you have no objection."

"No objections from me," he said, taking another bite of his dinner. "Should I meet you here tomorrow?"

"That would be fine. I'll be ready to go at noon." The nurse glanced at her watch and rose to her feet. "Do you have a place to stay?"

"I don't. Any recommendations?" Zane stood and watched as she took one last sip from her coffee cup.

"There's a hotel about four blocks from here. It's nothing fancy, but it's clean and the prices are fair. If you turn left when you reach the street out front and keep walking, you can't miss it."

"Thank you, Nurse Brighton. I appreciate the information and your offer to help. I'll see you tomorrow."

"Tomorrow," she repeated, giving him one last, lingering look before she turned away from him.

"Oh, and Nurse Brighton?" He closed the distance she'd placed between them. When she turned around, she nearly bumped into his chest. His grin widened as he held her arms to steady her.

"Did you need something?" she asked in a breathy voice.

"I'd sure like to know your name."

She tipped back her head and looked at him. He could have sworn her eyes turned from bright to a dark, forest green when she smiled. "Billie. It's Billie Brighton."

Without waiting for him to reply, she spun around and left the cafeteria.

Zane watched her go, curls bouncing and skirt swishing, before he sat down and finished his meal.

Billie Brighton.

Beautiful Billie.

Quite a name for quite a girl.

★ *Chapter Two* ★

With all the quiet stealth of a jungle cat stalking its prey, Billie closed the door and tiptoed across the foyer at the rooming house where she lived with a dozen other women.

An old Victorian mansion had been remodeled as an establishment that offered affordable, clean rooms to young women. Billie had lived at The Cascadia Hotel ever since she started working at the veteran's hospital five years ago. The hotel was only three blocks from the hospital and a coveted place of residence by the nurses who labored there.

After working late, she didn't want to disturb anyone, least of all the nosy owner of the property, Miss Gladys Burwell. The woman was a stickler for rules, schedules, and "proper comportment."

Billie had just reached the stairs when the creak of a floorboard behind her let her know she'd been caught.

Slowly, she turned around and smiled at her matronly landlady. "Hello, Miss Burwell."

"Miss Brighton, you are five minutes past curfew. Again." Miss Burwell pointed to the old pocket watch she held in her hand. The woman regularly consulted the timepiece as though the world might stop spinning if she allowed time to proceed without her constant checking to confirm it marched continually onward. "Are the telephones no longer functioning at the hospital?"

"Yes, ma'am, I mean, no, ma'am." Billie sighed, trying to hide her frustration. "The phones are working, but I didn't plan on being late. I was almost out the door when a doctor requested help with a patient. It only took a minute, and I ran all the way here, hoping to make it on time." Billie shrugged. "I apologize for being late."

The woman glowered at her then assumed a haughty stance. "Well, see that it doesn't happen again. You had a similar occurrence just last week."

"Yes, ma'am." Billie tamped down the urge to grind her teeth in frustration. She didn't know why the beak-nosed old spinster cared what time she came home as long as she was respectful of the other tenants, paid her rent, and obeyed the important rules like keeping her room clean and not allowing men inside.

"Aren't you due for a day off soon?" the woman asked, moving closer as Billie backed up the steps, hoping to make an escape.

"The day after tomorrow," Billie said, not willing to impart the knowledge she had half a day off tomorrow. No doubt, Miss Burwell would grill her about her plans if she mentioned it.

Perhaps the woman was just lonely. Billie gave the thought a moment of consideration, but she was too tired to dwell on it. She just wanted to take a hot bath and collapse in her bed. "I better head up, Miss

Burwell. Have a pleasant evening."

"Evening has come and gone, my dear." Miss Burwell gave her another disapproving look then retreated to her personal rooms located off the entry foyer.

Billie turned and rolled her eyes, then hurried up the steps. She waved to two girls as they stood in the hall quietly chatting before she unlocked her door and stepped inside. The room was spacious with a lovely view of the backyard. Cream wallpaper accented with pale pink and buttery yellow flowers blooming amid green vines made her feel as though she'd found her way to a peaceful garden. A double bed, two matching night stands, and a chest of drawers, all made of exquisite birds-eye maple, added a hint of elegance to the room. A desk and chair, a square table with a hotplate, a small book shelf and a floor lamp enhanced the homey feel.

After removing her nurse's cap and kicking off her shoes, Billie plopped onto an overstuffed chair and rubbed her aching feet. She'd sprinted all the way from the hospital, hoping to make it home before old burr-in-her-blanket Burwell realized she was late. When a doctor asked for help, Billie gave it, regardless of the time or the state of her weariness. She loved nursing, loved caring for others, and doing her best to make a difference in the lives of others.

If it disrupted Miss Burwell's perfectly ordered world to have her return home five minutes after the absurd curfew of nine-fifteen on a week night, then so be it.

Billie removed her clothes, wrapped a robe around her, and gathered the basket in which she kept her toiletries. She opened her door and stepped into the hallway. Six bedrooms, three on each side were bracketed at each end of the hall by bathrooms. Billie's room was located next to the bathroom on the east end of the second floor. A similar arrangement existed on the floor above her, too.

Glad the bathroom was unoccupied, Billie hurried inside and turned on the water to start filling the tub. She added a bit of vanilla-scented bubble bath and stirred the water with her fingertips.

The moment fragrant steam wafted into the air, she slid into the hot water and sighed. With her head resting against the back of the massive claw foot tub, she closed her eyes and thought about meeting Lieutenant Zane West. Rock had spoken of him so frequently, and with such affection, she felt as though she already knew him.

When Rock was feeling particularly low he would study a photo taken of him and Zane in front of a plane. In the image she'd seen on numerous occasions, the two young men were full of life and mischief. She should have recognized Zane the moment she'd turned around and seen him standing at the counter in the hospital. Yet, the sight of him — broad shoulders, icy blue eyes, and lips positively made for kissing — had rendered her so addled she hadn't realized who he was until he said his name.

Mercy, but the man was far more handsome in person than he'd been in Rock's photograph. And he smelled wonderful, too. Like sunshine and leather, and something masculine she couldn't quite describe. No doubt, the soldier left a string of broken hearts in his wake, considering how the nurses working with Billie couldn't stop raving about him from the few minutes he'd spoken to her at the nurse's station.

Billie had no business giving the man a second glance. She certainly had none volunteering to go with him tomorrow afternoon to look for Rock. Soldiers were off limits as far as she was concerned and that was a rule she had no intention of breaking. The men who risked their lives had her full admiration and she'd give her last ounce of energy caring for them, but she couldn't let her heart get entangled with one. She knew first-hand the sorrow a woman faced when she loved a man who might never come home.

With her water swiftly cooling, Billie washed her hair and finished her bath. She readied for bed, and returned to her room with her head swathed in a thick, sun-kissed white towel.

In her room, she combed the tangles from her hair then fluffed it with her fingers until it was nearly dry. Quickly twisting small sections of her golden locks, she pinned them in place, then tied a silk scarf over her head to keep her hair smooth while she slept.

After turning out her light, she draped her robe over the desk chair and slid between cool cotton sheets. Nestled into the comfort of her bed, she turned on her side and watched her white curtains dance in the breeze from the open window.

As exhaustion overtook her, she wondered if Zane had found a room for the night. Thoughts of him, of his broad shoulders and dimpled smile, kept her company as she drifted off to sleep.

The next morning, Billie rushed to get ready for work and carefully packed a bag with a change of clothes. She ate a hurried breakfast with the other girls in the dining room, grabbed her bag, and left before Miss Burwell could begin asking questions.

Billie's morning passed quickly as she worked with a variety of patients and problems. The worst moment was when one misbehaving patient tossed his breakfast tray at her and she barely missed being hit in the head with a bowl of oatmeal.

At a quarter to noon, she changed her clothes, adding a fresh application of lipstick, and finger-combed her curls.

"Who's the lucky fella?" her friend Peggy asked as she leaned against the wall near the mirror in the nurse's breakroom and held out Billie's hat.

Billie took the navy and cream fedora and settled it on her head at a saucy angle. She tugged on a navy jacket, piped in cream trim, and adjusted the bow on a cream blouse accented with navy polka dots.

"What makes you think there's a man behind my changing clothes? I often change if I have errands to run." Billie adjusted one errant curl around her ear and gave herself another critical glance.

Peggy grinned. "You might change, but not into one of your best outfits. Besides, you usually run home to do it. What's his name?"

"Lieutenant Zane West. He's the man who came in yesterday looking for Rock Laroux. I offered to help him search for Captain Laroux today. That's all."

Peggy gave her a knowing look. "Of course, searching for a lost patient requires wearing your new shoes and carrying your favorite handbag."

"Of course," Billie said, winking at Peggy in the mirror. She turned and hugged her friend. "Thank you for taking my uniform home for me. I'll swing by your room when I get back."

"Just don't be late or Miss Burwell will have your head."

"Don't I know it." Billie frowned. "She got after me last night and I was only five minutes late. Dr. Johnson needed help with a patient and that's why I was late. She's not particularly understanding of our work."

A derisive snort rolled out of Peggy. "She's not particularly understanding of anything that goes against her line of thinking, way of doing things, or her scheduled plans." Peggy brushed a speck of lint from Billie's shoulder. "Is Lieutenant West the cutie who had the girls all in a dither?"

Billie nodded as she pulled on a pair of cream gloves. "One and the same. He's meeting me out front in a few minutes."

Peggy playfully shoved her toward the door. "Well, for gosh sakes, don't be late."

Billie glared at her over her shoulder then broke into a grin as Peggy looped their arms together and they hurried downstairs to the main entry.

A handsome man walked up the steps as they reached the front doors.

Peggy whistled softly. "I see why the girls couldn't stop talking about him. Have fun, Billie."

"We aren't planning to have fun, Peg. The whole point of going with him is to try and find Rock." Billie scowled at Peggy, then reached for the door. "Just stay out of trouble while I'm gone and be careful around Sergeant Haney. He's been in a foul mood today."

"Don't worry about anything here. Go on and enjoy the company of that handsome solider."

Billie rushed out the door just as Zane reached the top step.

"Hello, Nurse Brighton. Beautiful day, isn't it?" he said as he offered her a snappy salute.

The soldier looked even more handsome out in the spring sunshine than he had inside the hospital the previous afternoon. Tanned skin, thick dark hair, and those incredible blue eyes captured her interest. How was a girl supposed to ignore all that? Regardless of how much she wanted to admire his masculine magnificence, she turned her thoughts to the reason he was there.

"It is a lovely day. We had a terrible rainstorm the day Captain Laroux disappeared, but the weather has been pleasant since then." Billie made her way down the broad steps in front of the hospital and followed Zane to a dark green car parked at the curb.

He opened the front passenger door and stepped back. "I thought it might be easier for us to search if we had something to drive. I wasn't sure if you had a car, so I rented this one."

"I don't have a car," she said, gliding onto the seat. "This one is a beaut."

"It is," he said, jogging around the car and sliding behind the wheel. "I sure like this color."

"It makes me think of a deep forest," Billie said, reclining against the fawn-colored seat. She brushed her hand over the leather upholstery. "Renting a car was a good idea."

"Is there a bus station nearby?" he asked, starting the car and putting it in gear.

"There's a bus stop there on the corner, but the nearest station is a few miles from here. You don't think Rock would have walked to it, do you?"

Zane shrugged as he pulled away from the curb and into traffic. "If he was desperate and determined enough, he might have."

"Turn west here," Billie said as Zane braked at a stop sign. He followed her directions and merged into traffic while she considered what Rock might have done in a moment of anxiety-driven panic. "I hate to think of him walking in the rain in his condition. Why, he could have..." She snapped her mouth shut, hesitant to say more about all the tragedies that could have befallen Rock in his weakened state.

Zane gave her a sideways glance then turned his attention back to the road. He observed one side of the road then the other as they drove.

"What are you looking for?" she asked.

"Places he might have stopped or stayed."

Billie looked at the businesses and buildings they passed. She couldn't imagine Rock taking refuge in any of them. Most would have been closed that time of night anyway. "There's the bus station," she said, pointing just ahead of them on the right.

Zane pulled into the lot and parked then hurried around the car to open her door. She certainly appreciated his fine manners. One of the tests Billie gave men she went out with was to see if they opened doors for her or remained standing until she was seated. Sadly, many of them got off on the wrong foot by failing to open her car door and the date would go downhill from there.

"Let's talk to the person in the ticket booth. They might remember seeing him," Zane said. He took out his wallet and removed a photo then tucked his wallet back into his pocket.

There were only a few people in line in front of them, so it didn't take long to reach the ticket agent.

"Where to?" the agent asked as Billie and Zane stood at the window.

"We don't want to purchase a ticket. We're looking for someone. By chance, did you see this man purchase a ticket?" Zane pushed a photo of him and Rock across the counter.

The agent picked it up and studied it a moment then handed it back to him. He shook his head. "Sorry, sir, but I haven't seen him. We've only had a few soldiers come through this week, and I don't remember anyone who looked like that."

"Are there other agents who may have been working Monday evening?" Billie asked. "It would have been after six-thirty."

The man nodded. "Jim Donner was working Monday night. You might ask him. He'll be on duty tonight."

"What time could we catch him?" Zane asked, stowing the photo of him and Rock in his front shirt pocket.

"His shift starts at five." The agent looked past Zane to the line of people waiting to purchase tickets. "Now, if you'll excuse me."

Zane nodded and stepped out of the way. Billie walked beside him back to the car. "Where should we go now?" she asked as he again held open her door.

He didn't answer right away, waiting until he was seated and had started the car to look at her. "Do you know how to get to Gales Creek?"

"I've never been there, but I think I could probably find it." Billie pointed across the street as Zane pulled out of the bus station parking lot. "There's a gas station over there. I'm sure they'll have a map of the area."

"Good idea." Zane zipped across traffic and parked the car. He rushed into the gas station and soon returned with two maps. He sank onto the seat and unfolded one, tracing the line of a road with his finger. "According to the map, we should be heading in the right direction."

He handed the map to Billie and pulled onto the street, continuing to head west.

"Rock said you were stationed in Hawaii, and it seems like he mentioned an injury. Are you doing better now?" Billie couldn't imagine what type of wound might plague a strapping male specimen like Zane West. He was the epitome of strength and health.

"I'm fine, now. I didn't want Rock to worry about me since he had plenty of his own troubles. I was flying a patrol when an enemy got the drop on me and shot down my plane."

Billie gave him a horrified look, scanning him for any visible injuries. Other than a scar on the left side of his forehead that ran into the corner of his eyebrow, she couldn't detect anything. "What happened?" she asked.

"The plane crashed, in spite of my best efforts to keep it in the air. I wound up with a slice of metal through my thigh. Since I couldn't use my leg and they wouldn't let me fly until it completely healed, I requested I be sent somewhere I could be of use." Absently, his hand rubbed across his right thigh. "I was pretty happy when I was assigned to train pilots in Pendleton. It was closer to Rock, even if I didn't make it to visit him, and gave me something useful to do while my leg healed."

Billie fought back the urge to reach over and press her hand to his thigh. Instead, she lifted her gaze to his face. "I didn't notice you limping at all."

"As long as my leg doesn't get too tired, I do just fine." Zane leaned a little closer to her. "And truth to tell, I work hard at hiding the limp. I hate not being able to fly and I'm chomping at the bit to get back to my regular duties." He grinned at her. "Come Monday, I'll be on the way back to my post in the Pacific."

"Doesn't it frighten you? Being so close to the Japanese opposition?" It would scare her spitless to be in the thick of things like he'd been. "Rock mentioned you being at Pearl Harbor when it was…

when the Japanese…" Tears stung her eyes, as they did each time she thought of the devastation wrought by the enemy in December.

Much to her surprise, Zane gave her hand a tender squeeze. "I think anyone with a lick of sense in their noggin is frightened when they're at war. It's just a matter of setting aside the fears and doing what is needed, what is necessary."

The modest, humble tone of his voice surprised her every bit as much as his words. She would have assumed someone as handsome as the lieutenant, and a hotshot pilot to boot, would have been quite full of himself and his accomplishments. She knew from Rock's bragging about his friend that Zane had earned a few distinguished awards for his exemplary service.

Honestly, the man intrigued her far more than any she'd met. It was for that very reason she had to safeguard her heart and keep matters strictly professional. Billie was not out on a leisurely drive with a good-looking soldier. She was trying to locate a lost patient.

Before she could think of something to say, Zane pulled off the road into an area that looked like a small park. Half a dozen picnic tables sat back under the cover of trees and two children played on a set of swings.

"Why did you stop?" she asked, looking at him as he parked the car and cut the ignition.

He grinned then hurried around to open her door. With a flourish, he held out a hand to her. "Might I talk you into a picnic lunch before we continue on our way?"

Resolved to ignore her rapidly growing feelings for Zane, she started to tell him she had no interest in a picnic or anything other than tracking down Rock. Hunger and common sense prevailed, though, as she took his hand and rose to her feet.

"You just happen to have a picnic lunch with you?" she asked, shooting him a dubious expression as he took a box from the backseat and started toward the nearest picnic table.

A shrug rode his broad shoulders, but he continued to grin. "I assumed you probably wouldn't take time to eat lunch before meeting me. I found a café close to where I rented the car." He set the box on the table and held out his hand for her to take a seat. "If you already ate, I'll hurry."

"No need to rush, Lieutenant West. I didn't have time to eat and a picnic would be lovely," she said, pleased he'd thought to provide lunch and had chosen a lovely setting. Sun filtered through the trees, creating splashes of light on the lush grass and highlighting the bright pink rhododendron plants lining the park with a beautiful hedge.

She glanced down at the bench and started to brush away lingering dirt, but Zane draped a starched white handkerchief over it. Billie accepted the hand he held out to her and used it for balance as she stepped over the bench and took a seat. "Thank you, kind sir."

"You're most welcome, lovely lady." Zane's gaze collided with hers as he held onto her hand far longer than she deemed appropriate. Something in his gaze — something warm and inviting — made her want to draw closer to him.

But that would never do.

She dropped his hand, leaned back, and forced her gaze to the box he'd set on the table. "What are we eating for lunch?"

Zane took a seat across from her and removed two paper-wrapped bundles from the box. "Turkey or ham?"

"Turkey," she said, accepting the sandwich he held out to her.

He set two bottles of Coca-Cola on the table, along with paper napkins, a small tin of potato chips, and two pickles.

"What a feast," Billie said, taking a handful of chips when he held the tin out to her. "Thank you, Lieutenant."

Zane lifted his left eyebrow, accentuating the scar visible there. "How about you just call me Zane? I've heard you refer to Rock by his first name and I expect you can do the same with me."

Billie thought agreeing to his request alluded to a familiarity she was determined wouldn't happen with the charming soldier. But since he'd brought along a delicious picnic lunch and had been kind and mannerly, she couldn't very well refuse. "Zane it is, but only if you call me Billie."

"Billie. I sure like the sound of that. Is it a nickname?"

She shook her head and dabbed at her mouth with her napkin. "I'm named after my Grandpa Bill. I think my father had his heart set on a boy, so when he got me instead, they switched from naming me William to Billie."

"What's your middle name? Is it after an

uncle? Your other grandfather? Something like Jack or Tom?" he joked.

"No," she scowled at him. "For your information it's Adaleen."

Zane's teasing smile broadened. "That's a pretty name for a pretty woman."

A blush soaked her cheeks with color at his flattery. She was accustomed to men paying her compliments, to flirting and flattering in an effort to woo her, but this was different. Zane's simple statement felt genuine.

"Thank you," she said in a quiet voice, then turned her focus back to her food.

Zane asked her questions about Portland, about how long Rock had been among her patients, and if she thought he'd been hovering at death's door like the doctor seemed to think.

"He was in a bad way, Zane. I won't make light of his situation." Billie looked off in the distance, thinking about the many times she'd sat beside Rock's bed as he slept, praying for him to make it through the night. "The thing none of us can figure out or understand is what's wrong with him. Doctor Ridley has been beside himself trying to discover the cause of what's making Rock so sick. His wounds from the crash are healing, although far slower than we'd expected. It's as though his life force drains out of him a little each day."

"And with him running off in a rainstorm, the hope is slim that he survived." Zane sighed then rolled back his shoulders. "I don't know how I know it, but Rock is alive. Maybe just barely, but he's alive."

Billie reached across the table and patted Zane's hand in a comforting gesture. "I hope you're right."

Zane gave her a long, studying look. "You seem pretty keen on my buddy. Was there more going on than him being a favorite patient?"

"Of course not!" Billie was appalled Zane voiced the thought. Then again, she supposed the way she'd talked about Rock with fondness and concern could lead to misunderstandings or questions. "Rock, as you probably know, is quite a charmer. He's sweet and gentlemanly, even on a bad day, and all the nurses appreciated his cheerful demeanor. He'll be missed by us all."

"But you're the only one who volunteered to help me look for him." Zane wadded up the paper from his sandwich then took a long drink of his pop.

"Rock is a good friend and a patient, that's all." Billie thought Rock had feelings for her, feelings she'd seen plenty of soldiers develop for their nurses. It wasn't real love or affection, but an emotion derived from gratitude. Then again, Rock teased her so much, she was never absolutely certain when he was being serious or not. In fact, he'd proposed to her at least once a week since he'd been at the hospital, but Billie never gave it a moment's thought. Rock Laroux would make some woman a wonderful husband, but it would never be her. Not when she considered him to be like the brother she'd always wanted and never had.

Zane finished his Coca-Cola and set the bottle in the empty box. Billie hurriedly ate the rest of her sandwich and pickle then wiped her hands on her napkin. She rose to her feet and followed Zane when he carried their garbage to a trash can at the edge of the park near the parking lot. Together, they walked to the car.

"Ready to go?" he asked and opened the car door for her.

She nodded and climbed in. For something to do, she sipped her pop as Zane drove to Gales Creek. "Do you know where his place is located?" she asked as they entered the small town.

"Not exactly, but he talked about the farm having a big blue barn." Zane drove through town. "I don't think it will be hard to find." A mile down the road, they stared at a blue barn visible from the car. It stood out against the green landscape, although it blended in with the vibrant afternoon sky.

"That has to be it," Billie said, pointing toward a lane that led to the farmhouse.

Zane turned off the road and they soon stopped in front of a freshly-painted fence around a neatly-trimmed yard.

A young man stepped out of the barn and waved to them.

Zane got out of the car, but Billie opened her door and stood before he could reach her. Together, they walked toward the man.

"Howdy, folks. What can I do for you today?" the farmer asked, offering a friendly smile as he approached them. A mottled, gangly mutt trotted next to him, tongue lolling out of his mouth and tail wagging in welcome.

"Is this the Laroux place?" Zane asked. He

moved closer to Billie and settled a warm hand on her back as they stopped in front of the overall-clad man.

She wondered if it was a natural instinct of Zane's to be protective. He appeared focused on the farmer and not her, so she assumed he meant nothing by his proximity that bordered on possessive or proprietary.

The farmer smiled. "This is the Laroux place. I've been renting it the last few years. Me and my missus sure like it here." The young man tipped his head to Billie. "Are you friends with Rock? There's sure been a bunch of hubbub about him disappearing from the hospital the other day."

Zane nodded. "I'm Lieutenant Zane West. Rock and I have been friends for years. I came to town to see him this weekend only to discover he's gone missing. He hasn't shown up here yet, has he?"

The young man shook his head. "No. I haven't seen him or heard from him. If he needed help, I think he knows he could call and I'd come get him." He reached down and absently stroked his work-roughened hand through the dog's fur. "I sure hate to think of anything happening to him. Rock's a real good egg."

Zane grinned. "He is at that. If you do see or hear from him, you'll call Doctor Ridley at the hospital, won't you?"

"Yep. I've got his number right by the telephone." The farmer motioned to the house. "Would you folks like to come in for a cup of coffee or maybe a glass of tea? My wife made some oatmeal cookies this morning that were top notch."

Billie glanced at Zane and he gave a slight shake of his head.

"We thank you for that offer, but we'll be on our way." Zane held out his hand. "It was nice to meet you."

The farmer shook it with enthusiasm. "It was a pleasure to meet you folks, too. You sure make a handsome couple. Been married long?"

"Married?" Billie spluttered. Much to her annoyance, Zane merely chuckled.

"Oh, you know how new brides are," Zane said, smacking Billie's cheek with a noisy kiss as he pulled her against his side. She could feel muscles through the fabric of his shirt and wondered what it would be like to truly be held by him, to be thoroughly kissed by him.

The young man laughed and waved as Zane turned Billie around and walked with her to the car.

"What do you think you're doing?" Billie quietly hissed.

"Having a little fun," Zane said, opening the door and handing her inside. He shut it then waved to the farmer again as he walked around the car and slid behind the wheel.

"I'll thank you not to do that again." She scowled at him as he turned the car around and drove down the lane. In truth she had no idea why she was acting so upset when she really wanted Zane to pull her close and hold her tight. Her gaze fastened on his enticing, entirely too kissable lips.

Unaware she leaned toward him, her entire focus was on his mouth. Intent, she pondered the flavor of his kisses. Would they be dark and rich? Seductive and decadent? Lost in her imaginings of his firm lips pressed to hers, she didn't hear him speak until he touched her arm.

"Billie?" Zane questioned. He cast a curious look her way as he turned onto the main road. "Everything okay?"

Hot embarrassment seared her cheeks as she realized she'd been about to kiss him.

"Fine. Everything is fine," she croaked and turned to stare out the window wondering how she'd survive being trapped in a car with Zane the rest of the afternoon. At the rate she was going, he'd think she was a… a… woman of slack morals.

Covertly, she glanced over at him, relieved to see he stared at the road ahead and wasn't paying any mind to her. Relieved, she released the breath she'd been holding and relaxed against the seat. Maybe he'd missed the fact she'd almost kissed him.

✦★★ *Chapter Three* ★★★✦

Every nerve ending in Zane's body bolted upright, instantly at attention. Billie was about to kiss him. The timing wasn't the best, but since he'd spent the past several hours fighting an overwhelming attraction to her, he was more than willing for her soft pink lips to tantalize his.

Although his primary focus was on finding Rock, Zane couldn't deny he felt some inexplicable pull to Billie Brighton.

The moment she'd set foot out of the hospital at noon, he'd been mesmerized. She looked like she'd walked right out of the pages of a fashion magazine in a navy and cream outfit that perfectly accentuated her lush curves. In spite of her diminutive height, Billie Brighton seemed larger than life when she offered him a smile and hurried his direction. She wore a pair of heels that elongated her legs and tugged his gaze to shapely calves visible beneath the hem of her trim skirt.

The slight hint of her fragrance teased his nose and ensnared his senses. If that wasn't enough to drive him half daffy, her golden locks, fashioned in an array of shiny curls, bounced on her shoulders with each step that she took.

Nonchalant, he kept one eye on the road while surreptitiously watching Billie as she leaned toward him. Her gorgeous green eyes glimmered with warmth and yearning, even as her lids began to close and her long eyelashes fanned her cheeks.

Then, just as quickly as he anticipated the impact of her kiss, she turned away, cheeks pink with color. Rather than comment or tease her for what nearly occurred, he feigned ignorance, purposely holding his gaze on the road.

He wondered what had stopped her. Although it was probably the smarter, wiser thing to avoid a kiss and any entanglements since he'd be leaving Sunday, disappointment settled over him. Billie failed to deliver something he suddenly realized he quite desperately wanted.

Confused and unsettled by his unexpected longing to hold Billie in his arms, to learn the unique and delightful flavor of her kiss, he gave himself a mental shake. The one and only reason he was in Portland was for Rock. Now that his best friend was missing, Zane needed to channel all his energy and attention into finding him, not letting a beautiful, engaging, fascinating woman turn his head.

Billie remained pressed against the car door, as though she considered jumping out. He cleared his throat and pointed to the road in front of them. "I thought it might be a good idea to drive back to Portland on a different road. Maybe we'll find a clue heading this way."

Curtly, she nodded, then fixed her gaze outside

the passenger window again.

Uncertain what to do to put her at ease, Zane turned on the radio and fiddled with it until the sound of Gene Autry singing "Back in the Saddle Again" filled the car.

Zane tapped his fingers on the steering wheel and whistled along to the tune. When the song ended, he glanced over to find Billie smiling at him.

"I take it you're a Gene Autry fan?"

"I do enjoy listening to him sing," Zane said with a grin. "What about you? Who do you like to listen to?"

"Oh, I like all kinds of music, but Bing Crosby is one of my favorites. No one can croon a song quite like he can." Billie's smile widened when a Bing Crosby song came on the radio just then.

Zane turned up the volume as Bing sang about being an old cow hand from the Rio Grande. "Nothing wrong with a little Bing," he said, smiling at her.

Billie giggled. "I think you found the western music hour. You must love cowpoke music."

He nodded. "I guess I do. It makes me think of the ranch and my growing up years."

"And that was in Texas?" Billie asked, shifting in the seat so she faced him. Her earlier embarrassment appeared to be forgotten, replaced by open curiosity. "What was life like there? I've never been any further than the coast, and it's only a few hours away. Is Texas as big and as grand as I imagine?"

"It is big and grand. Where the ranch is located, it can get blistering hot in the summer, and we've even had a few blizzards in the winter. The wind often blows. It's located in Northern Texas, in an area considered part of the High Plains. Cactus even grows on the far end of the ranch."

"Really? I've always wanted to see a cactus in person," Billie said, raptly listening to his description.

"They aren't all that fun, especially if you land in a patch of 'em." Zane winked at her before he continued describing the region where he grew up. "Amarillo is the closest big city and it's been a transportation hub in the region for quite a long time. There's a big ol' canyon in the area, too. When I was no bigger than a grasshopper, we'd go there for picnics sometimes or just to ride our horses for fun. They opened up a park a few years back on almost thirty-thousand acres, even though the canyon spans about twenty miles in width and runs for about a hundred miles. Palo Duro basically means hard wood. My dad always said it was because of all the mesquite and juniper trees that grow there."

"It sounds amazing." Billie continued giving him her full attention. "Do people live in the canyon, or just visit the park?"

Zane nodded. "Natives have lived there for thousands of years. One time, my brother and I found a big bone. Dad took it to a friend of his who works at a university. Turns out, it came from a mammoth."

Billie's eyes widened in astonishment.

"Apache lived there for a while, and then the Comanche and Kiowa moved in until the cavalry swooped in to transport them to Oklahoma. The Indians weren't too eager to go until the Army captured more than a thousand of their horses and destroyed them. With no means of transportation, they surrendered."

"That's horrible." Billie pressed a hand to her chest. "Those poor horses, and people."

"It was a sad thing. There were also a few ranchers who lived in the canyon. One named Goodnight had more than a hundred thousand head of cattle in his heyday."

"What about your ranch? How many cattle does your family run?"

Due to his brother's contempt and mismanagement, Zane hadn't set foot on the ranch since his father's funeral. After the attorney read his father's will, his brother had engaged him in a fist fight. Zane could have easily ended him, but instead he'd knocked him out, packed his things and left. Until Floyd got his head on straight or changed his ways, Zane wanted nothing to do with him, even though he missed the ranch.

Aware Billie awaited his response to her question, he tamped down his worries about the ranch and his brother, and pulled his thoughts from the past. "We generally run about three thousand head."

"That's a lot of cattle. Do you raise crops?"

"No. Just feed for the animals."

Zane slowed as they neared a produce stand. It was closed, but something about it wriggled loose a memory of something Rock had shared with him. "Did Rock ever mention going to a produce stand with his dad?"

Billie looked out the window at the tidy place. "Once when I'd brought him a cup of peaches to eat he said the best peaches he'd ever had came from a produce stand close to his home, but I have no idea where it was located."

"Me either. He mentioned it a few times. Seems like the name of the family who owned it was oriental. You suppose they all had to report to the assembly center?" Zane decreased his speed even further and they both looked at the cheery yellow bungalow and large produce stand as they drove past.

"Most likely. I think anyone who is even part Japanese had to report this week or face dire consequences."

"I read about it in the newspaper." Zane increased his speed and continued on his way.

Billie nodded then waved out the window to a little boy with bright red hair and a face full of freckles as he raced through a pasture. The rascal waved both hands over his head in greeting without breaking stride.

"He looks like he's a full bucket of fun," Zane said, glancing back at the child.

"I bet he's a handful." Billie looked over at him and grinned. "I can't help but wonder if people said that about you as a child."

Zane slapped a hand over his heart. "I'm wounded, Nurse Brighton. I'll have you know I sang in the church choir and won a much-coveted chocolate bar for reciting the most Bible verses at Sunday school."

"That covers Sundays." Her eyes held a spark of mischief. "What about the other six days in a week?"

Zane grinned. "That's a whole different story."

She gave him a knowing look. "That's what I thought."

"What about you?" Zane asked. "Did you excel at Sunday school and regular school. Did you run circles around your siblings?"

Billie's smile faded and the brightness in her eyes dimmed. She looked away, staring out the window again. "No. I don't have any siblings."

"What about your parents?"

She shook her head. "My father died when I was two and I lost my mother when I was seven. I went to live with my mother's aunt, but she could barely take care of herself, let alone me, so I was sent to a friend of my mother's. From there I was passed from home to home until I turned sixteen."

"What happened then?" Zane gave her a concerned glance.

"I decided to take care of myself, so I did."

He wanted to reach across the seat and squeeze her hand in understanding. Instead, he gripped the wheel tighter. "How did you come to be a nurse?"

"I always liked helping people, blood never made me squeamish, and it seemed like a good career. There's never a shortage of jobs for a good nurse. It took me two years of waiting tables and sharing a one-bedroom apartment with three other girls to be able to save enough to go to nursing school, but I'm glad I did it. I love being a nurse."

Admiration for Billie, for what she'd

accomplished in spite of her challenges, filled him. Not only was she beautiful, but he could add intelligent, determined, and dedicated to her list of attributes, too.

Zane shot a quick glimpse her way as they entered the outskirts of a small town. "How long have you been at the veteran's hospital?"

"Five years. I worked two years at the city hospital in a variety of positions before I got the job." Billie looked over at him. "Not that I didn't enjoy my work there, but I'm grateful for the opportunity to work at the veteran's hospital, especially now. It makes me feel like I'm contributing my little part to the war effort."

"You haven't been knitting socks or saving grease to take to the butcher?"

She laughed. "No one ever taught me how to knit, so you'd have to pity the poor soldier who received a pair of socks I made. And the place I live includes meals, so I don't cook."

"Don't cook or can't cook?" Zane asked. Didn't all women know how to cook? Wasn't that a rite of passage into womanhood, learning their way around a kitchen?

"Both. Again, learning to cook and sew weren't high on the priority list when I was younger. Maybe one of these days I'll learn."

"You mean when you get married and settle down and raise a little family of your own?"

"Something like that. The cook where I live has taught me a few things, but I don't have much time for learning." Billie studied him so intently, he wanted to squirm under her perusal. "What about you? Will you go back to Texas and live on the ranch when the war is over?" she finally asked.

Zane shrugged. "I doubt it. My brother runs it now. I've been in the military for a while and I like it just fine. I'll probably stay in it after the war ends."

He watched shutters drop inside Billie's eyes, as though she found it imperative to withdraw from him, to create a barrier between them. Although she didn't move, she might as well have leaped from the car and hit the ground running for all the distance that suddenly separated them.

Zane drove into the heart of town and parked. Together they got out and walked from business to business, showing the photo of Rock and asking if anyone had seen him.

As they made their way through town, Zane admired the swept sidewalks and painted storefronts that gave the place a pleasant appearance. It seemed like the type of town where everyone was friendly and welcoming. A great place to raise kids.

In all his twenty-nine years, Zane had never considered settling down and getting married. But after spending a few hours around Billie, he could suddenly envision himself herding a little boy and girl with bright green eyes and his dimples into the grocery store they'd just left.

Where in the heck had that vision come from?

Determined to clear all domestic delusions from his mind, he inhaled a cleansing breath as they made their way back to the car. They stopped in each town they came to, inquiring if anyone had seen Rock, but no one had.

Tired and disheartened, they were on their way back to Portland when Billie pointed out the window at the marquee sign above a small movie theater. "Oh, look at that."

Zane glanced at the name of the movie playing and grinned. "Want to see it?" he asked, slowing the car.

She started to say no. He could almost hear her decline, but then she nodded her head. "I'd love to. And it looks like something you might enjoy. At least it should be funny."

"Let's do it, then." Zane drove around the block and parked the car. Together, they hurried to the ticket window. "Two for *Ride 'Em Cowboy*, please."

"Here you are, sir," the ticket agent said, taking Zane's money and sliding the tickets to him. "Enjoy the show."

"Is it as funny as I've heard?" Billie asked.

The ticket agent grinned. "It's a barrel of laughs."

Inside, Zane guided Billie to the concession stand. "Popcorn? Candy? Pop?"

"Yes," she said, grinning. He ordered popcorn and a bottle of Dr. Pepper while she chose a box of milk duds. "Mind if we share?" she asked, pointing to his drink and popcorn.

"Not at all," he said and started to take out his wallet, but Billie insisted on paying for the treats.

Zane balked at her paying, but instead of making a scene he let her. Perhaps she didn't want him to get the idea they were on a date, which they weren't. They merely needed a break from the exhausting and utterly fruitless search for Rock.

They found seats at the back of the nearly empty theater and settled in to watch the show. A newsreel showed clips of the British army battling against Germans, the Flying Tigers with their planes, and cadets at West Point training.

The footage made Zane eager to get back into action with his comrades instead of being grounded at Pendleton Field. Not that the work he'd been doing there wasn't important, but he missed being in the thick of things.

When the newsreel showed a Japanese submarine and American planes bombing it, Billie reached over and squeezed his hand. He turned his over, glad she didn't pull back when their palms connected. A jolt, like he'd grabbed onto a live wire, skittered up his arm and down to his toes. She turned to him in the muted light and smiled.

In that moment, Zane decided he'd relish the time he spent with her in the darkened theater and not worry about the world outside. At least not until the end of the movie.

Five minutes after the movie started, she dumped her box of candy in with his popcorn and told him it was much better that way, then she'd stolen a sip of his pop and cast him a flirty smile.

If the movie hadn't been too hilarious to ignore, he would have spent all his time focusing on Billie. Each time she glanced at him, each time their fingers brushed when they both reached for popcorn, each time she bumped against his shoulder, it fired all of his senses until he felt like his nerve endings were ablaze and attuned only to her.

For the next hour and a half, Zane chuckled at the antics of Bud Abbot and Lou Costello as they portrayed two peanut vendors from New York who wound up as cowhands on a dude ranch out West. The merriment was a welcome diversion both from his worries and his attraction to Billie. From the way she laughed and giggled, he figured she needed the lighthearted reprieve, too.

When the theater lights came on and the credits rolled, she dabbed at the moisture in her eyes and released a long breath.

"Oh, I haven't laughed like that in forever. Thank you, Zane."

"It was your idea to stop, so thank you." He grinned at her as he stood then held out a hand to help her to her feet.

She placed her hand in his and stood, but didn't untangle their entwined fingers as they made their way back to the lobby.

"I'm going to freshen up, but I won't be long," she said, making her way to the restroom.

Zane tossed away their garbage, washed his hands in the washroom, and then returned to the lobby. He took out the photo of Rock and asked the people working there if they'd seen his friend, but no one had.

He couldn't fathom how Rock had so completely and thoroughly disappeared, but he had.

"Any luck?" Billie asked from beside him as he stared at the image he held in his hand.

"Nope." He tucked the photograph in his pocket then turned to her. "Ready to go?"

"Yes, I am." She walked out the door he held open for her and together they returned to the car. Once again back on the road, Zane glanced at his watch. "The ticket agents should have changed shifts at the bus station. Would you like to go with me to talk to the man the agent mentioned earlier or would you prefer to go home?"

Billie leaned back against the leather seat and turned her head his direction. "If you've no objection, I'd like to go with you."

Pleased she wasn't tired of his company, at least not yet, he nodded. "That's great. Maybe we can have dinner afterward."

"I'd like that. I know a nice little restaurant if you like good old American cooking."

He smiled. "That's my favorite kind."

Half an hour later, he parked at the bus station, opened Billie's door, and took her hand in his. They moved into the ticket line and waited their turn to speak with the ticket agent.

As they waited, Billie intermittently whispered funny lines from the movie and quietly giggled. Zane had all he could do not to burst into all-out laughter each time she did it. She was the most fun female he'd ever been around, and he'd been around many.

Mostly, he'd date a girl once or twice and move on before she heard wedding bells chime or started choosing wallpaper for the house they'd never have together. He had no desire for lasting attachments or long-term relationships. Not when his country needed his full attention and devotion.

But Billie Brighton was exactly the type of girl

who could make a man wish for a cozy home and a happily ever after. Despite his head telling him to keep up his guard and not let Billie work her way past his defenses, his heart encouraged him to open the door and invite her in.

"Where to, folks?" the ticket agent asked when they reached the front of the line.

"Have you seen this man?" Zane asked, handing the photo he'd shown to dozens of people that afternoon to the agent. "He would have purchased a ticket Monday evening. Might not have looked well."

The agent studied the photo, holding it up to examine it in better light, then scratched his chin, deep in thought.

"I kinda do recall seeing a soldier who looked like him. He acted either drunk or sick, I couldn't tell for certain. Only had thirty cents and wanted to know how far that would take him." The man handed the photo back to Zane.

"Did he buy a ticket? Where did he go?" Zane asked impatiently.

Billie settled a hand on his arm and nudged him over. She gifted the agent with a sweet smile and leaned toward him. "He's a dear friend and we're concerned about him. Anything you can remember would be so helpful."

The agent stared at Billie in open admiration and nodded at her. "Well, it seems like he took the bus to Beaverton. It's right over there if you want to ask the driver, but no hitching a ride without a ticket."

Billie's smile widened. "Thank you. You've

been most obliging. Have a lovely evening." She grabbed Zane's arm and tugged on it, pulling him out of line.

He glared at her as they walked to the bus. "Use those feminine wiles often to get your way?"

She batted her eyelashes at him in an exaggerated fashion, then wrinkled her nose and stuck out her tongue, making a silly face.

Zane couldn't help but smile. "You're a loon, Billie Brighton."

"So I've been told," she said, then stepped behind him as they reached the bus.

Zane hurried up the steps and held out the photo to the driver. "Did you see this man on Monday evening? He might have had a ticket to Beaverton and he probably didn't act quite right."

The man nodded his head. "Sure did. He sat right there," the man pointed to a seat in the front. "Fell asleep about a minute after we left the station. He slept through his stop and it was three or four miles later before I realized he was riding for free. I sure hated to kick him off the bus with a storm brewing, but I can get in trouble for that kind of thing."

Zane glanced back at Billie with a hopeful look. "That's great news. Do you remember exactly where you let him off?"

"Well, I'm not sure. I probably could remember on the route, but…"

"We'll follow you in our car. When you get to the stop where you let him out, just honk your horn." Zane backed down the steps. "Do you remember anything else about him? Did you see where he went once you let him off?"

"Nope. He acted like he was drunk or in a stupor. I assumed he'd find somewhere to sleep it off. Is he in trouble?"

"No. Just sick. Very sick." Zane stepped off the bus. "Thank you for your help. And remember to honk when you get to the right stop."

"I will." The driver looked over the heads of people getting on the bus and nodded once at Zane.

He took Billie's hand in his and they hurried back to the car.

For the next hour, they drove behind the bus, following it and waiting with growing frustration at each stop.

Finally, the bus pulled in at a stop out in what seemed to be the middle of nowhere. No one was waiting to board and no one on the bus got off, but the driver honked three times and waved a hand out the window.

Zane parked the car and he and Billie got out, walking around the stop, looking for clues. None were forthcoming.

Billie sank onto the bench under the small cover at the stop. "If it was you who'd been in the hospital, diagnosed to die, and you decided to go home. What would you do?" she asked, glancing up at Zane. "If you were tossed off the bus at this stop, in the dark and the rain, what would you do?"

Zane looked up and down the road. "I'd walk that way, but I don't know if he'd stay on this road or go a different direction."

Billie stepped beside him again. She pointed west. "Is that a crossroad in the distance?"

"Yep, it sure is." Tired, overwrought with emotions, and angry that Rock had done such a reckless thing, he kicked a rock and tamped down the urge to punch something.

Much to his surprise and delight, arms wrapped around him from behind and gave him a hug. Billie's warmth enveloped him — her sweetness infectious, her kindness contagious.

The tension that had been twirling through his midsection loosened and he drew in a deep breath before turning around and returning her hug. Several moments, several heartbeats passed before either of them moved.

When she pulled back, he tenderly clasped her chin in his hand and smiled. "Thank you for that, Billie, girl. I didn't realize how much I needed a hug."

"We all need hugs, Zane. Even rough and tumble cowboys turned soldiers like you." She walked toward the car and grinned at him over her shoulder. "Come on, let's see if we can figure out which direction Rock went."

Five minutes later, they stopped in the middle of the road, staring at the crossroad ahead of them. Billie pointed to the left. "Isn't that the produce stand we drove past earlier?"

"It sure is," Zane said, turning onto the side road they'd driven on earlier. He drove in front of the house, gravel crunching beneath their tires and parked. "Shall we see if anyone is home?"

"Yes," Billie said, hurrying out of the car and preceding Zane down the walk after he opened the gate to the yard.

They went up the steps and he tapped on the door. Silence echoed around them as they waited.

Zane pulled open the screen door and rapped loudly on the wooden door then let the screen slap shut.

Still nothing.

He tried to peer in the window by the door, but the house looked empty. Forlorn. Abandoned.

"I don't think anyone is here."

"If this did belong to the Japanese family Rock mentioned, they're most likely at the assembly center." Billie gave his hand a squeeze then turned and led the way back to the car.

Neither of them spoke as they drove out to the road. "We didn't see anything earlier when we were on this road," Zane said, feeling defeated. "I don't know which way to go to look for Rock."

"It's entirely possible someone picked him up and gave him a ride. We know he made it as far as the bus stop back there," Billie pointed down the road in the direction they'd come. "And we also know he has not returned to his family farm. It means he has to be somewhere between the two points."

"Unfortunately, there's more than twenty miles between those two points and any number of places he could be." Zane sighed and removed his hat, forking his hand through his hair. He cast a quick glimpse at Billie and caught her watching him with an odd look on her face. One he couldn't quite decipher. "Shall we eat dinner, then try this again tomorrow? I don't think we'll find any more clues tonight."

"That sounds like a good idea," Billie said, giving him an affirmative nod.

"Tell me how to find that restaurant you mentioned earlier," he said as they headed back toward Portland.

Two and a half hours later, Zane pulled up in front of the rooming house where Billie lived and parked. He turned in the seat to face her and took her hand in his. "Thanks for coming with me today, Billie. In spite of the reason, I truly enjoyed spending time with you."

"I enjoyed the day with you, too. The movie was perfect." She squeezed his hand then cast a cautious look at the big Victorian house. The flutter of curtains in a front window made her stiffen. "I better get going. The warden is watching out the window."

Zane chuckled. "And I bet she's a stickler for rules, especially no boys allowed. Is that right?"

"Why, Lieutenant West, have you been here before?" she gave him an observant look. "You've no doubt snuck in to one or two places you shouldn't have been. Is that right?"

He started to answer, but she held up a hand. "No, don't tell me. I don't want to know."

She reached for his hand again, giving it a final squeeze. "Thank you for everything, Zane. If you want help searching tomorrow, let me know. I have the day off."

"Why don't I pick you up after breakfast and we can drive back to where we left off this evening?" He hated to say good night, to tell her goodbye, but at least he had one more day with her before he had to leave. If they persisted, perhaps they'd discover Rock's whereabouts tomorrow. It was as though he could feel the presence of his friend nearby, but he had no idea why, or where to look for him.

"I'll be ready. Have a nice evening, Zane."

"You, too, Billie, girl."

Zane started to get out to open her door, but she shook her head. "It's better if I just go in. Good night."

She opened the door and jumped out of the car, hurrying up the walk. At the front door, she turned and gave him a brief wave before disappearing inside.

Zane smiled all the way back to the hotel where he was staying, wondering why he'd finally met a girl who could turn his heart to mush when he had no time for such foolishness.

His father had once said something about love knowing no time or season. Evidently, his dad had been right.

***★ *Chapter Four* ★**•

"I'd so hoped we'd find him today," Billie said as she and Zane sat at a picnic table in a small park and ate the hamburgers he'd insisted on buying for their dinner.

Zane looked as crushed as she felt that their search for Rock hadn't turned up a single lead. After he picked her up at the boarding house early that morning, they'd driven back to where the bus driver said he'd kicked Rock off the bus. They stopped at every house, every business, every wide spot in the road between there and the farm, but not a single person had seen him.

Disheartened, they'd driven back to Portland. Billie was glad when Zane suggested they get some dinner and take it to a nearby park to eat. She wasn't ready to say goodbye to him, even though she knew he had to leave in the morning for California. Although she'd only met him a few days ago, she felt like she'd known him forever. When he left, he'd take a piece of her with him. A part of her heart she vowed she'd never give away.

Perhaps that was for the best. With Zane, there was no danger of her becoming too attached to him since she'd likely never see him again.

If she believed in fairytales and whirlwind romances, she'd admit she'd fallen head over heels in love with him the moment she turned around and saw him in the hospital. But that was ridiculous. Wasn't it?

Of course it was. She had her nursing career and plans for her future. Plans that absolutely did not include a soldier, no matter how handsome, charming, sweet, and kind that man happened to be.

Zane slumped across the table from her, leaning on one elbow as he toyed with his French fries instead of eating them. "I was just sure we'd find him, or at least find someone who'd seen him. How could he just disappear? Maybe someone with underhanded schemes happened upon him? What if..."

Billie reached over and placed her hand on Zane's. "Don't say it, let alone think it. Rock will turn up one of these days, and when he does, we'll all be surprised."

Zane nodded, although it was a half-hearted effort at best. He ate a few more fries then leaned back and looked around the park. Since they were the only ones there, he'd left the radio playing in the car to break the quiet that settled around them.

Thunder boomed overhead and they both looked up. Billie didn't relish the idea of getting soaked, but the sky wasn't that dark. A chance existed the storm would roll on by.

She gathered the trash from their meal and carried it to the garbage can then brushed off her hands. Drops of rain started to fall and she looked up as Zane stepped in front of her.

"Care to dance with me?" he asked, holding out his hands.

Billie knew the smart thing to do was to climb in the car, shut the door, and wait for him to drive her home. But her heart overruled her head.

"I'd like that," she said in a low voice she barely recognized as her own. Zane swept her into his arms as the singer on the radio crooned "The Very Thought of You."

While a soft spring rain fell around them, Zane danced her around in circles, humming along to the song. Billie wondered if he had any idea what he was doing to her or the damage the romantic song combined with the even more romantic moment was inflicting on her heart.

"It's just the thought of you," he whispered as the singer sang the last line of the song.

One moment they were dancing and the next Zane had bracketed her face with his hands and was kissing the rain drops from her eyelids, her cheeks, her lips.

The second his mouth brushed hers, Billie felt the impact of the touch throughout every cell of her body. When he wrapped her in his arms and lifted her up, she slid her arms around his neck and gave herself over to the passionate exchange.

Oh, the man could kiss! His lips tantalized hers in a dance far more exquisite than any their feet might have executed. And he tasted heavenly — rich, dark, and decidedly decadent.

In that moment, Billie knew she was lost. Lost to emotions she hadn't anticipated, to a love she'd most certainly not expected. Lost to the possibilities of what the future might hold with Zane by her side.

Finally, he lifted his head and grinned at her. The dimples popped out in his cheeks and his teeth gleamed in contrast to the tan of his skin. "That was the best dance I've ever had, Billie, girl."

She felt heat burn her cheeks as she thought about how she'd been behaving, but she couldn't muster enough guilt to truly care. Zane was still leaving tomorrow and this might be her only opportunity to experience such bliss.

"Shall we take another spin," she asked, pressing her lips to his before he could answer.

Several minutes later, he raised his head again, but continued to clasp her against him. He held her gently, but with a fierce possessiveness that stole her breath.

"I better get you home, Billie, or I might decide to keep you out dancing in the rain all night." He spoke close to her ear, stirring the curls with his breath while stirring her heart with the temptation to cast caution aside and fall completely, irrevocably in love with him.

But she couldn't.

It was going to be hard enough to tell him goodbye as it was without spending more time with him. Reluctantly, she nodded and he kissed her cheek. He carried her over to the car and set her inside before he jogged around and got behind the wheel.

A fire smoldered in his eyes, one that made her blood zing through her veins. "What are you doing all the way over there?" he asked with a smirk as he faced her.

Before she could reply, he'd tugged her so close the warmth of his thigh seared against hers. "That's better." He winked at her then put the car in gear. He took his time driving her back to the rooming house. The little rain storm had passed and a rainbow popped out in the evening sky.

"That's beautiful," Billie said, pointing to it as he parked in front of the rooming house.

"So are you, Billie, girl." Zane took her hand in his and brought it to his lips, kissing the backs of her fingers with such deliberate care, Billie thought she might melt into the leather seats.

"Zane," she said in a pained voice full of longing. Longing for things she couldn't have. Longing for things better left alone.

"I sure hate to say goodbye to you, Beautiful." Zane's thumb traced a circle around and around on the inside of her wrist, causing sensations Billie had never experienced to weaken her knees. "You have my address, though. Will you promise to write to me, even if you don't hear from Rock?"

"I promise," Billie whispered, wanting Zane to hold her again, to kiss her like he had at the park.

The reality that she may never see him again crashed around her. Heedless to what Miss Burwell might think, Billie wrapped her arms around his neck once more and pressed her cheek to his. "I'm so glad I met you, Zane West. I'll think of you often and always keep you in my prayers. Be safe and promise you'll look me up if you ever get back to Portland."

"I promise, Billie. I promise." Zane burrowed

his hands into her hair and she heard him inhale a deep breath before his lips touched hers in a gentle, reverent kiss. "I better let you go. Walk you to the door?"

"No. Let's make this goodbye." She opened the door and started to get out, then looked at him. She trailed her hand over his firm jaw, committing everything she could about him to memory, convinced it would be the last time she ever saw him. Before she flung herself into his arms, she jumped out of the car, dashed up the walk and hurried inside without looking back.

"Who is that man?" Miss Burwell demanded before the door clicked shut.

Billie spun around, not in the mood to deal with the crotchety busybody. "No one," she said and ran up the stairs to her room.

Hours later, long after she should have been asleep, Billie sat with a book on her lap, staring at the pages but unaware of the words. Devastated by the thought of never seeing Zane again, she wanted to pout and fuss. And cry. Oh, how she wanted to cry.

However, she wouldn't indulge in the luxury of tears. From the start, she'd known Zane would leave. Known it was foolhardy to allow feelings for the handsome soldier to escalate like a blazing wildfire the last two days. Billie should have stuck to her rule of never, ever letting a man in a uniform turn her head.

Yet Zane had. There was no use in denying it. Denying the stirrings she felt in her heart, in her very soul for him.

With her heart aching and her thoughts muddled, she didn't hear the quiet knock on her door until the knob rattled. Billie had locked it earlier to make sure Miss Burwell left her alone, not that it would stop the woman since she had keys to all the rooms.

Quickly unfolding her legs, having tucked them beneath her in the overstuffed chair, she hurried to the door. Expecting to find Miss Burwell standing there, she was taken by surprise when Peggy and three other girls pushed past her and plowed into the room.

"What's going on?" she asked as her friends hustled over to the window. Peggy pushed it wide open and waved her hand at someone outside.

"There's a certain handsome man down there quite eager to see you," Peggy said with a grin. She motioned for Billie to join them at the window.

Shocked, Billie wasted no time in leaning out the window between the girls and peering down in the darkness to see a man in a uniform looking up at her from the backyard. She waggled her fingers at him and he waved back, then jumped up and caught a hold of a limb in the big old white oak tree that grew near the house.

"Is he climbing up here?" Peggy asked, slipping an arm around Billie's shoulders and giving her a squeeze. "Gracious, but he's intent on seeing you. He's been throwing rocks at windows for half an hour, trying to find you. He woke up Suzie, Marlene, and Joann, hitting their windows with rocks. My window was open and the rock he tossed in hit me on the arm. When I got up to see what was going on, he asked if I'd come get you." Peggy's grin broadened as Zane continued climbing the tree. "He's absolutely marvelous, Billie."

"We all think so. Not only is he dreamy, but romantic!" Suzie said, holding her hands beneath her chin with a giddy look on her face.

"Hush, or you'll have ol' burr-under-her-blanket Burwell up here," Peggy cautioned the younger girl.

The five of them lingered in the window as Zane continued up the tree. When he reached a limb close to Billie's window, he held his arms out to his sides for balance and deftly walked to the end of the thick, sturdy branch.

Just watching him made Billie dizzy. All five girls sucked in a gasp when he leaped off the limb and grabbed the edge of her windowsill.

"Are you crazy?" Billie asked in a soft voice as Zane pulled himself inside.

"Just for you, doll," he said with a teasing smile as he swung in his legs and landed on his feet.

Billie fisted her hands on her hips, trying to appear stern. "You're going to get me kicked out of here, you know."

"Oh, I don't think so. Your friends are all good eggs. They'll keep the warden occupied for a few minutes." Zane offered charming smiles to the women. "Won't you, girls?"

"Of course," Peggy said, herding the other three girls out of the room. "But I'm leaving the door open."

Billie absently nodded to her friend as she stared at Zane. He wore the same clothes he'd had on all day, although he'd removed his tie. His shirt was wrinkled and his hair looked as though he'd forked his hand through it multiple times, but he appeared so appealing and handsome, it was nearly more than she could handle in her current frame of mind.

"I had to see you again, just for a minute," Zane said, taking a step forward. He opened his arms and Billie was instantly in them, pressed against the solid warmth of his chest. For the first time since her parents died, she felt like she belonged, like she'd found her home. But how could that be? Zane was a soldier, here today and gone tomorrow. She'd never have a future with him. Not ever. But right then, tomorrow seemed so distant and Zane was so enticingly real and near.

Determined not to think about the future while she was captivated at that moment, she squeezed him a little tighter.

She felt his kiss on top of her head as he held her close. "I'm glad you came back even if Miss Burwell tosses me out on my ear."

"She won't. I promise," Zane said, pressing a kiss to her temple. "I thought I'd never find your room. I've been out there for half of forever tossing rocks at windows. I figured I'd either break out a piece of glass or find someone awake who'd be willing to come get you. The first two girls who stuck their heads out their windows should be more careful about what they say to strange men." His tone held a hint of disgust and censure. "I sure was glad when Peggy came to her window."

Billie tipped back her head and smiled at him.

"Peggy is a good friend. In fact, right now, I'd say she's the very best."

Zane smiled, dimples dancing enticingly in his cheeks. "I'd have to agree." He loosened his hold and took a step back, giving her room a cursory glance before turning his attention back to her. "I know I shouldn't be here, Billie, but I just needed to see you one last time."

"I'm glad you came, Zane," she said, then decided she needed to end whatever little fantasy the two of them had created the past few days. "It's been grand spending time with you and I've enjoyed every minute of it, but..." She hesitated, uncertain what to say.

"But what, Billie, girl?" Zane asked, giving her a pleading look. "If you're gonna tell me it's been swell getting to know you but not to start planning the wedding, I was thinking I should say something along those lines, too."

Relieved, yet oddly upset by his words, she nodded. "Oh, good. No hearts will be broken and no expectations will go unmet. We'll still be friends, though, right?"

"Absolutely, doll. Meeting you has been one of the nicest, best things that's happened to me in a long time." A teasing gleam glimmered in his gorgeous blue eyes. "But just because we're friends doesn't mean you won't give me a goodbye kiss, does it?"

"I think one last kiss could be arranged." She stood on her tiptoes and slid her hands along Zane's muscled arms. Heat radiated from him as his lips hovered just above hers. She knew she was playing with fire, but she didn't care. Not when thoughts of Zane's kisses chased every bit of sense right out of her head.

What might have happened next, she'd never know because Peggy rushed through the doorway, wide-eyed and out of breath from racing up the stairs. "She's coming. Hide!"

Zane started toward the window, but Billie pushed him in the direction of her bed. "Climb under there and be quiet."

Although it was a tight squeeze, he somehow managed to wedge himself beneath her bed. She kicked at his left foot as it stuck out from below her ruffled floral bedspread. He yanked it underneath the cover and Billie plopped down in her overstuffed chair. She whipped open the book she'd been unable to concentrate on earlier, then realized she held it upside down. Quickly righting it, she willed her pounding pulse to steady.

Peggy leaned against the doorframe, as though she'd dropped by to chat, and caught the emery board Suzie tossed her as she raced past on her way to her room. With slow, lazy strokes, Peggy brushed the board back and forth over her nails and snapped a piece of gum.

"What are you girls doing up? It's past time for lights to be out and you know I don't like you talking this late at night." Miss Burwell stood in the doorway, hair tightly bound against her scalp with little curlers that looked like rubber plugs. The disapproving sneer on her face matched the imperial gleam in her eyes as she glared from Peggy to Billie then back to Peggy.

"I'm sorry, Miss Burwell. It's my fault," Billie said, rising to her feet as her landlady marched into the room and looked around, as though she expected to find the girls engaged in a questionable activity. She walked over to the window, slammed it shut and locked it, then whirled around, glowering at Billie.

"See that it doesn't happen again. Now, Peggy, get yourself to your room and the two of you get some sleep. Aren't you both scheduled to work early tomorrow?"

"Yes, ma'am," Peggy said, pushing away from the doorframe and giving Billie a wink once Miss Burwell's back was turned. "Night, Billie. See you in the morning."

"Good night, Peggy. Have a pleasant night, Miss Burwell." Billie offered the older woman a repentant look.

"Humph!" the woman said, then made her way down the hall to the stairs.

Quietly, Billie closed her door and waited a few seconds before opening it to make sure Miss Burwell hadn't crept back to it. Assured the woman made her way down the stairs, Billie shut the door and hurried to her bed. "You can come out," she whispered.

Zane tried to scoot out, but remained trapped when he couldn't angle free from the bed frame. Finally, Billie dropped to the floor and hefted one side up until he could squirm out.

"Whew, that was close," he said, sitting beside her with a goofy grin on his face that she found particularly endearing.

"You've got to go, Zane. If Miss Burwell comes back up here, she'll…"

Zane silenced her. Much to her surprise, his lips settled over hers in a sweet, tender kiss. The next thing Billie knew, she was sitting on his lap, arms around his neck, while his masterful kisses blocked every thought from her mind except how much she wanted to be with him. Only him. Forevermore him.

Eventually, Zane lifted his head and smiled. "Kisses like those are definitely worth getting stuck under your bed. In fact, I'd crawl all the way here from the train depot on my hands and knees with a bed on my back, in a blizzard, for another kiss like that."

Billie buried her face against his neck, breathing deeply of his unique, masculine scent. His fragrance made her think of open range, wild horses, and summer sunshine. "I'm going to really miss you, Zane. Promise you'll write?"

"I already told you I would. I don't break my promises." Zane gave her a kiss on her nose then set her on her feet and stood. "But I better get out of here before you really do get in hot water with your landlady. From what I saw, the ol' gal could teach Hitler a new way to dance a jig."

Billie giggled quietly and he grinned, brushing his thumb across her cheek. "I just had to see you one more time before I left in the morning."

"I could go with you to the train," Billie offered. She'd have to find someone to cover for her at work for an hour, but it was doable.

"No, Billie. I know you have to work and I've

already wrangled up enough problems for you." Zane's hands burrowed into her hair then slid around to the back of her neck where his thumb gently brushed over her skin, making a shiver of delight trickle down her spine. "I'm sure glad I met you, though. Be a good girl and stay out of trouble?"

"Without you here, what trouble will there be for me to get into?" Tears burned her eyes, but she willed them away. Suddenly wanting to give Zane something to remember her by, she opened a drawer and dug through the contents until she found a photograph Peggy had talked her into posing for last autumn. Her hair had been shorter in the image, but it looked nice, and she wore one of her favorite dresses. Quickly, she wrote a message on the back of the photo then tucked it inside a cardboard photo holder.

From another drawer, she pulled a green silk scarf she'd saved weeks to purchase and handed it, along with the photo, to Zane. "I want you to have these, so you won't forget me." She shrugged. "Maybe the scarf will be like a good luck charm or something."

"I could never forget you, Billie Brighton. Not in a million years." He glanced down at the photo and grinned. "Thank you." He wrapped the scarf around the photo and tucked it in his pocket and stepped over to the window, but jerked back.

"Well, that's not going to work," he said, pointing outside, careful to remain unseen from below.

Billie leaned over and looked out the window.

Miss Burwell stood in the middle of the lawn, staring up at the bedroom windows, as though she knew something was amiss.

"Come on." Billie grabbed his hand and led him out of the room and down the hall. She stopped and tapped on a door near the stairs. Peggy poked her head out, then grinned when she saw Zane.

"Making an escape?" she whispered.

"Trying. Burwell is on guard out back so he can't leave the way he came in," Billie said as Peggy left her room and crept with them down the stairs. "Can you watch her while he sneaks out the front?"

"I'm on the job," Peggy said. At the bottom of the stairs, she offered Zane a snappy salute then hurried through the dining room to the library where she could keep an eye on Miss Burwell.

"You really do have nice friends," Zane whispered as he and Billie made their way to the front door.

Billie turned the lock as quietly as she could and eased the door open. Zane looked both ways before he stepped outside. Assured they were alone, he pulled Billie out on the front porch. His arms encircled her as he tantalized her lips with an urgent, intense kiss. When he finally pulled away and tossed her a rascally grin, she grasped onto the support post to keep her balance.

"Be safe, beautiful Billie. Goodbye." He ran down the steps, across the yard, and out to where he'd parked his car on the other side of the street.

Although she wanted to linger and watch him go, she closed the door, turned the lock, and ran through the house to where Peggy hid behind the curtain in the library.

"He's gone," Billie whispered, motioning for Peggy to move away from the window.

"It's a good thing, too. Miss Burwell is heading back in. Let's go." The two women scrambled up the steps and, after Billie offered Peggy a brief word of thanks and a hug, they both rushed into their rooms and shut their doors. Billie turned off her light, changed into her nightgown, and slid into the bed.

The thought of Zane coming back to see her, climbing the tree just to give her a kiss, filled her dreams with a bliss unlike any she'd previously known.

*★★★ *Chapter Five* ★★★*

"Hey, Jimmy. How are you doing this evening?" Billie asked a pallid young soldier as she set his dinner tray in front of him.

A ghost of a smile skipped across his lips before his face settled into its continuous morose expression. "I'm fine, Nurse Brighton."

"Aren't you hungry, Jimmy?" she pushed his tray a little closer. "The food is really good if you'd give it a taste. You can't beat the mashed potatoes. Try just a bite." She held a fork out to the young man.

The private took it and poked at the potatoes, eventually taking a small bite before he set down the fork then pushed away his tray. The soldier was so despondent and lethargic, she'd watched him waste away over the past two weeks since he'd been at the hospital. The poor young man had lost both legs in an explosion, but he also seemed to have lost his spirit and will to live.

Billie had no intention of letting him die when he had so much life ahead of him. He just needed to realize how fortunate he was to be alive and work past his grief and the mire of pity sucking him down into such a dark place.

She moved the tray then fluffed his covers. "What was your favorite candy bar when you were younger, Private Harwood?"

He gave her a strange look. "It was a coconut bar dipped in chocolate. I haven't had one since I left home in December." He licked his bottom lip, as though he could taste the candy. "Boy, I sure would like to have one."

Billie asked him the name of the candy and pried a list of his favorite foods out of him as she took his pulse and got him settled for the night.

The next morning, Billie dressed in one of her favorite outfits, sent her uniform to work with Peggy, then set out to find a candy bar for Jimmy.

She walked to a nearby grocer's store, but they had never heard of the candy. Billie went from one store to the next. At the fifth store she tried, she finally found the candy and purchased the last dozen candy bars. She also bought a package of cookies Jimmy mentioned he liked, and a handful of comic books, including Bugs Bunny and Goofy. The last thing Jimmy needed was to read anything about the war. It was essential to his survival he relax, laugh, and take his mind off what had happened.

If she could get him to do that, then they could work on getting him on the road to recovery. Once he got his head in the right place, his body would follow.

Out of time to walk all the way back to the hospital, Billie flagged down a cab. For the fifth time in as many minutes, she glanced at her watch, a pretty little thing set with marcarsite stones that had been a gift from the grateful wife of a patient. However, if the cab driver didn't hustle, she'd be late for her shift at the hospital, and that would never do.

The moment the driver pulled up at the curb, she paid the man and bounded out of the cab with a paper sack full of treasures for Jimmy. She turned around and nearly collided with a well-dressed man.

"Pardon me," he said, tipping his hat with a smile. His thorough perusal began at the emerald green hat on her golden head and ended at the open toes of her matching high-heeled shoes. "You look fetching today, Nurse Brighton."

Billie narrowed her gaze as she stared at the man. Something about him seemed familiar — his blue eyes, the shape of his jaw, the charming smile. Recognition washed over her along with excitement. She squealed and wrapped her arms around Rock Laroux.

"Good golly, Captain Laroux! I was sure you'd passed on to glory after you ran away," she said, hugging him tighter, relieved he was not only alive, but appeared to be thriving.

Rock returned her hug, then released her and took a step back. "I didn't run away, I merely left without asking Doc's permission."

"Well, I'm glad you did. I never expected to see you looking like this," she said. She took in the hat on his head, the expensive, well-cut suit, and the polished shoes on his feet. He looked healthy and happy. Pleased for him, for his returned health, she smiled broadly. "It's good to see you, Rock."

"You too, Nurse Brighton." Rock squeezed her hand and gave her cheek a quick kiss. "Thank you for taking such good care of me while I was here. I appreciate everything you did."

Guilt assailed Billie. Obviously, there was something, some major component of his care, the hospital, the doctor, or the nursing staff had failed to deliver. Rock had nearly died at the hospital and most likely would have if he remained there.

"It was all part of the job, Captain." She glanced at her watch again, aware she was about to be late, and took a step toward the door. "I'm truly happy to see you well. Take care of yourself."

Rock gave her another smile. "You too, Nurse Brighton."

Shocked by Rock's appearance, she spun around, rushed up the steps, and inside the hospital. The heels of her shoes clacked across the floor as she made her way to Jimmy's room. She walked into the room, tamping down her astonishment over seeing Rock, and smiled.

"Jimmy, today is your lucky day," she said, smiling as she walked over to the young private's bed.

He pushed himself up from his pillows and shook his head. "I think my luck ran out a while back." His glance settled on the blankets below his knees that should have covered his legs. Instead the blankets were flat, a stark reminder of what he'd lost.

"I don't believe it, Jimmy. In fact, what I have here proves otherwise."

He appeared the slightest bit curious as Billie

reached into the paper sack and pulled out a candy bar.

"It can't be!" he exclaimed, reaching for the candy bar.

"It can and it is," Billie said, fighting back tears as he ripped off the paper and bit into the candy.

Jimmy closed his eyes and moaned in pleasure as he savored the first bite. When his eyes opened, he gave her a huge grin that transformed his face and added color to his pale cheeks. "I don't know where or how you found this, but thank you."

"You're welcome, Jimmy." Billie set the package of cookies on his bed tray.

"Cookies, too?" Jimmy took another bite of his candy bar then fingered the package of cookies with his other hand. "You're an angel, Nurse Brighton. A pure angel."

Billie laughed. "Oh, there are many who would disagree with you, Jimmy, but I'm glad you like the treats." She handed him the comics, then showed him the other candy bars before tucking them into the drawer of his nightstand. "Now, you be a good boy and start eating your meals, and you can have a candy bar as a reward. How does that sound?"

Jimmy grinned at her. "Like I'm six years old again and Ma is trying to bribe me to do something I don't want to." He reached out a hand to her. She took it in hers and gave it a gentle squeeze. "I can't thank you enough for this, Nurse Brighton. It means a lot to me."

"It's my pleasure, Jimmy." She gently set his hand on the bed. "But I better get going or I'll be unforgivably late for my shift."

Before he could say anything else, Billie rushed to change into her uniform and get to work. All the nurses were abuzz about Rock showing up out of nowhere. A few hours later, Billie had the opportunity to ask Doctor Ridley if he'd seen Rock.

"I gave him a thorough exam. From what I can see, Rock is perfectly healthy and his wounds are finally healing like they should be. He said he's been living on a farm eating lots of good, fresh food. Seems to be doing the trick," the doctor said. "Before I forget, I should send a note to his friend that was here a few weeks ago looking for him."

Billie had been so stunned to see Rock, so taken aback by his miraculous recovery, and then her concerns about Jimmy, that she'd not given a thought to letting Zane know Rock was alive and well.

"Do you think you could send a telegram to Lieutenant West?" Billie asked. "I'm sure he'd love to hear the news as quickly as possible."

"I'll take care of that right now. I didn't even think to mention to Rock he had a friend looking for him."

Billie shook her head. "I didn't say anything either. I was so caught off guard by his unexpected appearance that I could scarcely remember my own name."

The doctor laughed. "Indeed, Nurse Brighton." He pointed down the hall. "Now, tell me what you did to Private Jimmy Harwood. That boy seemed like a whole new person when I checked on him a few minutes ago. He was sitting up in bed laughing — actually laughing — as he read a comic book."

"Well, I..." Billie described what she'd done for the patient.

By the end of her shift, Billie was exhausted, but in a good way. After she'd asked to have a special meal prepared for Jimmy, she'd taken it up to him and had felt entirely gratified when he'd cleaned up every bite of the chicken and dumplings along with a serving of tender green beans. As a treat, she'd given him another of his precious store of candy bars.

Billie had asked the store to let her know when they had more in stock. Hopefully, Jimmy's supply would last for a while. At any rate, Jimmy looked like a new young man as he'd finished the last bite of his candy.

Billie checked his vitals, settled him for the night, and smiled when he reached out and grabbed her hand. "Thanks again, Nurse Brighton. The comics are perfect. Just what I needed."

She gently squeezed his hand. "When you finish those, let me know and I'll see what else I can find."

"I will."

With her heart lighter than it had been in a while, Billie tiredly made her way home. Since it was late, she'd eaten dinner at the hospital and barely made it in the door before Miss Burwell's curfew.

The woman scowled at her as she entered the house, but didn't say anything when Billie plodded up the stairs to her room. After taking a bath, Billie wrapped herself in a soft robe and sat down at her desk, intent on writing Zane a letter.

She started three times, tossing away her attempts before scowling at her waste of paper. Whatever she wrote next was what he would receive. Her pen scratched against the stationery, filling three pages. She signed her name, tucked the sheets of paper into an envelope and addressed it before she changed her mind. She thought about tucking in a little something for Zane, but had no idea what. She'd already given him a photo and her favorite scarf, like a lovesick schoolgirl. He probably thought she was an idiot. If he did, she couldn't blame him. She'd certainly acted like one around him, losing her sense as though she didn't own a healthy portion.

Regardless, she wanted Zane to know Rock was well and nearby. Billie was happy for Rock. So grateful he'd survived and come out the victor over whatever had been robbing his very life. For the hundredth, or perhaps thousandth time, she wondered what had been making Rock so sick. Doctor Ridley said they'd likely never know for sure, but thought perhaps it might have been something at the hospital, or a mixture of medications.

At least Rock had been wise enough, or desperate enough, to take charge of his life and get well.

Now, if she could just get Private Harwood back on track. She thought back about how happy he'd been to get the candy and cookies, as well as the comic books. If Billie had to do battle every day to get the cook to make something Jimmy would eat, so be it. But she was making sure that young man got well and returned to a normal life, or as normal as it would be for a twenty-year-old who'd lost both of his legs.

With no energy left to expend, Billie removed her robe, turned off the lights and climbed into bed, thinking about Zane.

A few days later, she'd just arrived home from work when Miss Burwell thrust a small package at her. "This came for you today," the woman said, frowning at her.

"Thank you." Billie took the paper-wrapped package, nodded once to the woman, and hurried upstairs to her room.

She never received packages, unless she'd ordered something through the mail, which was a rare occurrence. In no rush to end the anticipation of what might be inside the package, one that was a complete surprise, she set the box on her desk, changed out of her uniform, and took her clothes down to the laundry room where she washed them then carried them out back to the clothes line to dry.

By then, it was time for dinner. She joined the other women who were there for the meal, presided over by Miss Burwell. The food was always plentiful and good, although Miss Burwell often served cold meals during the warm months. Tonight's menu included chilled cucumber soup with fresh dill, seared fish, cottage cheese, and tomato slices. Dessert was a bowl of fresh strawberries from the plants in the garden at the back of the house. As the women had time, they helped in the large Victory garden, all wanting to do their part.

Full of the good meal and ready to discover what was in the box in her room, Billie didn't linger downstairs after dinner. She made her way to her room, picked up the box and settled into her overstuffed chair. She tried to read the return address, but it had been smudged so badly it was completely illegible. With a dainty pair of sewing scissors she rarely used, she cut away the string that encircled the box and removed the paper. A small envelope was tucked beneath the pink ribbon tied around a box wrapped in pale pink paper decorated with dark pink and blue flowers.

She opened the envelope and took out a single sheet of folded paper. It smelled of leather and sunshine — and Zane.

Hello, Billie, girl!
You probably thought you'd gotten plumb shuck of me when I left, but here I am, turning up like a bad penny.

"Hardly," Billie whispered. She smiled as she returned to Zane's letter.

I made it to the base in California. My orders are to return to Hawaii and rejoin my unit there, so I'll be shipping out tomorrow. A few fellas and I decided to have a high time out on the town before we left. Since I'm not one for drinking firewater, as my daddy always called it, a buddy named Bud (his real name is Lawrence Muldoon, but everyone calls him Bud) and I wandered past shops, seeing what we could see. When I saw this in a store window, it

*made me think of you. Hope you don't think it's too
personal of a gift, especially between friends.*

*We are still friends, aren't we, beautiful Billie?
I sure hope we are, because meeting you was one of
the best things that's ever happened to me.*

"Me, too, cowboy," Billie said, then glanced at
her open door, hoping no one heard her talking to
herself. She got up, closed the door, then returned to
the letter.

*By now, I am praying Rock has been found and
he's well. I still can't help but think if something
awful had happened to him, I'd know. That
probably sounds like I've gone daffy, but Rock is
closer to me than my own brother.*

*Anyway, I need to finish this note so they can
send it with the gift.*

*Take care of yourself, doll, and know there is
one ol' Texas cowboy that you've made a little
happier with just the memory of your sweet smile.*

Until next time!

With kindest regards,

Zane

*P.S. In the event a whole slew of homesick
soldiers are writing to you, this is Lieutenant Zane
West, the one who climbed in your bedroom window
to steal a goodbye kiss. And, man, what a kiss that
was!*

"As if I could ever forget you, Zane West,"
Billie admonished quietly. How many men did he
think she let climb into her room, or kiss her for that

matter. Zane had been the first man she'd spent any time with, outside of work, since before Thanksgiving. No matter what anyone thought or assumed, Billie spent far more of her time and energy on work than she did thinking about handsome men. She had no interest in marrying just for the sake of marrying and she most adamantly would not entertain the notion of a relationship with a soldier.

However, thoughts of Zane's kisses, the warmth of his smile, and how good it felt to be in his arms made her consider how wonderful it would be to belong to a man like him.

No.

Not a man like him, but him. Zane was unlike the other men she'd met and dated. He was… oh, she didn't even know how to put into words what he was, but Zane was special. She was smart enough to know that and wise enough to keep her distance from it.

Or so she told herself as she carefully unwrapped the box and set aside the paper.

A smile brightened her whole face as she opened the box and lifted out an exquisitely cut glass bottle of her favorite perfume.

How had Zane known what perfume she wore? Had he recognized the scent? It had been very popular a few years ago. Although many girls had moved on to a different fragrance, Billie still favored the slightly exotic tones of Tabu.

Pleased by the gift, and even more delighted by Zane's note, she quickly sat down and wrote to him. The next morning, she rushed down to the nearby grocery store and purchased candy bars, cookies, crackers, and several packages of chewing gum, boxing them up and sending them to Zane along with her letter. She knew it would take weeks to reach him, but she hoped he enjoyed the surprise when it arrived as much as she appreciated the gift of perfume.

The reason why she wanted to make Zane smile was one she didn't care to examine.

After all, they were friends. Just friends.

⋆⋆★ *Chapter Six* ★⋆⋆

"Mail call!" A loud voice cut through the typical cacophony on the military base. "Mail call!"

Zane glanced over at Bud as the two of them walked back toward the barracks on a sunny afternoon. The air carried just enough of a breeze to keep the humidity in check, making for pleasant weather.

Not that Zane had much time to enjoy it. Since he returned to his squad, he'd immediately been pressed into duty, flying search missions that carried him hundreds of miles away from the Hawaiian Islands.

Concerned about another attack from Japan, patrols kept an eye on potential targets as well as possible problems.

"Mail call!" the voice sounded again.

"Want to go see if you got anything?" Zane asked. Although he rarely received mail, Bud came from a big family and often had letters and packages awaiting him. In fact, Bud was good about sharing cookies and treats his family sent. Although Bud was amiable and good-looking, he didn't have a wife or steady girl, saying he was married to the military, until the war was over, anyway.

"Sure," Bud said with a shrug.

The two of them veered toward a Jeep where a mail clerk stood in the back. Surrounded by bags of mail, the clerk distributed each piece to its rightful owner. The clerk was on the letter C as he called out names, so Zane and Bud stood at the back of the group and watched their fellow squad members.

One of the men received an oddly shaped package. Two of the jokers in the group took it from his hands and began shaking it, tossing it back and forth.

"What do you suppose it is, Marv? A football?" one teased.

"It's a stuffed coon. Aren't you from the hicks, Marv?" the other one said.

The soldier named Marv grabbed his package away from them and hurried on his way.

As the mail was handed out, some made comments on packages or bulky envelopes. A few men looked forlorn and disappointed when their names weren't called. Zane knew how hard it was to build up hope of getting word from home and ending up forgotten. He'd been in the military long enough it no longer bothered him, but he felt a twinge of pity for the new men who were still lonesome for home.

The past ten years, Zane had been at West Point and then at various posts with the United States Army Air Force. His brother had threatened to shoot him if he set foot on the ranch, so home was wherever he was based.

"Muldoon!" the clerk called, holding a box out

their direction, along with several letters.

"Hot diggety!" Bud grinned at Zane as he rushed forward and nabbed his mail before the jokesters could grab it. He returned to Zane's side, shuffling through the letters and giving the box a gentle shake.

"What'd you get?" Zane asked with a grin.

"Letters from three of my sisters, my aunt Alma, and the box is from the folks. I sure hope Ma sent some cookies."

Zane smirked. "I hope she did, too."

Bud looked over at him and raised an eyebrow. "What makes you think I'm sharing?"

"Because you always do," Zane said, nudging Bud with his elbow. "Ready to go?"

"Aw, let's wait and see who else gets mail. Who knows, maybe you'll even get a letter."

Zane shrugged. "I doubt that, but we've got nothing better to do at the moment." In truth, Zane had hoped to hear from Billie. He'd sent her a note and bottle of perfume the night before he left California, and he wondered if it had been a little too brash for her taste. Billie might be beautiful, and she might be used to soldiers flirting with her, but he knew she was a good girl. One who wouldn't take his kisses or intentions lightly.

He was glad she'd agreed they would part friends, since he had no time or energy to devote to a relationship. Billie seemed like a sensible, well-grounded girl who would understand he'd enjoyed her company, but she likely wouldn't see him again.

Then he'd gone and sent her perfume, of all things, along with that stupid note. If he'd had his head on straight, he wouldn't have done either. He would have waited a month, sent her an impersonal note, and left it at that.

But he couldn't.

He'd promised her he'd keep in touch. And even if he hadn't promised, he wanted to. He wanted to know how she was doing. He wanted to picture her marching around the hospital, bullying the patients into doing her bidding. He wanted to dream of her as she'd looked when he'd climbed in her bedroom window — relaxed and comfortable, and so gorgeous he could hardly think straight.

When it came to Nurse Billie Brighton, Zane was in big, big trouble. Which is why it was a good thing an ocean and a war separated them.

At any rate, Zane had been nearly beside himself with relief when he received a telegram from Doctor Ridley letting him know Rock was not only alive, but in excellent health. He'd sent a message back and acquired Rock's new address and mailed his friend a letter. He hoped to hear from Rock soon. He wondered if Rock would try to rejoin, since he'd been honorably discharged. From what the doctor said, Rock's arm injury prevented his hand from working properly. It would be hard for a pilot to do his job without two good hands, but not impossible.

However, he didn't think the military would be interested in taking a chance. For Rock's sake, he hoped his friend found a new occupation, one that kept him far away from enemy fire and battlefields.

"Walker!" the clerk called, brandishing an envelope over his head.

"Almost there," Bud said, as he held his mail to his chest like a precious treasure, which it was. "I'll bet you a chocolate bar that you get mail today."

"You're on," Zane said, shaking Bud's hand. "I think I want a…"

"West! Zane West!" the clerk called, flapping an envelope at Zane.

"You owe me a Snicker's bar," Bud crowed, giving Zane a shove forward.

"And I'll happily pay that debt." Zane hurried forward and claimed his mail. An envelope with delicate, feathery script made him tamp down the urge to rip it open right there in front of everyone. He held it up to his nose and took a whiff, inhaling the slightest hint of Billie's perfume.

"He's got a sugar report, boys," one of the jokesters teased, trying to snatch Zane's letter.

He gave the young upstart a fierce scowl. "Don't you have somewhere you need to be, Corporal?"

"No, sir." The corporal's smile broadened. "Aw, come on, Tex. You never get mail, especially not from a girl. Who's the Jane?"

"Just a nurse I met when I was in Oregon. We're friends, that's all." Zane didn't know why he felt the need to explain his relationship with Billie to the group of men gathered around him. It wasn't anyone's business.

"Aren't ya gonna see what she has to say?" the corporal asked.

"In due time."

"Private Zuchowski!" the mail clerk called, and passed out the last of the mail. "That's all she wrote!" The clerk hopped off the Jeep as the men dispersed.

"Come on. I'll buy you that candy bar I owe you and we can see what we got in the mail," Zane said, giving Bud a playful punch to the arm.

Fortified with bottles of cold Coca-Cola and candy bars, they found a shady spot on a swath of lush grass to sit and read their mail.

Zane watched as Bud opened his box. Inside was a carefully packed tin of homemade molasses cookies. They might have started out soft and chewy, but by the time they spent weeks making their way to them, the cookies were dry and hard. However, from past experience, Zane knew the cookies tasted delicious dunked in a cup of coffee. Bud also received a tin of crackers, toothpaste and razors, a new comb, and several magazines.

"We can save the cookies for later, if you're interested," Bud said, piling his goodies back into the box then opening one of the letters.

"Sounds good, Bud." Zane watched as Bud shook out a piece of thin stationery. "I appreciate you sharing."

Bud glanced over at him and pointed to the letter Zane still held in his hands. "You gonna read that or just imagine what she might have said?"

Zane smiled. "I'm letting the anticipation build."

Bud rolled his eyes. "You're full of applesauce, Tex."

Zane didn't mind that some of the men called him Tex, thanks to the slight drawl he never quite managed to erase from his speech and the fact he grew up on a sprawling Texas ranch. Most of the men had a nickname, or two.

The man sitting next to him was an easy-going sort who befriended everyone, hence the nickname of Bud. From what he'd shared, Bud had grown up on a farm in Oklahoma, the youngest of four brothers and five sisters. He'd wanted nothing more than a military career. Bud had worked his way up to Second Lieutenant. Zane was sure the cheerful soldier had a promising career ahead of him, if they didn't all get killed during the war.

Unwilling to let morbid thoughts darken his day, Zane slowly opened the envelope from Billie and pulled out three sheets of paper. In spite of his determination to feign indifference, he held the stationery up to his nose, breathing deeply of her scent.

"Must be quite a girl," Bud muttered as he watched him out of the corner of his eye.

Zane scowled at him then unfolded the sheets of paper and smoothed them out against his upraised knee. He was amazed the letter had reached him so swiftly, based on the date written in the corner. Perhaps Billie knew someone who was willing to speed things along. It wouldn't surprise him if she had a contact or two who could have made sure the letter was flown over as quickly as possible.

No matter how he came to have it, he was glad she'd written. With a steadying breath, he began reading.

Dear Lieutenant West,

The most miraculous thing happened today. I bumped (quite literally, as I was about to make a mad dash up the steps of the hospital after climbing out of a cab at the curb) into Captain Rock Laroux. Oh, my gracious! I hardly recognized him. In fact, it took me a moment after he said my name to realize who he was.

Good golly, but he looks wonderful. His skin is a healthy color, his cheeks are no longer sunken, and he could walk with no trouble at all. His wounds appear to be healing quite nicely. Best of all, I don't think there is any need to worry about his demise rapidly approaching based on the healthy specimen he appeared today. I spoke with Doctor Ridley, who gave the captain an examination, and he affirmed my thoughts on the subject.

By now, I'm sure you've received the news from Doctor Ridley. He said he would send you a telegram, but I did want to send a note, just in case you didn't receive it for some reason.

I'm sure the relief I'm feeling at seeing Captain Laroux's improved state of health is nothing compared to what you are experiencing. It must be a fine thing indeed to have a friend you value so dearly that you'd go to the great lengths you did to find him.

From what the doctor shared, Rock is staying on a farm and taking in all the fresh food and sunshine he can get. What a fabulous prescription! There are days I'd like to give it a go myself.

Or at least bottle it up and share it with some of

my patients.

A vision of Billie basking in the sun, stretched out on a blanket, made Zane's collar uncomfortably tight. He tugged at it and returned to the letter.

There is a young private I've been taking care of the last few weeks. He lost both legs in a terrible explosion, but more tragic, he seems to have lost his will to live. I've tried everything to get him to eat, to exercise, to engage in the world around him, but nothing works. I finally got him to tell me the name of his favorite candy. It took me all morning to track it down, but when I brought him that candy bar, it was worth all the effort. His face lit up and he smiled — the first smile I've seen since he's been here. I brought him some silly comic books, too. He started reading them, and laughing. My gracious, but I wish I'd thought to do that when he first arrived. I'm hopeful he'll begin to recover now instead of letting his life ebb away.

I'm sorry. That's probably the last thing you want to hear about.

Nothing else exciting has taken place here, although I think Captain Laroux's sudden appearance is about all the excitement I can handle for a while. I'm just so deeply grateful he is well.

Zane experienced a spurt of jealousy. What, exactly, were Billie's feelings toward Rock? And did Rock have feelings for her? Zane thought Billie merely cared about Rock as his nurse, but what if there was more to it than that?

Mindful his imagination was about to run away with him, he reined it in and resumed reading Billie's note.

Despite the reason we spent two days together when you were here, I'm glad we had the opportunity. It was lovely to meet you, Zane. You were such fun, and a gentleman, (a rare thing, let me assure you). Many times, I've thought of how much I enjoyed getting to know you, even in the brief time we had.

Thank you for making me feel special, even though I'm sure you have oodles of girls flocking around you every time you set foot out of your plane. Our friendship is something I'll always treasure.

I pray that you'll keep safe and unharmed in these trying, harsh days of war. And no matter where you go, remember there's a nurse in Oregon who'll be thinking of you.

With the warmest affection,
Nurse Billie Brighton

Zane assumed the perfume he'd sent had not arrived by the time she mailed the letter, or she would have mentioned it. Perhaps he'd guessed wrong and it wasn't the fragrance she wore. No, he was certain of it. At least mostly certain.

He leaned back and pictured her running into Rock. A low chuckle rolled out of him and Bud cast him a curious look.

"What made you laugh?" his friend asked.

"I told you about looking for Rock and him

turning up a few weeks later."

Bud nodded. "Yep. You mentioned just a few days ago the doctor had sent you a telegram that he was alive and kicking."

"Well, there was a nurse at the hospital who helped me search for him. She's the one I sent the perfume to. We struck up a friendship, I guess you'd call it, while I was in Portland. Anyway, she was writing to let me know about Rock turning up. She said she bumped into him on the hospital steps and I was just picturing the surprise on her face when she realized who Rock was." Zane grinned. "I bet it left her plumb flummoxed."

Bud snickered. "I'm sure it did. What else did she say?"

"Oh, not much. She mentioned a soldier she's been taking care of, trying to get him to eat. Sounds like she hunted down his favorite candy and got him back on track."

Bud frowned. "How come we don't get nurses like that? The old battle-axe I had was meaner than a two-headed dragon."

Zane laughed and gave Bud a shove that almost knocked him over. "They brought her in special, just to take care of you."

Bud snorted. "I knew it!"

They joked around a few more minutes, then Bud finished reading his letters while Zane read through Billie's twice. He was just tucking the letter back into the envelope when Bud held out his hand. "I won't read it, but do you think I can take a whiff of it?"

Zane wanted to tell him no, but there wasn't

any harm in him merely sniffing the paper. He handed the letter to Bud who drew in a deep breath.

"Hmm..." Bud handed the letter to Zane then leaned back, bracing his arms behind him. He closed his eyes and appeared contemplative. "She has blond hair, curly. Petite. Curvy. Quite pretty. Great smile." He opened one eye and glanced at Zane. "Am I right?"

Zane's gaze narrowed and he glared at his friend. "How do you... how could you possibly describe her?"

"Well, a pretty nurse, you know... word gets around. Why, I bet she's got dozens of soldiers drooling at her doorstep. A girl like that..." Bud stopped and let the tension coil between them before he sniggered. "If you get any more worked up, that vein throbbing in your neck might just explode." The man grinned and waggled his finger at Zane. "I'm just yanking a knot in your rope, Tex. A few times, I've seen you looking at a picture of a girl with light hair and assumed it must be her. Can I see her photo?"

Zane gave him a long, harsh look before he took out his wallet and removed the photo Billie had given him. He'd taken it out of the cardboard holder so he could always carry it with him. The reason why he wanted to do so wasn't one he cared to examine. All he knew was he felt better, calmer, with that picture kept where he could look at it whenever the mood struck.

Bud whistled. "She is a sweet gumdrop." He handed the photo back to Zane. "How did an ugly cuss like you get a lovely girl like her to give you the time of day?"

Zane shrugged and got to his feet. "Pure, dumb luck I suppose. But we really are just friends."

"And I'm up for promotion as the general," Bud said in a teasing tone. He gathered his mail and hopped up, then thumped Zane on the shoulder. "What's her name?"

"Billie. Nurse Billie Brighton." Zane's voice caressed her name as he said it.

Bud shot him a knowing look. "Yep, I can tell you're just friends."

Zane glowered at him as they made their way toward their barracks. "Just shut yer yap trap. Let's hide your plunder and grab some chow. Last night the pickings were mighty slim by the time we made it through the line and I don't plan to eat the dregs tonight."

"I'm with you on that," Bud said as he stashed his mail at his bunk then hurried to the mess hall.

After they finished eating, they made their way out to check on their plane. Bud served as Zane's copilot. The B-17 they flew had a navigator, a bombardier, an engineer who doubled as the top turret gunner, a radio operator who also served as a gunner, a ball turret gunner who rode in a cramped little space in the belly of the plane, right and left waist gunners, and a tail gunner. Their crew was a good bunch of men who not only got along well, but were also trained and skilled. Every last one of them could do their job without hesitation and fill in for one of the other crew members as needed.

"The Tornado looks good," Bud said as they walked around the Flying Fortress, as the B-17s were known.

"Yep," Zane said, stopping to study the nose art newly painted on the plane. As the pilot, he got to choose the name and, with the agreement of his crew, settled on Texas Tornado. The art showed an outline of the state of Texas with a tornado spinning over it. In the center of the Tornado was a perfect yellow rose in full bloom.

Their navigator had practically begged them to go with Yellow Rose as the name and an image of a naked girl holding a yellow rose painted on the nose, but Zane had seen too many of those. He was all for boosting morale, but art exploiting naked women just seemed disrespectful to him, especially when some of the soldiers used photographs of their wives or girlfriends for the designs. Zane was sure most women would be mortified to find their faces stuck on those bare bodies.

"Wish you'd given in and gone with Yellow Rose?" Bud asked as they turned and started back toward the barracks.

"Nope. Not at all." Zane grinned at his friend. "How about you?"

Bud shrugged. "I was holding out for Naughty Nancy."

Zane thumped him on the back and chuckled. "You were not. Do you even know someone named Nancy?"

"Nope, but if I meet a Nancy someday, I could tell her she was the inspiration for the dame on our plane."

Zane rolled his eyes, but before he could offer any comments, an officer approached them.

They stood at attention as the man stopped in front of them.

"At ease, gentlemen," the colonel said. "Everything in ship-shape order with your plane?"

"Yes, sir," Zane said, wondering what was behind the colonel's question. He assumed it wouldn't take long for the reason to come to light.

"Good. Your crew will fly out in the morning for a new post. Be ready by 0400 hours for further instruction. That will be all."

"Yes, sir," Zane and Bud said in unison, watching the colonel and his assistant walk off.

"I guess we better tell the others and pack our gear," Bud said as they turned toward the barracks.

Zane glanced back at the colonel and noticed him stop another pilot in their squadron. "Looks like things are about to get exciting."

✦✦★ *Chapter Seven* ★✦✦

"You'll be flying to Midway today, men. The Japs are planning something and we're gonna be ready for them," the colonel said as he walked around the room, briefing the crews who had gathered there before dawn. "I want wheels up in an hour. Once you reach the island, you'll be given your orders. Fly smart and stay safe."

Zane and Bud, along with the other crews, hurried out to load their bags on the planes and get ready to take flight. Bud sent the tail gunner to the mess hall to bring them back something to eat. Pancakes wrapped around sausages filled their empty bellies as they made final preparations before lining up on the runway.

"You suppose the Japs are really planning an attack on Midway?" Bud asked as Zane zoomed down the runway and the plane lifted into the air.

"They must be or the colonel wouldn't be sending us there." Zane glanced at the other planes making the trip to Midway. He knew there were already B-17s on the island making daily search missions, along with Navy Catalina patrol bombers. The Catalinas, waddling things that they were, rarely got past a slow, piddling speed, regardless if they were climbing, flying, or landing. Armed with only .30 caliber machines guns, the rumbling amphibians were a death trap when cornered by Jap fighters. However, the planes could fly almost all day long without refueling.

"There she is," Bud said, pointing out the window hours later as they approached Midway. The island was really an atoll, a ring of coral reef encircling a lagoon.

"Looks pretty from up here," Zane said, grinning at his friend. "Did you know Midway is part of a chain of volcanic islands that run from Hawaii all the way up to the Aleutians?"

"I do now, professor." Bud smiled. "Been reading the encyclopedia again?"

Zane shrugged. "Maybe. Better than walking around like a dunce."

Bud laughed and said something Zane couldn't hear over the roar of the engines.

He looked down, admiring the blue water. The barrier reef stretched nearly five miles in diameter while the island offered several sand islets. The two most significant pieces of land, though, were Sand Island and Eastern Island. Not only did seabirds call it home, but so did many military men who'd been working to fortify the atoll.

Zane knew the location of Midway had been important to the military before America entered the war. It was a convenient place to refuel on transpacific flights, and a vital stop for Navy ships. Airstrips, gun emplacements, and a seaplane base were built in 1940 on the island, along with a submarine base. Early in 1941, President Roosevelt created a naval defense area in the Pacific territories, establishing Midway Island Naval Defensive Sea Area. Only U.S. government ships and aircraft were permitted to enter the naval defense areas at Midway.

And Midway was second only to Pearl Harbor on the list of importance to protect from a Japanese attack. In actuality, Midway was attacked by two Japanese destroyers the same day as the enemy unleashed terror on Pearl Harbor. Those defending Midway successfully triumphed over the Japanese that day in the first American victory of the war. A Japanese submarine had bombarded Midway in February, but again the Americans prevailed.

Now, it seemed, the Japs were planning a third attack on the tiny island.

"I like the runway," Bud said, pointing to the three paved runways that criss-crossed to form what appeared to be a large A on the island.

"I'll like it better once I know we can land smoothly," Zane said, lowering the landing gear and expertly setting down the plane.

The wheels glided easily over the surface of the runway and they came to a stop, along with the other planes in their group.

It didn't take long to surmise the island was overcrowded. In addition to Marine Corp, Navy and Air Force planes, the island had two good search radars, and plenty of artillery. Nearly three thousand men in Army and Marine units had dug in and were protected by bombproof shelters throughout the island.

Cooperating with the Marine ground forces on the island, the plane crews serviced their own planes and refueled them, leaving them ready to take off at a moment's notice.

Tired, dirty, and hungry when they finished readying the Tornado for flight, Zane and his crew made their way to their temporary bunks. Everywhere they turned was crowded — with men and supplies. Fear and anticipation lurked around corners while determination and hope lingered in the air.

Restless as they awaited further orders, Zane and Bud went to check on their plane then meandered to the beach.

"What do you think is gonna go down?" Bud asked as they strolled along a stretch of white sand. "Do you think we'll see some action?"

"I do, Bud. They wouldn't have sent us out here just for kicks." Zane stopped and picked up a seashell. He wondered if Billie would like it. She'd mentioned going to the Oregon coast. Did she enjoy the beach? Annoyed with himself for letting thoughts of her trickle into his head, he pulled back his arm, ready to send the shell swirling into the ocean. Just before he let it go, he dropped his arm and stuffed the shell into his pocket.

Bud grinned at him but wisely refrained from commenting on his odd behavior.

"There are so many men here, they look like ants overrunning a picnic basket," Bud said, pointing to where soldiers dug trenches in the distance.

Zane nodded in agreement. "I reckon they do."

He tipped his head toward the mess hall. "You bring any of those cookies your folks sent to you?"

"Sure did." Bud whacked him on the back good-naturedly. "Maybe you can wrangle up some milk or coffee to go with them."

"Consider it done," Zane said, heading toward the mess hall.

Although that evening proved peaceful, an undercurrent of expectation and worry washed over them all as they turned in for the night.

Early the next morning, Zane and his crew ate breakfast then hurried to their plane for a search mission. The admiral in charge wanted daily sweeps flown at least seven hundred miles out to make sure the Japanese weren't sneaking up on them.

As they flew, Zane gave Bud the controls for a while and watched the water and clouds below them. It would be easy to miss an enemy ship beneath the cover of clouds, but they did their best to keep an eye out.

The next few days were like living in a loop that replayed over and over. Eat, fly, search, return, service the plane, eat, and finally snatch a few hours of sleep before starting it all over again.

By the time he made it to his bunk to rest, Zane was exhausted. In the past two days, they'd been in the air more than thirty hours, and had yet to see anything. The following day, he and his crew entered the mess hall to find the Japanese had dropped bombs on Dutch Harbor in the Aleutian Islands where two American bases were located.

"I think it's a diversion," Bud said as he and Zane sat at a table with others. "They want to split our resources, draw us away from Midway."

"I agree," Zane said as he lifted a fork heaped with mashed potatoes to his mouth. "Midway has to stay the main focus now."

The men had just finished their meal when word trickled in that one of the Catalina pilots had spied Japanese ships.

Zane and his crew, along with eight other crews, raced to their B-17s to take to the skies. Realizing he'd forgotten something important, at least to him, Zane sprinted back to his bunk and grabbed the scarf Billie had given him.

He didn't believe in good luck charms, but he hadn't flown without it since she'd placed it in his hand and he sure wasn't going to start now. Quickly tucking it inside his pocket, his long strides carried him to the Tornado. As soon as he climbed behind the controls of the plane, they rushed to the runway and took off to attack the convoy.

"We're gonna nail 'em, but good, Tex!" Bud exclaimed as they zoomed across the sky toward their destination. The men were in high spirits as they crossed more than five hundred miles and came upon the Japanese ships.

Under the direction of the officer leading the charge, Zane's crew dropped bombs from high in the sky and watched geysers erupt when the bombs exploded in the water. In total, more than thirty demolition bombs, each weighing six hundred pounds, had been dropped before they flew back to Midway.

"You think we wiped 'em out?" Bud asked as they fell into formation on the flight back.

"I don't know, Bud. It's hard to tell from this height. I doubt we got them all, but hopefully it shook them up enough they'll think twice about continuing with their plans, whatever they might be." Zane glanced down at the clouds below them, wondered how many more enemy ships drew closer to Midway.

The enormity of what they needed to do, what was at stake if they failed to defend the island, washed over him, leaving him nervous, yet determined.

The crew hadn't settled down, full of anxious energy, when they landed at Midway. While Zane wanted nothing more than some peace and quiet to get his thoughts in order and settled on the task at hand, the men wanted to recall every moment of their flight. Unwilling to do anything to dampen their good spirits, he encouraged them as they spoke with bravado of what they hoped to accomplish tomorrow.

The next morning, Zane and his crew were up before dawn and ready for their orders. One of the Catalina pilots who'd gone out on a search mission an hour earlier radioed a report that enemy planes were heading toward Midway.

"In the air! Get all the planes in the air!" orders were called over the arising chaos.

Zane and Bud hustled the men of their crew to board the Tornado so they could get in line for take-off.

"Shake the rust off your joints, Smitty, and move it!" Zane shouted over his shoulder to their belly gunner as they ran toward the plane.

The man, who was all of five-foot-four if he stretched, tossed Zane a cocky grin. "It ain't rust, Tex. You long-legged giraffes just make it hard to keep up."

By six that morning, the only plane left on the ground was an old single-float biplane.

With orders to head north and attack the Japanese carriers, Zane mentally prepared for the battle ahead. When they reached the Japanese carriers, they dropped their load of bombs then dipped down low enough to strafe a carrier's deck before pulling back amid heavy anti-aircraft fire.

"Did they bring the whole dang Japanese Navy?" Bud asked as they pulled back up while explosions of flak burst around them.

"It sure looks like it," Zane said, zooming away from the enemy fire.

The war raged throughout the day. Dive bombers, Wildcat fighters, and B-26 planes carrying torpedoes joined in the battle as the Americans valiantly fought to protect Midway from invading Japanese forces.

When Zane and his crew finally returned to Midway, it was to find the installations there badly wrecked by enemy bombers, but still in American hands, with the runways intact. Bombs had taken out mess halls, barracks, shelters, even a hospital, along with the powerhouse on the East Island that resulted in the loss of the refueling system.

Zane and the other plane crews that returned to the island had to service their planes with the cans and drums they could find amid the debris.

Although the majority of the fighting took

place on June fourth, the battle wasn't declared over until a few days later. In that time, the American forces had lost one of three carrier ships. The *Yorktown* had been hit on the fourth and abandoned. When a salvage party went over on the sixth on the destroyer *Hammann* to attempt to bring her back to port, a Japanese submarine put one torpedo into *Hammann* and two into *Yorktown*. The great carrier that had survived the Battle of the Coral Sea sank in the early morning hours of June seventh.

Additional American losses included an estimated one hundred and fifty aircraft and more than three hundred good men. However, the Japanese had lost four carriers, numerous ships, more than three hundred planes, and an estimated three thousand men.

The victory was hard-won and provided a much needed boost to the morale of American troops and those on the home front.

"The Japs won't soon recover from the lickin' we gave them," Bud said as he and Zane once again worked with the crew to service the plane. The men were beyond exhausted, but a time for rest was forthcoming.

"I hope they don't. It seems like things are a little more balanced now. Maybe they'll think twice about coming at us again like that." Zane wiped his hands on a greasy rag and motioned to his men. "Let's get the Tornado fueled then see what we can round up for grub."

"You're always ready to eat, aren't you, Tex?" Smitty asked as he polished the plexiglass bubble on his belly gun turret.

Zane smiled. "I reckon I am, but only if there's something tasty to be had." Unbidden, thoughts of Billie Brighton, of her delicious kisses snuck into his thoughts. Subconsciously, his hand patted the pocket where he kept her scarf, feeling closer to her with it there.

Before his lips ever settled on hers, no doubt had existed in his mind that she'd taste as sweet as candy. But he'd been unprepared for the entirely luscious, decadent flavor of her — something far sweeter than he imagined, layered with depths he couldn't begin to fathom.

Much to his dismay, his mouth started to water every time he thought of kissing her. His arms ached to hold her. His ears longed to hear her voice, her laughter.

How in the world would that ever happen when he had no idea if or when he'd ever set foot in Portland again?

✶✶★ *Chapter Eight* ★✶✶

"Have you heard any more news?" Billie asked as she stopped by the nurse's station where a radio played nonstop since the Battle of Midway began a few days ago.

"Nothing new," Peggy said as she stood from the desk and patted Billie's shoulder before she left on her rounds.

Billie, like so many other Americans, waited anxiously to hear if the United States would win the battle and prayed for the safekeeping of those engaged in the fight. She knew one of the Navy's few carrier ships had been hit and abandoned. The battle-weary *Yorktown* had limped back to Pearl Harbor after the Battle of the Coral Sea only to be sent right back out again. She hoped the crew onboard at least had time to rest between battles.

It was beyond her ability to comprehend how the men could function on so little sleep, sometimes little food, and often with an injury. The human body was capable of incredible feats, and it seemed like the war provided an opportunity to test the limits of what man could endure.

Although she wasn't in a front line hospital or

medic tent, Billie had seen some terrible, horrible wounds in the past months. The visible, physical injuries were hard to bear, but it was the hidden wounds in the hearts, minds, and spirits of her patients that proved the hardest to heal.

As she had so many times in the past few days, Billie closed her eyes and sent up prayers for the men in Midway, and all the men fighting in both the Pacific and Atlantic battles. She hated war, hated the devastation and destruction it brought, the way it split up families and left children without fathers, or both parents. Hated it all.

But she loved her country and would do what she could to support the war efforts.

She collected a handful of folders and returned them to their proper spots in a filing cabinet with one ear tuned to the radio. Her thoughts wandered to Zane, as they did with increasing frequency. Although she had no idea where he was, or if he was safe, she had the strangest feeling he was in danger.

She knew he was based in Hawaii, but wondered if he'd been sent to Midway. The majority of those involved in the battle were from the Navy and the Marines, but she'd heard a few reports mention aircraft from the Army Air Force joining the fight. What if Zane was in one of those planes?

Had he already been shot down? Was he injured? Taken prisoner?

At the thought of him being tortured by the Japanese, she sank onto the desk chair, no longer able to stand on her wobbly legs. She couldn't bear the thought of something tragic happening to him.

Tears burned the backs of her eyes as she buried her face in her hands and willed the raging gale of worry to recede. One deep breath, then another, helped calm the storm. Quickly gathering together the frayed edges of her composure, she got to her feet and went about her duties.

When she stepped into the room of Private Harwood, he looked up at her with a smile from his seat in a wheelchair.

"Hi, Nurse Brighton. How's it going?" the young man asked.

Billie couldn't believe the difference a few weeks had made in his appearance and attitude. From time to time, Jimmy struggled to accept his limitations, but he'd made tremendous progress. Just that morning, he'd spent a productive hour in therapy. He'd even warmed to the idea of artificial limbs making it possible for him to walk again.

"It's going along just fine, Jimmy. How are you doing?" she asked, taking his pulse. She studied the color that had gradually returned to his face. He appeared to be putting on a little weight. Considering his previous near-skeletal state, that was a great achievement.

"I'm doing great. Doc says if I keep making progress, I can maybe try walking with crutches in another month or so." Jimmy beamed at her as he pushed his wheelchair close to the bed then used his arms to pull himself up into it.

Billie helped settle the sheet and light blanket over his lap then stepped back. "I'm so proud of you, Jimmy. You're doing fantastic."

If she thought his smile could light up a room before, it practically illuminated the space now.

"Aw, thanks, Nurse Brighton." He pushed himself up into a more comfortable position then glanced at her. "Have you heard more about Midway?"

She shook her head. "Nothing new to report. I'm sure we'll hear something tomorrow."

"And you'll let me know when you hear something?"

"You know I will, Jimmy. If things go like we hope, we'll be celebrating an American victory." She gave him a warm smile, made a note on his chart, and moved toward the patient in the next bed. She looked back at Jimmy. "Do you need anything? Still have enough candy bars?"

"I've got three left and I'm saving them for a special occasion." Jimmy tossed her a grin. "Like that victory at Midway."

"Don't pay to count your eggs before they hatch, especially when there's a devil in the henhouse," grumbled the patient in the bed next to Jimmy's.

Billie had tried everything to cheer the grumpy man, but nothing seemed to help. He had been in the Army for more than twenty years, joining when he was fifteen to fight in the Great War.

A seasoned veteran, he'd been injured when a grenade accidentally went off during a training exercise at a west coast fort where he was helping whip new recruits into shape. Sergeant George Haney had been sent to the hospital in Portland to recover from his wounds and would most likely never return to active duty, unless he'd settle for a desk job.

His left hand had been blown off and he suffered from burns on the left side of his face and body. The hair on the left half of his head had been scorched away, and he'd insisted on having his head shaved.

To say the man was bitter was an understatement. Jimmy may have been lethargic before Billie found a way to reach him, but at least he hadn't hampered the progress of other patients. Sergeant Haney could be cruel and cutting with his words. He threw out biting comments and lobbed insults with the only thing Billie had seen him express that was close to pleasure. He'd tossed so many trays of food at the nurses and the volunteers who came to help, no one but Peggy and Billie would willingly take him his meals.

"My granny always said don't put all your eggs in one basket." Jimmy grinned and shrugged. "Guess that means about the same thing. Me, I'm gonna put all my bets on the fellas defending the Stars and Stripes. They won't let us down."

"I agree, Jimmy," Billie said, smiling at the young man as she reached out to take the sergeant's pulse.

The gruff man slapped her hand away and scowled at her.

"Hey, Sarge, no need to be that way," Jimmy said, raising himself up on his arms.

"Mind your own business, kid. Who are you to tell me what to do why, I..."

Billie shoved a thermometer in the sergeant's

mouth, effectively quieting him, at least for a second or two, until he took it out and flung it at her. She caught it before if fell to the floor and broke.

"If you don't like it in your mouth, I can find someone to hold you down while we go another, much less pleasant but far more invasive route," Billie said, fisting her hands at her hips. She cocked an eyebrow and glared at the disgruntled, grizzled man. It didn't make a lick of difference to her that he outweighed her by a good hundred pounds and had to be at least a foot taller. She'd put up with about all of his nonsense she was willing to take. "You know I'll do it, too."

Sergeant Haney muttered something Billie chose not to hear and opened his mouth. She stuck in the thermometer then took his pulse. In truth, she didn't need his temperature, but she was tired of listening to him pick on Jimmy. The young man had come such a long way, the last thing she needed was for anything or anyone to impede his progress.

She'd asked the doctors about moving the sergeant, and they agreed everyone would be happier if he had his own room, but they were so short on beds, there wasn't anywhere to place him. Until a solution presented itself, poor Jimmy was stuck with the sourpuss.

Billie took the thermometer from George's mouth, checked the reading then entered the information on his chart.

She spent a few minutes with the four other men who shared the room, then stopped back by Jimmy's bed before she left.

"Any requests for breakfast tomorrow?"

The young man grinned. "All this talk of eggs has me craving an omelet. A big fluffy one with cheese and maybe some ham."

Billie smiled at him. "I'll see what I can do." She adjusted his pillow and set a comforting hand on his shoulder. "Have a good night, Jimmy. I'll see you in the morning."

"Thanks, Nurse Brighton. Night."

Billie completed her rounds and returned to the nurse's station where she joined Peggy. The two of them walked home together.

They both had put in a long day and were tired. Miss Burwell was waiting for them when they walked inside the rooming house. In no mood to deal with the woman, Billie pasted on a smile and took a quick step toward the stairs.

"You both received mail today," the woman said, pointing to letters in a basket on the table near the door.

"Thank you, Miss Burwell," Billie said, snatching a letter postmarked from Hawaii and then gathering the letter and magazine marked with Peggy's name. "Have a lovely evening."

Billie handed Peggy her mail and the two of them rushed upstairs.

"From Zane?" Peggy asked, glancing at the letter in her hand as they reached the top of the stairs.

"Yes." Billie no longer felt tired. Instead, she could hardly wait to read the letter.

"Enjoy it. I plan to sit in front of the window and thumb through my magazine until I fall asleep."

"Just don't sleep in your chair again. You practically put a permanent crick in your neck last time." Billie shot her friend a teasing smile as Peggy opened her door. "And I'm not going to massage it for you if you do."

"Some best friend you are," Peggy said with a huff, then grinned. "Have a nice night, Bill."

"You, too, Peg."

Billie hurried to her room, gathered her things, and took a quick, cool bath. After brushing her teeth and rubbing violet-scented cold cream into her skin, she returned to her room, picked up the letter, and climbed into bed. Enough light spilled in the open window, she didn't need a lamp to read.

Her fingers traced over the black ink on the thin envelope, imagining Zane sitting at his bunk writing it to her. Or maybe he'd been outside, sitting on a sandy beach or beneath some exotic tree in a patch of shade.

With deliberate movements, she opened the flap of the envelope and pulled out a sheet of paper. The note had been written the day he'd left Portland. She wondered why it had taken so much longer to reach her than the gift of perfume.

She closed her eyes, picturing Zane on the train, balancing the letter on his knee while chugging down the tracks.

Greetings, Nurse Brighton!
Although it was just last night that I climbed up to your window to tell you goodbye, I find my thoughts lingering on you today as I head south to California.

It was a pleasure to meet you, even under the trying circumstances that made my visit necessary.

Zane went on to describe some of the scenery they passed, the fellow passengers on the train. She laughed as he described a *"chubby little rascal who looks like a chipmunk dressed in the best brown plaid suit Meier & Frank has to offer."*

Billie giggled and continued reading the letter. It wasn't long or even all that personal, until she reached the end.

Meeting you, beautiful Billie, has been a blessing to me. I won't ever forget that gorgeous smile. Stay well and don't forget to write. I truly would enjoy hearing from you.
With deep fondness,
Zane

Billie read the letter a second time before tucking it into the envelope and placing it in a box of keepsakes she hid in the bottom of a dresser drawer.

A heaviness settled over her as she climbed back in bed and slid down to rest her head on the soft pillow. Where was Zane now? Was he safe? Was he looking up at the night sky and thinking of her, too?

Fears for him, for his safety, tightened her throat until she could barely swallow while tears rolled down her cheeks. This was why she refused to get attached to a soldier. To let one turn her head.

The waiting and worrying, the doubting and not knowing were torturous. How did women endure it? How did mothers send their sons off to die? How did wives send their husbands — the men they cherished as lovers and partners in life — off to fight in battles they might never win?

"I hate the war," Billie whispered as she turned on her side and soaked her pillow with her tears.

Dreams of Zane being shot at, of his plane crashing haunted her sleep. In the morning, she was bleary-eyed and unsettled as she readied for work. At the breakfast table, her jittery fingers couldn't hold onto her cup of tea and twice she dropped her spoon in her bowl of oatmeal.

"What is the matter, Bill?" Peggy whispered, leaning toward her.

"Nothing," Billie replied, unwilling to discuss her feelings with so many listening ears. As soon as she finished eating, Billie plodded upstairs, gathered her things, then had to almost run to get to the hospital in time for her shift.

The day proved to be a busy one with three new patients arriving. Billie and Peggy oversaw the process of adding beds to already crowded rooms to squeeze them in.

Jimmy had welcomed the newcomer to their room with a jovial greeting while George had merely glowered at the man.

That evening, as Billie finished a few things at the nurse's station, "The Very Thought of You" began to play on the radio. Unable to hold back her emotion at hearing the song she would forever connect to Zane, she ran to a supply closet and stayed there until her deluge of tears passed.

When she walked back to the nurse's station, the women loudly cheered as the newscaster proclaimed an American victory at Midway.

Billie hugged Peggy then hurried to tell Jimmy and the others in his room. The men who were awake, with the exception of George, shouted and whooped with glee.

"Told you we'd lick them Japs," Jimmy said, giving George a knowing look.

George closed his eyes and feigned sleep, but the other men rehashed what they knew of the battle and speculated on the rest.

Billie went home in better spirits, but still had no idea if Zane was among the casualties listed. Why, oh why, had she ever given him more than a passing glance?

*★★★ *Chapter Nine* ★★★*

"Well, would you look at that," Bud mused as the mail clerk held out a pile of mail to Zane. Two letters and two boxes could almost compete with the six letters and two boxes waiting for Bud when their crew returned to the base in Hawaii.

They'd spent several days after the Battle of Midway flying ongoing search missions to make sure the Japanese weren't planning another assault on the island before they received orders to return to Hawaii.

After they landed, they all appreciated the appearance of the ground crew who would service and fuel the plane without Zane and his men having to take care of it.

Once they'd settled into their barracks, cleaned up, and eaten, Bud decided to see if he had any mail when the mail clerk announced mail call.

Zane was every bit as shocked as Bud to see he had not one, but several pieces of mail to open.

"Come on, let's see what your girl has to say," Bud said, giving Zane a teasing grin as they wandered over to the shady spot beneath a tree where they tended to sit when they had free time.

"What about you? Did each one of your siblings write to you?" Zane asked with a grin as Bud sorted through the envelopes.

"Not all, but several of them. One box is from the folks. I bet there are more cookies. And the other one is from Aunt Luella. She can't cook worth a darn, but she was always heaps of fun when we were kids." Bud motioned to the two boxes Zane had received. "Who sent you goodies?"

"Billie sent one box and I'm guessing the other might be from Rock by the Oregon address." Zane opened the box from his friend. He smiled at the package of razors, shaving lotion, soap, toothpaste, and other necessities Rock knew a soldier appreciated receiving. He opened the letter, written in Rock's bold hand, and read about the man's half-delirious decision to leave the hospital, wandering through the rain, then being taken in at a farm where he was nursed back to health.

"I wonder if that farm is one where Billie and I stopped." Zane questioned aloud.

"What's that?" Bud said, looking up from a letter he read.

"Nothing." Zane looked over at Bud. "What did your aunt send you?"

Bud held out the box and Zane could see several packages of candy and chewing gum.

"You'll rot your teeth out," he teased before returning to Rock's letter.

Rock wrote about milking cows, tending the garden, and meeting the neighbor boy who was full of mischief and fun.

Keep yourself safe, my friend, and know that you are always in my thoughts and prayers. Come see me if you make it to Portland again. I'm sure sorry I missed you when you were here.

"Me, too, buddy," Zane muttered, then finished reading the letter. He placed it back in the box and looked at the other two. One from his brother made him roll his eyes, wary of what he'd find inside.

Deciding to get it out of the way, he opened it and read his brother's brief, terse note, insisting he come home to help on the ranch. The majority of the hired men had left to join the Army and the few that were left weren't capable of doing the work necessary. Floyd was worried about the ranch continuing to prosper with the cowboys gone, and demanded Zane do something to help. His brother had banned him from the ranch and ended what little bit of a relationship remained between them when their father passed away. Even if he was inclined to help Floyd, which he wasn't, he certainly couldn't just leave his responsibilities as an officer and pilot.

"Not going to happen," Zane said. He wadded the letter into a ball and tossed it on the ground next to him.

Bud gave him a curious look. "I hope that isn't from your girl."

"My idiot brother," Zane said with disdain. He picked up the other letter. It was from Billie. He took a deep, calming breath before he opened it, shoving thoughts of Floyd and the ranch to the back of his mind.

The letter was written weeks ago, but he was glad to receive it. It was mostly a newsy note, talking about the garden Billie and the other women at the rooming house had planted, the young soldier who she desperately wanted to help, and the flowers that were blooming after they had a few days of steady rain.

The letter could have been sent to anyone who was a friend, but it lightened the weight in Zane's heart. He opened the box she'd sent. The date on the letter in it was a few days before the letter he'd just read.

Dear Zane,

Imagine my surprise when I came home today to find a package from you awaiting me. Miss Burwell would have liked nothing better than to see me open it, but I took it up to my room. For all I know, the nosy ol' gal opened it then wrapped it back up before I got home. I like to think she wouldn't stoop to such snoopy tactics, but you never know.

Zane thought of the pinch-faced woman he'd seen lurking outside, hoping to catch someone doing something she deemed wrong. She probably kept the girls at the rooming house on their toes all the time.

Thank you, thank you for the perfume. Tabu is my favorite scent. Even if it has peaked as the top fashionable fragrance to make way for newer options, I think it shall always be tops on my list.

"Mine, too, Billie, girl, as long as you're the one wearing it," Zane thought as he read the letter.

You certainly didn't need to send me anything, but I do so appreciate the perfume and the fact you went to the trouble of purchasing it and having it shipped. It came wrapped in the loveliest paper. What a wonderful surprise, especially when it isn't my birthday.

"The thirtieth of July," Zane said, recalling the date she'd mentioned during the hours they'd talked.

"What's the thirtieth of July?" Bud asked, glancing over at him as he munched on jelly beans his aunt had sent while he read one of his many letters.

"Billie's birthday."

Bud gave him a knowing look. "Mark that day in red on your calendar, Tex. Better yet, you ought to send her something special, but you best get to it if you want it to arrive in time for her to get it by then."

His friend was right. He needed to go shopping, and soon, if he had any hope of getting something to Billie by her birthday.

"I'll think of a gift," he said. Bud muttered something about clothes and candy as Zane turned his attention back to Billie's letter.

Truly, the perfume is much appreciated and I'll think of you when I wear it.

By the way, you wrote at the bottom of your note a reminder of who you were, in case I'd forgotten. How many bold, brash soldiers do you think I let climb in my window and steal a kiss? Perhaps I don't want to know your answer, but I assure you, Lieutenant West, you are the first. From the way Miss Burwell has kept a diligent eye on my every move, you will be the last, too. I like living here too well to get myself ousted.

Besides, being a nurse and doing my part to help with the war efforts here at home leaves no time for anything else. (But if you return to Portland, I would make an exception to my rule.)

"I should hope so, Billie, girl." Zane grinned and continued reading.

I pray for your safety, Zane, and thank you for what you are doing to help win the war. I know enough from Captain Laroux's stories to realize you are a brave man who embraces risks for the good of his country.

Take care of yourself and know I'm thinking of you, my friend.
With deep affection,
Billie

"Well? What's she got to say?" Bud asked as he leaned back and looked at Zane.

"She thanked me for the perfume I sent. Took me to task for something I said in the letter, and promised to keep me in her prayers."

Bud grinned. "She's sweet on you."

Zane shook his head. "I don't think so. She finished her note calling me her friend and signed it 'with deep affection.' That's something a grandmother might write, not a girl who's in love."

Bud shrugged. "Time will tell, Tex, but I think she cares for you more than either of you dare to admit." He nudged the box sitting on Zane's lap. "What did she send you?"

Zane pulled out cookies and crackers, assorted candy bars, and several packages of his favorite spearmint chewing gum. In the bottom of the box was a Mark Twain book he hadn't read. He'd mentioned to her he never had much time for reading, although he enjoyed Mark Twain's tales. She must have remembered what he'd shared.

"Yep, that's a girl who doesn't like you at all."

Zane slugged Bud's arm with a light punch then the two of them got to their feet and wandered back to the barracks.

That night, Zane lay in bed, arms crossed behind his head, trying to think of a perfect gift to send Billie for her birthday. It took three days before he got a chance to leave the base and do a little shopping, but when he did, he hoped Billie would like what he chose to send. Even if it didn't seem like it at first glance, he knew the birthday gift held pieces of his heart. Pieces he was sending across an ocean in hopes to make her smile.

*** Chapter Ten ***

"I don't have room for more patients, sir," Billie said, glaring at the doctor. The idiot seemed to think she could magically find empty beds and places to put them for the dozen soldiers who'd just arrived at the hospital.

"Figure it out, Brighton," the man barked then turned and strode off.

Billie wished Doctor Bartle would go back to wherever he'd come from. He'd joined the staff at the hospital a few weeks ago and had been rude to the nurses, disrespectful to senior physicians, and acted superior to anyone he deemed beneath him, which was most everyone. He'd even terrorized a few of the patients with his dire, and totally unfounded, predictions of their imminent demise.

The only person in the entire hospital who seemed to admire the man was a cranky, crotchety nurse who'd been treating patients since before the Great War. Rock Laroux had called her Horrid Homer and that title, sadly, hit the mark. Billie had been thrilled when Nurse Homer had been moved to a different floor and she rarely had to see her.

Doctor Ridley was working to find a way to

have Doctor Bartle transferred, but until that happened, they were stuck with him. If they wanted to dream big, Billie hoped he took Nurse Homer with him when he went.

"Take a deep breath," Peggy whispered as she stepped beside Billie. "Doctor Bartle is..."

"Detestable. Arrogant. Obnoxious. A bubble-headed blowhard." Billie grinned at her friend. "Was that what you were going to say?"

Peggy giggled. "No, but that'll do." She looked at the stack of patient files in Billie's hands and sighed. "I guess we better see about getting these poor soldiers settled. I'll have maintenance scrounge up more beds from basement storage. Do you want to figure out what rooms we can squeeze more beds into?"

"I don't want to, but I will," Billie said with a cheeky smile as she strode down the hallway.

An hour later, she'd made room assignments for the new patients then she and Peggy supervised the transfer of the patients to the beds made with fresh, crisp linens.

By some miracle, Doctor Ridley devised a plan to keep Doctor Bartle busy so he wouldn't bother the new patients. After being transported from various points around the country, the last thing they needed was the wretched man filling their heads with morbid thoughts.

Billie, Peggy, and two other nurses checked in at their station before they went to oversee delivery of the evening meals to the men on their floor.

"Have you heard from that yummy pilot again?" a cheeky nurse asked as she applied a fresh coat of lipstick.

"Not for a while," Billie said, hurriedly adding information about their new patients to the appropriate files in the filing cabinet behind the desk.

June had rolled into July and she hadn't heard anything from Zane in the past three weeks. She had no idea if he'd fought at the Battle of Midway. If he'd been injured — or the unthinkable. But she'd faithfully written to him twice a week using the new V-mail forms.

When Billie first heard about the program, she'd been amazed how it worked. She could write a letter on the special form, send it, and the letter would be captured on film. The film canisters were shipped overseas then each letter printed and given to the recipient — in two weeks or so. She'd heard of standard letters taking six to eight weeks to reach soldiers overseas. The poor men surely felt like they'd been forgotten or abandoned when weeks went by with no mail. V-mail helped the soldiers keep in touch with loved ones more frequently. Additionally, the V-mail forms also cut down on weight and bulk on the planes carrying them.

She just hoped Zane liked the letters she sent. Since she was determined they would be nothing more than friends, good friends, she wrote him newsy notes about the rooming house, their garden, things she'd seen or done, and stories about her patients. She'd even written to him about bitter Sergeant Haney and how even on his worst day, he hadn't been able to dampen Jimmy's newfound enthusiasm for life.

That fact made her grateful. Based on his current progress, it wouldn't be long before Jimmy was able to walk again. He gained strength by the day and he'd even managed to walk a few feet yesterday using his crutches. The look on his face when he took those steps made Billie's heart climb up in her throat. She'd been so overcome with raw emotion at how far he'd come in the last weeks all she could do was smile at him when he asked her if she wanted to dance. She promised Jimmy she would dance with him when he was ready.

Thoughts of dancing brought Zane to mind and the day he'd held her close in the rain.

Desperately, she wanted to hear from him, to hear that he was healthy and whole. Her prayers always included a petition for Zane's safekeeping, wherever he might be.

"I'm sure he's off fighting the Japs and keeping us all safe," another nurse said, giving Billie's shoulders a hug, pulling her back into the moment and out of her worrisome thoughts.

"Shall we get back to it, girls?" Peggy asked, drawing the conversation away from Zane and his whereabouts.

Amid groans and half-hearted protests, the women returned to their work.

Billie felt like she was dragging hundred pound weights on each leg by the time she collapsed in her bed that night. In spite of her exhausted state, she had trouble sleeping, dreaming of Zane's plane crashing.

The next morning, she stumbled out of bed and

drank two cups of coffee, needing the jolt of caffeine to awaken her enough to function at work. At the hospital she made her rounds, spending extra time with the new patients.

One man in particular pulled at her heartstrings. Something about Sergeant Klayne Campbell reminded her of Zane and Rock Laroux. The sergeant was quiet, clearly a man used to being alone. Yet, something in the determined set of his jaw, the intense resolve in his eyes made her think of Rock and Zane.

She smiled as she took his pulse and made notes in his chart for the doctor. "How are you feeling today, Sergeant Campbell?"

"Well enough," he said, giving her a cautious glance before he looked back at a book he held clasped in his right hand.

"You enjoy reading?" Billie asked as she tried to see the title of the book, but couldn't with the way he held it.

"Yes," he answered, not meeting her gaze.

Billie took a step back and surveyed his injuries. A deep, red scar, edges jagged, ran from his left eyebrow across his eyelid and continued along his cheek down to his jaw. Smaller scars, in various stages of healing, dotted the right side of his face. Another red, angry scar ran straight across his hairline on his forehead, as though he'd nearly been scalped. She'd noticed a filmy appearance to his left eye, where it had been scratched beyond hope of healing. His left arm and leg were both in casts.

The scars on his face would no doubt enhance

his rugged appeal when they fully healed. Sergeant Campbell was a handsome man and probably had more than his share of girls chasing after him.

She recalled reading something in his file about a crash landing in China and sudden recognition set in.

"You're one of the Doolittle Raiders, aren't you?" she asked in a hushed tone.

He glanced up at her, his clear right eye pinning her with a cool stare. "That's right."

She leaned slightly closer and patted his good arm. "Thank you for what you did, Sergeant Campbell. I can't even begin to imagine what you've gone through, but the hope your raid gave our country is beyond measure."

His stiff posture relaxed and the beginnings of a smile pulled at his lips. "I'd do it again tomorrow if I could." He gave her a long look, one that wasn't perusing, but more observant. "Since I'll be here a while, why don't you call me K.C. Most of my friends do."

"That sounds fine, K.C. You may call me Nurse Billie if you like." She fluffed his pillows and settled him more comfortably. "If you let me help you, we'll have you back on both feet and out of here as soon as possible."

He grinned at her. "When do we start?"

"Now, that's the kind of attitude I like." Billie offered him a smile. "We'll begin tomorrow."

Yesterday, when she'd made room assignments for the new patients, she'd just been intent on finding them all a place to rest. She was glad she'd placed K.C. in the same room as Jimmy.

She had a feeling the two men might be good for each other. Who knew? Maybe some of their positivity would rub off on Sergeant Haney.

"You ready for that dance?" Jimmy asked in greeting as Billie checked his vitals and made notes in his chart.

"Not quite yet, Jimmy, but I want you to promise I'll be the first girl you dance with."

He held a hand to his heart and grinned. "You betcha you'll be the first, Nurse Billie."

Sergeant Haney was even more cantankerous than usual and threw his breakfast tray at the teen girl who brought it to him. The edge of the metal tray caught her just above her eye, leaving a cut.

"How dare you?" Billie said, racing over to the girl and pulling a gauze pad from the pocket of her skirt. She pressed the gauze against the cut while glaring venomous daggers at George Haney. "We've done our best to help you, Sergeant, to be kind in our care and assist in your healing, but this is enough. I won't stand for another outburst from you or you'll find yourself out on the street regardless of what kind of shape you are in! Am I understood, soldier?"

The man stared from her to the young girl who was crying and trembling with fear. Before he could speak, Billie led the girl out of the room and to the nurse's station. She had Doctor Ridley take a look at the cut to confirm it did not require stitches before she cleaned the wound and placed a small bandage over it.

"You go on home now, Dorothy. I do hope you'll come back again, but if you don't want to,

we'll understand," Billie said, giving the girl a hug after she'd walked her to the door.

"I like helping, Nurse Brighton, and I'll come back. But may I please be excused from helping that man?"

"Of course." Billie waved at the girl as she left then returned upstairs to her floor. She marched back to the room where she'd left the men gaping at her after her outburst. A repentant appearing George Haney bent down, cleaning up the mess he'd made with his good hand.

Shocked to not only see him up, but doing something helpful, she glanced at her patients. From the looks on the faces of the eleven other occupants of the room, she had a feeling more than one of them had taken the man to task.

"Thank you, Sergeant," Billie said in a soft voice, taking the dented tray he held out to her.

He didn't speak, but nodded at her, oddly contrite, before he slumped on his bed.

Billie left the room, hoping the bitter man had perhaps turned a corner. On her lunch break, she wrote a letter to Zane, sharing about the new patients and how they struggled to make room for them, of Jimmy's wonderful progress, and the incident with Sergeant Haney. She posted the V-mail letter at the mailbox on the corner then raced back inside to begin her afternoon shift.

With each soldier she helped, she prayed for Zane. Prayed he was somewhere safe and unharmed.

∗∗★ *Chapter Eleven* ★∗∗

Billie swallowed back her disappointment as she completed her morning rounds at the hospital. Today was her twenty-sixth birthday and no one remembered.

Not that she had any family to wish her well, but Peggy was like a sister to her. Many of the hospital staff fulfilled the roles of her extended family. Loath to admit it, her feelings were hurt they'd all forgotten her birthday.

She made it a point to celebrate the birthdays of those she considered friends. She even tried to do something special for the patients if she knew their birthday was approaching. Yet, not a single person had bothered to offer a word of congratulations or cheer to her today.

Bothered but determined to hide it, she decided she'd grab a sandwich for her lunch and eat in the courtyard where she could pout in solitude. She'd just started for the stairs to go to the cafeteria when someone called her name.

She turned around and watched as Peggy hurried toward her.

"Man alive, Billie! I've about run my legs off

looking for you," Peggy said, trying to catch her breath.

"What's wrong? Is it one of the patients? Where am I needed?" Billie asked, placing a hand on Peggy's arm and taking a step toward the nurse's station.

"Room seven. There's something going on in there you need to see," Peggy panted.

"Who's hurt? Did Jimmy fall trying to walk? Is it Klayne? Or Sarge?" Billie fired questions at Peggy as the two of them hurried past the nurse's station then turned down a long hallway.

Room seven housed what Billie thought of as her favorite patients. After the incident with Sergeant Haney tossing his tray and hurting the young volunteer, he'd suddenly started to improve both physically and in his attitude. The men in that room all needed special help and attention, and Billie would have done anything for them.

When Peggy didn't answer her questions, Billie frowned at her. "Please tell me they're all breathing and no one is bleeding."

"No one is bleeding. In fact..." Peggy pushed Billie into the room and a bevy of shouts and cheers greeted her. Streamers and balloons hung from the ceiling and a big cake sat on a cart someone had pushed into the room.

"Happy Birthday, Nurse Brighton," the men chorused.

Heat soaked her cheeks with embarrassment at all the unexpected attention while tears burned the backs of her eyes. She smiled and took a step back, grabbing Peggy's hand and pulling her next to her.

"You could have given me some warning," she whispered out of the corner of her mouth while maintaining a smile.

"Where's the fun in that?" Peggy said with a saucy grin. "Enjoy it, Billie. When I mentioned your birthday the other day, the men practically begged to have a party. Let them enjoy it."

"It's sweet of them, and you." Billie gave Peggy a hug then stepped into the circle of her friends. Her favorite staff members were crowded into the room among the tightly packed beds of the recovering men.

Peggy handed her a knife to cut the cake, which Billie did, serving Jimmy the first piece. They enjoyed cups of punch along with the layered white cake, created with a precious supply of sugar.

A basket sitting near the cake held an assortment of cards that Billie looked forward to reading when she could sit and savor each one.

"How many years young are you?" one of the older men asked.

"Aw, shoot, Ed," Jimmy said with a cheeky smile. "Don't you know you can't ask a girl her age?"

Everyone laughed and Billie winked at Jimmy. To her surprise, she watched the young girl George Haney had clocked with the breakfast tray speak to him and laugh at something he said before she turned her attention to Jimmy. With the moony eyes Jimmy cast toward the volunteer, she could tell the affection between the two of them was mutual. Dorothy was as sweet and kind as she was pretty. The girl would make a wonderful match for

Jimmy's exuberant personality.

Many of the men in the room tired quickly, so the party didn't last long, but it brightened Billie's day unlike anything had in a while.

She and Peggy decided the balloons and streamers could stay until the end of the day, since they brought such a festive mood to the room and the men.

"Our card is the one attached to the box in blue paper," Jimmy said as Billie picked up the basket of cards.

"Now, you fellas sure didn't need to get me anything," Billie set the basket down and pulled out a small gift wrapped box with a card tied to the top of it. She opened the envelope and removed a card with birds and flowers on the front. Inside it read "happiest birthday wishes to the best nurse in the world," and was signed by all twelve men in the room.

"Go on, open it," Jimmy urged her.

She blinked back tears as she stared at the box in her hands. Carefully, she unwrapped the paper and opened the box to find a scarf the same mossy green shade as her eyes. It was expensive, beautiful, and made the tears she'd subdued roll down her cheeks.

"This is wonderful. You all are the best patients a girl could have." Billie took a handkerchief from her pocket and dabbed at her tears. "Thank you so much."

"Do you really like it?" Sarge asked, leaning forward as he sat on his bed.

"I love it. It's perfect." Billie gave each of

them a warm smile.

"They talked me into picking it up for you," Peggy said, giving Billie's shoulders an affectionate squeeze. "But they decided on what to get you without any help from me."

"It's perfect. Truly it is." Billie rubbed the silk of the scarf between her fingers and thought of the one so very similar she'd given to Zane. Did he still have it? Peggy knew she'd given him the scarf, so she'd known a replacement would be a welcome gift.

Overwhelmed by the kindness of the men and her friends, Billie took a deep breath and tamped down her emotion. "You fellas sure know how to make a nurse feel special. I think this is the nicest birthday I've ever had."

"Well, you deserve the best, Nurse Billie," Klayne said with one of his reserved smiles.

"Thank you all."

Billie and Peggy cleaned up the mess from the party and spent the afternoon discussing their plans for that evening. They both got off work at six, so they planned to hurry home, change, and go out to dinner and then to the movies. Billie hadn't gone since the afternoon she and Zane had watched Abbott and Costello in the silly comedy.

The diversion a movie would provide was exactly what she needed, especially since she hadn't heard from Zane other than a brief note to let her know he was being transferred and had no idea when he'd be able to write to her again.

Although she knew he couldn't tell her where he was going, she had her suspicions it would be somewhere dangerous, right in the thick of things.

Throughout the afternoon, people stopped Billie to offer birthday greetings. She didn't know if it was Doctor Ridley's special gift to her, or a coincidence, but Doctor Bartle was attending a seminar in Seattle that day and Nurse Homer was nowhere to be seen.

A few minutes before six, Billie stopped in room seven. She thanked the men again for such a lovely remembrance of her birthday and promised to wear her scarf that evening.

"You should take a picture in it," Jimmy said as she stood at the door bidding them all a pleasant evening.

"Maybe I will," she said, giving him a cheeky smile before she joined Peggy at the nurse's station and the two of them left.

The sun was shining brightly in a cloudless sky as they walked home. It was a beautiful July day, with a slight breeze that kept it from being too hot.

"Did you enjoy your party, Bill?" Peggy asked as they sauntered along.

"It was wonderful, Peg. I know you played a big role in planning it, so thank you. And the scarf truly is perfect. I can't believe the guys all chipped in for it."

"Well, believe it," Peggy said, grinning at her. "When Jimmy heard me say something to Doctor Ridley about your birthday coming up, he told the other fellas they had to chip in and do something nice since you're always doing extra things for them. They asked me for suggestions and I gave them some options, but they decided on what to get. Sarge was the one who said the scarf should be the same color as your eyes. If I didn't know better, I'd think you won him over."

Billie smiled, so full of joy she could barely contain it. The feeling of being appreciated and remembered with friendly affection made her wonder if her heart might burst from the pleasure of it all.

"We have a few minutes, Billie. Let's go check on the garden," Peggy said, grabbing Billie's hand and pulling her around the side of the house and into the backyard. Streamers hung from the trees and a table, draped in a white cloth, was filled with a picnic supper. Another small lace-covered table held an assortment of colorfully-wrapped packages.

The residents of the rooming house jumped from behind trees and bushes, yelling "Surprise, Surprise!" The women circled around Billie giving her hugs and laughing.

"All this is for me?" Billie asked, hardly able to acknowledge the party and elaborate efforts were on her behalf.

"All for you," Peggy said, giving her a tight hug. "Let's run up and change, then we can have supper."

The two of them raced upstairs and changed their clothes. Since she'd promised the men she'd wear the scarf they'd given her, she tied it around her curls like a headband, fastening it with a jaunty bow, then hurried downstairs and out to the yard.

Miss Burwell even gave her a stiff hug. "Felicitations to you, Billie."

"Thank you, Miss Burwell. And thank you for

allowing the party. It's very kind of you." In truth, Billie was shocked the woman permitted it. But by the color in her cheeks and the twinkle in her eye, she had an idea the persnickety woman was enjoying it every bit as much as Billie.

"You're welcome." Miss Burwell pointed to the table. "Now, we should all be seated and enjoy this meal the cook prepared before the heat spoils it."

"Yes, ma'am," Billie said, taking a seat next to Peggy.

Dinner was a lively affair with the women laughing and talking, sharing stories and teasing one another. The cook brought out a cake, sweetened with honey, and topped with whipped cream and berries from their garden.

"This is delicious," Billie said, smiling at the rotund woman who mostly hid in the kitchen, preferring not to be seen.

The cook blushed and scurried back to the kitchen.

When they'd finished eating dessert and carried the dishes inside, the women gathered around the table as Peggy passed gifts to Billie. She took her time opening each one.

Her friends presented her with a variety of gifts including everything from a new writing pen and beautiful floral stationery to a box of fancy chocolates she loved but rarely indulged in purchasing. Peggy had crocheted a pair of airy lace gloves. Much to her surprise, Miss Burwell had knit a stunning burgundy sweater. Billie looked forward to wearing it when the weather turned colder.

Billie thanked each giver for the gifts with true gratitude. After her parents died, no one cared to celebrate an orphan girl's birthday. Even when she'd grown up, few friends knew the date and those who did hadn't made a big fuss. But this year, Peggy had gone to quite a lot of work to ensure her day was properly celebrated.

For that, Billie owed her a debt of gratitude and one of sisterly love.

"There's one more box," Marlene said, picking up a package that appeared to have arrived in the mail.

"That just came today," Miss Burwell said as Marlene set the box in front of Billie.

The postmark from Hawaii buoyed her hopes it was from Zane. Had he truly remembered her birthday? She'd barely mentioned it in passing, although she'd made note his birthday was in January.

She untied the string, removed the paper, and opened the box. An envelope rested on top of layers of tissue paper. She slit open the flap and removed a letter, glancing down at the bottom to see Zane's name.

Determined to savor what he wrote at her leisure later, she tucked the letter inside the envelope and folded back the tissue paper.

"Oh, my," she whispered, lifting the most unique handbag she'd ever seen from the box.

"Why, that's bamboo," Suzie said, wonder thick in her voice. She leaned across the table and reverently ran her fingers across the glossy surface.

"Imagine that."

The handbag, handle, and even the clasp were crafted of bamboo.

"Open it," Peggy urged from beside her, nudging her with her elbow.

Billie twisted the clasp and lifted the top to reveal additional treasures nestled in the depths of the small bag.

"What else is in there?" Peggy asked, peering inside.

Billie grinned and took out two fine linen handkerchiefs embroidered with bright tropical flowers in the corners.

"Those are gorgeous," Peggy said, taking them from her and passing them around for the other girls to see.

Next, Billie removed a small tin. "Macadamia nuts. Popular here," was written on a scrap of paper in Zane's hand on top of some strange, round nuts.

"You'll have to dig out a nutcracker," Peggy said, passing the tin down the table.

Billie took a delicate pink sea shell from the bag and held it in her hand, gently pulling free a tiny slip of paper sticking out of it.

"Found this on Midway. Thought of you," Zane had written. That confirmed her thoughts he'd been there, engaged in the pivotal battle that had been such a needed victory for America.

She tried to hide the note, but Peggy snatched it and got the goofiest, dreamiest look on her face before she passed it, along with the shell, to Marlene and the others.

The last thing in the handbag, which had the

richest, most exotic aroma, was something padded with tissue paper. Slowly, she folded back the paper and sucked in a breath at the sight of a silver barrette inlaid with luminous pieces of shell in a floral design.

A note scribbled on the tissue paper made her smile. "I pictured this in your golden curls."

She quickly folded the tissue and tucked it inside the handbag before Peggy could read it.

"I think that young man is quite taken with you," Miss Burwell said. For once her tone didn't sound full of censure. Instead, it held a hint of amusement or perhaps it was indulgence.

"Oh, we're just friends, Miss Burwell," Billie hurried to explain, which made all the women break into laughter. Billie blushed, but then joined them in their jollity.

They sat beneath the shade of the trees until the sun dipped into the horizon. Finally, Billie stood and gave each of them a hug and thanked them for making her day so special.

She gave Miss Burwell an extra squeeze. "The sweater is lovely and I can't wait to wear it when the weather cools. You do such beautiful work."

The woman looked quite pleased and gave Billie a rare smile. "You're welcome, dear. Enjoy it."

Peggy helped Billie gather her gifts and carry them up to her room. Billie gave her friend a long hug and thanked her profusely for making her day so memorable.

"It really is the nicest, best birthday I've ever had, Peg. Thank you."

"You deserve it, Billie. You're the one who always makes things special for others. Have fun reading your letter from Zane." Peggy gave her a knowing look then left her alone in her room.

Billie put away her gifts, spending time admiring each one. She still hadn't opened all the cards and notes she'd received at work, so she took her time reading them. Tears welled in her eyes and her heart threatened to overflow from the kind, heartfelt words that had been expressed.

She closed her eyes, full of gratitude for her friends, her life, to feel so loved. More loved than she'd felt since she could remember. With both parents dying when she was young, she'd just been one more unwanted mouth to feed and body to clothe. Even in the places she'd been genuinely welcomed, she never belonged. Not truly.

Here, among her friends, at a job she loved, Billie felt like she was in a good place, a right place for her. Yet, something — some incredibly elusive thing — kept her from saying she felt at home.

Home was something she'd dreamed of for years. In her mind's eye, she pictured a farmhouse with a broad porch, a plethora of flowers, a gangly dog, and apple trees in the distance. She'd never been to an apple farm, had no idea how one even operated, but her dream was always the same. The place she dreamed of calling home also included a man with dark hair who caused excitement to swirl in her stomach while love flooded her heart every time she looked at his broad back. She had no idea what his face looked like, but she hoped someday she'd meet the man she envisioned. At least he wasn't a soldier. A farmer was a good, solid option for a husband. And farmers were needed so badly now to support the war effort and provide food on the home front.

Lest thoughts of the war dim the joy of her day, she took out Zane's gift. Her hands caressed the smooth wood, so different and foreign from anything she'd seen. The fashionable handbag, so cleverly styled, would be something she treasured. But of all the gifts Zane had sent, the seashell was her favorite, because he'd picked it up on a beach while he was thinking of her.

Did he think of her even half as often as she thought of him? At night, when she finally found her way to bed, her thoughts lingered on him. On the deepness of his voice. Those enticing dimples and his smile. His far too kissable lips. And that rich brown hair with the little swoop in the front that practically begged for her fingers to run through it.

Falling for Zane was stupid, crazy, and destined to break her heart. Yet, she couldn't help it. Couldn't stop it. Honestly, she didn't want to. What she wanted was to love him without restraint, without fears or doubts, without the knowledge that loving a soldier would end badly. So badly.

For tonight, though, she would pretend he wasn't a soldier, but a cowboy from Texas who'd swept her off her feet, which he most certainly had.

She set down the handbag, opened the letter he'd sent, and held the seashell in her left hand, fingers rubbing over the edges of it as she read what he'd written.

Hiya, Billie, girl!

Bud and I were joking around the other day and I suddenly remembered you have a birthday coming up in July. I had to wait for permission to leave base for a few hours to do my shopping, but I hope you like the handbag. It just looked like something a fabulous, fashionable girl like you might enjoy.

"Indeed, Zane West," Billie muttered, not taking him seriously.

A little old woman, missing half her teeth, had a table on the sidewalk where she was selling all sorts of things, like leis. (If it wouldn't have wilted into a musty mess on the way there, I would have sent you one of those!) Anyway, she had a pile of handkerchiefs she made and was so proud of them, so I thought you might like them, too.

The nuts are grown here on the islands. I've heard a professor from somewhere back east thinks they could be mass manufactured. I don't know if that will happen or not, but they're pretty tasty. We've had them raw, or baked into cookies, and such. You can toast 'em, too, and add them to dishes. If you want a taste of the tropics, mix the nuts with some pineapple, coconut, and whipped cream. Yum! That's pretty good eating.

Billie wondered if she could find a fresh pineapple somewhere, or at least canned slices. She'd have to check at the grocery store. It would be fun to make a dish with the nuts that she could share with the other residents of the rooming house.

When we were in Midway, Bud and I were walking along the beach. I reached down and picked up that shell and immediately thought of you. I think because it was just so dang delicate and pretty.

A blush warmed her cheeks. "You are full of flattery, aren't you Lieutenant?"

I hope this arrives in time for your birthday. Bud has assured me I should have mailed it last week. He's always helpful that way, you know.

Billie grinned, imagining the teasing that went on between the two men.

I'm sorry I can't be there to wish you a Happy Birthday in person, but please know I'm thinking of you today. Look outside your window at the brightest star you see. I'm looking up at it too, envisioning you sitting in your room, pretty as a picture, just like the last time I saw you.

You're a swell girl, Billie. Beautiful, smart, sweet (I can't think of anything sweeter than your kisses), and tender hearted. You're the kind of girl a guy admires, respects, and can't get out of his head or heart.

No matter what the future days may bring, please know how much joy you've given this lonesome ol' soldier through your letters and the memories of those few incredible days I spent with you.

Best wishes to you, Billie, girl, for a wonderful birthday and happiness always.

Yours,

Zane

"Mine?" Billie questioned. What had he meant by signing the letter "yours?"

If Zane inferred he was hers, he belonged to her, is that what she wanted?

Yes, her heart whispered.

Her head protested. What on earth would she possibly do with him? He was a soldier, one who'd already had nearly a decade-long career in the military. Zane wouldn't give that up. Not for her. Not for anyone. What good could come from giving him a place in her life? How could she willingly fall for him, knowing the outcome?

Love him, demanded her heart. *Just love him.*

⋆⋆★★ *Chapter Twelve* ★★⋆⋆

"I can't see a blasted thing in this rain, can you?" Bud asked as they flew through a driving rainstorm in the South Pacific.

"Not much," Zane said, keeping his eyes peeled for the runway on New Caledonia where they'd been transferred.

With the Japanese hustling to build a runway on Guadalcanal and take over the South Pacific, American forces were equally determined to stop them. Zane's bombardment group had been ordered to take their B-17s and fly to Plaines Des Gaïacs in New Caledonia. The island location south of Guadalcanal would allow them to fly search and bomb missions throughout the area, adding to the efforts to thwart the Japanese.

At least it would if they could find the runway through the torrential sheets of rain falling around them.

"I have a feeling we're not gonna dry out for a while," Bud said as he stared out at the gray skies around them.

"Look on the bright side," Zane said, grinning at his friend. "We could be in the middle of a lightning storm, or maybe hail the size of baseballs."

"You got me there. That would be worse." Bud sat forward and tapped on his window. "Down there. Isn't that the runway?"

"We should be coming right over it, Tex," the navigator's voice crackled across their radio system.

"Copy that, Stretch. Over." Zane brought the plane around and lined it up with the runway. Thanks to work done by troops stationed on the island before the Battle of the Coral Sea, there was a runway, barracks, and an established base there.

In spite of the rain and low visibility, Zane made a perfect landing and brought the plane to a gentle stop. With their service crews still at sea, they took care of the plane, filled it with fuel, and went to find a place to bunk.

The next morning, they took off on their first mission over the Guadalcanal area. They snapped photos of Japanese working on an airstrip there, and flew along the north coast, capturing images, per the general's orders. The cameras were borrowed from the Navy and the photographer who rode along was a Marine, but they got the job done.

The men got their first taste of fighter opposition when Zeros intercepted them during their flight. The Japanese planes opened fire, but Zane's crew, along with the rest of the squadron on the mission, returned fire as they flew back toward the base.

In the next few days, they hardly slept, either flying missions or servicing the Tornado. The landing strip had been hacked out of a swamp and was coated in red dust, high in iron oxide. The dust sifted through everything, including the filters on the plane, causing mechanical issues. The B-17s were doing well to fly six hours with a full load of oil.

The rare moments Zane had to himself, his thoughts drifted to Billie. She'd been faithful in sending him letters when he was in Hawaii. With the new V-mail, he'd received at least a letter every week, sometimes two, and the news was never more than two weeks old. Other than her birthday present, he'd only managed to send her one letter before he'd been sent to the South Pacific. He hoped she'd understand the silence from him since he had no way to get her a letter right now. As it was, he had no idea when he'd receive mail, either.

He'd brought along every note she'd written him and reread them until he had the words memorized. In the midnight darkness when sleep eluded him, he'd close his eyes, picture her smile, and pretend he could hear her voice as he replayed her letters in his mind. Sometimes, he'd even sleep with her scarf beneath his cheek, just to inhale the delightful scent of her.

Relentless in his teasing, Bud continued to inform him he was far past smitten with Billie.

Zane would have argued with him if the man hadn't been right. Each letter he received from her only made him fall more in love with the woman. And that was something Zane had vowed he'd never do.

He'd been married to his career for a long time

and had no plans to change that. If he guessed correctly, Billie had no interest in marriage either. Yet, in spite of what his head knew, his heart yearned for her in ways he'd never imagined possible.

Unable to remove her from his mind or untangle her from his heart, he shoved thoughts of her into a corner during the day so he could focus on his work.

July was nearly at an end when Zane and the members of his squadron were given orders to report to a new base northeast of their current location that would put them closer to Guadalcanal.

"Well, what kind of rinky-dink set up did they send us to, Tex?" Bud asked as they circled the newly-constructed runway on Espiritu Santo.

The island had previously been a no-man's land, but was positioned directly in the path of a possible thrust from the Solomons. A Navy admiral was adamant a base there would give them an advantage as the Americans took Guadalcanal away from the Japanese.

Zane glanced down at the runway. Completed just days ago, the airstrip had been hacked out of the jungle and a coconut grove. At two hundred feet wide and several thousand feet long, crushed coral and a Marston mat provided the landing surface.

"Have you landed on one of those before?" Bud asked, pointing to the long strip of interconnected metal that created the mat.

Pierced steel planking consisting of steel strips punched with holes set in rows, along with a formation of U-shaped channels between the holes, comprised the mats. Marston mats had been developed to provide an almost instant place for military planes to land. Hooks were formed along one side of each piece with slots on the other edge that gave the mats the ability to connect. The hooks were held in place with steel clips and stakes were driven in at intervals to keep the assembly in place. The design of the mat, perforated and channeled, created strength and rigidity, as well as providing sufficient drainage which was necessary on the humid, damp islands where they were used with growing frequency.

"I have a few times," Zane said. He wholeheartedly agreed with Bud's statement about it being a rinky-dink place, but refrained from saying anything. The base there was so new that barracks had not yet been established. In fact, it looked like not much of anything had been wrested from the jungle beyond a place to land and a spot to park the planes.

Zane carefully set the plane down, noticing the revetments were barely deep enough to keep the Tornado's nose off the runway and so narrow, he worried about taking out a tree with a wing tip.

When his crew crawled inside the plane to sleep that night, Zane wondered what they'd been sent into. Even the colonel was asleep on the ground beneath a B-17 wing. No barracks, beds, or mess halls existed in this primitive place.

Poor Smitty had screamed like a girl when he'd wandered off to take care of personal business and happened upon a snake bigger around than a three hundred pound pugilist's hefty arm. They'd all run through the thick growth of jungle, expecting to find him being packed off by cannibals or eaten by a wild animal. Instead, Smitty stood with his pants around his ankles, frozen in place with a look of terror on his face as the snake lifted its head and stared at him from a few feet away. Bud had nearly laughed himself silly as the snake turned, as though dismissing Smitty as not worth his time, and slithered back into the jungle.

Zane wouldn't admit it, but he wasn't any fonder of snakes than Smitty.

The lack of service crews, and nearly everything else, left little time for worrying about their new base.

The very next morning, they prepared to fly to Guadalcanal under the protection of bad weather. Zane and his crew, along with others from their squadron, dumped bombs from fourteen-thousand feet, striking at the landing strip. Others ravaged supply dumps at Lunga Point with the bombs they dropped. Little resistance met them, as though they caught the Japanese by surprise.

By then, it was determined Lunga Point held the biggest concentration of supplies and personnel for the Japanese. It became the top priority to destroy. Daily, crews took full bomb loads from Espiritu Santo to Guadalcanal. They dropped them on nearby Tulagi, too, an island also under Japanese control.

During those hectic, harrowing days, Zane had never longed so much for the ranch of his childhood with cattle as far as the eye could see. He'd be thrilled with a cactus or sagebrush, too. He never thought he'd wish for a day of dry heat, maybe with a hot wind blowing, but it sounded like a slice of heaven at that moment.

Between the encroaching jungle, snakes and unfamiliar creepy-crawlies, and rain that turned the foot-deep black soil into a quagmire, he dreamed of his boyhood years on the ranch in Texas where the sun would beat down on the hard-baked earth.

Smitty had complained he was going to start growing moss soon if they didn't dry out and Zane didn't think the scrappy little gunner was wrong. Even when it wasn't raining, everything felt damp, and humid, and musty.

The option of keeping dry, or rested, didn't exist with their limited supplies at Espiritu Santo. Everything, from clothing and food to fuel and housing had to be brought in by ship. Without fuel trucks or water carts, just servicing the planes proved unbelievably difficult. Steel drums of fuel were dumped over the side of a supply ship, floated ashore in nets, hand-rolled under trees and dispersed into smaller containers. These were rolled onto stands then emptied into tank wagons that serviced the B-17s.

One early August day, during a driving, blinding rain storm, all available hands worked a bucket line for hours on end to put twenty-five thousand gallons of gasoline aboard the planes. Zane looked up from the line, wiping the water from his eyes, and saw both the colonel and brigadier general passing along buckets.

When the crews finally took off in the early morning hours, a man stood beside each wing tip to guide pilots out to the short taxiway. Bottles of oil with wicks made of paper flickered along the runway to illuminate it while the headlights from a Jeep marked the end of the strip as they took flight, prepared to deliver more destruction to the Japs.

In the past week, they'd dropped bomb loads on Japanese airfields, supply dumps, ships, docks, and troop positions with hardly any resistance, other than a few Zeros chasing them and anti-aircraft explosions from the ships that did no damage. While the bombers focused on destroying what they could from the air, Naval support moved in and Marines took to the ground on Guadalcanal and Tulagi.

Zane felt sorry for the men at Guadalcanal, an island that appeared forgotten in time. A mixture of rain forests, stinking malaria-plagued swamps, thick grasslands and undergrowth, and steep, treacherous mountains made for round-the-clock challenges. The Marines quickly secured the airfield and sent out scouts to deduce what the Japanese who'd fled into the jungle had planned.

Tulagi was a different story. The Japanese there offered stiff resistance, but the Marines prevailed and had the island completely under their control with nary a Japanese soldier left in a matter of days.

Yet the battle was only beginning. The Japanese seemed to have unlimited resources as they snuck supplies to troops left on the islands, dropped bombs at night, and used the cover of darkness to harass American troops. But the Americans were determined to prevail.

Zane and his crew, along with a handful of other planes, had been on a mission to drop bomb loads on an enemy carrier. The timing left them flying back to Espiritu Santo in the dark. The Tornado acted sluggish, so they'd fallen behind the rest of squadron as Zane babied the plane along.

They hadn't seen any enemy planes, so he wasn't too worried about a group of Zeros getting the jump on them as they limped back to the airfield.

As they flew through the dark sky, Zane thought of their struggling base. The supply situation on the island had become critical. No spare parts existed for broken turret doors. Regulators as well as flight and engine instruments were acting up. Some engines were so full of muck and mire, they necessitated constant engine changes.

"What a beautiful day for an adventure," Bud quipped with heavy sarcasm as the clouds thickened and it began to rain. "I bet we can look forward to another delicious meal of rice and canned meat for supper. If I never see another can of that stuff, I'll be glad from now through the rest of eternity." He glanced over at Zane. "Hey, speaking of beautiful adventures, how do you suppose that nurse of yours is getting along? Any chance she'll get transferred overseas while you're gone?"

Zane hadn't even given a thought to Billie leaving the states with the nurse's corp. He thought most of the nurses at the hospital were civilian, but he didn't know Billie's status for a fact. What if she'd been sent off to a war zone? She could be on her way to one of the island bases or to a hospital in Europe right then and he'd have no idea how to find her.

He hadn't received a letter from her since he left Hawaii more than three weeks ago. A lifetime of experiences might have transpired the past month. She could be injured, taken captive, forced to...

With effort, he shut down his derailing train of thought and glanced over at Bud. "She's a civilian nurse, I think. There shouldn't be an issue of her leaving."

Billie seemed to love her job at the hospital, so he couldn't imagine her leaving. What she did for the men there, many of whom would never return to active duty, was essential and necessary. Even Rock was convinced without Billie's care, he would have died before he had the chance to escape.

"We got company, Tex," the tail gunner's voice crackled over the radio.

"Copy that, J.J. Eyes wide open, men." Zane cast a quick glimpse out the side window and thought he could see something approaching through the dark.

"There's one on our tail," J.J. reported.

"I've got one on my side," the left waist gunner noted.

"I can see one, too," Smitty said.

"Be ready to fight," Zane said, pushing Texas Tornado to reach Espiritu Santo before the approaching Zeros shot them out of the sky.

The crack of enemy fire burst around them and Zane felt the plane lurch as it was hit. His gunners opened fire and they watched a Zero burst into flames.

Another exploded to their right, hit by Smitty.

The men cheered as they pressed onward through the night sky.

"They're lighting a shuck and running, Tex," the tail gunner said.

"They're scared of a Tornado sweeping them up and spitting them out," Bud replied, grinning at Zane.

Only Zane didn't notice. He had a failing engine and he was sure the fuel tank had been hit, unless that gauge had suddenly malfunctioned.

"How far are we from the airstrip?" he asked the navigator.

"Should be coming up on our right, Tex."

The tropical rainstorm drenched the airfield with a consuming blackness that made it seem like they'd fallen into the inky depths of a bottomless well. Water poured from the skies over the plane, leaving visibility nearly nonexistent, especially without any illumination on the landing strip to light their way to the ground.

"Tex?" Bud asked, his voice holding a note of worry and concern as their plane pitched to the right and they started losing elevation.

"Brace yourselves!" Zane bellowed as he sent up prayers they'd survive the landing.

The engines coughed, sputtered, then fell quiet. Eerie silence enfolded them as the ground rushed up with alarming speed. Zane banked hard to the left as a ball of flame shot up in front of him. Explosions burst around them and the sound of ripping metal screeched through the air along with the screams of his men.

He glanced at Bud as the plane ripped apart then the darkness swallowed him.

*★★★ *Chapter Thirteen* ★★★*

"What's that you got there, Klayne?" Billie asked as she happened upon the soldier as he rested in the courtyard. He'd walked out there on his own, as part of his therapy to strengthen his wounded leg. If all her patients were as determined as Sergeant Klayne Campbell, they'd have a lot fewer men in the hospital.

His hand clenched around a bit of fabric as he shot a guarded look her direction.

She raised her eyebrows in question, but didn't move closer to where he sat on a bench in a patch of sunshine. Billie had no idea where the summer had gone. August would soon give way to September, bringing with it the first hints of autumn. She hadn't heard a word from Zane since her birthday, but she'd continued writing to him twice a week. She'd even sent him a package a few weeks ago with more cookies, chewing gum, and a selection of magazines she thought he might enjoy.

Instead of worrying about where he was, she sent up another prayer for his safekeeping and refocused her attention on the man sitting in front of her.

With her best schoolmarm expression in place, she stared at Klayne until he shifted on the bench, like a misbehaving boy squirming to get out of his punishment.

Finally, the man sighed and held out his hand.

Billie looked at a woman's handkerchief. It might have been lovely at one time, and had no doubt been white, but now it was gray, stained with spots of dried blood, the edges beginning to fray.

"Does that belong to someone special?" she asked, noting the skilled embroidery work. Someone had gone to much effort to make it a thing of beauty, even if it now looked more like a rag.

Klayne nodded. "My wife."

"Your wife?" Billie's mouth dropped open in surprise and she had to force it shut. She spluttered a few minutes before she turned her disbelieving stare on Klayne. "You have a wife?"

He nodded again.

"Well, good golly, man! Do we need to notify her that you're here? Do you want to write her a letter? What can I do to help?" Billie knew for a fact Klayne's file didn't list a wife. No relatives were listed and no one had been contacted on his behalf.

Klayne gave her an anxious look. "No. Delaney doesn't need to know. I don't want her to see me like this."

"Delaney? Is that your wife's name?" Billie asked, wondering why men were so stupid. If her husband had been as gravely injured as this man, she'd want to know where he was, how he was doing. She'd want to be right by his side. Billie couldn't imagine Klayne's wife would be any different.

"Delaney is her name. I call her Laney, but her friends call her Dee." Klayne glanced down at the handkerchief then held it to his nose and took a whiff before stuffing it inside the pocket of his robe.

He gave her a sheepish look. "The scent of her wore off months ago, but I can imagine it's still there. I hope you don't think I'm completely loony."

Billie sat beside him and placed her hand on his back, like she would if she offered comfort to a small, frightened child. "Not at all, Klayne. I think it's sweet you keep that close to you. It's obviously been with you through your trials and tribulations."

Another nod.

"When did you marry Delaney? Have you known her a long time?"

"No. We met at a New Year's Eve party and I married her the next month, just before I shipped out to begin training for the raid."

Billie knew the raid meant the Doolittle Raid when a group of brave men dropped bombs over Tokyo and a few other Japanese cities. In spite of the odds that they wouldn't survive, the men had gone anyway. Fortunately, most of them had made it through the experience, although several bore life-altering injuries.

"She must be so proud of you. Of what you did."

Klayne gave her a wary look then glanced across the courtyard. "I'm not sure she knows. I haven't been in touch with her since I left. I did write her a note in April and arranged for her to receive a gift for her birthday last month. Before I shipped out, I sent it to her friend to give her in case I didn't make it back."

Billie stiffened beside him. "Let me get this straight? You met a girl and married her a month later, then left for a dangerous mission she has no idea you went on, and you've not reached out to her since? Is that about right?"

"Yep." Klayne continued staring into the distance.

"What is wrong with you, Klayne Campbell? That poor woman is probably beside herself with worry and fear, desperately praying you'll come home. You have to write to her. If you want, I'll even help you place a long distance telephone call."

"No." Klayne's voice held a hard edge. One she'd not heard before. "I don't want Delaney to see me or hear from me until I can walk up to her. I'll be there soon. Doc said he figures he'll release me next week."

"You've made remarkable progress, Klayne. We're all so impressed with how far you've come since you've been here." Billie studied his profile since he refused to look at her as they talked. He'd allowed his hair to grow, both on his head and his face. A beard covered the scars on his face while his overgrown hair hid the scar on his forehead.

She stood, moving in front of him.

He tipped his head back and looked at her.

Her hands fisted on her hips and she glowered at him. "You absolutely must get a haircut and shave off that mess before you go home to her. No

177

wife deserves that." She waved a hand toward his unkempt hair.

Klayne offered her one of his rare smiles. "Yes, ma'am."

Billie reached out and clasped his good arm in her hand. "Come on. If you want to get home to Delaney, we've got work to do. I want you to take four more laps around the courtyard then walk to the cafeteria and tell them I said to give you a big glass of tomato juice." She laughed when he wrinkled his nose. "Don't you turn up your nose at me, young man! It's good for you."

The soldier was a few years her senior, but she had no problem taking him to task. "Once you drink that juice, and I mean every last drop of it, you work on the strengthening exercises we've been doing."

"Yes, ma'am." He offered her a snappy salute then started walking with his cane along the courtyard path.

Billie watched him take a few steps then made her way inside the hospital. She'd miss Klayne when he left. His gentle presence had assisted in keeping a balance in room seven. Although she'd never heard exactly what he'd said to George Haney the day he'd thrown the tray and hit Dorothy in the head, Jimmy had told her that Klayne had given the man an earful along with an ultimatum that had straightened the man right up.

Although he was an unassuming, quiet man, a few words from him could settle an argument or diffuse a potentially heated situation.

She hoped, for his sake and his wife's, he

would soon be on his way home. How his wife must have suffered his absence, his silence. Billie hoped Delaney would be accepting of Klayne and welcome him back into her life, because he was clearly besotted with the woman.

Billie grinned as she thought of another besotted patient. Jimmy was so head-over-heels for Dorothy, it was almost funny to watch him when the girl worked as a volunteer. And Billie greatly admired Dorothy for seeing past Jimmy's lack of legs to the sweet, wonderful boy that he was.

Two of the twelve patients in room seven had been discharged just that morning, leaving empty beds that would no doubt soon be filled. The hospital was already treating more patients than they could adequately care for. Beds were crammed into rooms until it made privacy impossible. Even the private rooms previously used for high-ranking officers now had two to four beds in them.

"Billie, can you give me a hand?" Peggy called as she stepped into the hallway on their floor.

"Coming."

The morning passed in a hectic blur of activity. Billie took only long enough to gobble a sandwich and drink a glass of milk before she returned to work for the afternoon.

When an orderly approached and handed her a stack of files, she tamped down a frustrated sigh. "More new patients."

"Where do you want them?" he asked. Billie and Peggy hastily worked to find beds for the ten new men, two of them landing in room seven.

Billie hadn't even taken time to read the files or

learn their names. There would be time enough for that when they were all settled.

One soldier in particular drew her gaze and stirred her compassion. White gauze encircled his head, wrapped over his eyes and looped beneath his chin. He had burn marks and stitches covering his torso, where he'd been hit with shrapnel. The skin around a bandage on his side felt hot, and she made note to check it as quickly as possible.

"You're safe now," she said, bending down and whispering close to the man's head.

He turned his face toward her, but remained silent. Something about him seemed familiar but she had no time to dwell on it. Not when her patients needed her.

An hour later, Billie returned to the soldier's beside with Doctor Ridley.

"Afternoon, soldier. I'm Doctor Ridley and I'm going to have a look at your side."

The soldier remained silent and unmoving. Billie would have thought he was sleeping, but he finally moved slightly, so his wounded side was more exposed, giving the doctor better access to it.

The doctor removed the bandage and handed it to Billie. She was grateful it was dry, a good sign the wound wasn't infected. With skilled hands, Doctor Ridley examined the stitches on the wound, felt around it, drawing a grunt from the soldier, before he glanced at Billie.

"The nurse is going to put a fresh bandage on you, but the wound is healing." The doctor moved back and jotted notes on a chart, leaving it with Billie. "Later, we'll do a full examination and take a look at those eyes, Private Timmons."

"I've got a bandage right here, Private. I'll just…"

"Billie!" one of the nurses scurried into the room, a stack of files in her hand. "That dimwitted orderly scrambled all the files. I think these belong to the men in here." She handed Billie two files, then picked up the one the doctor had just written in. "Private Timmons has his arm in a cast and his right foot is broken. I think he's in room three."

"Well, who's this soldier?" Billie asked, opening the file. Her knees buckled as she read the name written in the file. Captain Zane West.

Zane? Her Zane?

Was he the blind soldier on the bed in front of her?

She scanned the file. Plane crash. Explosion. Shrapnel wounds and burns. Loss of crew member. Concerns over patient's mental state as well as physical health.

For the first time in her life, Billie thought she might faint. Her throat felt thick, her ears rang, and her eyes swam.

"Nurse Billie?" Jimmy asked in a voice that sounded far away.

Unable to remain upright, she tilted toward the floor.

"Someone catch her!" Jimmy yelled.

Billie felt hands guide her to the bed behind her, the one Klayne normally occupied.

"Put your head down and take a deep breath," Doctor Ridley ordered, pushing on the back of her neck until her head was between her knees. She

SHANNA HATFIELD

sucked in a gulp of air, then another.

The doctor picked up the files that had fallen from her hands.

"Oh, I see," he said, aware of Billie's friendship with Zane. "We should move him to one of the officer's rooms."

"No." The wounded soldier said, speaking for the first time since his arrival. "No. I'll stay here."

Billie drew in another lungful of air then slid off the bed on wobbly legs. She moved to the side of the man she'd spent the last several months worrying about, wondering about, while praying for his safety.

"Zane? Oh, my poor Zane." Gently she took his hand between both of hers and pressed a kiss to the back of it.

"Billie?" he asked, turning his head slightly, as though he thought he was dreaming. "Beautiful Billie Brighton? Is it really you?"

"It's me, ol' lonesome cowboy." She pressed another kiss to his hand. "Fancy meeting you here."

The hand she didn't hold lifted and touched their joined hands then tentatively searched for her face. The rough calluses on his palm scratched across her cheek while his thumb wiped at the tears she didn't even realize streamed from her eyes.

"Billie," Zane whispered, as though he couldn't force any other words from his throat.

She had no idea how long they remained there, so close, but miles and months apart.

A hand on her shoulder finally drew her back to the present. To the other men who needed her assistance. She glanced at Doctor Ridley.

182

"Let him rest, Nurse Brighton. Let him rest for now."

She nodded and released his hand, tenderly setting it on the covers of the bed near his side. Her fingers brushed through the hair not bound down by his bandage. "I'll be back, Zane. I promise."

He nodded once, then released what sounded like a pleased sigh. Tension he'd held coiled in his shoulders melted away and he appeared to relax as he settled back against the pillows.

Billie didn't want to leave his side, not even for a single minute. But she had other patients depending on her, patients who needed her. She gave Zane one more look, relieved he was alive, but her heart aching over his wounds. Of more concern to her were the wounds she couldn't see, those that picked at his mind and ravaged his soul.

Unsure and disconcerted, she buried her thoughts and trepidation in her work.

The important thing was Zane had returned and if she had anything to say about it, he'd once again be whole and well.

*** **Chapter Fourteen** ★★★

"What do you think, Doc?" Zane asked as Doctor Ridley shined a light in his eyes. Zane could sense the light. In fact, it made him want to flinch at the pain it caused, but he still couldn't see.

"Tell me what you remember from the plane crash," the doctor said, removing the light.

Zane could hear him doing something, but he had no idea what. "We'd flown a night mission. Some Zeros caught up to us on the way back to the base and shot at us, hit the plane worse than we realized. We were almost to the airfield, but the rain had doused the landing lights and it was thick darkness all around us. The engines failed and we fell out of the sky. I tried to make a landing, but we crashed."

"Lie back," the doctor said, pushing against his shoulder until Zane rested on his back on the examination table. "I'm going to rinse your eyes. It shouldn't hurt, but it will feel cool and may be uncomfortable."

Zane nodded. To distract himself from the procedure, he kept talking. "I banked too far from the landing strip. There was a ball of flames, an explosion, and screeching metal." And the pain-wrenched screams of his men. Men who'd entrusted him to get them safely back to the base. "I woke up in a plane being transported to Hawaii, unable to see."

"They obviously stitched you up there. Did they treat your eyes at all?" the doctor asked as he trickled liquid over Zane's eyes.

"No. The doctor took a look at them and said either the explosion or the fire must have blinded me. He did say I didn't get any shrapnel in them, but that I wouldn't see again."

"Hmm," the doctor said. "And how did you end up here at the hospital?"

"After I found out Rock's whereabouts, I changed my home address from Texas to his. I put in a request if anything happened to me, I be sent to Oregon so I'd be close to Rock. I guess that includes when I'm unfit to serve and have to recuperate at a veteran's hospital." Zane had been so out of things, sedated with drugs for the consistent, horrid pain in his head he'd suffered from since the crash, he hadn't realized they'd brought him to the hospital in Portland until he heard Billie's name.

He thought he recognized her voice and scent when she first stepped near his bed, but he figured he was hallucinating. It wouldn't be the first time he'd imagined her presence, or his mind had conjured her fragrance.

Then he'd heard someone say her name. From the scrambling and shouting, he assumed she must have figured out who he was, too, and nearly fainted. Then she'd taken his hand in hers and kissed it and nothing else mattered at that moment. He'd felt her tears, heard the shaky fear mingling with relief in her voice when she spoke.

Zane knew in that moment his love for her was far greater than he'd allowed himself to believe, but he couldn't and wouldn't pursue it. Billie deserved far, far better than to be saddled with a helpless blind man.

He wouldn't burden her with his disability, but he knew someone who would gladly welcome him into his home.

"Do you think you could let Rock know I'm here?" Zane asked the doctor.

"Of course. I'll telephone him myself if Nurse Brighton hasn't already done so," the doctor said. The man dabbed at the liquid that ran down the sides of Zane's face and pooled beneath his head. "Go ahead and sit up."

Zane sat and forced himself to stillness when the doctor held the light to his eyes again.

"It's too soon to tell, but I'm not convinced you'll be permanently blind. I've seen a few cases like this in my lifetime. It might just be a flash burn." The doctor turned off the light and stepped back.

"Flash burn?" Zane asked.

"Have you ever stared at the sun then been unable to see for a second or two when you looked away?"

"Sure. What ornery little boy hasn't done that, even when his ma is hollering at him not to do it?"

The doctor chuckled. "Indeed. Well, it's sort of

that same principal. I believe the explosion, or perhaps the ball of flames, might have created a temporary burn on your corneas. Given enough time and healing, you might be able to see again. I can't make any promises, but we'll do our best for you, Captain West. And if I remember correctly, congratulations are in order. Weren't you a lieutenant when you were here back in the spring?"

"I was, sir, and thank you."

The doctor patted his shoulder. "Just relax, Zane. Give your body the time it needs to heal. Now, I'll go find a nurse to take you back to your room."

Zane half hoped it would be Billie, but at the same time dreaded it. He didn't want her to see him like this. Injured and weak, and unable to even feed himself because he couldn't see a blooming, blasted thing.

"Let's get you back to your bed, Zane," Billie said in cheerful tone as she entered the room.

An orderly had brought him to the examination room in a wheelchair, but Billie placed one hand around his back, her other on his arm, and led him from the room.

"We're going down the hallway," she said, as he slid his feet along the floor in a pair of slippers. "The floor is tile, there are no bumps, ridges or steps, and miraculously, no one left anything sitting out in the way today."

Zane might have smiled if he hadn't been listening so intently to her voice. The smooth cadence of it struck something deep inside him. He wanted to keep her talking, hold her close, never let her go in spite of his intentions to push her away.

"I promise I won't let you fall," she said when he continued taking small, shuffling steps. She stopped and he could picture her sizing him up. "Zane West, I know for a fact you can walk like you aren't an ancient old woman. Now lift those feet and walk like a man."

Annoyed by her command, he forced himself to forget he was blind and walk as he had before the crash. Before his career ended. Before he'd killed his friends.

The weight of his guilt and burdens caused his feet to stumble. He tripped, but Billie somehow kept him upright.

"It's all right, Zane. You're doing fine," she said, pressing a hand against his chest as they stood in the hallway. The heat of embarrassment burned up his neck. Frustrated and flustered, he wanted to hit something, to kick something, to run until his lungs burned, deprived of air.

Instead, he kept his chin lifted, back straight, and ignored what the touch of Billie's small hand did to him. Nerves jangled, it felt like her warm palm might sear right through his skin. He refused to wear a pajama shirt or a robe because the fabric rubbed on his wounds. The shrapnel he'd taken in his side had cut him up like a frying chicken. The worse wound, the one on his side, felt hot and hurt deep inside. Even a sheet brushing over it left him unable to rest comfortably.

Billie had touched him plenty in the one day he'd been in her care, but her touch as a nurse was far different than how she touched him as she did now — as a woman who cared about him, for him.

What a stupid fool he was to let her into his head and heart. How could the woman possibly see him as anything but an invalid, a cumbersome weight, in his current state?

Distraught and despondent, he stiffened and she dropped her hand from his chest. He wanted to grab her fingers in his, press them back against his skin. But he didn't.

"Come on. We're almost there," she said, guiding him forward by pressing a hand against his back. "Eight more steps then we'll turn left and go into the room."

He counted the steps in his head then felt the pressure of her hand against his back again and turned to the left.

"That's great, Zane. Now, nine steps to your bed."

She guided his hand down to the mattress and he sank onto it, wishing she'd leave him alone while silently begging her to stay.

Her hand brushed through his hair and lingered at the back of his neck for just a moment. A moment of bliss. A moment charged with longing. A moment filled with memories from those hopeful days in May.

"Stay out of trouble and try to get some rest," she whispered close to his ear.

He drew in a deep breath, inhaling her perfume along with the essence of a fragrance that was uniquely her. The scent washed over the jagged edges of his soul, bringing a brief feeling of peace and cleansing.

The soothing murmurs of her voice comforted him as he listened to her tend to the other men in the room. When she finished, her footsteps carried her to his bed. She touched his foot, giving his toes a gentle squeeze before she left the room.

When she was gone, a whiff of her scent lingered and Zane breathed it in.

"You have to spill the beans, Cap," the voice of a young man to his right said. "How do you know Nurse Billie?"

Zane didn't feel like being friendly or chatty, but he'd be stuck in this room with these men for who knew how long and he'd make the best of it. He settled himself more comfortably on the bed then turned his head to the right. "I met Nurse Brighton in the spring. I came here to check on one of my buddies before I shipped out to my next assignment."

"Is your friend well?" An older voice, one that bore the craggy depths of too many years of hard living and too many packs of cigarettes, spoke from the bed to his immediate right.

"He wasn't at the time, but he is now." Zane relaxed and let his natural talent at telling stories surface. He told the men about Rock walking out of the hospital on a cold, rainy night, of him getting kicked off the bus and left in the storm to fend for himself. He regaled them with the adventure he took with Billie trying to track down Rock. He even told them about climbing in her window and almost getting caught by Miss Burwell.

"But Rock is doing great now. He's living on a farm and regaining his health," Zane said, finishing his story.

"What about Nurse Billie?" This voice came from his immediate left. "She's certainly happy to have you back."

"Yep. She sure never looks at any of us the way she looks at you," the young man he thought was named Jimmy said.

"Nah. She's just doing her job," Zane said, refusing to admit there was more to it than that. Billie deserved far better than a blind man. He wanted to tell them no sane woman deserved a blind man, or half a man, or a man who'd always fight the ghosts he battled in his dreams. But he refrained. These men had enough to deal with without him adding more concerns.

He was almost asleep when he heard voices in the hallway and a steady tread making its way toward him across the floor.

"You ornery ol' cuss. I should have known a life of SPAM and rice would make you desperate for a vacation," said a voice Zane well recognized.

"Rock Laroux! Who are you calling an ornery ol' cuss, you dog-ugly, contrary, three-footed mule." Zane pushed himself back against the headboard and held out his hand in greeting.

Rock grasped it firmly and gave it a long shake with both hands.

"Boy, is it good to see you," Rock said, taking a seat on the edge of the bed and patting Zane on the arm. "Are you doing okay? Can I get you anything?"

"I'm fine," Zane lied, forcing a grin. "I'm surprised you got word so soon. They just brought me here yesterday afternoon."

"I know, but your favorite nurse called to give me the scoop." Rock's voice held a teasing note. "It's sure good to see you, Tex."

"I wish I could say the same," Zane quipped in an attempt to keep the conversation light. "But I'm glad you're here. Now, tell me what's new with you. Are you still staying on the farm where you recovered, gorging yourself on fresh butter and strawberries?"

Rock chuckled. "I am still on a farm. In fact, I bought one. It's called Double J Farms now. I don't know if you remember, but I told you about a produce stand I used to go to with my dad when I was a kid. Well, that's the place I bought."

"Wasn't it owned by a Jap family?" Zane asked.

"It was," Rock said, sounding hesitant.

"I got no use for Japs, no matter where they came from or how American they might pretend to be. No use for them at all." Zane declared with enough venom to take down a whole swarm of Zeros. "But I don't want to talk about that, tell me more about your farm."

"Well, I've got a crew of high school students who work for me," Rock said. "And there's something else, too."

"What's that?" Zane asked, leaning forward slightly.

"I got married."

"You what?" Zane's voice rose in volume, emphasizing his shock at Rock's announcement. He pushed back against the headboard, shocked by this bit of news. "You're yanking my rope."

"Nope. I'm dead serious. She's a swell girl, Zane. About as sweet as the good Lord makes them."

Zane grinned. "Well, how about that. Congratulations, Rock. I didn't think the woman existed who could tie you down to a permanent state of bliss, wedded or otherwise."

"I didn't either, but she did. I can't wait for you to meet her."

"What's her name? How did you meet?" The pain throbbing in his side forced Zane to lie back. Exhaustion pulled at him, but he fought to stay alert, awake.

"I'll tell you all about it another day. I think I'll stop in to see Doctor Ridley while I'm here. Do you need anything before I go?"

Zane felt Rock's weight lift from the mattress when he stood. "No. I've got everything I need. Will you come back again and visit?"

"You can count on it." Rock patted his leg in a brotherly gesture then moved away from the bed.

Zane listened as he took a few steps back. "I'll look forward to it. Thanks, Rock."

"Anytime, my friend."

✦★★ *Chapter Fifteen* ★★★✦

"You know we'll miss you, Klayne, but we wish you every happiness in the world," Billie said as she watched Klayne Campbell pack his meager belongings in his duffle bag.

He tossed her a grateful smile as he finished packing. "Thank you for taking such good care of me, Nurse Billie. If it hadn't been for you, I wouldn't be on my way home."

Billie sniffled, determined she wouldn't cry. But it didn't stop her from giving Klayne a hug. She stepped back and pinned him an admonishing glare. "Now, you absolutely promise you'll get that disgusting, bushy mess shaved off your face and your hair properly trimmed before you see your wife." It wasn't a question, but an order she expected to be followed.

Klayne grinned and nodded his head. "I promise I'll take care of it before I get on the train headed home."

"Best of luck to you, Klayne," George Haney said, holding out a hand to Klayne. "If you're ever in Salem, come look me up."

"I'll do that, although I hope I never leave

Pendleton again."

"Make sure you treat your wife like a queen," Jimmy instructed as he reached out to Klayne, shaking his hand as the man passed by his bed.

"I plan on it. I've got a lot to make up for," he said, glancing back at Billie. "You all take good care and if you're in Pendleton, come say hello. Just ask for directions to Sage Hills Ranch."

"Safe travels," Billie said as Klayne left the room, ready to return to civilian life. He'd mentioned his interest in working at Pendleton Airfield, training new recruits, once he fully regained his strength. She hoped he'd be able to, since it seemed important to him to keep helping the war effort in any way he could.

Billie turned back and surveyed the room. Klayne's departure and that of one of the other occupants of the room yesterday left her with two empty beds in the room. Doctor Bartle had informed her that morning he wanted to shift some of the patients around. By tomorrow, the room would be full again.

Doctor Bartle's incompetent work and horrid behavior with staff and patients alike had infuriated her to the point she wanted to snap at him. The lack of staff to meet the growing needs of the patients left her frustrated.

But the fact Zane had pushed her so far away she didn't think she'd ever be able to reach him, made her want to run to the rooming house, climb in her bed, and pull the covers over her head.

She, Peggy, and several of the other nurses often worked double shifts. Billie had given up her last three days off because the hospital simply needed all the helping hands it could get.

Dorothy, bless her sweet young heart, had coerced several of her friends into volunteering. While the girls could carry trays of food, read to the soldiers, boost morale, and perform basic care, what they really needed were more trained nurses.

Weary, and heart sore from Zane's rebuffs, Billie knew she should leave well enough alone. She'd lectured herself multiple times throughout the summer that she had no business, not a single speck, getting involved with a soldier.

Yet the moment she'd realized Zane was the blind man in one of her beds, she'd felt like the bottom had dropped out of her world and she was falling through an endless sky.

Zane was back, yet he wasn't. This quiet, withdrawn, infuriating man wasn't the one she fell in love with. No. It seemed he'd been left in a South Pacific jungle on a rainy, stormy night.

Doctor Ridley assured her Zane needed time to adjust to things. To the idea he was no longer a pilot, no longer needed in the military, no longer able to see. Regardless, Billie sensed the demons chasing Zane had far more to do with something else, something he refused to discuss.

She'd even asked their resident psychiatrist to speak with him, but Zane would hardly say more than a few words to the physician.

Exasperated and out of ideas on how to reach him, how to help him heal, not just from his visible injuries but the hidden wounds in his mind and heart, she was at the point of giving up.

The other men in room seven must have sensed her struggle because several had offered encouraging words. Even Sarge had told her not to give up on Zane.

"If you can get through to me, you can help anybody," he'd said, giving her shoulder a fatherly pat.

She just hoped they were right.

Billie checked on the men in room seven, made sure they were all settled for the moment, and then went to find someone to strip the empty beds and remake them.

It was late evening when she found herself standing at the foot of Zane's bed, wondering if he was awake or asleep. The soft breathing and light snores of the other men in the room let her know they rested peacefully.

However, Zane appeared tense, the sheet clenched in one hand while his legs moved restlessly.

In the week he'd been at the hospital, she'd taken over bathing his eyes in the soothing rinse Doctor Ridley prescribed. Twice a day, she poured the cool liquid over his eyes. Twice a day she wrapped the bandage back over them. Twice a day, she reminded him that there was still plenty of hope his sight would return.

But dozens of times a day, she longed to touch Zane, to hold his hand. To hear his laugh. To taste his kiss. She would have given a king's ransom just to see him smile a genuine smile.

Unable to help him until he was ready to help himself, she prayed for him. Wept for him in the dark midnight hours when sleep refused to give her fatigued mind and body relief. Ached for him, for the losses he'd suffered, the pain he'd endured, and the devastation he had to be working through so stoically on his own.

"You're such a stubborn idiot, Zane West," she whispered, as she quietly feathered her fingers through his hair. Rather than wrap his eye bandage around and around his entire head, she kept it just on his eyes, leaving his rich brown hair free to fall over his forehead. Free to tempt her to run her hands through it.

Most likely, she'd claw the eyes out of any nurse she caught touching Zane as she was now. But this was different. Zane had signed his last letter as "yours" and she intended to hold him to it. Since he couldn't return to the military, to life as a soldier, she was more than willing to explore a future with him as a civilian.

It didn't matter a whit to her if he was blind or had perfect vision. Her concern was in him staying by her side, not rushing headlong into battle on the other side of the world. That option was no longer a possibility and removed the one obstacle her head had insisted she not try and overcome before his injury.

"I'm so glad you're here." She spoke in a hushed tone as she continued stroking her fingers through his hair with one hand while she picked up his hand with her other and brought it to her lips.

He stilled and released a long breath. Visibly, he relaxed, so she kissed his hand again then held it pressed to the base of her throat where he could feel the steady beat of her heart while her fingers toyed with his hair.

"That feels so good," he mumbled, his voice husky and drowsy.

Startled, Billie would have squeaked if she wasn't afraid of waking up everyone else in the room.

"You do this for all the soldiers who have bad dreams?" he asked, his tone more alert.

"No, Zane. Only one," she whispered close to his ear. "Be a good boy and go to sleep. You need your rest."

"Yes, ma'am," he said, his drawl evident. The hand she wasn't holding reached out and connected with her arm. He skimmed it slowly over her shoulder until it cradled her cheek. His thumb brushed over her skin several times before his hand slid to her jaw and around to the back of her neck. He pulled her down until their lips connected.

The kiss was brief, but it held a world of emotion in it, a world of promise.

"Good night, Billie, girl."

Billie squeezed his hand then straightened. Before she left, she placed a light, butterfly kiss to his lips then walked out of the room.

She'd taken only a few steps down the hall when she heard a crash and darted into a room to help Peggy settle a patient in the throes of a nightmare. It took both of them, plus an orderly and a doctor to calm the man and get him settled for the night.

"I don't know when I've been so tired," Peggy said, her voice drained, as she and Billie finally left the hospital and made their way home.

"I can't imagine it getting better anytime soon." Billie glanced up at the stars overhead, not realizing how late it was. Miss Burwell would be in a tizzy, no doubt.

"I caught Nurse Homer whispering in a corner with Doctor Bartle twice today. Something about those two seems off to me." Peggy glanced at Billie. "Have you noticed anything odd?"

"Nothing I can pinpoint, but it seems to me the patients in Nurse Homer's care have not been doing well. Perhaps she's recently had some very tough cases, but…"

Peggy cut in. "You can't help but wonder what she's doing to them. Let's keep an eye on both of them when we can."

"Agreed." Billie used her key to unlock the front door to the house and she and Peggy stepped inside. Much to their surprise, Miss Burwell wasn't around, but the stair lights had been left on and an envelope bearing their names rested on the table where they collected their mail.

"What's it say?" Peggy asked as Billie pulled out a note.

"Miss Burwell said if we're hungry, she had the cook leave food for us in the warming oven." Billie grinned. "How do you like that?"

"Quite well," Peggy said, motioning Billie to follow her to the kitchen. "I missed lunch and didn't even give a thought to dinner. Food, a bath, and sleep all sound so good."

"I know exactly what you mean." Billie took the plates out of the warming oven while Peggy poured glasses of milk and gathered silverware and napkins.

The girls tucked into the good, filling meal, too tired to carry on a conversation. They drained their glasses of milk, washed the dishes, then trudged up the stairs to get ready for bed.

"Have a good night, Peggy, and sweet dreams."

Peggy gave her a knowing smile. "Mine won't be as sweet as yours with dashing Zane West in them."

"He might dash through my dreams, but I don't think I'm in his. Not any longer," Billie admitted.

"Give him time, Bill. If he was just another patient, not the soldier you fell in love with, what would you say we should do to help him get back to normal?" Peggy leaned against her door, waiting for Billie to answer.

"I'd say we should encourage him, but push him, too. Make sure he eats well, gets plenty of rest, sunshine and fresh air, and exercise." Billie sighed. "And let him heal in his own good time."

"Right there you have it. The best program for a wounded soldier to get well." Peggy gave her a hug. "Get some rest. Morning will be here before we're ready."

Billie went to bed, determined to heed Peggy's advice.

★ *Chapter Sixteen* ★

Even though he couldn't see, Zane had learned many details about the fellow occupants of room seven and the hospital staff he interacted with each day by using his ability to listen.

Sarge, in the bed next to his, was a lifelong military man who'd fought in the Great War. The man was crusty and slightly bitter, but Zane could sense him healing more than just physically. The man had told him about losing a hand to a grenade an eighteen-year-old newbie had accidentally pulled the pin on and set off. When Sarge was ready to leave, he had a choice of retiring from the military or going to a base in Washington where he could still train enlistees.

On the other side of Sarge, closest to the door, was Jimmy. The private seemed about as happy and carefree as anyone could be, but Zane knew from Billie's letters the young man had lost both his legs. At one time she'd worried about the boy giving up his will to live. As he listened to Jimmy joke and tease the other patients, he knew it was because of the work Billie had done.

Being around her every day was both torturous

and heavenly. He loved listening to her voice, hearing her laughter, picturing her smile. He could almost feel her presence before she set foot in the room. By now, he knew her footsteps, and, of course, he recognized her fragrance.

The moment she stepped into the room, the atmosphere changed, as though every single man there revered and respected her. Truthfully, it was more than that, but Zane couldn't even put to words what that feeling encompassed.

All he knew was that Billie's presence brought a lightness and brightness to these men they otherwise wouldn't know. Billie was an excellent nurse, highly skilled and expertly trained, but it went far beyond her ability to help them heal physically. It rested in her ability to encourage the men, make them believe they could get better, be better.

Zane hated being blind. Hated being confined to his bed or at the mercy of someone to lead him around like a dog, but he had no choice in the matter. Unlike Rock who'd walked himself out of the hospital and to a better outcome for his life, Zane couldn't even do that much.

Rock had been to see him three times in the past two weeks, and he was grateful for his friend's presence.

When he'd come yesterday, Rock had brought him a few treats, and a wooden puzzle he could put together by feeling the tabs and slots as they slid into place. The puzzle at least gave him something challenging to do during hours of boredom, besides brood about his mistakes and regret his past.

He'd tried to pry more detail out of Rock about his wife, but the man had changed the subject quite abruptly. He didn't know if Rock was already regretting his marriage, or what the problem could be. Had Rock made a hasty decision to wed based on his recent brush with death?

Thoughts of illness and death sent his mind chasing along a path guaranteed to put him in a maudlin mood. He'd finally been ready to read the details of the report about his plane crash just that morning. Since he couldn't see, Billie had taken him to an exam room where he'd be able to have privacy and read it to him.

Zane knew he'd missed the runway and crashed in the jungle. What he didn't know was that the plane had taken so many hits from enemy fire it had knocked out the engines and drained all the fuel.

So many other things were already malfunctioning on the plane due to a lack of parts and supplies, not to mention trained service crews, it was a wonder they'd made it back to the island at all.

When the plane crashed, a fiery ball had shot up, burning Zane's eyes. Shrapnel from the torn hull of the plane had sliced through him and Bud, but Bud had survived.

Zane was sure all the other men on his plane had died, but he discovered the only casualty was poor Smitty who'd been in the belly turret. He'd been crushed the moment the plane hit the ground.

Unable to contain his emotion — a charged mixture of relief that so many of his men survived, and grief over the scrappy little gunner's death, he barked at Billie to leave him alone. When she placed a hand on his arm in comfort, he'd brushed it off and yelled at her to get away from him.

She'd left him without saying another word. Ten minutes later, an orderly helped him back to his bed. That was right after breakfast and it was nearing time for supper. He'd had hours to mull over his need to apologize to her, if she returned to the room. Maybe she'd request someone else take over, or perhaps she'd have him moved to a different floor.

As much as he hated to admit it, he needed her daily visits, even more than the other men. In spite of everything, he thought of Billie as his.

"You have a visitor, Captain West," a feminine voice said from the foot of Zane's bed, pulling him from his thoughts. He recognized it as belonging to a young girl named Dorothy who volunteered at the hospital. If he hadn't missed his guess, she was sweet on Jimmy and the feeling was returned tenfold from the young private.

"Thank you, Dorothy," he said, forcing a smile in the direction of where the girl spoke.

Zane pushed himself up against the headboard, glad his side no longer felt like someone constantly rammed a hot poker through it. Other than occasional twinges if he turned wrong and a bit of heat radiating from it, he thought it was healing quite nicely.

"Well, Two-Bit, what have ya done to yerself?" a nasally voice twanged from the end of his bed.

Panic, irritation, and fury rolled into one distasteful lump in his throat. Zane swallowed it down, sat up a little straighter and lifted his chin.

"Howdy, Floyd. What brings my big brother all the way from Texas?" Zane had no idea what dire calamity would have forced his brother to travel to Portland to see him. He knew he wasn't dying. He was certain even his demise wouldn't spur Floyd to travel that far.

"Well, shoot it all to heck and back again, Two-Bit. Yer as blind as a foggy-eyed frog. I reckon they ain't been a lyin' to me."

Zane could feel a faint stirring of air in front of his face and assumed his brother was waving his hand in front of his eyes to make sure he couldn't see. He resisted the urge to reach out and grab his brother's hand, or punch Floyd in the nose.

Irritation swelled in him until he could hardly keep it subdued. "What do you want, Floyd? I know you didn't come all the way here just to make sure I was receiving adequate care."

Floyd laughed, an annoying sound that always reminded Zane of a witch's cackle. "No beatin' around the bush with ya, is there, boy?"

Zane barely refrained from grinding his teeth or clenching his jaw. "Just get to the point, Floyd."

"Well, shoot, Two-Bit, it ain't like ya can chase off somewhere. Seems to me ya got all the time in the world. 'Sides, I ain't clapped eyes on ya since Pa up and died." Floyd's weight settled on the edge of his mattress.

The mention of their father caused Zane to bristle. He fought the temptation of kicking his brother onto the floor. "Only because you chased me off the ranch and told me not to come back."

Floyd released a sigh, the stink of his alcohol-laden breath tainting the air. "I may have been a bit hasty. After all, we're family."

Zane held his tongue and waited. Floyd was on a fishing expedition and he had no intention of taking the bait. His brother cleared his throat. Zane pictured him rubbing his fingers across the felt of the big ten-gallon hat he always wore.

"Ya never did answer my letter asking for ya to come back to the ranch and help. We lost all the hands to the war except ol' Darnell and Cookie. They've both been picking up the slack."

Zane had loved the foreman and bunkhouse cook as though they were his uncles. He'd spent many, many hours learning life lessons and skills from both men. He hoped Floyd wasn't working them into their graves, but he wouldn't put it past his brother.

"It's not like I could just walk away from my responsibilities, Floyd. The military frowns on that sort of thing," Zane said, listening as his brother's clothes rustled. No doubt, Floyd was fussing with his suit jacket, tugging at the sleeves. He'd had that habit for years and it always meant he was fixing to bamboozle someone.

"Right," Floyd said. "At any rate, with the shortages on meat starting now that it's rationed, we've had problems with cattle rustlers. They stole a dozen head just last week."

"I'm sorry to hear that," Zane said, and he was. Cattle rustlers had been plaguing the West family since his great-grandparents first started the ranch right after the Civil War.

"Look, Zane, I can't keep the ranch by myself and ya'll sure ain't in any shape to help. I want to sell it, but to do that, I need you to sign a paper. Will ya do that?"

Anger blazed in him. "No, I'm not going to do that. That ranch has been in our family for generations. It's survived Indian wars and raids, floods, famine, infestations, cattle rustlers, blizzards, droughts, and fire. If you think I'm gonna stand by and watch you lose something our family has worked so hard to keep, you've lost your ever-loving mind!"

Floyd got off the bed. The stench of his overpowering cologne mingled with the odor of his foul breath. The smell nearly gagged Zane as he leaned down close to him. "See, Two-Bit, right there is the problem. Ya can't watch nothin' because ya went and lost your sight. Now sign the dang paper so I can be on my way."

"No. I'm not signing it." Zane pushed himself up, swung his legs over the edge of the bed. He would have stood, prepared to engage his brother in a round of fisticuffs, if a small hand hadn't settled in the smack dab middle of his bare chest and pushed him back.

"Captain West, you stay in that bed and do not move." Billie's voice, full of authority and fury, brooked no room for argument.

He heard the swish of her skirt as she spun around. "As for you, Mr. West, I must ask you to leave this room and the hospital. We simply will not allow visitors to upset our patients. It's quite clear Captain West is more than ready for you to leave.

Please do so posthaste."

"Aw, shoot, lil' lady, me an ol' Two-Bit grew up goin' at it quite regular. It don't mean nothin'."

"Well it does to me," Billie said, her voice laced with steel. "If you refuse to leave, Mr. West, you'll leave me no choice but to have you forcibly removed. You can walk out of here on your own or be hauled between two orderlies who were boxing champions during their school days. It makes no difference at all to me."

"Now, there ain't no need to get all het up about things," Floyd said. Zane could hear his boots clomping toward the door. "I'll come back tomorrow."

With that, Floyd was gone. Zane listened as a huff filled the air and then the men in the room all started talking at once.

"Man alive, Nurse Billie, I thought I saw flames shooting from your eyes."

"That's the way to set him straight."

"Boy, I'm glad you're in our corner, Nurse Billie."

Zane would have joined in the commentary, but he was still fuming from Floyd's visit and highly embarrassed Billie came to his rescue.

The years hadn't changed his brother at all. If anything, Floyd was even more detestable than he recalled.

"That's your brother?" Billie asked, sounding upset as she spoke in clipped tones.

"That's him."

"Well, I could have run into him on the street and would never have made the connection," she said as she fluffed his pillow and adjusted his covers. "You don't have to see him tomorrow unless you choose to."

"I know. I don't really want to, but there are some things I'd like to know about the ranch, questions I'd sure like him to answer. Rustlers taking a dozen head of cattle shouldn't throw the finances off kilter. Something else is going on and I want to know what."

"What happens if he sells the ranch?"

"After the bills are paid, we'd split the profits." Zane sighed. "Honestly, I took the few things that meant the most to me when my father died and left them with an old family friend. He promised to keep everything until I had a place he could send it."

"That's good," Billie said, continuing to fuss over him.

He grabbed her hand as it brushed over his arm and held it between his. "Listen, Billie, I'm sorry about this morning. I had no right to yell at you and I wasn't mad at you, just myself."

"You shouldn't be, Zane. You did your best in a horrible situation and saved the lives of all your crew but one. I'm sure your men would agree if it wasn't for you and your skills, you'd all have been dead."

"But Smitty is." Zane choked as he said the gunner's name.

Billie squeezed his hand then she was gone.

The following afternoon, Zane and Sarge had gone for a walk around the courtyard. Billie had decided they made a good team. Sarge guided him and if the older man got tired, Zane had enough strength to help him get to a bench and sit down. Between the two of them, they managed to get in their daily quota of exercise. On their walks, Sarge talked about his years in the army and the horrors he'd seen during the first World War. Zane shared about his experiences at West Point, growing up on a Texas ranch, and his lack of plans about his future since he'd always assumed he'd enjoy a long military career.

The two of them had just returned to the room from their walk and settled back into their beds when Zane heard the distinctive step of boots on the tile floor and smelled his brother's cologne.

"Lookin' all bushy-tailed but not so bright-eyed are ya, brother?" Floyd jeered as he seated himself on the end of Zane's bed.

"Go away, Floyd. I'm not going to sign anything. At least not until you tell me the truth. Why do you want to sell the ranch? And don't try and feed me that pig wallow about rustlers. How many head have you lost total?"

"Close to seventy."

That was a sizeable number, but not enough to upset the ranch's finances that badly. "So what's the real reason you have this sudden urge to sell and how did you even find me?"

"Well, Uncle Sam sent me a telegram when ya were injured. After a few telephone calls, I found out ya'd been moved here. I can't even begin to guess why. Sure didn't make it convenient for me to travel here from home."

"And?" Zane asked, hoping to prod his brother

into finally telling him the truth. Not that Floyd would recognize the truth if it bit him on his flabby backend. The man had manipulated the truth, twisted and turned it for so long, reality was a complete stranger to him.

"Ya know it's powerful hard being in charge of a ranch that size. There's overseein' and decisions, and a man gets lonesome. Needs a diversion from time to time."

Zane bit his tongue until he tasted blood. If the conversation was headed in the direction he feared, he might just strangle his brother with his bare hands.

"What kind of diversion?" he asked, his voice tight and tense.

"Mostly at The Crystal. A little drinkin', and availin' myself of the services, and…" Floyd hesitated. Zane knew what was coming, knew what his brother was going to say before the word came out of his thin lips. "Gamblin'."

"You ran the ranch into debt with your gambling problem. Is that what this is about, Floyd? Hmm?" Zane sat forward and wished he could see just enough to lay his brother out cold on the floor. "Wouldn't Mama and Daddy be proud of you," he said, his voice dripping with sarcasm and disdain.

Floyd stood. Zane could hear him pacing back and forth in front of his bed before he moved so close the hate rolled off his brother in a palpable force, battering against him.

"Listen up good, ya blind, helpless whelp! Ya got no future and I sure ain't takin' ya in, so you might as well sign the paper, let me sell the ranch, and I'll split what's left after I pay off the debts."

A vein in Zane's neck began to throb. He could feel it with each pulse. "How much do you owe?"

"That don't matter. They ain't gonna give me any more time. I need the money, now."

"How much, Floyd?" Zane asked again.

"Almost seventy-thousand."

Sarge whistled from the bed next to him. Even with his blindness, he could practically see Floyd glaring at the older man.

"How did you get that deep in debt? You just don't know when to fold and walk away, do you?" Zane asked, no longer capable of hanging onto his rising temper. "Dad dragged your sorry hide out of trouble twice before. A smart man would have learned his lesson. Even a dumb one would know not to get that deep into a hole he couldn't get himself out of without crawling to family for help."

Zane's head snapped back when Floyd hit him. He scrambled off the bed, going purely by instinct, and landed a blow to Floyd's gut. Elation flooded through him when Floyd grunted in pain.

"Enough!" a voice boomed so loudly from the doorway it nearly rattled the windows. "Out! Get out of the here, you nasty, horrid man. Out of the hospital, out of this room, but most especially out of your brother's life. I'll have you arrested if you set foot back in this room today. How dare you come in here, upset my patients, and strike one of them. I won't have it. Not at all, you filthy, low-down skunk! Now, out!"

Zane was shocked Billie could yell that loud. He heard scuffling sounds as though his brother scooted away from her fury.

"I'll be back with a lawyer and we'll settle this Two-Bit. I'll have you declared incompetent and keep every penny for myself."

"Just try it, Floyd," Zane said, listening as his brother's footsteps faded. He reached behind him, searching for the bed. Something wet trickled over his lip, and he only then realized his cheek throbbed where Floyd had hit him.

"You're cut, Zane. Rest while I get something to take care of it." Billie helped him back into bed then hurried from the room.

"That is one fine gal," Sarge mused after Billie left the room.

"She's like a mama bear defending her cubs," another man said with a laugh.

"No offense, Tex, but she sure set your four-flushing brother on his ear," Jimmy crowed. "I wish you coulda seen the way she poked him in the chest as she let him have it."

Zane wished he could have seen it, too.

And Sarge was right. Billie Brighton was one fine gal.

✶✶★ *Chapter Seventeen* ★✶★✶

Raised voices from room seven urged Billie down the hall to investigate. She feared Zane's brother would return and hadn't been surprised to find him there.

What had shocked her was to see Zane jump out of bed and sock the disgusting man in the stomach. She had no idea how Zane had managed it, but silently cheered him on. With blood trickling down his cheek from a nasty cut, she assumed Floyd threw the first punch. She certainly wasn't going to allow him to land another.

What kind of man attacked his blind, recovering-from-a-fiery-plane-crash brother in a hospital room? The despicable, detestable kind — like Floyd West.

Billie knew from past conversations with Zane there was no love lost between him and his only sibling. But Floyd's animosity toward Zane was like a living, breathing thing, intent on doing harm.

She had no idea how two siblings could be so different. It wasn't just their personalities that were worlds apart. Where Zane was broad-shouldered and muscular, Floyd was skinny and lean to the point of scrawniness. The brothers looked nothing alike.

Well, that wasn't entirely true. She could see a faint resemblance in the shapes of their noses, and they had the same shape to their hands, but that was where the similarities ended. Floyd had dark, almost beady eyes, thin lips, and a pallid complexion. She would have assumed a Texas rancher would have skin tanned and weathered from time spent outdoors. However, it sounded as if Floyd spent most of his time at some deplorable establishment gambling, drinking and who knew what else.

Not finding the supplies she needed at the nurse's station, she hurried to the supply closet and filled a small metal container with bandages and medicated ointment. She was just about to step out when she heard two men talking and recognized Floyd's Texas twang.

"It's a sorry thing you're having trouble with your brother," she heard someone say as they passed by. She waited a moment, then looked out, seeing Floyd with Doctor Bartle. Curious what the two of them might discuss, she followed them when they turned the corner and walked toward the doctor's office.

Billie hid behind a gurney when Doctor Bartle glanced her way before motioning Floyd inside his office. Thankfully, they left the door open so she could hear every word they said. She knew she shouldn't eavesdrop, but as the conversation progressed she was glad she had.

"My brother's always been a soft-hearted fool. He never would've been able to handle the ranch like I have," Floyd said.

"What seems to be the trouble?" Doctor Bartle asked.

"I need him to sign a paper givin' me authority to sell our ranch. We own equal shares of it and I can't sell it without his agreement."

"How's a blind man going to know any different?" Doctor Bartle asked.

Indignation and anger began simmering in her belly, making her wish she could lambast both of the thick-headed, horrible men.

Floyd offered a short, derisive bark of laughter. "That's just the thing of it. He can't see to sign, even if he knew what the paper said. I got me a feelin' he won't sign a thing without someone readin' it to him, otherwise I'd figure out a way to have him sign over the whole place to me."

"What are you doing?" a voice whispered in Billie's ear.

She clapped a hand over her mouth to keep from screaming and spun around, glaring at Peggy.

"Shh. Listen to this," she said low enough only Peggy could hear as she pointed to Doctor Bartle's office.

Peggy leaned closer, listening to the two men talk.

"You know, for the right price, I might have a solution to your problem. Not all the patients here survive. Some become terribly ill and pass away despite the valiant efforts of our staff. I have a nurse who'd be more than willing to help bring about his death."

"Ya don't say," Floyd said, his tone full of

curious wonder. "I'd dearly mourn the passin' of my beloved little brother."

Both men chuckled before Floyd spoke again. "What's it gonna set me back?"

"For a thousand dollars, we can take care of things for you. Half to do the job, and half when it's finished."

"It's a deal. How long will it take before I'm the sole heir of the ranch?"

"Well, we can do it two ways. Zane's health can slowly decline, with a little help. The nurse can mix up his medication or mess with his food, depending on what is needed to get the job done."

"Is there a faster solution?" Floyd asked.

"I like the way you think," Doctor Bartle said with a wicked chuckle. "I can give him a shot that'll end him like that." The sound of fingers snapping carried out to Billie. "Then you'd be free to do as you wish."

"How about ya give him that shot in the mornin'? I can act like the grievin' brother when I come to see him and he's dead. Here's yer deposit. I'll bring the rest of the money with me tomorrow."

The sound of a chair scraping against the floor sent the two women racing down the hall and around the corner.

"Did you hear that? They're planning to kill Zane," Billie said, stunned by the revelation.

"Even worse, Doctor Bartle has done it before. I bet I know which nurse is helping him."

"Me, too. We need to tell Doctor Ridley about this right away," Billie said. The two women hurried down the hall to the doctor's office.

"I knew something was wrong with Bartle, but couldn't place my finger on it," Doctor Ridley said after Billie and Peggy relayed what they'd discovered. "That's it. I'm not going to stand by another day and let him run amuck in my hospital. Your word against his won't likely result in his arrest, but we must do something. Perhaps I can go to the board and we can have his license revoked at the very least. Also, we must determine if Nurse Homer is the nurse he mentioned."

"Doctor Ridley? What if Zane wasn't here and someone else was in his bed, waiting for Doctor Bartle and Nurse Homer in the morning?" Billie asked, a plan quickly formulating in her thoughts.

The doctor stopped pacing around his office and stared at her a moment. A slow smile creased his face and he nodded his head.

"Go on. What do you have in mind?"

"Well, what if…"

Twenty minutes later, Billie practically ran down the hall to room seven. The blood had dried on Zane's cheek when she returned to his side.

"My apologies for taking so long to get back to you, Zane. Something popped up quite unexpectedly." She dabbed at the blood with a soft, warm cloth until it loosened, then she cleansed the wound. It didn't require stitches, but was a nasty gash that had to sting. "I'm afraid that might leave a scar."

"It'll match the rest," Zane said, with a wry grin as she carefully applied medicated cream over the spot.

"What did he hit you with?" A faint design was

visible along the edges of the wound.

"His fist, but he wears a big ol' ring with a raised lion in the middle of it." Zane lifted his hand to his face and gingerly touched the bandage she'd just secured over the cut. "That's what caused the cut. If it wasn't for that ring and the fact he was fighting a blind man, he'd still be trying to pull himself up off the floor."

"I think a bit of fresh air would be just the thing for you right now, Zane. Are you up to it?" Billie asked, eager to get him alone so she could explain what was about to take place.

"I reckon I can muster enough juice to get myself outside." He rose from the bed and Billie guided him from the room. Peggy saw them coming as Doctor Bartle stopped by the nurse's station and asked the doctor to accompany her to see a patient down the opposite hall.

Billie knew she'd owe her friend for that.

Together, she and Zane made their way out to the courtyard. She waited until Zane was settled on a bench in the warm sunshine before she sat beside him.

"What's going on in that pretty head of yours, Billie, girl?" Zane asked. It was as if he could read her mind even though he was unable to see her face. "I know you didn't bring me out here because I needed a stroll in the fresh air. There's a storm brewing and if I'm not mistaken it has something to do with my lunkheaded, conniving brother."

Billie explained what she'd heard Floyd and Doctor Bartle discussing, the plans she'd made with Peggy and Doctor Ridley, and how Zane had to pretend he knew nothing the rest of the day.

"Are you sure the other fellas will be okay in the room? I don't want one of them getting hurt," Zane said, rubbing his thumb across Billie's palm as she held his hand.

"We'll tell them what's happening in the morning and give them the choice of being moved to another room temporarily. If I know those men at all, though, not one of them will go anywhere."

"Probably not." Zane released a long, beleaguered breath. "I'm sorry to cause work and trouble for all of you."

Billie gaped at him. "Are you crazy, Zane West! You didn't do anything wrong. This is all on your brother and Doctor Bartle, and Nurse Homer if we can catch her helping to carry out their devious plans. What kind of man plots to have a fine, upstanding war hero such as yourself killed?"

"I'm no hero, Billie, but Floyd is a disgusting excuse of a human." Zane ran a hand through his hair and sighed. "It's kind of hard to imagine him hating me that much, but it doesn't exactly surprise me. He's never cared about anyone but himself."

"Was he that awful to you when you were kids?" Billie asked. "And why does he call you Two-Bit, other than the fact it clearly irritates you."

Zane turned his face away, as though he gathered his thoughts. Billie wished she hadn't asked questions that obviously upset him.

When he remained silent, she placed a hand on his shoulder. "You don't have to answer my questions, Zane. Forget I asked."

"No. It's fine, Billie." He inhaled a deep breath

then turned toward her. "My brother was six when I was born. Since he'd spent so much time as the spoiled and pampered lone child on the place, he viewed me as an interloper. When I was just about a year old, we'd gone to town. Floyd was supposed to keep an eye on me while Mama was in the store. One of the old-timers happened upon us and offered to give Floyd two-bits for me as a joke. My brother took the money and left me with the old man, telling him I wasn't worth two-bits, but he'd have to keep me since they made a deal. Dad thought it was hilarious. Mama was livid Floyd let me out of his sight. And my brother decided I would be called Two-Bit from then on. Anytime someone would say something kind to me, Floyd would tell them I wasn't even worth two-bits."

"He sounds like he's always been a horrible person, even as a child."

Zane nodded his head in agreement. "You have no idea. He was lazy, mean, and lied so often, no one knew when he was actually telling the truth. The sad thing is he only got worse as he aged."

"What did your parents think of Floyd?"

"Dad thought he'd grow out of it, learn to be a good man by example. I think he knew how Floyd was, but he just kept hoping he'd change. Floyd didn't fool Mama, though. I was only seven when she died in childbirth, right along with my newborn sister. She loved children and wanted a houseful, but had a lot of trouble carrying them."

"I'm so sorry, Zane. There is no good age to lose a parent, but that age is particularly hard." Billie laid her hand against his back and gave it a comforting rub. "What about your father?"

"Dad passed away three years ago. His horse stepped in a hole and threw him. Dad landed on a pile of rocks and crushed his spine and messed up things inside. He spent five days in the most intense pain anyone could imagine before he passed away. Thanks to the ranch foreman getting in touch with me right after it happened, I was able to get home and see him the day he died. It meant a lot to me to be able to tell him goodbye. Right after the funeral and the reading of the will, which gave Floyd and me equal shares of everything, Floyd threatened to shoot me if I ever stepped foot on the place again. He was expecting Dad to leave him the whole ranch, free and clear. It put quite a crimp in his tail that he had to share with me."

Zane leaned forward then straightened back up, favoring his still tender side.

"If you were gone, Floyd would have the whole ranch to himself and could do as he pleased. And if you're still around, he has to run decisions like selling the place past you and get your official approval. Is that correct?"

"That's right," Zane said, getting to his feet and walking back and forth by the bench.

Billie hated to see him restlessly pacing, but she was glad he was comfortable enough in his surroundings to move normally without the fearful hesitant steps he generally took. Maybe he was still so worked up over Floyd that the need to move overruled everything else.

"We better get you back to your room. There's much to be done before your ride to freedom arrives."

Zane's hand clasped hers tighter as she led him toward the hospital door. "Are you sure Rock doesn't mind?"

"Not at all. When Doctor Ridley spoke with him, he said Rock sounded quite pleased at the idea. He'll be here after supper, once everyone has settled down for the night."

"Good."

Billie guided Zane back to his bed and while the men were occupied with their evening meal, she quickly packed his bag. He'd just have to wear a robe when he left, but that couldn't be helped at the moment.

Under the guise of gathering dinner trays, she managed to stash his bag on the bottom of a cart and roll it out of the room. She hid the bag in Doctor Ridley's office then returned to her duties.

Her nerves were jangled by the time the men settled down for the night and the hallways grew quiet.

It was a little past ten when Rock Laroux appeared at the nurse's station. Peggy and Doctor Ridley had remained behind to help carry out the plans. The doctor quietly made his way into room seven and led Zane to the door while Peggy made sure no one would see them. She arranged pillows on Zane's empty bed so a nurse walking by would think he still slept there.

With the doctor on one side of him and Rock on the other, they snuck Zane down the back stairs and out a little-used door to where Rock's car waited behind the hospital. Billie carried Zane's bag and Peggy had a basket full of medical supplies they thought Zane might need while he stayed at Rock's place.

Rock had agreed it might be best for Billie to come along and get Zane settled for the night, so she climbed in the car.

She sat in the backseat with Zane, his head cradled on her lap as exhaustion pulled him into sleep. Her fingers stroked across his brow and through his hair, seeking comfort from the motions as much as offering it to him.

While Rock drove, they spoke little, concern for Zane's wellbeing uppermost in their thoughts.

It took almost an hour before Rock turned off the road and pulled up a short driveway. Gravel crunched beneath the tires as he drove around to the back of a house she and Zane had visited when they were trying to find Rock.

"We looked for you here, back in May," Billie said, peering through the darkness to the house aglow with lights. "Zane and I stopped here, but no one answered the door."

Rock glanced at her in the rearview mirror. "I wouldn't have been in any shape to answer the door, let alone hear you knock."

Before Billie could ask questions about who else might have been there, who cared for him, Rock parked the car.

"The bedrooms are closer to the back of the house. I thought it would be easier to go in this way." Rock glanced over the seat at Billie then hurried out of the car.

He opened the back door of the sedan and

placed a hand on Zane's arm as he sat up, groggy with sleep.

"Hey, Zane, we're gonna get you inside and settled now. Just follow my lead." Rock helped him out of the car and looked back at Billie. "If you leave those things, I'll come back and get them." Before she could reply, Rock guided Zane up the back steps and through the door.

Billie left Zane's bag but grabbed the basket and hurried to catch up to the men. The hand-carved screen door on the back entrance featured a crane in a grouping of cattails and appeared to have been made by a talented artist.

She opened it and stepped inside, going down a hallway into a brightly lit kitchen decorated in cobalt blue and white. Tidy, neat, and filled with decorative touches, the air smelled of chocolate and coffee, reminding her empty stomach she hadn't made time for lunch or dinner.

"Welcome to our home. You must be Nurse Brighton. I'm Mrs. Laroux." A tall woman with black hair motioned for Billie to follow her as she left the kitchen and went down a hallway into a bedroom.

Billie hardly paid any mind to the comfortable, homey room where Rock helped Zane settle into a large bed. She was too focused on her patient.

Zane's skin no longer looked healthy, but pale, and beads of sweat dotted his upper lip. She took his hand in hers, finding it clammy.

"It's so kind of you both to open your home to him, especially under these trying circumstances." Billie spoke in a quiet tone, hoping Zane wouldn't hear.

He rolled his head toward her and grinned. "Aw, just tell it like it is, Billie, girl. My brother's the biggest horse's patootie that ever lived."

His words sounded slurred, almost like he was drunk.

Worry gnawed at Billie as she began digging through the basket of supplies she'd brought from the hospital. She glanced over her shoulder to where Rock stood with his arm resting around the waist of his wife. "May I please have a warm cloth for him and perhaps a glass of water?"

"Of course," Rock's wife said, disappearing from the room. She quickly returned with a cool glass of water, a warm cloth, and a shallow basin half-full of steaming water.

"Is there anything else he needs or I can help with?" the woman asked in a soft, articulate tone that gave Billie the impression the woman was educated, perhaps even well-to-do, yet kind.

"No, this is perfect. Thank you." Billie sponged Zane's face, hands, arms and chest then checked the bandage on his side.

Rock and his wife both left the room, but Rock returned a few moments later carrying Zane's bag, setting it at the foot of the bed out of the way.

"Is there anything else we can get him? Get you?" Rock asked.

"No. I think we have everything we need, don't we Captain West?"

"Oh, drop the captain business, Billie, girl. Ain't we all just dandy friends?" Zane's grin looked lopsided as he turned his face toward her.

SHANNA HATFIELD

Rock walked around the bed and moved so he stood close to the headboard on the other side. He reached out and placed his hand on Zane's shoulder, giving it a gentle squeeze. "I'm sure happy to have you staying with us for a while, Tex. It'll be just like old times, except there's no cranky sergeant to kick us out of bed or bark orders at us."

"Remember when ol'…" Zane's voice faded and his head tilted to one side.

Billie wasn't sure if he'd gone to sleep from exhaustion or passed out. Either way, he needed the rest.

"Will he be all right?" Rock asked, giving her a questioning glance.

"I think so. I'll sit up with him tonight, but I'll need a ride to the hospital early in the morning."

"You can take our car whenever you want to leave." Rock walked back around the bed and followed her into the hallway. He turned off the light in Zane's room and shut the door until it remained open just a crack.

Billie shook her head. "That would be disastrous for your car since I've never learned how to drive."

"Well, that does present a problem." Rock gave her a studying glance. "You need to be at the hospital bright and early to carry out the rest of your plans, don't you?"

"I do. They could make do without me, but I think I can get the boys to cooperate better than someone else."

"I'll take you back now. Miko can keep an eye on Zane. She's pretty handy when it comes to

228

nursing sick soldiers."

"She's the one who nursed you back to health?" Billie asked, surprised by this bit of news as she and Rock returned to the kitchen.

Rock's wife, the woman he called Miko, had her back to them as she poured coffee. Slices of chocolate cake set on pretty plates at the kitchen table.

"Do you take cream?" Miko asked as she turned to Billie and smiled.

"No. Black is fine," Billie said, trying not to stare at the beautiful woman who looked nothing like she pictured. She assumed Rock would marry a woman who resembled... well, her. He seemed the type to choose a petite, blond-haired, curvy woman with all-American appeal.

Miko was tall and graceful, lithe and lovely. She could have passed as a movie star with the way she carried herself so elegantly. It wasn't Miko's finely tailored dress, the perfect style of her glossy black hair, or even her friendly smile that drew Billie's admiration.

What struck Billie the most was the love shining in Miko's eyes and glowing on her face when she looked at Rock — like he alone had hung the moon and stars glistening outside in the night sky.

She glanced at her former patient and saw he returned his wife's deep affection.

Their love for one another was so strong, so clearly evident, she could almost feel it filling the kitchen as she took a seat at the table.

A hundred questions poured through her

thoughts, but she kept them to herself. Rock had found a woman he adored and that was good enough for her. In truth, she was glad for him, for the love he'd found and the life he was building. He deserved every moment of happiness that came his way. And so did his gracious wife.

✯✯★ *Chapter Eighteen* ★✯✯✯

Billie and Peggy crept up the hospital's back stairs in the pre-dawn hours of the morning and made their way to Doctor Ridley's office.

One final time the three of them reviewed the details of their strategy to catch Doctor Bartle. When they finished, the doctor went to find an orderly he felt they could trust while Peggy and Billie went to room seven.

Two of the men were awake, the rest not yet stirring when they entered the room. Peggy stood watch in the hallway while Billie awakened the men who were sleeping and shared their plans.

"Under no circumstances can Doctor Bartle, Nurse Homer, and Captain West's brother know anything is amiss. We have to convince them the person in that bed," Billie pointed to the bed that had been Zane's, "is Zane and none other. If you're afraid of what might happen or just don't want to be in the room, now is the time to tell me. I'll find somewhere to place you until after all this is over."

Not a single man wanted to move. In fact, a few of them volunteered to take down Zane's brother if he showed his face again.

"What kind of yella-bellied skunk would hire someone to kill his own brother?" Sarge asked, indignant fury puckering his heavy brow.

"The kind like that dandified snake wearing snakeskin boots who was here yesterday," another man said. "Count me in. I'll help."

"Thank you," Billie said, smiling at the men she considered "her boys."

An hour later, they'd all had breakfast before she and Peggy whisked away their trays. While Peggy wrapped gauze around the head of the orderly the doctor had asked to help, Billie snuck down to the floor below them to see if Nurse Homer had arrived for the day.

After spying the woman at the nurse's station, Billie rushed upstairs and let Doctor Ridley know the nurse was there. She then returned to room seven and surveyed Peggy's efforts to make the orderly look like Zane.

"We need to make his hair swoop in the front," Billie said, using her fingers to style the young man's hair that was nearly the same shade of dark brown as Zane's. With the gauze bandage wrapped over his eyes and most of his nose, he could pass as Zane to someone who didn't know him well.

She wasn't sure Doctor Bartle had ever actually looked at Zane, even if he'd been in the room before.

"Thank you so much for helping us, Colin. We really appreciate it." Billie finished brushing the young man's hair and took a step back, surveying her work.

"I'm happy to do what I can, Nurse Brighton."

The orderly grinned at her. "Just tell me what you want me to do."

"All you need to do is pretend you're asleep. That's it."

"I won't get in trouble if I really take a nap, will I? I've been on duty since three yesterday afternoon."

Billie laughed softly. "No, you won't get in trouble. By all means, sleep while you can."

After getting him settled in Zane's bed, Billie and Peggy reminded the men to keep their lips sealed and went to Doctor Ridley's office. The two of them weren't scheduled to work for a few more hours and didn't want to give anything away with their presence.

When two police officers arrived at a quarter to seven, Billie watched as Doctor Ridley accompanied the men from the room and down the hallway. They figured Doctor Bartle would sneak in before breakfast, which they generally served the men at eight in the morning.

Billie and Peggy peered out Doctor Ridley's office window and watched Doctor Bartle arrive a few minutes past seven.

"I hope this works," Billie said to Peggy as they turned away from the window and paced around the office, waiting.

"It's just got to, Billie. Goodness only knows how many other patients we've lost due to Nurse Homer and Doctor Bartle. It makes me wonder if he's even a real physician," Peggy said, plopping down in one of the two chairs in front of Doctor Ridley's desk.

The hands on the clock seemed to move in slow motion as they waited. Twenty minutes after they'd watched Doctor Bartle arrive, a commotion down the hall made them both race to the door. They yanked it open and watched as Nurse Homer tried to beat Doctor Bartle with an empty bedpan while the officers attempted to get them both into handcuffs.

Doctor Ridley followed the group to the elevator, letting the two criminals know what he thought of them.

Billie ran down the hall to room seven with Peggy right behind her. Colin sat up in bed, the gauze they'd wrapped around his eyes on his lap as he laughed with the other men.

"Well, it's about time you got here," Sarge said, grinning at Billie as she and Peggy skidded into the room.

"You're all fine?" she asked, quickly surveying the men to make sure everyone looked well.

"Better than fine," Jimmy piped in. "That's the most fun we've had in a while."

"You shoulda seen that quack, Nurse Billie. He and Horrid Homer tiptoed in here and we all pretended to be asleep. They sidled right up to Colin, thinking he was Zane, see." Sarge leaned back against his pillows, excited to tell the tale. "Nurse Homer grabbed his arm and yanked away the covers while Bully Bartle lifted a needle, ready to stab him, telling him his brother sent his best regards. But before he could give him a shot, Doc Ridley and the officers jumped out from behind that screen and caught them by surprise. You shoulda seen their faces." Sarge hooted and slapped his leg with his hand.

Billie glanced at the screen in the corner by Jimmy's bed. It had made a perfect hiding spot to hear what was said and watch the drama unfold.

"Colin did a dandy job of pretending to be Zane," Jimmy said, his grin growing broader. "I don't think they realized it wasn't him at all."

"Most likely not," Billie said, gifting each man with a beaming smile. "I think this occasion calls for another round of breakfast. Who's hungry?"

The men cheered and laughed as she and Peggy oversaw the delivery of more food. A few hours later, Billie looked up from the nurse's station and saw Floyd West walking down the hallway with an evil gleam in his eye and a pleased look on his face.

When he saw her watching him, he quickly schooled his features into an expression of grief.

"Everything okay with Zane today?" he asked as Billie met him outside the door of room seven.

"No. No it isn't," she said, wanting to stand on a chair and slap the living daylights out of the repugnant lout. "Doctor Ridley would like to speak with you in his office."

Floyd sauntered down the hall beside her. When he reached over and ran his hand over her backside outside the doctor's office, she spun around and elbowed him in the gut.

A dark scowl replaced his cocky sneer as she stepped into the office and announced his presence. A police officer awaited him there, but, much to her dismay, Floyd somehow wriggled out of the officer's grasp and took off running.

"Stop that man!" Doctor Ridley yelled as Floyd flung open the door to the stairs and raced down them.

"He's faster than I would have given him credit for," Sarge said from the doorway of room seven.

Billie turned and shook her head, hoping the authorities would catch him before he escaped and made his way back to Texas.

✶✶✶★ *Chapter Nineteen* ★✶✶✶

Sleep left Zane slowly, like a tide in no hurry to ebb and roll back to the sea. He rested on his uninjured side, one hand tucked beneath a soft pillow that smelled of sunshine and Oxydol detergent.

Awareness seeped into his consciousness and he realized the background sounds were different than what he'd grown accustomed to hearing at the hospital. He heard music playing on a radio in the distance. The whoosh of water running through pipes. The moo of a cow.

"A cow?" he mumbled in his half-awake state and sat up in bed. His hands brushed over cotton sheets that carried the scent of fresh outdoors and a soft blanket that felt nothing like the coarse one he'd had at the hospital.

He stretched out his arms then his legs, discovering he slept in a large bed, not a small hospital bed.

Fingers exploring, he traced the smooth wood of a headboard and trailed over a bedside table. He leaned farther to the right and felt the cool glass of a lamp.

Memories of the previous day, of Floyd's threats and Billie coming to his rescue with the help of her friend Peggy, Doctor Ridley, and Rock filled his mind.

Aw, that was it. He was at Rock's house.

Zane had been so weary when he'd arrived, he hadn't even been properly introduced to Rock's wife. The fuzzy recesses of his mind recalled gentle hands lifting his head and giving him a drink when he'd awakened in the middle of the night. She'd hummed a song, one he didn't recognize, as she wiped his brow with a warm cloth and encouraged him to go back to sleep.

A creaking to his left drew his attention that direction. He assumed the hinges of the door could use a little oil as they continued to protest at being used.

"Morning, Zane. How are you feeling?" Rock asked. Zane counted his friend's footsteps as he crossed the floor. Rock took three before the steps sounded muted, like he walked on a carpet. He felt a hand on his shoulder and then Rock patted his back. "Do you feel like eating breakfast?"

"I could do with some food," Zane said, grinning at Rock. "Do you think after I eat, I might be able to take a bath or shower?"

"I think we can take care of that. Or I could haul you out to a pond and toss you in. I might even be able to find one with leeches."

Zane recalled a summer afternoon years ago when he and Rock had gone swimming in what was nothing more than a glorified mud hole and both came out covered in leeches.

"That won't be necessary." He swung his legs over the edge of the mattress and placed his feet on a plush carpet. When he stood, Rock's hand on his arm steadied him. "Would it be okay if I sat at the table? I'm about plumb worn out of staying in bed."

"The table it is," Rock said with a smile evident in his voice.

Zane tried not to feel useless as Rock helped him slip on the robe he'd worn from the hospital then guided him into a hallway. "Turn right and you'll run into the wall at the end of the hall. Turn left, and it's about seven steps to the kitchen door on the right or five steps to the bathroom door on the left. Our bedroom is another ten steps down the hall.

"Let's make a stop in the bathroom." Zane tamped down his embarrassment and irritation at the need to have Rock help him before they went to the kitchen.

The welcome aroma of coffee and bacon mingled in the air, making Zane's mouth water. He couldn't even remember the last time he'd eaten crispy, perfectly fried bacon. The toe-tapping sounds of Cab Calloway performing *The Jumpin' Jive* adding a lively undertone to the welcoming atmosphere of Rock's home.

"Good morning, Captain West," a cultured, feminine voice spoke from in front of him.

Zane pasted on a smile and nodded that direction. "Good morning, Mrs. Laroux. It's sure a pleasure to meet you."

"The pleasure is mine, sir. Rock has spoken of you with great affection. Truly, it is wonderful to have this opportunity to make your acquaintance."

Zane's smile became genuine. "I hope he didn't tell you about any of the crazy, stupid things we used to do."

A melodic laugh danced around his ears. "Oh, he's told me a few stories, but I'd love to hear more. Maybe you'll tattle on him. According to Rock, you were the one who always led him astray."

Zane turned his head to his right, where he knew Rock stood. "Is that so?" he asked, lifting an eyebrow in question.

Rock chuckled and nudged him forward, placing Zane's hands on the back of a chair. "I was the fair-haired child who never thought of doing anything ornery or naughty."

Zane snickered as he felt his way around the chair and sat down. "Rock single-handedly got our entire barracks in trouble one time."

"Now this sounds like a great story," Rock's wife said, amusement ripe in her voice.

"I like to think it is, Mrs. Laroux." He heard a chair scrape against the floor to his left, the swish of skirts, and a noise that could have been a kiss as the chair was scooted in. It was easy to picture Rock seating his wife and giving her a quick kiss. Even if he couldn't see, he could feel the love that flowed between the couple. Their happiness enveloped the entire house and everyone in it.

Rock's footsteps moved around the back of his chair, and then he took a seat on the other side of Zane.

A thin hand with incredibly long fingers settled on top of Zane's. "Please, Captain West. I hope you'll call me Miko. All my friends do."

Zane had never heard that name before. Miko sounded foreign, but it could stand for anything he supposed. He offered his best friend's wife his most charming smile. "I'd be happy to do that, Miko, but only if you call me Zane."

"Zane it is," she said, then gently guided his left hand to the edge of his plate. "If you pretend your plate is a clock, your toast is at noon. It's already buttered and I added jam. I hope you like strawberry."

"Perfect," Zane said, grinning at her.

"There are two fried eggs at four and bacon at eight. Milk and coffee are at one o'clock just above your plate, and silverware is to your left."

Grateful Miko made it easy for him to locate what he needed, he bowed his head as Rock asked a blessing on the meal, on the day ahead of them, and gave thanks for the privilege of Zane staying there with them.

His friend's words brought a lump to Zane's throat and he realized it had been a while since he'd spent some quiet time in prayer. God had spared him, even if he hadn't quite yet accepted the gift of grace, or allowed himself to accept the forgiveness he needed for his part in Smitty's death.

Determined not to dwell on dark thoughts, he joined in the conversation between bites of the best meal he'd had in months. The toast was made from homemade bread, yeasty and light, topped with freshly churned butter and sweet strawberry jam made from berries grown right there on the farm.

"The eggs," Rock said, "were yanked right

from the roost this morning and the glass of milk is straight from the source."

"I thought I heard a cow mooing earlier," Zane said. He took a bite of crispy, salty bacon and barely suppressed a moan. It tasted so good.

"We have two cows, Amos and Andy. John and Lucy Phillips, our neighbors on the other side of the pasture, are building up a dairy," Rock said, and then he chuckled. "Just wait until you meet their son. Petey is an all-around, couldn't-be-better kind of boy."

"He saved our lives," Miko said quietly.

"He what?" Zane asked, shocked. The piece of toast he'd been about to bite into dangled in his fingers as he turned toward Rock. "What happened?"

"Well, there was a salesman who kept coming around. The man was deranged, to put it mildly," Rock said. Zane heard him release a long breath before he continued. "Anyway, he got it in his head he was going to take this place, regardless of the fact I'd just purchased it and held the deed. One afternoon when I was gone, he snuck in here, tied Miko to a tree and left her unconscious while he ransacked the house. He was in the midst of tearing the place apart looking for the deed when I walked in and he shot me. Petey Phillips just happened to come over and you wouldn't believe what that boy did."

"What did he do?" Zane asked, eager to hear more of the story.

"Petey is pretty handy with a slingshot. He filled a bucket with rocks and rotten fruit and waited for Norman to come out the back door. The little rascal had spread marbles across the step so thick, Norman didn't have a chance. Every time he tried to move, Petey would blast him with another shot. Anyway, if it wasn't for Petey, I'm quite sure Norman would have killed us both.

"When did this happen?" Zane asked, realizing it had to have been a recent occurrence since Rock hadn't been married more than a few months.

"About six weeks ago."

Shocked by this revelation, he bumped his arm against Rock's. "And you didn't think to tell me before that you'd been shot by a madman?"

Rock chuckled. "Well, it was just a graze, right above my ear. Miko took good care of it."

"And you weren't injured?" Zane asked, turning toward Miko.

"No, I was fine. The young people who work for us came and helped clean up the mess in the house and Petey became a local celebrity for a while." Miko laughed. "He still mentions it from time to time."

"I look forward to meeting Petey. I reckon the little sprout is in school now. Didn't it just start back up?"

"Yes, last week," Miko said. "I miss having him around all the time. He keeps things lively."

"I'm sure he does." Zane asked about the farm, the crops they raised, and what they had left to harvest. "Are you picking produce today?"

"We are," Rock said. "We've got green beans coming out our ears. Miko is going to get a bunch of them canned today."

"Is there anything I can do to help?" Zane assumed the best thing he could do was stay out of their way, but he wanted to at least make the offer.

"I might put you to work snapping beans," Miko said with a warm smile in her voice. "If you feel up to it."

"I think I could do that much," Zane said, using the tip of his fork to make sure he hadn't left any food behind on his plate. He found one last bite of egg and finished it, then drained the glass of milk. After drinking canned or powered milk in the South Pacific and what the hospital had to offer, the fresh farm milk tasted more like cream. He wondered what the chances were of getting a glass of buttermilk. It had been ages since he'd had any.

He listened as chairs scraped back and dishes clanked. Rock's hand settled on his shoulder. "Shall we see about getting you cleaned up?"

"Sure," Zane said, getting to his feet and turning toward the sound of running water where he imagined Miko washed the breakfast dishes. "Thank you for the best meal I've had in a while, Miko."

"You're welcome, Zane. If there is anything in particular you'd like to eat for supper, let me know. We're having roast beef sandwiches for lunch."

"That sounds delicious." He took a few steps with Rock. "And I'm not a picky eater. Rock can attest to that."

Miko laughed softly then he heard her take a few steps toward him. "Oh, I almost forgot about rinsing your eyes with the solution Nurse Brighton left behind. When would you like to do that?"

Zane wanted to tell her he'd like to not do it at all. He hated the treatments, but Billie had assured him if he wanted his eyes to get better, he had to have them.

"Maybe Rock could help me do it while I'm getting clean," Zane suggested. It would be an easy enough thing to pour the liquid over his eyes while he was in the bathtub or shower.

"Sure. I can take care of it," Rock said, as they took steps forward. Zane could feel the difference in the floor as they stepped from the linoleum of the kitchen onto the hardwood in the hallway. "Miko better be the one to change the bandages, though."

Zane was happy to discover Rock and Miko's bathroom had a showerhead in the bathtub. After turning on the water, handing him a bar of soap, and helping him step over the edge of the tub, Rock left Zane to enjoy the steamy spray.

To be able to stand up and take a shower seemed like such a trivial thing, but it meant the world to Zane at that moment. There were times in the past few weeks he began to think he'd never leave the hospital. He couldn't imagine how Rock must have felt after spending months there, getting worse instead of better.

Zane got down to the business of getting clean then managed to turn off the water. He'd just wrapped a towel around his waist when Rock returned and rinsed his eyes with the solution. The light hurt so badly when he opened them, he could hardly stand the intensity of the pain. Despite that, though, he thought his eyesight was starting to come back. Rather than seeing nothing when his eyes were open, he was beginning to discern fuzzy shapes. Encouraged by that fact, he continued to endure the treatments and hoped for the best.

Rock guided him to his room where Zane dressed in a clean pair of pants. He didn't bother with a shirt since Miko would have to bandage the wound on his side. Back in the kitchen, he sat on a chair while Miko wrapped a strip of gauze over his eyes then applied ointment to the healing injury on his side. She covered it with a thick gauze pad and taped it in place.

"You're set for the day," Miko said, brushing her fingers over the bandage to make sure the tape would hold.

When Billie changed his bandage, Zane felt like he might spontaneously combust each time she touched his bare skin. The slightest contact seared his flesh and made his blood zing through his veins.

With Miko, he felt nothing other than appreciation that she was willing to help him.

"We're going to go out and start picking the beans, Zane. Do you want to stay in the house or come out on the porch?"

Zane hated to admit it, but he was tired and ready for a nap. "I think I'll stay inside, if you don't mind."

"We don't mind at all. Make yourself at home. If you turn about sixty-degrees to your right and walk straight, you'll find the doorway to the dining room. It's a straight path through it to the living room and the couch," Rock said. "Would you like some help?"

"No. I'll find it," Zane said, offering what he

hoped was an encouraging smile to his friend. "I'll be ready to snap those beans when you come back."

"I'll hold you to that," Miko said, placing her hand on his arm again. "I left a plate of cookies on the table and a glass of buttermilk in the refrigerator in case you need a snack."

Buttermilk and cookies? The woman must have read his mind. "You're an angel. You should have waited for me instead of marrying this gangly galoot." Zane placed his hand over Miko's where it still rested on his arm and gave it a squeeze.

Miko laughed and stepped away from him. "I kind of like this gangly galoot. Besides, I've almost got him trained the way I like. I'd hate to have to start all over again."

Zane barked with laughter as the couple walked down the back hall and outside.

With his hands in front of him, he turned and took cautious steps forward. The linoleum changed to hardwood when he stepped into the dining room. His left hand grazed across the back of a chair. He eased past it and continued forward.

A floorboard groaned beneath him and his shin bumped into a low table. He felt his way around it to the couch and sank down into the comfortable cushions. In moments, he was asleep, dreaming of a nurse with golden hair and a brilliant smile.

Two hours later, he awoke feeling rested. Afraid of knocking over something he couldn't see, he carefully sat up and felt his way back to the kitchen. It wasn't until he reached the room he realized Miko hadn't told him where to locate the refrigerator. He stepped to the left until he bumped against a counter and felt his way forward.

He found the sink, the enamel surface cool to his touch. He longed to turn on the water and splash it over his face, but it would only soak the bandage over his eyes and make more work for Miko. He continued in his quest, hand connecting with the warm door of the oven. Was something baking inside or did the heat linger from something Miko had baked earlier that morning?

A few more steps and another length of counter, and he found the refrigerator. Pulling on the door latch, he opened it and stood in the blast of cool air that swirled around him. Hesitant of knocking over something he couldn't see, he reached a tentative hand inside and felt along the top shelf. His hand connected with a glass and he stuck the tip of his finger in it, tasting the liquid.

He grinned and removed the glass. It was definitely buttermilk. He carried the glass across the room to where he thought the table should be and felt with his foot and hand until he connected with a chair. He sat down then reached out, searching for the plate of cookies. A napkin covered it, but Zane set it aside and pulled the plate closer.

He bit into a bar cookie that was moist, packed with nuts and coconut. It was nothing like anything he'd had before, but he liked the flavor. Cool, tangy and slightly tart, the buttermilk slid down his throat with a refreshing smoothness that perfectly complemented the cookie.

Zane leaned back in the chair, wishing Bud was there to share the treat with him. Bud with his love of cookies would enjoy the bars Miko had made.

Thoughts of Bud and his crew darkened Zane's otherwise bright start to the day. He'd had a letter from Bud, letting him know he and the rest of crew were all recovering nicely from their wounds. Bud had burned his left hand and a length of shrapnel had pierced his right shin, but had suffered no other wounds and expected to be back in a plane in another month or so. The rest of the crew, with the exception of Smitty, escaped with nothing more than cuts, bruises, and a few broken bones.

Bud told him his warning to brace themselves before they crashed allowed them to prepare for the impact and minimize the damage. In spite of his friend's assurances that without him there may have been worse injuries or many deaths, Zane didn't feel comforted by the words. He felt guilty. No matter how many times he tried to think of a better way he could have landed, nothing came to him.

His landing gear was stuck, the engines were dead, and he barely had control of the plane. His head knew there was nothing more he could have done, but his heart protested. Surely there was a way Smitty could have been spared.

Before he could tumble headlong into his dark thoughts, Rock and Miko returned. He heard them setting down something heavy, he assumed baskets full of beans.

"I'll be back for lunch," Rock said then left.

For the next hour, Zane sat at the table and snapped beans. He had a feeling he probably hindered Miko's work more than he helped, but sitting in the kitchen with the radio playing quietly in the background and the smell of something baking in the oven took him back to his childhood when he'd sometimes helped his mother when she was busy canning. It was a time when he could enjoy her attention without Floyd's interference. He owned many special memories of moments spent with her there in the sunny kitchen of his youth.

"You're doing great, Zane. Thank you for helping me," Miko said, taking the bowl of beans he'd filled and setting an empty bowl in front of him. "I think you've done this before."

He smiled as he snapped the ends off another bean. "I used to help my mama sometimes. My brother wasn't much for work of any kind, but he especially hated being stuck in the kitchen." Zane shrugged. "I didn't mind, though. Mama made the work fun and I got to spend time with her."

"She sounds like a special person. Rock mentioned she and your father are both gone. I'm sorry for your losses."

"Thank you," he said, nodding his head. "What about your folks? Do they live nearby?"

"They are in Portland, along with my younger brother and my grandparents. Rock goes to see them every Tuesday and takes them produce from the garden."

"You don't go along?"

"No," she said, cautiously.

Sensing he'd made her uncomfortable, he changed the subject to her preferred brand of canning jars and if she thought he might be able to sample one of their fresh pears.

"I'll have Rock bring in a few pears after lunch. They're just starting to ripen," she said, the smile back in her voice. "Now, you have to tell me at least one unbelievable thing you and Rock did in the wild days of your youth."

Zane told her about the watering hole with leeches, making her laugh. She was still giggling when Rock returned for lunch and demanded to know what was so funny.

Lunch was a light-hearted affair as the three of them teased and joked like they were all old friends instead of Zane and Miko brand-new acquaintances.

After lunch, Zane went outside with Rock. The warm September sunshine bathed his face as they walked around the yard. Zane hadn't put on shoes, instead liking the feel of the lush grass beneath his bare feet. The air carried a pleasing assortment of aromas on a spice-laden breeze. He could pick out the hint of ripening pears and apples, the sharp odor of manure, and the loamy smell of earth as it blended with the sweet fragrances of flowers.

"I know I can't see a blasted thing, Rock, but this sure seems like a nice place."

"I love it here. I actually bought the place before I married Miko because I just couldn't imagine being anywhere else." Rock released a contented sigh. "I think I'm happier here peddling produce with her beside me than I've ever been in my life."

Zane wanted to tell him he was crazy, but he couldn't. Not when he'd so often dreamed of creating a life with Billie. When he'd left in May, she'd made it clear she didn't want to be more than friends. However, since he'd been her patient, he'd sensed a change in her. He couldn't understand it, but there it was all the same.

He and Rock returned to the porch. Zane settled onto a padded chair and tipped his head back, falling asleep almost immediately. He awoke to the feel of fingers brushing through his hair and the fragrance that was all Billie Brighton ensnaring his senses.

✳✳★ *Chapter Twenty* ★✳✳

Dust covered the toes of Billie's shoes as she stopped at the end of Miko and Rock's front walk. She needed a moment to catch her breath and gather her composure before she knocked on the door.

A glance at the front porch made her smile as she started up the walk. Asleep in a wicker chair, Zane rested with his head tipped back and lips slightly parted.

Silently, she made her way up the porch steps and waved at Rock when he came to the screen door. She placed a finger to her lips, letting him know she didn't want to awaken Zane. Not yet.

The temptation to kiss him out of slumber, to press her lips to his, almost overtook her. Instead of surrendering to the desire, she removed her gloves and tucked them in her handbag then reached out with one hand and brushed it through Zane's thick, dark hair. He was barefooted, without a shirt on, wearing only a pair of khaki trousers. The sun stroked his golden skin, tantalizing her to follow the path of the sunbeams over his broad chest and muscled midsection.

Zane stirred and tilted his head as he drew in a

253

deep breath. "Hiya, Billie, girl," he said, somehow knowing she was there. The smile he gave her brought his dimples out of hiding and threatened to turn her knees into softened putty.

She wondered how he knew she was the one ruffling her fingers through his hair. Had he been awake the whole time she'd stood next to his chair, admiring his handsome face and muscular form?

After grazing her fingers through the short wave of hair above his forehead one more time, she pressed the back of her hand to his cheek. It was warm, but not overly so, and beneath the white of the bandage covering his eyes, his skin looked healthy, not sallow.

"I think farm life agrees with you," she said, taking a step back to study him. Something about him seemed different, but she couldn't say what exactly. How had he changed in the short time he'd been there? Zane appeared more rested, more relaxed, more comfortable than she'd seen him since he'd arrived at the hospital a few weeks ago.

"How are you feeling?" she asked.

"Good. Better than I have for a while." He stood and turned toward her. "What are you doing here?"

"There was too much news to share over the telephone and I wanted to see how you're doing." Billie glanced over at Rock as he pushed open the screen door and stepped outside. She nodded at him and placed her hand on Zane's arm, guiding him toward the door. "I took the bus out here as soon as I left work. I only had to walk about a quarter mile from where it let me off."

"Please phone us anytime you need a ride out here," Rock said, holding open the door as she and Zane stepped inside. "We could at least pick you up at the bus stop."

"I'll do that next time," she agreed, looking around the spacious living room. To her left was a room that appeared to be an office with bookcases lining the walls and a solid wood desk occupying a large space.

She returned her glance to the living room, taking in brown leather wingback chairs sitting like sentinels on either side of a fireplace. A velvet tufted sofa in a lovely shade of yellow sat across from the fireplace. Tables with lamps flanked both ends. A large Philco radio kept company with a rocking chair and a basket of yarn beneath a side window. Slivers of sunbeams snuck through the glass, refracting through a pale yellow chandelier hanging above their heads and dancing along the far wall in colorful prisms.

"You have a beautiful home here, Rock," Billie said as they walked through the dining room.

"I can't take any credit for it," Rock said as they stepped into the kitchen. He went straight to where Miko stood at the stove stirring a pan of gravy and kissed her cheek. "Supper ready?"

"Yes. As soon as I finish the gravy we can eat." Miko turned and smiled at Billie. "It's so nice to see you again. Did you have supper yet?"

"No, I haven't, but I don't want to impose." Billie realized she should have waited to come until after the evening meal. She hadn't even given a thought to arriving just as the Laroux family was about to sit down to eat. She'd merely wanted to reach Zane and share her news with him.

Miko motioned one hand toward the table. "It's no imposition at all. We just need to add another place setting. I hope you don't mind eating in here instead of the dining room."

"I much prefer in the kitchen," Billie said. "Unless there's a big group or a party, dining rooms seem rather formal and stuffy. Kitchen tables are so much friendlier."

"I agree," Miko said, spooning the gravy into a serving boat while Rock added a place setting to the table. She looked at Zane and grinned. "I'm glad to see Sleeping Beauty awake."

"I didn't mean to sleep away the day," Zane said, rubbing a hand over his head, then along his shadowed jaw. Billie wondered if Rock would help him shave. One of the orderlies was good at shaving the men and had scraped away Zane's whiskers two days ago.

"You sleep all you like," Miko said, carrying the gravy to the table. "If you'd want to wash up, Nurse Brighton, the bathroom is just through that doorway."

"I would like to wash away the dust," Billie said. She removed her hat and left it and her handbag on a little stool by the telephone on the wall then went to the bathroom where she took a moment to freshen up. After washing her hands and tucking a few loose curls back into the roll she wore pinned at the back of her head, she returned to the kitchen where Rock helped Zane into a chair.

Rock seated Miko then held out a chair for

Billie. She nodded to him politely and sat down on Zane's other side.

After Miko asked a blessing on the meal, she placed Zane's left hand on the edge of his plate. "Roasted chicken at noon. Green beans at four, mashed potatoes at seven, and a roll with jam at ten. A glass of juice is at one o'clock above your plate."

Zane smiled at the woman and picked up his silverware then took the napkin she handed him and draped it over his lap. "Is there more of that good butter on the dinner roll?"

"Of course there is," Miko said with a smile. "What good is a roll, hot from the oven, without butter melting into every little bit of it?"

"Now you're talking," Zane said, biting into the roll.

Billie might have felt a prick of jealousy if Miko hadn't already been married to Rock. She knew the woman was trying to be helpful, but it annoyed her that Miko and Zane already seemed to have established a good rapport. Zane acted like Miko was a long-lost sister. Considering the fact he viewed Rock as a blood brother, and with great reason in light of his biological brother, she could understand why he might slide into an easy friendship with the lovely woman.

Not that Zane knew she was lovely, but still.

Billie hated to admit it, but she was the tiniest bit envious that Rock had gotten past the crush she was sure he had on her nearly as soon as he left the hospital. Apparently, he'd swiftly fallen in love with Miko.

Before jealousy turned her into a ranting,

raving lunatic, she shoved it away. She was happy for Rock and genuinely liked Miko. She also reminded herself how good Zane looked, how happy he seemed, after only one day at the farm with his friend. Too bad she couldn't bring more of the men out to soak up whatever elixir existed in the fresh air and sunshine at Double J Farm.

As soon as they finished the meal, three faces bearing expectant looks turned to her.

"I suppose you're all waiting to hear what happened today," she said, smiling at Miko and then Rock.

"We've been waiting, Billie, girl, since the moment you got here," Zane said, leaning back in his chair. "Tell us about today."

"Our plan worked perfectly to catch Doctor Bartle and Nurse Homer. Doctor Ridley hid behind a screen in the corner, along with two officers, and they heard every word Doctor Bartle and Nurse Homer said. We had an orderly pretend to be Zane and when Doctor Bartle started to give him a shot, the orderly yanked the gauze off his face, grabbed the needle and almost scared the daylights out of our two criminals."

"Did they confess to plotting to do me in?" Zane asked.

"They did. Doctor Bartle admitted he'd struck a bargain with your brother. You won't believe it, but Doctor Bartle is a nephew to Nurse Homer. It seems in the last few years, she's done horrible things at the hospital. She gave a full confession, but it's just terrible." Billie felt tears sting her eyes.

"What did she do?" Rock asked. His hand

reached out and settled over Miko's. Billie watched as Miko turned her hand over so their palms connected and fingers meshed together. Even that small touch spoke of their love.

"Billie? Nurse Homer? What did she do?" Zane asked, a hint of impatience in his voice.

"The last two years, she's, um... well, she killed more than a dozen patients."

"What!" Rock's face bore a look of shock while Zane's jaw tensed. "How could that happen? At the hospital, no less."

"She would choose her victims based solely on their family records. If they had no family, no one who might claim what was theirs, particularly officers, she falsified documents listing her as the sole heir and made sure they were filed. She then made it look like they died of natural causes."

"That's one of the most horrible things I've ever heard," Miko said, glancing from Billie to Rock. "Do you suppose..." Miko's voice caught, unable to finish her question.

"You're wanting to know if she was trying to kill Rock?" Billie asked then sighed. "She didn't list his name, but that doesn't necessarily mean anything. From what Doctor Ridley shared, she only included the names of men who had actually died due to her tampering."

"Tampering? What does that mean?" Zane asked.

She could see frown lines creasing his forehead above the white gauze of his bandage.

"Sometimes she gave a patient too much of their medication. Other times she withheld the medicine they needed. Or substituted something that would make them ill. She also admitted to suffocating two patients when they lingered longer than she deemed necessary."

"So all that was about money? Stealing an inheritance that didn't belong to her?" Zane asked.

"So it seems."

Rock shook his head in disbelief. "I'm so glad she won't be able to harm anyone else. What about her nephew?"

"Apparently he's done things like give patients fatal shots before. His father is a muckety-muck of great importance. Anytime Bartle got into trouble, his father would move him someplace new to start over. This is the first time he's been arrested and there are too many witnesses for him to get away this time." Billie was so glad the two people who'd been terrorizing the hospital wouldn't be able to hurt anyone again, but she grieved for the lives taken by their greed. Guilt assailed her as she questioned whether she'd missed some clue she should have noticed about Nurse Homer's actions.

As though they could read her mind, Rock placed a hand on her shoulder while Miko reached across the table and took her hand.

"I'm sure there is nothing you could have done," Rock said. "People like that are good at hiding what they do, who they really are."

Zane turned toward her. "Don't you take on any guilt when you went to so much effort to stop them, Billie. Everyone should be grateful to you, Peggy, and Doctor Ridley for catching them before anyone else was harmed."

Billie blinked back tears and nodded her head.

"What about Floyd? Is he in the calaboose with them?" Zane asked.

"No, Zane. I'm sorry. He managed to get away during his arrest and the police haven't been able to find him."

"He most likely hot-footed it to the train station and caught the first train heading east." Zane shoved his hand through his hair, sending it into a state of disarray. He looked as though he wanted to get up and pace the floor as nervous energy fairly jounced around him. "Or he's hiding out somewhere planning to finish the job."

"We'll keep you safe." Rock hurried to offer reassurance.

"That's why I took the bus out here. I figured if he was watching me, he'd get lost after I switched buses the third time."

Zane grinned and visibly calmed. "That's my girl."

"In light of the fact Floyd is still on the loose, I do think it best if Zane remains here," Rock said.

Billie nodded in agreement. "I do, too. What do you think, Zane? Will you stay here a while longer? Or would you rather be back at the hospital?"

"I'll stay here if Miko will serve a piece of that apple pie I can smell."

Miko smiled and rose from her chair. "That, I can do."

Later, after the dishes were washed and the evening shadows grew long, Billie sat on the front porch with Zane. Rock offered to drive her home, but she hated to use up his gas rations, so she agreed he could take her to the bus stop in Beaverton when she was ready to leave. From there, it was an easy bus ride home.

"It's sure a nice evening," Zane observed. He looked relaxed and content.

"It's lovely out here. No wonder Rock healed so miraculously if this was where he regained his health." Billie leaned back and breathed deeply of the rich night air, redolent of flowers, approaching autumn, and country life.

"I'm glad you came out, Billie. I wanted to say thank you. It's because of you I'm still alive and kicking." Zane started to reach out to her, then paused, as though he was uncertain he'd find her hand.

She clasped his hand between both of hers and smiled at him as he sat beside her. Rock had suggested he put on a shirt after dinner. Zane appeared slightly embarrassed he'd forgotten he hadn't worn one at all. Billie rather hated to see him cover up all that glorious skin, but it was too cool for him to go without a shirt in the crisp evening air.

"You're welcome, Zane. I have a particular interest in you staying alive and especially in getting you well."

"And what might that be?" he asked. His voice sounded low and husky as he spoke.

"I think you know, but in case you don't, I look forward to the day you'll dance with me again. Maybe even climb up the tree into my room, although I'm not sure you could sneak past Miss Burwell a second time."

Zane grinned, dimples popping out in his

cheeks. "I'll look forward to that day. How is Miss Burwell?"

"Better, actually. She's been a little more accommodating with us since we've all been working extra hours and can't always get home on time. And she even made me a wonderful sweater for my birthday."

"That was nice of her," Zane said, lifting her hand to his mouth and pressing a kiss to the back of it. "Did you have a good birthday?"

"I did," she said, realizing he must not have received the last month's worth of letters she'd mailed. "My birthday was the nicest one I've ever had, and everyone spoiled me so much, I felt quite overwhelmed by it all."

His second kiss to the back of her hand nearly unsettled her. The first had created a swarm of butterflies in her stomach, but now they threatened to take flight. She tried to focus on anything but the intense, frightening, entirely magnificent feelings he stirred in her. The thought of pulling her hand away from his never entered her mind, though. Not when it felt so right to have his rough callused skin pressed to hers.

"I loved the handbag you sent, and the other gifts, too," she said, snatching up the thread of conversation about her birthday. "I gave the cook at Miss Burwell's some of the nuts and she made the most divine cookies. All the girls raved about them. If I can talk her into making them again, I'll bring you some."

"I'd like that," Zane said, grinning at her. "Did you have cake on your birthday?"

She laughed. "Twice! Peggy, that sneak, arranged a party at work and another at home. It really was so sweet and I received some lovely gifts. The boys in your room at the hospital even chipped in and bought me a scarf."

"Oh, they did? What color was it?"

"Green, like the one I gave you."

Zane frowned. "I'm sure sorry, Billie, girl, but your scarf was destroyed when the plane crashed."

"You… you carried it with you?"

He nodded. "In my pocket, close to my heart. I took it with me on every mission, along with your picture. Bud decided you could do a whole lot better than this ol' cowpoke from the sticks."

Taken aback by the thought he cared enough about her to carry her scarf and photo with him, she didn't know what to say.

"You really did too much for my birthday, Zane. The handkerchiefs would have been plenty."

"No," he said. His hand skimmed up her arm until he reached her face, then he tenderly cupped her cheek. "I needed to fill up that little bag for you."

"I'm glad you did. I think the shell was my favorite gift, though."

He scowled. "That was just a silly thing I found on the beach."

"I know, but you said you thought of me when you picked it up and that's what makes it special." Billie rose before she exposed too much of her heart to this man. She loved him, of that she had no doubt, but what to do about it remained a question she was too tired to contemplate. "I better head back or I'll miss the last bus."

He stood, hands at his sides, as though he was afraid to reach out to her. "I'm glad you came, Billie. Be safe."

"I will, Zane. And if you need anything, promise you'll let me know." She stood on her tiptoes and kissed his cheek.

He grinned and wrapped his arms around her, giving her a hug. "I promise, beautiful. Now, go on and get out of here. Rock's been peeking out the door every little bit for the past ten minutes."

"I have not!" Rock denied, then realized he'd been caught.

Zane laughed and Billie felt her cheeks heat with embarrassment.

She thanked Miko for dinner, squeezed Zane's hand, and then followed Rock out to where his car was parked at the end of the walk.

Did she dare give Zane her heart? Would he stick around and cherish it or would he leave and break it? Only time would tell.

⋆⋆⋆ *Chapter Twenty-One* ★★⋆⋆

In the three days he'd been at Rock and Miko's farm, Zane felt as though he'd turned a corner in regaining his health. Each day he felt stronger, more like himself. And even though he couldn't see, his hope returned that he eventually would.

Miko fed him delicious, nourishing meals made from fresh, wholesome ingredients. He rested well and often. In between naps and eating, he soaked up the warm sunshine or helped do simple tasks.

Since it was Saturday, the high school students that worked for Miko and Rock were all there. He'd met three girls who worked in the produce stand and a handful of boys who helped with the harvesting, weeding, and watering. Today, the boys picked boxes full of pears while the girls alternated between picking tomatoes, pulling carrots, and working the counter at the produce stand.

The lack of sight didn't keep Zane from being amused by the innocent flirting taking place among the young people. He sat in a patch of sunshine in the side yard on a bench, shucking ears of corn Rock had picked early that morning. He'd filled two dozen gunnysacks to sell in the produce stand, and brought two more to the house for Miko to can.

Zane volunteered to shuck the corn. He'd shucked plenty in his day and set to work, content with the world around him.

The hum of conversations blended with the music playing from a radio in the produce stand. It seemed Rock and Miko had a radio on nearly all the time. He supposed Rock didn't want to miss any news about the war and the way Miko sometimes hummed along to a song gave him the idea she enjoyed listening to the music.

When Roy Acuff started singing about the "Wabash Cannon Ball" on the radio, Zane whistled along while his toes tapped, keeping time to the music.

"I'll tell it to the world, but you sure can whistle, mister," a voice said from nearby.

"Thank you." Zane turned his head toward the boy. "Do you know how to whistle?"

"Sure I do," the boy exclaimed then proceeded to share a few shrill blasts.

A warm, wiggly body that smelled of dog, sunshine, and licorice plopped down beside him. "Who are you?" the boy asked.

Zane heard him pull back the husk on an ear of corn as the bench vibrated. He pictured the boy swinging his feet back and forth as he worked. He tipped his head toward the youngster and smiled. "I'm Captain Zane West. Rock and I have been friends for a long time."

"Well, how about that," the boy said, suddenly growing still. "Another Captain. Golly, but that's swell. Cap, that's what I call Rock, and Miko are

SHANNA HATFIELD

both the bees knees. If you're a friend of Cap's, then I s'pose you're a real humdinger, too."

A little hand, sticky with corn juice, connected with his. "I'm Petey Phillips. We live on the other side of the pasture behind the barn."

Zane shook the small, grubby hand and smiled. "It's nice to meet you, Petey. Miko and Rock told me you're quite the hero."

"Well, shoot! You already know my story of glory," Petey said, returning to shucking corn and swinging his feet. "How long are you staying here?"

"Until I'm feeling better."

The feet stopped swinging again and there was a long, quiet pause. "Did you get hurt flying planes like Cap?"

Zane nodded. "I did. My plane crashed in the jungle last month."

Zane felt the boy press against his leg, as though he wanted a close-up look at Zane's face.

"Did you hurt your eyeballs?" Petey questioned.

Rock had suggested Zane might be more comfortable wearing sunglasses instead of the bandage wrapped around his head. The pair he'd given him blocked the light as well as if not better than the gauze. He wore them constantly, except when he was sleeping. It made him feel less like an invalid without the bandage covering his eyes.

"I did injure my eyeballs, Petey. That's why I'm wearing the glasses. The light makes them hurt."

"Well, that's a dirty rotten thing to happen to someone like you." Petey patted his arm then

268

returned to wiggling his feet and shucking corn.

"Did I hear you have a baby sister?" Zane asked, dredging up tidbits of conversations he'd had with Miko about the neighbors.

"Yep. Mom and Dad brought home the princess about the same time Grandpa and Grandma Yamada went away." Petey sighed. "I sure miss them, but I like the princess just fine. She's kinda cute, if a fella has to be stuck with a sister. I'm trying to teach her to say my name, but so far all I can get outta her is something that sounds like a lamb bleating."

Zane chuckled. "You take good care of your princess. Not every guy gets a baby sister, you know."

"Oh, I know." Petey stopped wiggling. Zane could feel the weight of the boy's stare as he studied him. "Do you have a sister?"

"Nope. My mama and baby sister died the same day."

A small hand patted his arm again in a gesture full of sympathy. "That's sure a rough ride, Captain West. Do you still have your dad?"

"Nope. He's gone, too. But I've got Rock and now Miko, so it's like having a brother and sister."

The jiggling resumed and Zane heard Petey relieving another ear of corn of its husk. "I'm pretty keen on them myself. But I've got Mom and Dad and the princess. Granny comes to visit a lot, too. It's been a rough row to hoe since my best friend had to leave, though."

"Where did he go?" Zane asked, tossing another ear of corn into the box at his feet.

"Well, his dad got hurt real bad at the Battle of Midday."

"Midway," Zane said without thinking.

"Were you there?"

Zane nodded. "I sure was." Too many good men were lost that day, but the fight hadn't been in vain.

"Oh, Ryatt's daddy's name was Mac. Mac Danvers. Maybe you met him. Anyhow, he got hurt real bad and died after that. Ryatt's mom left him at our house to go make arrangements." Petey stopped and sighed as his little body slumped against Zane's side. "I just everlastingly hate that word now. Arrangements. Seems to me arrangements are the cause of all kinds of troubles."

Zane couldn't argue with the boy. The childish logic might be slightly skewed, but there was truth in it, too. "What happened?"

"She ran her car off the road on the way to make those arrangements and died. Poor Ryatt. He was a mess. The princess wasn't very big so Granny came to take care of her while Mom and Dad tried to handle Ryatt until his aunt Delaney could come get him. She took him to her ranch in Pendleton. Gee, but I'd like to see a real cattle ranch."

"Pendleton, huh?" Zane awkwardly reached down and gave the boy's back a comforting pat. "I was stationed there for a while in the spring."

Petey's body straightened as enthusiasm flooded back through him. "Did you see a ranch there? With cattle and horses and a sea of wheat?"

Zane chuckled. "I did see a few ranches there and the hills are covered in so much wheat, it almost looks like an ocean rolling around the town. But I'll tell you something, Petey."

"What's that, Captain West?"

"I grew up in Texas on a big cattle ranch."

"Well, that's a jim-dandy thing," Petey declared and leaned against Zane again. "Did you have a horse of your own and a dog and everything?"

"I did." Zane told him a little about the ranch and the name of his favorite horse and the dog he had when he was a boy.

"Do you have a dog, Petey?" Zane asked, able to detect the slight whiff of dog still clinging to the boy.

"No, but I found one in the trees at the edge of the pasture. He's kind of scrawny, like someone dumped him out 'cause they didn't want to feed him. I've been taking him scraps. He's a good mutt. I was thinking about naming him Tuffy."

"That's a good name. Have you asked your folks about bringing him home with you?"

A sigh must have rolled up from the boy's toes for the way his whole body shook when he expelled it. "Mom doesn't want a dog, especially not a stray, with the princess."

"Have you mentioned the dog to Rock and Miko?"

"Not yet. I was kinda keeping him just to myself for a little while. If Miko casts her opticals on him, that dog won't know anyone else exists 'cause Miko's a real royal-stepper and even the animals know it." Petey jumped off the bench then bumped into Zane's legs. "Have you been to visit the three little pigs yet?"

Zane nodded. "Rock took me on a tour of the barnyard yesterday. I met Amos and Andy, the pigs, and his horses."

"He hasn't had the horses long. He bought them from Ryatt's aunt. Me and Ryatt used to ride them all the time. Now Cap and I do."

"Does Miko ride?"

Petey laughed and it sounded like he slapped his hands together in glee. "Does Miko ride? Now ain't that a question. Do birds sing? Do peaches ripe from the tree taste like candy? Do stars shine up in the sky?"

The boy didn't wait for a reply before he continued. "Of course she rides. I betcha my life there ain't a thing you can think up that Miko can't do, 'cause that's just Miko." Petey leaned closer and lowered his voice, as though he shared a great secret. "I was gonna marry Miko, but when Cap asked if I'd mind stepping aside so he could, I gave him the go ahead. But I told him if he ever makes her cry, I'll dip him in honey and leave him for the bears."

"I don't think you have to worry," Zane said with a grin. "I think Rock is pretty set on Miko."

"Set on Miko? I guess it's hard with you not being able to see, and all, but Cap is plumb loony for her. All she has to do is look at him, and Cap almost trips over his feet to do whatever she wants."

Zane laughed. "I'd sure like to see that."

"Gee, Captain West. Are you a real, true Texas cowboy?"

"I sure am, pardner. If I ever get my vision

back, I'll show you some rope tricks. How would that be?"

"By jingo, that'd be dandy." Petey bumped against him again. "Do I have to call you Captain West?"

"No. How about you call me Tex? Some of my friends do and I hope we'll be great friends."

"I betcha we'll be great buddies, Tex. I better get going. I promised Mom I wouldn't stay too long. I'm in charge of weeding the garden and the weeds are about to stage an all-out revolt in the potatoes. I got my orders to get things in order."

"I hope to talk to you again soon, Petey."

"Oh, I'll be back before you know it. I might even bring Tuffy when I come."

"You do that, Petey."

Zane listened as the boy ran off, whistling as he went. He tried to picture Petey from the description Rock and Miko had given him. The rascally imp was every bit as full of life and fun as they'd said.

After lunch, Zane rested for a while, taking a nap for about an hour. When he awakened, he made his way to the kitchen where he could hear Miko working.

"Did we tire you out this morning?" Miko asked over the sound of jars rattling in a pressure cooker. The air in the kitchen felt moist and thick, heavy with the scent of fresh corn.

"Not at all. I didn't mind shucking corn. Do you have more I need to do?"

"Not today. I've got all I can get put up this afternoon," Miko said. He heard water running in the sink and then the sound of a knife scraping. He envisioned her cutting the golden kernels off the ears before she packed them into jars to process in the hot water bath of the pressure cooker. He'd watched his mother go through the process enough times to remember each step.

"What can I do to help? I could attempt to fold laundry or is there something I could do outside?"

"Well, why don't you..." Miko gasped. "Oh, no! We forgot about your eye treatment this morning. Would you like me to do it now?"

"No, Miko. It'll wait until this evening. You've got enough to do."

"How are your eyes? Does the light hurt them as much? Are the sunglasses helping?"

"I like the glasses much better than the bandages. I think they do a better job of blocking the light, too. It's nice to be able to not have my eyes pressed shut all the time."

"Can you see anything yet?" Miko asked as she continued cutting corn off cobs. He listened as she plunked the bare cobs into a metal pail on the floor.

"A few fuzzy shapes, but not enough to be able to tell what anything is."

"But that's wonderful progress," Miko said encouragingly. "Just think, in another..."

A loud rapping at the back door interrupted her. Before she could take a step, the door opened and it sounded like a stampede of cattle raced down the hall and into the kitchen.

"Golly, Miko, your kitchen is even more gummed up than Mom's and she's got Granny over there helping her." Petey's unmistakable voice made Zane grin.

"What are you up to, Petey?" Miko asked. Zane could hear the indulgent affection in her tone as she spoke.

"Pop went into town with a list of errands. Mom and Granny are wading in a river of corn and green beans, and the princess is off to dreamland. I decided to see if I could find more milkweed pods and thought Captain West might like to come along. We could check on Tuffy, too."

"Who's Tuffy?" Miko asked.

"A dog I found in the trees over on the far end of the pasture. He's friendly, but hungry."

Zane could hear Petey shuffling his feet on the linoleum, as though the boy found it impossible to stand still.

"How long has that dog been there?" Miko asked with concern.

"Since last weekend. I've been taking him scraps. And before you snap your cap, Mom and Pop both know." Petey bumped against Zane then grabbed onto his hand. "Do you wanna come with me?"

"Well, I suppose I could. But you have to promise not to let me fall in a hole or trip over a log."

Petey huffed, clearly insulted and released his hand. "Gee, Tex. What do you take me for? A cracked egg with a heaping side of spoiled applesauce? No, siree! That's balled up baloney for certain. I'll get you there and back again. I'm on the job. You can trust me."

Zane grinned and took a step forward. "Then let's get to it. What are you gonna do with the milkweed?"

A sigh rolled out of Petey. Zane heard the boy's hands smack together. "I see an education is in order. By jingo and golly, you'll know gobs by the time I'm through. Tell 'em about my milkweed, Miko."

"The military is using the fibers found inside milkweed pods to make life preservers. Many children in the area have been collecting the floss all summer," Miko explained. "The local extension office has been running a contest for the child who collects the most pods. They'll win a bicycle."

"Boy, it's a rip-roaring dandy, too," Petey said, excitedly. "Wanna guess who's in the lead so far?"

Zane chuckled. "It wouldn't be you, would it, Petey?"

"It sure is! Gosh, that bike is swell. It's dark blue with a red and white stripe, just like Uncle Sam himself painted it."

"Then we better get out there and see if we can find more milkweed floss."

"Here, take some cookies with you." Miko placed a handful of cookies on Zane's palm. "Be sure you bring Captain West back if he gets tired, Petey."

"I will, Miko. If his motor runs down and he hits empty, I'll make a beeline back here." Petey tugged on Zane's arm. "Let's go."

Five minutes later, Zane walked through the pasture with Petey leading the way. They munched on the gingersnap cookies Miko had sent along. Petey whistled and Zane listened to the sound of something loping toward them. The boy giggled and a dog woofed softly. Zane could picture Tuffy washing Petey's face with friendly licks.

"Mercy! What is that horrible smell?" Zane asked, wrinkling his nose.

"Aw, that's just Tuffy. I think he got tangled up with a skunk or maybe rolled in something that was dead. I tried to give him a bath in the ditch, but he wasn't having any part of it."

"Well, let's see if he'll follow us to Rock and Miko's house when we go back. I bet Rock would help you give him a bath." Zane sniffed again. There was the stench of skunk in the air, but something decaying, too. He wondered if the poor dog had a sore Petey hadn't noticed. Zane held out one of his cookies in the direction of the sound of panting.

The cookie was gobbled up in a jiffy and a wet nose nuzzled his fingers. "It's nice to meet you, Tuffy. I'm Zane."

The dog woofed and pressed against his legs. Zane hunkered down and gently rubbed his hands over the canine. Ribs stuck out, his fur was matted and full of burrs, and he felt the dog wince when he touched a spot beneath his chin. He leaned closer and could smell something putrid. The dog definitely had an infected sore. Zane rubbed the dog's head, scratched behind his floppy ears, then stood. "Shall we get back to the business of finding your milkweed?"

"Yes, sir!" Petey charged ahead with the dog barking. He heard hurried steps as the boy came back and grabbed onto his hand. "Sorry, Tex. I forgot you need a little help getting there."

Zane held a gunnysack while Petey picked the pods that grew alongside a ditch. Eventually, they made their way back toward Rock and Miko's place. Petey led Zane over to a fence where he found a few more milkweeds growing.

"There aren't many pods to be found with Cap on duty. The weeds know better than to grow here," the boy said.

Zane had an idea it wasn't that the weeds knew better, but that Rock and Miko endlessly worked to keep them pulled. Since he'd been there, the couple hardly stopped working from early morning until late in the evening.

"What's this place?" Zane asked, as his hands trailed over a fence covered in some sort of vegetation. With the toe of his boot, he traced the edge of a stepping stone, then reached out with his foot and touched another in front of him.

"Just a fence. It's sure pretty. Sometimes flowers bloom on it." Petey tugged on his hand again. "I see Cap. I wanna ask him about giving Tuffy a bath. Come on!"

Zane had to hustle to keep up with the rambunctious boy. He stumbled over a large rock and took a few hasty steps forward to keep from falling.

Petey stopped and placed a little hand on his back. "Are you okay, Tex? I'd be ten kinds of a low-down, belly-slithering goof if you got hurt on my watch."

Zane ruffled the boy's thick hair. "I'm fine, Petey. No harm done. Maybe we could find Rock without running, though."

"Deal," the boy said, keeping such a sedate pace Zane almost told him he could go faster, but refrained. The smell of the dog didn't fade, so he assumed Tuffy accompanied them.

"What'd you find?" Rock called to them.

Zane could hear water running and wondered if they were close to the barn or the garden. He sniffed the air, but all he could smell was the dog with undertones of little boy.

"I found Tuffy last week, Cap, but Mom laid down the law with an iron fist set in concrete. I can't take him home. Would you and Miko maybe want to keep him? He's a dandy dog."

Zane heard Rock's footsteps as he approached them. Rock whistled softly and Zane listened, imagining his friend petting the dog, giving him a thorough onceover.

"Under his chin," Zane said quietly as he bent forward, getting a lick on his cheek from the dog.

"I see," Rock said. "How about we find a tub and give this fella a bath? Can you stay to help, Petey, or do you need to get home?"

"I can stay until supper time, but then I'm heading home. Pops promised to bring home hamburgers from town and I don't want to miss that. Where's the tub, Cap? I'm on the job."

"You're always on the job, Petey," Rock teased. "I'll help you get the tub because it's heavy. Zane, maybe you could ask Miko to heat up some water for us?"

"I can do that," Zane said, turning to his left.

"You're about six steps away from the back gate if you walk straight ahead," Rock called to him.

"Thanks!" Zane walked to the gate, felt his way through it, then continued to the back stoop. He made it up the steps, tapped once on the door, then walked down the hallway. The kitchen was still humid and hot, but the sound of Bing Crosby crooning "Sweet Leilani" made him smile.

"Did you have fun with Petey?" Miko asked amid the clanging of pans.

"I did enjoy myself. We brought the dog back and Rock asked if you could provide hot water for a bath. The dog stinks to high heaven, but the real problem is he's got an infected wound. I didn't say anything to Petey since I can't see it, but I think Rock noticed it too. Petey's going to help give the dog a bath."

"Oh, that poor thing. I'll bring out some water, soap and rags in a minute." Miko paused and he could feel her studying him. "Are you staying in or going back out?"

"I'm feeling pert at the moment and haven't yet run out of juice, as Petey would say."

Miko laughed. "Then tell Rock I'll be there in a moment."

Zane retraced his steps and found Rock and Petey in the backyard with a washtub. Rock had turned on the hose and was filling it with water while Petey giggled and the dog woofed. From the noises they made, Zane assumed a game of chase was afoot.

"Miko said she'll be out in a minute."

"Good," Rock said, then lowered his voice. "That spot under his chin is definitely infected. Poor mutt. Looks like he's about starved to death, too."

"That's what I thought, at least from what I could feel. If we clean him up and treat that wound, fill that hollow spot between his ribs, he might make you a good dog." Zane grinned at his friend. "If you keep him, you'll at least have a buddy to share the doghouse with when you get into trouble with Miko."

Rock snorted. "There'll be no doghouse sleeping for me, my friend. I don't plan to get into that kind of trouble."

"Petey!" Miko called as she stepped outside. "Your mother just phoned. She said your dad is back from town and to come straight home."

"I'm on my way. Bye, everyone. Take good care of Tuffy!" And in a whirl of pounding steps and the squawk of the gate, Petey left.

"Here, let me take that," Rock said.

Zane listened as water was poured into the tub and he felt steam rising from the water.

"Is that enough or do you need more? I could drain the water from the canning kettle," Miko said.

"This should be fine," Rock assured her. "You might as well go back in the house. No need for all of us to get dirty with this job."

Zane took a step toward the door and grinned. "That's nice of you to excuse me."

Rock laughed and Miko giggled. "I wasn't talking to you and you know it. Get back over here and help me wash this filthy, disgusting animal."

Zane dropped down on his knees next to the tub, glad he was wearing an old pair of Rock's jeans instead of his uniform pants. The footlocker Zane had left in Hawaii was on its way, but until it arrived, he didn't have too many clothing options.

He whistled and the dog ambled over to him, pressing against his side. "Tuffy, this is gonna be worse for us than it is you, so just bear that in mind."

Rock picked up the dog and set him in the tub then Zane held him in while Rock soaped him. They both worked to pry burrs from his coat.

Before they let him loose, Rock had Miko bring out more hot water with a heaping spoon of salt mixed into it. He held hot compresses to the sore below the dog's chin, trying to draw out the infection.

When the wound broke and spewed out nasty, yellow pus, Zane was glad he couldn't see it, but he could smell it, especially when it ran down his arm.

"I hope that's it," Zane said as Rock scrubbed the spot on the dog with a clean rag and dabbed on some of Miko's special ointment.

"Look who's here," Miko said, stepping outside. "Nurse Brighton and Doctor Ridley are just in time for supper. I think we should eat out here at the picnic table."

"That's a grand idea," Rock said.

Zane felt the dog lunge forward and couldn't stop him. He heard the dog shake himself and Billie squeal. A smile broke across his face as he pictured the dog soaking her as he shook off his bath water.

"Oh, my," Miko gasped.

Rock and Doctor Ridley made futile attempts to hold back their chuckles.

"Let's get you inside," Miko said and two sets

of footsteps hurried up the back steps.

The men all burst into laughter and Zane felt the dog bump against him again. "Mind looking at a patient?" Zane asked, placing a hand on the dog's head.

"Not at all," Doctor Ridley said, as he drew near. "What's wrong with this fellow, other than he looks hungry."

"He's a stray the neighbor boy found," Rock said, hunkering down by the doctor. Zane could feel Rock get a firm hold of the dog, tipping his chin up. Zane continued rubbing Tuffy around his ears and letting the dog rest against his legs. "He has a sore on his neck, and it broke open during his bath. We put a little ointment on it, but don't know what else to do."

The doctor was silent for a moment and the dog whined once. Finally, Doctor Ridley cleared his throat. "You did a good job of cleaning the spot, getting most of the infection out. I'd say put hot compresses on it once or twice a day. Salt is good to draw out the infection, then a medicated ointment is good, if he'll leave it alone. Don't try to bandage it because he'll likely paw at it. Give him plenty of milk and eggs. He should be fine in a few weeks."

"Thanks, Doc. He's a nice dog. Hate to see someone just turn him loose to die." Zane continued rubbing the dog's head. "I bet you didn't come all the way out here just to look at a stray mutt, though."

"No. I wanted to check on you and Rock promised he'd send me home with pears, potatoes, and fresh corn. Perhaps I could wash up and then take a look at your eyes and check on how your side is healing?"

"Sure, Doc. Let's go inside." Rock led the way inside the house where the men all washed up in the kitchen since Billie was in the bathroom repairing the damage Tuffy had done. Miko dashed outside to give the dog a bit of meat to keep him close to the house until they returned outside.

Zane peeled off his shirt and let the doctor poke and prod his side. He listened to his murmurs and mumbles. "It's healing nicely, Zane. The flesh is no longer hot to the touch and there's no sign of infection. The stitches need to come out and I can take care of that now if you like. After that, you can leave off the bandage."

"Go ahead, Doc. Rip 'em out."

He sensed Billie's presence as the doctor carefully removed the stitches. Her perfume tantalized his nose even if it mingled with the smell of wet dog. He grinned, thinking of Tuffy soaking her. Boy, he wished he could have seen it.

"It's not that funny," Billie whispered as she stood close to his ear while he sat on a kitchen chair, stretched over slightly on the table to expose his side for the doctor to work on.

"Yes, it really is," he said, tamping down the urge to laugh aloud.

"Done. That didn't take long," Doctor Ridley said as he removed the last stitch. "Now, let's take a look at your eyes. Is there a dark room we can use?"

"The office would probably work best. If you pull the curtains closed, it's fairly dark in there," Rock said, guiding them to the office. Zane sat down in a leather chair and listened as curtains swished closed.

The doctor's bag settled with a soft thump in the chair next to him.

"I'll shut the door," Rock said, then left Zane alone in the room with the doctor and Billie.

"Let's see how they look," the doctor said, removing his glasses and handing them to Billie.

Zane knew that because he could barely discern the blurry outlines of their hands.

"What can you see, Zane? Can you see my fingers?" the doctor asked.

Zane blinked and blinked again. Something lingered in the distance, but he couldn't tell what. "No. It's too fuzzy."

The doctor took a step closer. "How about now?"

Zane squinted, trying to see.

"Don't squint, just look as you would under normal conditions." Doctor Ridley moved another step closer.

"There. I can see your hand. It's blurry, but you've either lost a finger or aren't holding up your pinky."

"Very good. I wasn't holding it up," the doctor said, patting Zane on the shoulder. "That's excellent. And you're still sensitive to light?"

"Yes, especially anything overly bright. It gives me a blistering headache."

"I'm glad the glasses are helping. I'll have to remember that trick." The doctor patted him on the shoulder again. "I'll let Nurse Brighton put some drops in your eyes. I can hardly wait to taste the corn. The whole kitchen smells just like my grandmother's used to."

Doctor Ridley left and Zane tried to focus on Billie. Her face was blurry, but he could see her blond curls. If he wasn't mistaken, she wore a pleased smile.

"Hey, beautiful," he whispered, reaching out and touching her cheek. It felt so smooth beneath his fingers, so soft, so much like he remembered.

"Hey, yourself, cowboy," she said, moving so close her face was just a few inches from his.

Although she still appeared out of focus, he reveled in the joy of seeing her again. Of knowing she was smiling without having to assume or guess.

"Ready for those drops?" she asked.

"Not particularly, but they have to be better than the wash you've made me endure."

"Poor baby," Billie teased and gave him a quick kiss on the mouth. He wrapped his arms around her and pulled her onto his lap.

She didn't put up a fuss or struggle. Billie slid her hands up his arms and wrapped them behind his neck, twining her fingers in his hair. "I've sure missed you," she whispered.

"I missed you, too, Billie, girl." His lips captured hers, claiming them, caressing them, then giving in to his need to hold her closer, kiss her deeply.

Footsteps heading toward the door broke them apart. Billie jumped off his lap, grabbed a bottle she'd set on the desk and lifted a dropper. She pushed his head back and let a drop fall in his eye.

"Ow! What is that? Acid?" he asked, blinking

his eye against the sting.

Rock opened the door, glanced at them both, and chuckled. "Supper's ready." He turned and left them alone again, but with the door wide open.

Billie placed a drop in his other eye, then kissed his cheek. "I'm sorry they sting. Doctor Ridley thought these might work better than the wash you've been using, though."

"I'm willing to give anything a try if it means I can see you again."

"You've always been able to see me, Zane."

Before he could reply, she slid his sunglasses in place, gathered her things and walked to the door. "Are you coming?"

"Yes, ma'am." He stood and followed her outside to where Miko served dinner on a picnic table in the shade of a tree.

Once the meal was over and Rock had loaded an abundance of produce in Doctor Ridley's car, the man cautioned Zane to get plenty of rest and to not over do it. He thanked Miko and Rock for the meal and the produce, then left. Miko and Rock offered a flimsy excuse of having a few chores to see to, leaving Zane alone with Billie.

Even if he couldn't sense her presence beside him, which he most certainly did, he could still smell a tantalizing whiff of her perfume. The odor of wet dog had dissipated, although the thought of Tuffy shaking himself on Billie made him swallow down a laugh.

"It's still not funny," she said, giving his arm a squeeze. "I'd be mad, but that poor dog looks like he's got enough trouble."

"He does, and he didn't mean anything by it. We just need to teach him some manners." Zane felt the dog bump into his legs again and reached down to pet him. He turned toward Billie as she pet the dog, too. "Is Rock taking you home later?"

"No," she said, with a bit of hesitancy in her voice. "I'm staying here tonight."

"What?" Zane asked, surprised.

"I don't have to work tomorrow. When I called and spoke with Miko earlier, she invited me to spend the night since I planned to come out again tomorrow anyway. I hope you don't mind. I won't be throwing off any big plans of yours, will I?"

"Well, I guess I'll have to cancel that hot date I have later tonight, but I'll make do with you." Zane waited only a second before Billie swatted his arm and huffed indignantly.

"You don't have a hot date, you arrogant man."

"I do now," Zane said in a husky growl, wrapping his arms around her. "That is I will if you'll sit with me on the porch later. We might get in a little spooning before Rock starts spying on us and tells us to come inside like we're a couple of misbehaving youngsters."

Billie laughed, the sound entangling Zane's heart much as her fingers meshed with his as they brushed over Tuffy's clean coat. "A date on the porch sounds wonderful. Now, tell me where you got this homely, pathetic dog that is going to completely steal my heart."

⋆⋆⋆★ *Chapter Twenty-Two* ★⋆⋆⋆

"I don't think this is a good idea," Billie said, glancing across the car at Zane.

"You need to learn to drive, Billie, girl. No time like the present." Zane sat back and rested his right arm on the edge of the door, elbow hanging out the open window. "Rock said the road going past their place doesn't have much traffic on Sundays. Besides, with his generous offer to let you use his car to practice driving, you've got nothing to lose.

Billie decided she'd gone loony. She'd never driven a car in her life, never even sat behind a wheel before. Here she was in Rock and Miko's very nice sedan, about to attempt to drive it, with a nearly-blind man giving her instructions. No doubt about it — she'd lost her ever-loving mind.

"What could possibly go wrong?" she muttered and put the car in gear.

Zane cocked his head her direction. "Now just ease up off the brake and gently push the gas pedal. Nothing to it."

Billie did as he said and the car crept forward.

Zane grinned at her. "That wasn't so hard, was

it?"

"No, but we haven't even driven past the house yet."

He chuckled. "You'll be fine, Billie. I promise. We just spent an hour with Rock showing you how everything works. It's time to put all that into practice."

"Fine," she said, distracted as they neared the road.

"Take your foot off the gas and push down on the brake when you get to the end of the driveway."

She stomped the brake and Zane put his hands on the dashboard to keep from cracking his skull on the windshield.

"Sorry," she said, offering him a sheepish look he couldn't see.

Rather than chastise her, he pointed to his right. "Just push up on your turn signal and look both ways. Is there any traffic coming?"

"No. The road is clear," she said, looking to her right then left and right again.

"Before you pull out, check one more time. It only takes a second for a vehicle to pop up out of nowhere."

Billie craned her neck, leaning forward to see as far as she could in both directions. She'd almost asked Miko for a pillow to sit on to give her a little boost of height, but refrained. She felt like a child playing grown up as she struggled to reach the pedals and see over the steering wheel in the car. Rock had tried to adjust the seat, but it didn't move enough to be any help to her.

"The road is clear," she said, glancing one

more time to be sure.

"Push into the gas, slowly, while turning the wheel in the direction you want the car to go. You won't have to turn it too much."

Hesitant, fearful, and cautious, she eased into the turn then straightened out the wheel when they were on the paved surface of the road.

"That's good, Billie. Now, just follow the road. Rock said there's another intersection up here in about a mile. If we take a right, then another, it will bring us back around by John and Lucy Phillips' place."

Billie kept her hands on the wheel and eyes glued to the road, but she smiled. "That Petey is something else. I've heard so much about him, it was fun to meet the little scamp."

"He seemed excited to meet you, too." Zane turned his head toward her. "He told me before he left that he thinks you're a straight arrow and might even be a royal-stepper like Miko."

"I'll take that as high praise." Billie smiled at Zane and wondered how much he could see. She knew his vision was improving up close. Doctor Ridley was hopeful he'd recover most of his sight, even if it never all quite returned. Billie prayed it would be so.

"You're doing just fine, Billie. As you drive, you want to be aware of what's going on around you at all times. Keep an eye behind you, to the cars around you, those heading toward you. Anticipate what might be coming so you have time to react to it. And don't let anything distract you."

"Distract me?" she asked, casting a quick

SHANNA HATFIELD

glance his way then looking behind her. "What on earth could possibly distract me?"

"Well, you shouldn't ever put on your lipstick while driving, or try to style your hair."

"I would never do that." Billie shook her head in consternation. "That would take at least one hand, possibly two, and mine are both holding tightly to the wheel."

Zane reached over and felt along the wheel until his hand connected with hers. "You don't have to strangle the life out of the steering wheel. You'll make your hands cramp if you keep that up too long. Just maintain a firm grip."

She relaxed her grip and felt the tension in her shoulders lessen. "What else might distract me?"

"What if you were alone in the car with a handsome, charismatic fella and he scooted over closer to you like this?" Zane slid across the seat until their thighs touched. He settled his arm around her shoulders and his masculine, alluring scent enveloped her. Even with a growth of scruff on his face, he was still far more appealing than any man she'd encountered. She loved the swoop in his thick, dark hair. The dimples in his smile. The seductive fullness of his lips. The tempting indentation in his strong chin.

"I'd tell that fella to behave like a gentleman or he'd be sorry."

Zane chuckled but he didn't move away. In fact, he pressed a little closer. The hand he'd draped around her shoulders toyed with her hair while he leaned near and nuzzled her ear. He pressed a warm, moist kiss on her neck and Billie

292

fought back a moan of pleasure.

"Road, Billie. Focus on the road."

She hadn't even realized she'd turned her head to give him better access and let her eyes drift half-closed. She popped them wide open and screeched as the car crossed the center line and headed toward the ditch on the other side of the road.

"Gently guide the car where you want it to go," Zane said in a calm voice as he moved back to his side of the car. His patience and unruffled demeanor helped settle her skittered nerves.

Billie got the car on the right side of the road then pulled over and stopped as soon as she came to the crossroad. She clenched the steering wheel in both hands until her knuckles turned white and worked to slow the breaths that came in frightened gasps.

Zane gave her an unreadable look, one nearly devoid of expression. "That's what I mean by a distraction."

"Oh, you... you... man!" Billie swatted his arm and he laughed, catching her hand and bringing it to his lips. He kissed each finger with such tenderness she thought she'd melt into the leather seats of the sedan. However, she was still so upset at him, she wasn't yet ready to succumb to his considerable charms.

"You could have gotten us both killed!" she yelled, but didn't jerk her hand away from Zane's thorough attention to each finger.

"Nah. I knew you'd do fine, and you did."

Zane kissed her palm and her heart stopped. His lips trailed up to her wrist and her heart jumpstarted then began a beat set in double time.

Swiftly gathering the rapidly unraveling threads of her common sense, Billie yanked them together and tugged her hand from Zane's. "We better continue with the lesson."

"Driving or kissing?" he asked. Even though she couldn't see his eyes, the look he gave her held such heat, she felt singed just sitting near him.

"Driving, cowboy. Just driving."

He chuckled and scooted back until his arm once again rested out the open window. "Put the car in gear, check to make sure no one is coming, and then turn right at the intersection."

"Can you see the stop sign? The intersection?" she asked, hopeful.

"No, but I have a good idea how far a mile is. I figure we have to be close."

"It's right in front of us." She followed his instructions, turned the car to the right, and started down the road.

By the time they reached the next intersection a mile later, she was feeling much more confident. Zane hadn't tried to distract her again. She wavered between feeling relieved he'd behaved and disappointed that he hadn't at least tried.

The feel of his lips on her neck, his leg pressed to hers, did things to her she'd never imagined. And mercy! His kisses to her fingers, her wrist. If he'd kept going, she wasn't certain what might have happened. But with each kiss, each inch he'd advanced, her resistance faded until she wasn't sure she'd have kept even a smidgen of it.

"You never told me much about your family,

Billie girl. You've met what's left of mine, such as it is. I'm sure sorry about my brother. Floyd is…Floyd."

"You aren't your brother's keeper, Zane. Don't take on his problems just because you're related. That's not right or fair. He made his choices." She sighed. "I just hope he really did return to Texas and doesn't pop up around here again. What do you think he'll do?"

"I doubt I've heard the last from him, but he's too big a coward to risk anything that might get him caught or into trouble right now." Zane studied her for a moment. "Now, let's hear about your family."

"There isn't much to tell." The day was too pleasant to dredge up her past. Since it was Sunday, Rock and Miko had held an impromptu church service in their living room. Rock read a few Psalms from his Bible and then the four of them sang several hymns they all knew.

Afterward, Billie helped Miko set out a cold lunch. They'd just finished eating when Petey Phillips arrived to check on the dog. Once he declared Tuffy a brand-new dog after his bath, the boy and canine rolled around in the grass until Petey decided he better run on home. That's when Zane landed on the idea to give Billie a driving lesson.

"There has to be more than what you shared, Billie. You told me your father and mother both died when you were young and that you got passed from pillar to post until you decided to make your own way when you were sixteen. What happened to your folks?"

Billie hated to think about the sadness of her youth, but she knew Zane would persist until he wheedled the truth out of her. "My father was ten years older than my mother. They wed when she was barely sixteen. Two years later, they had me, and a year after that, my father decided he needed to do his part in helping knock the Germans down a peg during the Great War. As soon as America joined the war, he enlisted. He died the following summer in a bloody battle. My mother never recovered from her grief and she died when I was seven. As you know, the elderly aunt who took me in couldn't provide adequate care, so I went to stay with one of Mother's friends. Then I went from her house to another, to another. By the time I was sixteen, I'd lived in twelve different homes. It was time for a change. I got a job waiting tables at a restaurant, found a few girls looking for a roommate and began making my own way. That's when I started saving my money to go to nursing school. I took any job I could find to put money away."

Zane's eyebrows shot above the sunglasses he wore, stretching toward his hairline.

Billie shook her head. "Well, not any job, but those I could do without compromising my morals or integrity. I waited tables, took in mending, made deliveries for a dress shop. I even worked in a hospital's laundry room just to get my toe in the door there."

"Wow, Billie. I had no idea. You really are full of pluck and determination aren't you?"

She smiled. "I try. I haven't had anyone to lean

on, to count on, since I was a tiny child. I've learned to take care of myself."

"And you've done an admirable job of it." Zane continued gazing at her, as though he tried to study her. "What about the future? If you could snap your fingers and make one dream come true, what would it be?"

Billie had never admitted it to anyone, but she felt compelled to share her dream with Zane. "Ever since my mother died, the one thing I wanted most in the world was a place to call home. When I close my eyes, I can picture it, Zane. It's a little place in the country, a farmhouse with a broad porch and flowers everywhere. Of course, there would have to be a dog, and some other animals, and I always picture apple trees in the distance. Lately, it seems that dream includes a handsome dark-haired man with the most intriguing dimples that come out of hiding when he smiles."

Zane turned away and didn't say another word for the length of several heartbeats, then he faced her again. "When I was here in May, why did you work so hard at keeping me an arm's length away?"

Billie didn't think she'd done a very good job of keeping her distance from him. Not at all. Yet, she had insisted they depart as friends, not potential lovers.

"I saw what happens to a woman who loves a soldier, Zane. Her heart shatters when she finds out he isn't coming home. I just couldn't put myself through that kind of misery. Years ago, I made it a personal rule to never get involved with a soldier."

"So what are we, then? What's this?" Zane

asked, agitation thickening his voice as he motioned between the two of them. "I could be wrong, but I think you've already bent that rule."

"I may have made allowances where you're concerned. However, you aren't going to be a soldier now, so that changes things."

"Oh, I'm still a soldier and I plan to get right back into the thick of things as soon as I can," Zane said, turning his face toward the window. "So you're telling me the only reason you've been smooching on me, cuddling up to me, is because you think my military career is over. Is that right?"

"That's not... I didn't mean..." Billie stammered, unable to refute what he said when he'd summed it up so well. She'd loved Zane from the moment they met, but she hadn't surrendered to the possibility of that love, to the opportunities of loving him, until he'd arrived at the hospital wounded and no longer able to fly. It wasn't that her love for him had changed. No, it had taken root and grown from that first day she'd looked into his amazing pale blue eyes and gotten lost in his dimpled smile. Now, though, she felt free to love him without the niggling worry he'd be killed in some foreign place by an unknown enemy.

Then again, he'd nearly been killed by a doctor in her hospital at the request of his own brother.

Maybe life was full of danger and she had to learn to accept it in all its forms. Lost in her thoughts, she didn't notice Zane had grown quiet until they passed an apple farm. From the road, the top of a farmhouse was just visible. Billie sucked in a gulp, convinced it was the house she'd always pictured in her dreams. Goose bumps broke out on her arms and she swiveled her head, trying to see more.

She didn't say anything about it, though, and continued driving. Not far down the road, they passed a large farm, one she recalled seeing when she and Zane had driven around in May, searching for Rock. She turned a corner onto a main road and grinned as a red-haired boy ran across the yard, waving and smiling.

"Oh, it's Petey's house," she said, nudging Zane. "We're driving past the yard and he's waving like we're a grand parade."

Zane smiled and waved his hand. "Hi, Petey!" he called.

"Hi, Tex! Enjoy the ride with Miss Brighton!" Petey yelled.

"I will!"

Billie glanced over at Zane and noticed he appeared less upset, although he didn't seem as happy as he'd been earlier. In the time it took to try to find a way to express her concerns, they arrived back at Rock and Miko's home.

"Thank you for the lesson, Zane. I won't soon forget it."

He nodded once and opened the door, making no effort to tease her or find an excuse to touch her as he usually did. "I won't forget it either, Billie."

Miko and Rock sat on the front porch swing, hands clasped, with Tuffy asleep at their feet. The dog had already made himself at home.

Billie got out of the car and walked around it to lead Zane through the gate. His arm was stiff in her hand, whereas before he'd been relaxed, eager to be with her.

"Did you have a good time?" Rock asked and rose to his feet, then pulled Miko up beside him.

"It was... informative and instructive." Billie gave Zane a quick look. He remained unusually quiet and a slight frown created a vertical line across his brow.

"Do you want me to run you into town now or would you rather stay for supper?" Rock asked.

"If you don't mind, I should probably head home," Billie said as they walked up the porch steps. "I can catch the bus if you wouldn't mind giving me a lift to the stop."

"I'm happy to take you all the way home," Rock said, giving Billie a smile then studying his quiet friend. "If you want, you could ride along, Zane."

"No. I'm feeling a little worn out. I better rest awhile." Zane tipped his head toward her, since she stood with her hand on his arm, and gave her a small, tight smile. "Thank you for coming out, Billie, and spending the day with us. Have a safe trip home."

With that, he turned and made his way inside the house.

Rock watched him go then shrugged and shook his head. "Let me grab my hat and jacket and we can be on our way."

"I'll gather my things, too," Billie said, following Miko inside and picking up the small overnight case she'd brought with her yesterday that held her toiletries, nightgown, and change of clothes. In spite of Zane's protests to take his bed, Billie had slept quite comfortably on the couch in the living room. It had been a lovely evening to joke and laugh with Zane, Rock and Miko. They'd enjoyed a delicious breakfast then shared in the time of fellowship that imbued her heart with peace.

The peace now seemed like a distant memory as she picked up her case and purse, and returned outside. Miko gave her a hug and the dog sat up, tongue lolling out of his mouth as he looked at her.

Billie set her things on a chair and bent down to pet the dog. "You keep Zane out of trouble, Tuffy. Can you do that, boy?"

The dog's tail whopped against the porch floorboards.

Miko laughed. "I guess we can take that as a yes."

Billie smiled and hugged her again. "Thank you so much for having me. It was so kind of you."

"Is everything all right with Zane?" Miko asked as they walked down the porch steps and out to the car.

Billie shook her head. "I'm not certain. One minute he was teasing me and the next he grew quiet. I don't think he's ill, but he could be tired. I'm sure my presence has kept him from resting like he should. If he isn't feeling well when he wakes up from his nap, please call me or Doctor Ridley."

"Of course, Billie."

Rock held the passenger door open for Billie then set her things in the back seat. He gave Miko a hug and kiss before sliding behind the wheel and they were soon on their way toward town.

Billie felt a sharp pain in her chest. Despite Zane's sudden sullenness, she'd left her heart on the farm with him.

302

✶✶✶★ *Chapter Twenty-Three* ★✶✶✶

Zane feigned exhaustion as an excuse to get away from Billie. When she'd basically told him the reason she wanted to be with him was because she assumed his military career was over, he'd wanted to punch his hand through the dash of Rock's car.

What was wrong with that woman? She fought getting close to him when he was healthy and whole, with perfect vision. But now that he was wounded and blind, she wanted to be his little snuggle pup. Well, he wasn't having it! No, siree!

If Billie didn't care about him enough to love him when he was a dashing pilot ready to take on the world, then he sure wasn't about to let her lay claim to his heart when he was a wounded has-been who'd never fly again.

Anger surged through his veins. He was angry at Billie. Angry he was blind and helpless. Angry his career had suddenly and unexpectedly ended. Angry Smitty was dead and his crew injured. Angry horrible men existed who made it necessary for America to go to war. He was especially angry at the Japs.

They'd bombed Pearl Harbor, cutting a wide path of destruction that not only killed his friends, but claimed civilian lives. Japs were the reason his plane crashed. Japs were the reason Smitty was gone. He hoped the men fighting in the Pacific wiped every single one of them from existence.

His conscience pricked.

Wrath and vengeance fit him like someone else's worn shoe or a pair of pants two sizes too small. Uncomfortable. Prickly. Painful.

He knew his hateful, spiteful feelings were wrong. Feelings like that led to bitterness and destruction, desolation and anguish. Determined not to let his mind or spirit go to such a dark place, to go down that nightmarish road, Zane slid off the bed and fell to his knees, spending a long time in prayer. When the storm blazing in his soul quieted, he sat on the edge of the mattress, introspective.

Zane was no idiot.

He loved his military career, but had no desire to be at war. War was a terrible, monstrous thing that left behind so much irreparable grief and devastation. But by golly, he'd do his part to serve, to keep the country he loved protected and the people there safe.

Why couldn't Billie understand that? She, of all people, should realize what a soldier was called to do wasn't always an easy thing. It was certainly never a safe thing.

He was still so mad at her he wanted to paint her back porch bright red. And if she'd been there at the moment, he might have just turned Billie over his knee and got the job done.

304

Instead, he propped his elbows on his knees and tried to think calming thoughts. Like a flock of hungry buzzards, his mind kept coming back to feast on his irritation with Billie.

Zane loved her so much. He was man enough to admit the truth. He'd loved her since the day he'd stepped into the hospital and seen her standing there. She was beautiful, of that there was no doubt. But he loved her spunk and sass, the way she took on the world without a care to her own safety, focused on those that mattered to her. He'd witnessed her selflessness, her willingness to go the extra mile for others.

It had been an enlightening experience to be among the men she nursed, particularly those in room seven. Zane couldn't see her in action, but he felt the genuine affection she held for "her boys" as she called them. She came in early, stayed late, and ran around in her precious hours off hunting up candy bars, magazines, or other treats that might brighten the day of one of the wounded men. Jimmy had told him how he'd been scraping against death's door when Billie brought him a candy bar that tasted like home. Whether it was the candy or the fact she'd spent an entire morning tracking it down, Jimmy turned a corner in his recovery and never looked back.

Generally, he could tell the moment Billie entered the room not because of the faint teasing hint of her perfume, but because of the feeling among the men when she was there. They relaxed. They seemed happier. Settled. Peaceful.

The way the whole bunch of patients talked

about Billie — like she was a cross between a saint, a pin-up girl, and their favorite childhood friend — made Zane so jealous he sometimes battled the urge to turn into a rampaging cavedweller and flatten them all.

Then the sane part of his brain would kick in and he'd realize what a blessing she was to the men in the hospital. She badgered them, pushed them, nursed them, made them laugh, brightened their days, and gave them a reason to look forward to tomorrow.

His fury toward her began to ebb. In her own way, Billie served her country with every bit as much dedication and honor as any man he'd known in the armed forces.

He could understand why she wanted the stability of a man who'd be home every night, one who wouldn't die in a hail of gunfire, or a cannon blast, or a fiery plane crash. No woman wanted her man going off to war, but thousands did.

Would his love for Billie, and hers for him, be enough to overcome the obstacles that rested between them? He certainly hoped it would, needed to believe it would, because he couldn't envision his future without Billie in it.

There were days her letters were all that kept him going. Filled with her wit and humor, her silliness and sweetness, he'd savored every word until he had them memorized.

Uncertain what to do about her, about them, he knew he wouldn't find the answer hiding in his room. He took the sunglasses he'd tossed on the bedside table and slipped them on then went to the kitchen. The room was oddly quiet.

"Miko?" He waited. Listened. Nothing.

He walked through the house, saying her name, but she didn't answer. He stepped out the front door and called her name, but more silence met him. Maybe she accompanied Rock when he took Billie into town, but he doubted it. Miko seemed to prefer to stay at home and he didn't think they'd leave him completely unattended.

It rankled that he had to have someone keep watch on him, as though he was a child in need of constant care. Even if he couldn't see, it didn't mean he was utterly helpless, although he'd proclaimed as much earlier in the throes of his self-pity about Billie.

He closed the front door, crossed the porch and made his way down the steps and around to the backyard. "Miko?" he yelled, raising his voice.

"Coming!" she called from a distance. He couldn't tell if she was at the barn or somewhere else.

He heard something bang and then her footsteps as she approached him.

"Is everything okay?" she asked as she neared him.

"Yes. I just wasn't sure if you were here," he said, annoyed he sounded like a lost little boy.

"I decided to take care of the chores so Rock won't have to when he gets back. He promised to bring home hamburgers for dinner. There's a place in Beaverton that's open on Sundays."

"That sounds good. I haven't had a hamburger for the longest time." Zane followed Miko as she walked up the back steps. "Did you finish the chores or can I help?"

"Nope. I'm finished." Miko held the door for him as he made his way inside.

In the kitchen, he listened to the familiar sounds of her straining the milk and placing it in the refrigerator. She washed her hands then crossed the floor toward him.

"Billie said we should put these drops in your eyes two to three times a day. Did she give you any drops before she left?"

"No." Zane knew that was his fault, for acting like a sulking baby.

"Want to do that now or wait?"

"Either way is fine with me," he said, wishing he didn't have to accept the drops at all. However, they were far better than the wash he'd endured the last few weeks.

"Why don't I give you the drops then we can sit on the porch and wait for Rock with Tuffy. If you prefer, we can rest in the living room and listen to the radio."

"Let's keep Tuffy company," Zane said, preferring to be outside whenever the opportunity arose. "The office seemed like a good place to do the drops, since it's darker in there."

"Then to the office we'll go," Miko said in a cheerful tone.

Zane followed her through the house and sat in the same chair he had yesterday when the doctor was there. He recalled the sizzling kisses he'd shared with Billie and wished he hadn't let her leave without talking to her. He hoped she'd come back soon and they could discuss the possibilities of a future together.

"Is it one drop in each eye?" Miko asked.

"That's what Billie did yesterday."

Zane removed his glasses, tipped his head back and stared upward. A woman's face appeared in his line of vision.

Miko was close enough he could make out black hair, an oval face, smooth skin. He'd known from the few hugs she'd shared with him that she was tall, nearly as tall as him.

As she drew nearer to give him the drops, his focus improved. He hadn't expected her to have dark hair or such dark eyes. They almost looked like glossy obsidian in the dim light. She bent closer and Zane sucked in a gasp at the same moment the drops fell into his eyes.

He blinked rapidly, wanting to see her again. To confirm what he'd seen. Make sure his eyes weren't playing tricks on him.

"Did that hurt, Zane? Do you need something?" Miko asked, her voice mirroring her concern.

"No. I'm fine." He stood and blinked again, desperate to focus on her face. "Can you come closer?"

"Sure," she said.

Her blurry form took on edges and curves. Zane moved two steps closer, until he was nearer to her than was proper, but he needed to see her face.

His gaze started at her slightly stubborn chin and moved upward to the warm smile on her nicely shaped lips. Small nose, perfect skin.

And eyes that belonged to someone who was Japanese.

Miko was Japanese.

Why hadn't Rock said anything? Why hadn't anyone told him?

Hate and fury tried to rise like acidic bile up his throat, but he swallowed it down. Miko had welcomed him into her home, nursed him, even in the middle of the night, and gone out of her way to make him feel welcome and sheltered. She'd joked with him, teased him, and he'd begun to think of her as the sister he'd always wanted and never had.

If he closed his eyes, none of that had changed. Miko was the same no matter her nationality, but it was still hard for Zane to come to terms with the unmistakable truth she was Japanese.

"Zane?" Miko asked, placing a hand on his arm.

Without thinking he shook it off and stepped back, sinking into the chair behind him with a thud.

"Can I get you something? A drink of water? A cool compress? Do you want to go to your room?"

"No, Miko. Just give me a moment, will you? I'll come outside in a minute."

"If you're sure," she said, sounding hesitant to leave him to his own defenses.

"I'm sure."

Zane waited until he heard the creak and slap of the wooden screen door before he slipped his sunglasses back on and drew in a ragged breath. His best friend married a Japanese woman.

Would he feel any differently if Rock had

married a German woman or an Italian woman, or a woman from Timbuktu?

If the woman was as kind and gentle, funny and caring as Miko, then no, he wouldn't feel any differently. He was thrilled Rock had found his one true love. His friend deserved a lifetime of happiness with a wonderful girl.

The fact that girl just happened to be Japanese made it hard for him to let go of his prejudice and see her for who she was, not where her ancestors had once lived.

See. Now that was the ironic thing about it all. He couldn't see anything more than a foot away from his face.

When he had to look at Miko through the eyes of blindness, he'd seen a beautiful person, one who was devoted to Rock, respected by her neighbors, and adored by the young people who worked for them. Petey Phillips had declared no one was any finer than Miko and he had an idea the boy didn't toss out compliments like that freely.

Miko was gracious and graceful, tenderhearted and hard-working. If he was angry no one had told him she was Japanese, he supposed the only person to blame was himself.

Numerous times, they'd been listening to news reports on the radio and he'd ranted about the stupid Japs. He even recalled saying something the other day about being glad the president had rounded up all the American Japanese like they were cattle and shipped them off where they couldn't do anyone harm.

Had he insulted Miko? Hurt her feelings?

Certainly, his cruel words must have stung.

Yet, she'd continued to be a friend to him, even when he didn't deserve it.

Embarrassed by his behavior and his attitude, he rose to his feet, knowing he needed to make things right even if she hadn't said anything was wrong.

He stepped out on the front porch and felt his way to a chair. The bright light made him squeeze his eyes shut, trying to prevent a headache. Outside, he still kept his eyes closed a good deal of the time, even with his sunglasses on, to block out the painful light.

"Miko?" he asked when all remained quiet.

"I'm here," she said, touching his hand as he settled into one of the padded wicker chairs.

A warm, wriggly body pressed against his legs as the dog made his presence known, not wanting to be ignored. Zane buried his hands in Tuffy's soft fur.

"What color is he?" he asked, realizing no one had told him what the dog looked like.

"A better question would be what color isn't he." Miko's soft laugh eased his tension. "When you and Petey first dragged him in, he looked almost black, but his bath removed a lot of dirt and grime. His back end and tail are dark brown. His chest is a tan color and his legs are more golden than brown. His face is tan with some white splashes, and his ears are brown. Rock said it would be impossible to guess his breed because it looks like a mix of many. Tuffy is all mutt, but a loveable one."

Zane scratched behind the dog's ears and along his back. Tuffy's tail brushed back and forth across the floorboards of the porch, hinting at how much he enjoyed the attention. He patted the dog's side. "His ribs aren't sticking out so much already. That's good."

"He's been eating like there's no tomorrow, but he'll fill up soon enough," Miko said.

Zane heard her chair squeak, like she'd shifted in it.

"Miko, I owe you an apology, a huge one. In fact, I don't think I deserve your forgiveness, but I'll beg for it anyway. I'm sorry for going on and on about the Japanese, but I'm especially remorseful for what I said about those who are American and have been sent to assembly centers. I've let the emotions of war color my opinions. Even worse, I've allowed them to alter my moral compass. It's wrong to carry around that kind of hatred for anyone, even our enemies. I'm truly sorry for anything I've said or done that may have hurt you."

All was silent for several moments, although he thought he heard a sniffle. Finally, Miko released a sigh and placed her hand on his arm, giving it a gentle pat. "When I put in your drops, you could see me? Is that what happened?"

He nodded. "Yes. I discovered yesterday if someone is really close, I can see them fairly well."

"That's wonderful. I mean, that your vision is coming back, not that you decided I was on your 'hate the Japanese' list."

Zane placed his hand over hers before she

could pull it away from his arm. "Miko, I don't hate you. In fact, up until I saw you, I'd decided you are the sister I've always wanted. Rock's been closer than a brother and I looked forward to extending that relationship with you. I'd still like to, if you think you can forgive me, for acting like a dunderheaded fool."

"I forgive you, Zane. I know you've been through terrible things and I can't even begin to imagine what it must have been like to be at Pearl Harbor, or Midway, or any of the other places you've had to fight against the Japanese. My ancestors may have come from there, but believe me when I say my family is about as American as they come."

He gave her hand a light squeeze then leaned back in his chair. He reached down and stroked the dog, as much for something to do as to comfort the dog. "Will you tell me about your family? How they came to be here? And how you came to know Rock? He's been oddly vague about the details, although now I understand why."

"I know. I wanted to tell you from the first day you arrived who I really was, but Rock was afraid you'd take the news he'd married the enemy badly."

Zane shook his head. "You most certainly are not the enemy, Miko. Not at all."

She cleared her throat and the chair creaked again. He pictured her settling in it more comfortably. "My great-grandparents came to Portland from Japan in the 1880s. My great-grandfather took any work he could find, saved

314

every penny he didn't have to spend. In a few years, they'd saved enough money to purchase a quarter section of land. People thought they were crazy for buying a place covered in brush and trees. But they cleared the acres at the bottom of the hill that was now theirs, planted fruit trees, berry bushes, and tilled the soil for a garden. The second year they were here, they added the produce stand. My grandfather was a little boy then. He grew up and took over the business. He and my grandmother built this house and a new produce stand when I was a young girl."

"Did you live here, too?"

"No. I often came and spent the summers here because I love working in the garden, but my parents lived in Portland. My father had his own real estate business and my mother was quite a socialite. My older sister, Ellen, was the perfect daughter, doing everything mother asked of her. She married a nice Japanese boy and they have two beautiful little girls. They're in California, in an assembly center there."

"Do you have other siblings," Zane asked.

"Just my younger brother, Tommy. He was a senior this year."

"And your family is in the assembly center in Portland?"

"Yes. Rock goes to see them every Tuesday and takes them fresh produce, and tins of food. It's a horrible place, from what I understand, although Rock refuses to let me go there. He's afraid they'd make me stay."

"They most likely would," Zane said in

agreement. "How did you come to be here with Rock if your family is all there?"

"Pastor Clark, he's the pastor of the Presbyterian Church we've always attended, has only one child, a daughter. Sally and I have been best friends forever. She lives on the coast and was expecting a baby back in the spring. Her husband had just been shipped overseas and she didn't want to be alone, so I went to stay with her after I was fired from my job. And before you ask, the reason I was fired is because I was Japanese, even though I'd worked there for years. Anyway, I stayed with Sally for several weeks. Her baby is just the sweetest thing. One Sunday afternoon in early May, my father called in a panic for me to rush home because we'd all been ordered to report to an assembly center. I tried to get home in time to report, but no one would sell me a bus ticket. Sally finally left the baby with me and went to purchase one. I was forced to wear a disguise of sorts just to get on the bus. Except on the last bus, I was caught and left by the side of the road about twenty miles from here."

"What did you do?" Zane asked, feeling sympathy for Miko and what she must have gone through. Overnight, she'd gone from a regular American girl to the enemy.

"I walked home. Rain started as a drizzle, then soon left me drenched. The night was cold and dark, one of the longest I've ever endured. It was nearly daylight when I made it here, hoping to catch my family before they left, but they'd gone the day before. I walked around to the back step to get the key and go inside, and found Rock sprawled across the step. I tugged him inside and spent almost two weeks by his bedside, nursing him the best I knew how and praying he'd survive. By that time, I'd become a fugitive and didn't know what to do. I couldn't leave Rock alone, yet each day I stayed, I feared someone would find me, turn me in. When Rock finally put the pieces together and figured out what I'd done by staying with him, he refused to let me turn myself in. Pastor Clark agreed with Rock and he married us across the river in Washington. Rock bought the farm from my grandfather with the agreement if Grandpa and Grandma ever want it back, they can have it. This farm has been in my family for generations and I just couldn't bear to see anyone take it. The man that shot Rock wanted to log all the trees."

What little Zane could see of the place, he couldn't imagine it stripped bare and left with nothing but ugly stumps. The farm was beautiful. A lush, green haven, especially with a towering tree-covered hill in the background.

"I'm glad Rock saved the farm, but I'm even more grateful he married you. I've never seen him this happy and content with life, Miko. That's because of you."

"Thank you, Zane. That means a lot to me, knowing how close the two of you are. I'm sorry we kept all that from you, but Rock didn't want you to judge me based on my heritage until you got to know me as a person."

"I have no right to judge at all, Miko, and I realize that now. I'm truly, truly sorry."

He heard the chair creak again as she rose to her feet and placed a hand on his arm. "How about we quit apologizing and I show you something I think you'd like to see."

"Sure," Zane said, feeling the camaraderie he'd so easily shared with Miko return.

She led him to a large storage building he'd not yet been in and pushed open the big door. The dim interior of the building made it easier for him to see. Fuzzy shapes of a tractor and truck took shape. Then he saw what looked to be a car. He bent close and was nearly blinded by the shiny chrome on the Packard convertible. He admired the white sidewall tires and buttery smooth leather seats.

"What color is it?" he asked, unable to distinguish it though the dark sunglasses.

"Laguna maroon. My dad calls it the luna mobile."

"Is it your dad's car?"

Miko laughed. "No, it's mine. I bought it when I was still gainfully employed."

"It's quite a car, Miko, for quite a girl."

"Want to go for a ride? I haven't taken it for a spin in a long time, mostly because I don't want to waste our gas rations, but Rock wouldn't care."

"Why not?" Zane grinned and stepped back as Miko backed the car out of the building. She pushed the door shut and grabbed a pair of sunglasses and a broad-brimmed hat she fastened with a bow beneath her chin, then she headed down the driveway. She followed the same route Billie had driven earlier, but rather than cautiously putting along, Miko zoomed down the road, barely slowing at the corners.

Zane hadn't felt so free since the last time he'd lifted off in a plane just for fun. She turned down the road that would eventually come out on the main road that ran past the Phillips place.

"That place over there," she said, pointing to her left as she rolled to a stop. "Mac and Carol Danvers lived there. Mac was killed at Midway and Carol died not long after. Their poor son is Petey's best friend."

"He went to stay with his aunt in Pendleton, is that right?" Zane asked, trying to focus his gaze. He could make out shapes of trees and the top of a house on the other side of a hill.

"Yes. Delaney wants to sell the place, but right now someone is taking care of this year's apple crop. It has a big farmhouse and barn, and several outbuildings. Mac always had horses and a few cattle, too. It would make a wonderful place for someone who's looking to settle down." Miko put the car in gear.

Zane didn't know if she was making the statement in general or hinting that he should consider it. What in the world would he do with an apple orchard? He knew ranching and flying planes. Even if he did want to settle down, was this where he wanted to do it? He'd always pictured returning to Texas and building a house on the ranch when he retired from the military.

Recent events made it clear he'd likely never return to Texas, at least not for an extended time. Floyd would figure out a way to keep the ranch just long enough to lose it or he'd sell it. Either way, it would never be Zane's home again. Truthfully, it hadn't been since he'd left for West Point.

Miko had given him much to think about, so much to consider. He had to mull over how Billie figured into his plans for the future. Without her, he just couldn't picture a future at all, at least not one where he was happy.

They drove to the main road and Miko turned onto it then tooted her horn as they passed the Phillips' place. Petey was outside playing on a tire swing. The boy waved both hands over his head in greeting and nearly fell off the swing.

"That boy is sure the cat's pajamas." Miko laughed and returned his wave.

"That he is," Zane agreed waving even though he couldn't see Petey.

She hit the accelerator and roared down the road. Zane heard her giggle as she turned right at the intersection and raced into the driveway just ahead of Rock as he pulled in behind them in the sedan.

"Is the sedan really Rock's car or yours?" Zane asked.

"Neither. It's my grandfather's car, but he told Rock when he bought the place that included everything here. Technically, it is Rock's now."

"Yours and Rock's," Zane corrected as Miko parked her car in the storage building and turned off the ignition.

"I'm gone for five minutes and my best friend tries to run off with my wife. Gee, what's the world coming to?" Rock joked as he parked and got out of the car.

Although their images were fuzzy, Zane could see Miko hurry over to Rock. He lifted her in a tight hug and gave her a kiss before he set her back on her feet.

"I've got dinner if anyone's hungry," Rock said, holding up two paper bags.

"I'm starving," Miko said. She stepped over and placed a hand on Zane's arm. "Come on, brother, we aren't leaving you behind."

Warmed by Miko's words as well as how readily she forgave him, Zane truly felt like he was with family, with people who loved him no matter what an idiot he'd been.

★ *Chapter Twenty-Four* ★

Zane pressed his head against the warm side of the cow and stripped the last of the milk from her teats. "You're a good girl, Amos," he said, patting the cow as he got to his feet and picked up the bucket of milk.

"Are you sure you feel up to being out here?" Rock asked, taking the bucket from him so he could strain the milk.

"I practically feel as good as new," Zane said with a grin. Each morning he awoke feeling more like himself. His side rarely hurt at all and the wound's angry red scar was slowly fading. Miko had given him some cream to rub on it and it had almost magical healing properties, or at least that's what he'd concluded.

Even better, his eyesight improved daily. Although things in the distance were still nothing more than fuzzy blobs, he could see objects a few feet away without much difficulty. He still wore sunglasses except when he was in a dark room or sleeping because the light made his eyes and head ache, but Doctor Ridley assured him his sight should continue to improve.

Grateful for what vision had returned, Zane trusted the rest would come back eventually. If not, at least he was thankful he could get around by himself without someone constantly watching over him and leading him around.

Just yesterday, he'd gone with Rock on his Tuesday trip to town. Rock left milk, eggs, butter, and some produce at a little store run by a friendly man that immediately made Zane think of Santa Claus. Rock bought them both a cold bottle of Coca Cola and they continued on their way to Rock's attorney's office where they spent more than an hour having papers drawn up that would prevent Floyd from carrying out his plans, even if he did the unthinkable and killed Zane.

From there, Rock drove Zane to the hospital where Doctor Ridley checked him over and congratulated him on his progress. Billie hadn't been there, but he had spoken to Peggy who assured him Billie was fine, just down in bed with a bad cold. He'd asked if there was anything he could do, but Peggy had laughed and said Billie had more care than she wanted, living in a house full of nurses.

Zane was concerned about Billie, about their relationship. She'd not been able to come to visit him since the Sunday he made her learn to drive, and he didn't feel comfortable calling her to talk. He'd thought of little else besides what he could do to make things better with her, since he'd let her leave on such an unsettled note.

Perhaps he needed to make an effort to do something special, something that would let her know how much he cared, how much he loved her.

He mulled over those thoughts as Rock drove out to the assembly center. Even with his limited vision, what Zane had seen there would haunt him. Regret tasted bitter in his mouth when he thought of saying the Japanese Americans deserved to be isolated in internment camps and assembly centers. As he looked around, he couldn't help but think no one deserved to live in such conditions, especially when they'd done nothing wrong.

Humble and contrite, he'd met Miko's grandparents, parents, and brother. Her grandfather was a jovial man, full of smiles. Her brother was like any other young man his age, full of energy and questions. Her father was polite and friendly. But the women were quiet. Stoic. Reserved. He could see bits of Miko in both her parents, as well as her grandfather.

This morning, as he milked the cow, his thoughts jumped between Billie and the plight of Miko's family. Zane had liked them and wished there was something he could do to help, but he knew there was nothing that could be done for any of them.

He agreed with Rock and Pastor Clark, whom he'd met Sunday afternoon when the man came for a visit and stayed for supper. Miko had no business being at the assembly center with her family. Besides, he'd learned that many of the women who'd originally been sent there had returned home to their Caucasian husbands. Miko was no different. Her place was with Rock and nowhere else, but he certainly understood why she remained at the farm and hesitated to leave.

"You look like you're thinking heavy thoughts today," Rock said, thumping Zane on the back.

"Just thinking about Billie and my future, what I want to do."

"When you figure it out, it'll all feel right," Rock said as he picked up a small pail of milk and set it down for Tuffy.

The dog eagerly lapped at the warm liquid then looked up at them with milk rimming his mouth and dripping off his chin.

Zane grinned and bent down, giving the dog a good rub. "He's really starting to look more like a dog than a half-starved wild beast."

"He is." Rock scratched behind the dog's ears before he continued the morning chores.

Zane volunteered to feed the horses while Rock took the eggs and milk into the house. He'd just finished watering them when he heard a shout from the house and hurried that direction.

Miko and Rock hadn't argued once or raised their voices since he'd been there and he couldn't picture them fighting now.

Worried something else was wrong, that someone else might be there, he ran past the barn and storage buildings and crossed the backyard in a few long strides. Through the open window, he heard Rock's raised voice.

"No, and I mean it. You aren't going!"

Zane hurried inside and found Miko weakly pounding against Rock's chest while sobbing hysterically. The woman wasn't one given to tears, at least from what he knew, so to see her in such a state made dread slither down his spine. "What's wrong?"

"Pastor Clark phoned. They're moving Miko's family today. He just happened to go for a visit and found out they'd been ordered to pack. They'll leave on a train in a few hours," Rock said. He rubbed his hands up and down Miko's back trying to comfort her when she sagged against him, burying her face in his neck.

"What do you need to do? Are you going to see them?" Zane asked.

Rock continued holding her, attempting to offer comfort through his touch. "I plan to, but Miko wants to go along, too."

Clarity set in and Zane understood the problem. Rock didn't want her to go in case someone tried to force her on the train.

"What if I go along and Miko and I watch from a distance. That way she could be there, but not get too close to things."

Miko snuffled and turned to look at him. "You'd do that?"

"Of course," Zane said, stepping closer and settling one hand on her back and the other on Rock's. "I'd do anything for either of you."

"I still think it's best she stays home," Rock said, kissing Miko's wet cheek and cuddling her close. "But I have a feeling if I don't take her with me, she'll drive herself anyway."

Zane smiled. "I think you're probably right."

Miko sniffed and wiped her tears away with a dishtowel Rock handed to her. "You're absolutely right, no probably about it."

"Let's get ready to go," Rock said, guiding Miko from the room.

Zane went to his room and changed into the nicest outfit he had, which happened to be his uniform. His footlocker still hadn't arrived, so he'd been borrowing a few clothes from Rock, even though they were a little big. He had purchased a few things when they went to town yesterday, but he hoped the rest of his belongings would arrive soon.

After combing his hair, he settled his cap on his head, stuffed his wallet in his pocket and made his way back to the kitchen, then they left. They'd stopped at the store where Rock sold milk and eggs and filled baskets with food that wouldn't perish like crackers and cookies, as well as medicinal supplies, bars of soap, toothpowder, and other things that might be of use.

When they reached the assembly center, Zane stood with an arm around Miko's shoulders, offering support. Rock spoke to her family as they waited in line to board a train. The windows of the train had been covered, so the occupants would have no idea where they were, and anyone on the outside would be unable to see the train transported Japanese Americans.

A uniformed man dug through the baskets, but finally let the family accept them after his inspection.

Zane balked at the way the families were being treated, but there was nothing he could do. Nothing any of them could do, other than pray for the people who were being treated less than human for no valid reason.

Miko stood stiff and unyielding, as though if she wavered even an inch her composure would shatter. He could feel her longing to go to her family, to give them hugs and tell them how much she loved them. However, Rock refused to relent on his orders for her to stay far enough away there would be no possibility of her getting shoved onto the train.

With a broad-brimmed hat cloaked with dark netting, and sunglasses hiding her face, Miko looked like a fashionable lady who'd merely come to observe the unfolding drama. Several people stood nearby, gawking as the passengers methodically boarded the train.

No one would guess Miko was the daughter of one of the families waiting to begin a new chapter in their uncertain future. Pastor Clark had tried to find out where her family was headed, but no one would tell him anything. Zane was of a mind to try to pry out details, but Rock counted on him to keep Miko safe.

When she lifted a handkerchief beneath the veil of her hat and dabbed at a lone tear sliding down her cheek, Zane's heart broke right along with hers.

She held herself together, waving as her family climbed up the train steps and disappeared inside.

As soon as they were out of sight, a sob burst out of her, followed by another. Immediately, Rock was there, taking her in his arms and guiding her to the car. Zane gave them a few minutes alone while he strode over to an armed guard.

"Remind me again where they're headed," he said with an engaging grin.

The private gave him a glance, noted his rank of captain, and stood a little straighter. "Idaho, sir."

"Oh, that's right," Zane said, as though he'd merely forgotten the detail. "Carry on, Private."

Zane strolled off, as though he had nothing better to do than wander past the train cars. He wanted to climb on the car where Miko's family had been loaded and wish them well, but he didn't. Abruptly, he stopped and stared at a boy who couldn't be any older than Petey, sitting on his little suitcase. An identification tag was pinned to the front of his shirt, his clothes neatly pressed. In his hand he held a miniature American flag attached to a wooden stick, the kind often seen at parades. A slight breeze slowly blew the red and white striped fabric back and forth.

The sight of the boy, of the flag in his small hand, made a lump rise to Zane's throat that he couldn't dispel.

Overwrought with emotions he couldn't begin to express, he turned away, closed his eyes, and drew in several deep breaths. When he had control of himself again, he returned to where Rock and Miko sat in the sedan. Miko's sobs had subsided, but she rested her head against Rock's shoulder as though weariness weighed her down.

"They're moving them to Idaho. Does that mean anything to you, Rock?" Zane asked as he slipped in the back seat and shut the door.

"Idaho? No, but I sure plan to find out." He sighed and started the car, then kissed Miko's cheek. "There's nothing more we can do today. Let's go home."

"If it isn't too much trouble, would you mind dropping me off to see Billie?" Although the words had popped out of his mouth rather unexpectedly, Zane liked the idea of checking on the feisty little nurse. It would also give Miko and Rock the time alone he sensed they needed.

"Are you sure, Zane? How will you get home?" Rock glanced over his shoulder at him.

"I can take the bus if I can't find a ride. I don't mind. Really."

Rock studied him in the rearview mirror for a moment then nodded once in understanding. He knew Zane wanted to give him time with Miko, but also that his friend needed to see Billie, needed the comfort of her presence.

"Just leave me at the rooming house. If she isn't there, I can walk to the hospital," Zane said as Rock took an exit and turned onto the street that ran in front of the hospital.

He turned onto a side street, at Zane's direction, and stopped the car in front of The Cascadia Hotel sign.

"She lives here?" Miko asked, glancing up at the grand Victorian home.

"Yep. I think about a dozen nurses have rooms here. It's handy for them since the hospital is just a few blocks away." Zane opened the door and got out, then leaned in the open passenger window. "I'll be back this afternoon."

"If you need a ride, call," Rock said, giving Zane a grateful look.

"I will." Zane tapped the side of the car once then stepped back as Rock pulled away from the curb and drove down the street.

Zane could have gone to the front door, knocked, and asked to see Billie, but there wasn't much fun in that.

He glanced both ways then jogged around to the back of the house. Not much had changed since he was there in May, other than the trees had already started changing their colors. He glanced up at Billie's window, but couldn't tell if it was open or closed.

The day was warm and pleasant, the sky bright and blue, and he had a girl to profess his undying love to.

Zane jumped up and grabbed a branch in the big oak tree and pulled himself onto it. His side protested as he climbed higher and higher. Unlike before, the height made him slightly dizzy. He ignored it and continued climbing.

Rather than walk out on the limb by Billie's window, he scooted across it, not trusting himself to maintain his balance. Her window was partially open when he got close enough to see it. The sound of music drifted out to him from a radio. When the singer began to croon "The Very Thought of You," Zane grinned, recalling the day he'd danced with Billie to the song.

The very thought of Billie left him tantalized, tormented, taunted. Like the singer, Zane knew the mere thought of her had distracted him numerous times when he should have been focusing on his work. He'd see her face when he glanced up at the

SHANNA HATFIELD

stars, or when he walked along the beach. She was there, in every flower, every moonbeam, making him long for her, wish he could take her in his arms and love her for a lifetime

And now that she was so close, Zane knew he wouldn't willingly let her go.

"Billie?" he called softly, edging toward the end of the branch. He could feel his weight pulling it down and knew he needed to move quickly. "Billie?" he said again, a little louder.

When she didn't answer, he got to his feet, prayed he wouldn't fall out of the tree, and jumped off the branch, catching the edge of the window sill. He pulled himself up, pushed the window open, and climbed inside. Without waiting for her invitation, he moved across the room until he stood next to her bed and could see her clearly.

Billie had been asleep, but she snapped upright, her hair a snarled tangle of curls, nose red, and eyes wide. She started to scream, but when she realized it was him, her mouth formed an O and she gaped at him.

"What on earth are you doing Zane Zander West? Trying to kill yourself? Or scare me half to death?" she asked, then dabbed at her runny nose with a handkerchief.

He grinned and hunkered down next to the bed, placing his hand against her cheek. Her skin felt hot and dry to his touch, confirming his assumption she was indeed quite ill.

"Hiya, doll. I heard our song playing and thought I'd see if you wanted to dance."

She rolled her eyes and flopped back against

her pillow. "That's the most ridiculous, stupid, romantic, wonderful thing anyone's ever said to me." She smiled at him, a joyous smile that was better than sunshine streaming from behind storm clouds. "What are you really doing here?" she asked.

"Rock dropped me off. I was at the hospital yesterday to check in with the doctor and Peggy said you were sick." He tucked her blanket around her and smoothed a curl away from her face. "I'm sorry you don't feel well, baby. How long have you been sick?"

"A few days. I don't want to give anything to the patients, so I've stayed here in my room." Her smile faded. "You shouldn't be here. The last thing you need is to get sick."

"Shoot, I never get sick. It'll be fine." Zane's palm cradled her cheek. "I sure have missed you, Billie. Missed your smile and your sass, and being bossed around every living minute of the day."

"You have not. Don't you lie to me, cowboy." She grinned then coughed a deep, rattling sound that made her press a hand against her chest as though it hurt. Zane didn't know what to do, other than rub her back and wait for the coughing spell to pass.

When it stopped, Billie looked exhausted. He handed her a glass of water from the bedside table and she took a long drink. After he settled her back on her pillow, he set the glass down and knelt beside the bed, her hands held between his.

"I really did miss you, Billie. I just needed to see you today." He buried his head in her covers and breathed in her fragrance mingled with a faint hint of soap. "And I owe you an apology. The other day at the farm, after your driving lesson, I acted like the south-end of a north-bound mule and I'm sorry."

"What upset you?" Her big green eyes gazed at him, filled with questions and worry.

"I know it's dumb, but it made me mad to think that perhaps the only reason you're willing to spend time with me is that I'll never be able to go back to flying. I just got the idea that you liked me better because I'm injured, and one of your patients. It made me wonder if you'd like me half as well if I was still able to fly. I guess it just made me angry and sad all at the same time to think you only like me when I'm less than whole."

Billie remained silent for several long, uncomfortable moments before she spoke. "The truth is, you weren't entirely wrong. With you injured, it felt safe to be more open to you than before. Under the assumption your military career is most likely over, I wouldn't have to worry about you going off and leaving me and never coming home. So I'll accept your apology, but only if you'll accept mine."

Surprised by her admission, he stared at her, unable to speak.

Billie brushed a lock of hair away from his forehead. "I realized something that day, too, Zane. You could just as easily have an accident on the way to the grocery store, or on the farm, or even in the hospital. I can't foresee the future, and I certainly can't control it. What I do have control over is living the very best life I can today. And if my very best means leaving my heart open to you, even if you someday return to flying planes, then so be it."

"I'm glad to hear that, Billie, girl." Zane cupped her cheek again and gave her a tender smile. "I do care about you, far more than you know."

As though she'd just noticed his attire, she jerked upright and gaped at him. "Why are you in your uniform? Zane, you can't possibly be shipping out somewhere. You aren't healed yet. You haven't gained back your strength. You..."

He placed a finger to her lips to quiet her. "I'm not going anywhere, at least yet. Miko found out her family is being sent away today. Rock didn't want her to come with him to say goodbye, but she wouldn't take no for an answer. My uniform is the nicest thing I have to wear right now, so I came along to keep Miko from running into the thick of things while Rock saw them off. We watched from across the tracks, but it broke my heart to listen to her silent tears and see how those poor people are being treated."

Tears welled in Billie's eyes as she rubbed her nose with her handkerchief. "I wondered how long it would take before you figured out Miko's family is Japanese."

Zane shook his head. "Her family is American. It's horrible what's happening to them, to the others who've done nothing wrong."

Billie smiled and patted his cheek. "I'm proud of you Zane. You were so adamant in your feelings about the Japanese, Rock was clearly afraid of what you'd do or say when you found out about Miko. She's a lovely person, regardless of her ancestry."

"She is a lovely person. A lovely, caring, genuinely kind person, which is why I decided she and Rock could use some time without their built-in chaperone."

"They both love having you there, Zane, but it's nice of you to give them time alone today. I'm sure Miko is beside herself. Do you know where her family is going?"

"A guard mentioned Idaho, but I don't know any more than that. Rock was going to see what he could find out later. Today isn't the day to press for answers to questions."

Billie sighed and leaned back against her headboard. "No, I suppose not." She sniffled and wiped her nose again. "I'm such a mess and you really shouldn't be here. What if Miss Burwell comes in? She'll toss me out on my ear."

Zane chuckled. "Perhaps, but it's such a cute little ear." His finger traced the rim of Billie's ear before trailing along her jaw.

"Zane," she whispered and closed her eyes, as though she needed something, longed for something. However, with her sick and him in a strange, somewhat pensive mood, today wasn't the time to speak from his heart. But soon.

"What can I get you, beautiful? Do you need some juice? Toast? A cup of tea?"

"No. The cook said she'd bring me something at noon." Billie glanced at the clock then her eyes widened. "She'll be here any moment. You really need to go."

"Oh, it'll be fine, Billie, girl. Besides, I don't think I have enough juice left in me to climb back down the tree." He gave her a pleading, boyish look. "Can't I stay a little while? Please?"

Before she could answer a tap sounded on the door.

Billie gave him a frightened look and pointed toward her closet. Zane stood, kissed her forehead, and then boldly strode to the door.

"Right on time," he said, swinging the door open with a charming smile.

"What are you doing up here, young man?" Miss Burwell asked, her features pinched with disapproval as she glared at him.

"I heard Billie was sick and stopped by to check on her. I hope that's okay. I just wanted to see for myself that she's on the mend." Zane took the tray from the woman's hands and set it across Billie's lap.

"Why on earth are you wearing sunglasses?" the old woman demanded.

"Well, when my plane crashed, there was a fireball that burned my eyes and left me blind for a while. The light still makes them hurt a might more than I can stand, so I wear dark glasses to help manage the pain."

"Gracious!" Miss Burwell said, placing a hand to her wrinkled throat. "And you can see now?"

"Mostly. I can see up close well, but things in the distance are still fuzzy. The doctor said he thinks I'll get most of my vision back, even though I'll likely never fly again."

"I'm sorry to hear that." The woman gave him

a long, studying glance, one he would have felt even if he couldn't see it. "If you are here in Miss Brighton's room, might I assume you are the legendary Captain West?"

"That's me, ma'am," Zane said, offering the woman a sharp salute. "You must be the legendary Miss Burwell."

She tittered and the hint of a smile tickled the corners of her thin mouth. "It's nice to meet you, Captain West. However, I can't allow any male to be here in the rooms with my girls. You may stay long enough to eat lunch with Miss Brighton, then you absolutely must go. I'll send the cook up with another tray."

"Thank you, Miss Burwell. That's very kind of you," Zane said, smiling at the woman.

"Yes, thank you, Miss Burwell," Billie said, finally regaining her ability to speak after she'd stared at Zane and her landlady in shocked muteness.

Miss Burwell gave them both a leveling look. "I'll leave the door open, so I better not find it closed when I return."

"It'll be open, ma'am," Zane assured her.

When she left the room, he pulled a chair over next to Billie's bed and sat down, stirring her cup of hot tea then handing it to her.

"Take a sip of that, Billie, and eat your lunch like a good girl."

Thirty minutes later, he finished the last bite from a generous slice of spice cake sweetened with molasses and loaded with nuts. The cook had brought him a tray with two thick, smoky ham sandwiches, a heaping portion of potato salad, a whole pickle, the piece of cake, and a tall glass filled with cold milk.

"Mmm. That was sure good," Zane said, wiping his mouth on a napkin and glancing over at Billie.

She'd nibbled at her toast, leaving it half-eaten, drank most of her tea, and then rested against the pillows. Her eyes had grown drowsy as she listened to him talk about things happening at the farm, how Tuffy gained weight, and amusing things Petey had said or done.

He knew he needed to leave, to let her rest, but he hated to go. Footsteps coming up the stairs let him know his time with Billie was at an end. Most likely the person heading their way was Miss Burwell.

Quickly setting aside the tray, he stood and cupped Billie's chin in his hand then kissed her cheeks, worried since she felt unnaturally warm. "You be a good girl and rest, and get well. When you do, I hope you'll come out to the farm. There are some things I'd like to talk to you about."

"I'll come, Zane," she whispered, eyes so heavy with sleep she could barely keep them open.

"Rest for now, Billie." He kissed her forehead then straightened. "I love you, Billie."

"Love you, too," she said with a sleepy smile as her eyes closed.

"Captain West, it's time for you..." Miss Burwell strode into the room, but quieted when she saw Billie asleep and Zane stacking the two trays and lifting them off the bed.

He carried them into the hall and she closed Billie's door. "Thank you, ma'am, for allowing me to eat lunch with Billie. I haven't been able to see her much lately and it was good to spend a few minutes in her company. She'll be okay, won't she?" he asked, expressing his genuine concern.

"Yes. The poor girl hardly gets a moment's rest when the others are here in the evening with them fussing over her." Miss Burwell motioned toward the stairs. "Would you mind carrying those trays to the kitchen?"

"Not at all, Miss Burwell. It was very kind of you to feed me lunch. We had a bit of a rough start to the morning and missed breakfast."

"I hope all is well now," Miss Burwell asked.

"Eventually it will be. At least I hope so."

The older woman led the way to the kitchen. The cook, a jolly round-faced woman, smiled at him as he entered and took the trays from him.

"That was a wonderful lunch. The cake was especially delicious. I can't think of the last time I had spice cake that good. Thank you."

"You're welcome, Captain. It was my pleasure to feed a hungry man. These girls eat like little birds half the time."

Zane chuckled. "But such pretty birds they are." At Miss Burwell's scowl, he snapped his mouth shut.

"I'll walk you out, Captain West."

"Yes, ma'am." He followed her to the door of the kitchen then grinned at the cook. "Thanks again for the fine grub."

Miss Burwell walked down the hallway with

staccato steps, back straight and curls tight against her pink scalp. She stopped at the front door and opened it. "The next time you'd like to visit Miss Brighton, might I suggest the front door. In your shape, you might have broken your neck shimmying up that tree."

Caught off guard by the woman's words, Zane couldn't help but stare at her in surprise.

She smiled and waved her hand out the door. "Go on, get out of here. And don't be telling anyone I broke my rules for you. Understood?"

"Yes, ma'am. Absolutely, ma'am. Thank you, ma'am." Zane felt like a school boy who'd just discovered the teacher didn't really hate him after all.

He jogged down the steps and out to the sidewalk, then turned and saluted Miss Burwell. When she waved at him, he shoved his hands in his pockets and whistled as he made his way to the bus stop.

✯✯✯ *Chapter Twenty-Five* ✯✯✯

Zane walked through the house, calling for Rock or Miko. Neither of them answered. He even opened the door to the basement and called, but only the sound of his voice bounced back to him.

"I wonder where they could be?" he mused aloud. He and Rock had spent the morning digging up potatoes and an assortment of root vegetables that would be stored in the cold recesses of the basement or sold in the produce stand.

After lunch, Rock went to work on an old harrow he'd bought for practically nothing at an auction the previous weekend.

Zane offered to clean the barn and had just finished spreading a clean layer of straw in the stalls when he decided to go for a ride on one of the horses. He'd brushed them, fed them, made friends with them, but had yet to ride one. The yearning to be in the saddle again was more than he could stand, so he went to the house to change from the old Army boots he wore around the farm into his cowboy boots.

His footlocker had finally arrived a few days ago and not a moment too soon. He was thrilled to have his possessions again. Additionally, the family friend who'd kept his things in storage had sent a few trunks of his belongings and they'd also arrived.

Ten days had passed since Miko's family had been carted off on the train to a location they still had yet to discover and he'd had lunch with Billie. He hadn't gone back to town, but he had telephoned and spoken with Miss Burwell once and Billie three times, assured she was getting better. The day she returned to work, she'd phoned that evening to tell him how the boys in room seven were so excited, it seemed like a party. She'd laughed and said they told her life at the hospital was too boring without her there to liven things up.

It was true.

Billie was such a bright light. One that shone on those around her. A light he hoped to claim for his own.

Zane yanked on his cowboy boots, fastened on his spurs, and grabbed his old Stetson off a hook by the back door. He jogged down the back steps and headed to the barn, wondering where Rock and Miko had disappeared. On a few occasions, they seemed to have completely vanished, but then he'd turn around and they'd be walking toward him, as if they'd been there all along.

Newlyweds, he reasoned, could disappear whenever they liked without justifying their whereabouts.

Zane whistled and Tuffy raced over to him, an always faithful companion. He reached down and gave the dog a playful thump then fed him a few scraps of meat left over from lunch.

The dog gobbled them down and gave him a look that was pure adoration. "Now, if I could get Billie to look at me like that, we'd be in business."

Tuffy woofed in agreement.

Although he hadn't ridden a horse in more than a year, Zane had no trouble saddling the blaze-faced chestnut gelding and leading him out of the barn. When he'd asked Petey the horse's name, he'd told him Ryatt always called the horse Big Red. Not a fancy name, but fitting since the horse stood a little more than seventeen hands high and had a broad chest and rump.

Zane swung into the saddle, one he'd had shipped from Texas, and released a sigh of contentment. This was one of the things he'd dearly missed when he was in the military — the ability to ride whenever the mood struck him.

The creak of the saddle, the smell of leather mingling with that of the horse, were familiar, comforting scents from his childhood.

As he rode away from the barn, he wondered if Billie knew how to ride. Rock had taught Miko, but, as Petey said, she was a natural at it. Then again, he was sure Miko could master anything she set her mind to.

Billie was the same in that respect, yet different, too. She'd grown up without the family support Miko had, but both women were strong and determined.

Zane's thoughts conjured up an image of sitting on a front porch years into the future. He and Rock both had gray in their hair as they laughed together, while Miko and Billie looked on with indulgent smiles.

In the perfect world of his dreams, Billie would agree to marry him, they'd have a long happy life together, and they'd live somewhere close to Rock and Miko so their kids could grow up as friends.

How had he gone from flying planes that dropped bombs on the enemy to wanting to bounce grandkids on his knee?

Zane shook his head, amused with his runaway thoughts. He better slow that train down since the only time he'd even told Billie he loved her was when she was so sick, he didn't think she remembered him saying it.

Their telephone conversations were lighthearted and brief, just enough to make him long to be with her. Before he got down on one knee and proposed, he knew they needed to discuss plans for the future and he sure didn't want to ask that all-important question while he was still wearing his sunglasses.

His eyesight continued to improve, but Zane doubted he'd ever see objects clearly in the distance again. Even if he did regain one hundred percent of his eyesight, he'd never be allowed to fly. That didn't mean he couldn't continue serving his country, though. The months he'd spent training pilots had taught him there were many ways to do his part, even if it wasn't as a pilot.

He rode down a path and along a fence that seemed to encircle the entire hillside. He'd built enough fences during his days on the ranch to know what a laborious project that would have been. The fence seemed to go on for miles and miles. Had Miko's grandfather built it? Her great-grandfather? He'd have to remember to ask her.

Tuffy barked and chased after a bird that darted up in front of them.

Zane grinned and watched the dog run in hopeless pursuit of something he'd never catch.

Was that him chasing after Billie? Would he catch her? Would she let him? Did she want him to? Questions buzzed around in his thoughts like flies at a forgotten picnic until he took a deep breath, and another, in an effort to calm the tumult in his mind.

Tuffy growled and his bark changed, as though something upset him. Zane reined the horse around at the precise moment the loud pop of a rifle echoed off the hill. A scorching burst of pain exploded in his left arm. He didn't have to guess who'd shot him — with unwavering clarity he knew.

"You never were a good shot, Floyd," Zane yelled. His voice carried a hefty measure of disdain and more than a bit of frustration. He glanced at the blood trickling down his arm from where the bullet grazed him, and shook his head. "Before you try to kill me, you might want to listen to what I have to say." He scanned the area, but everything in the distance appeared blurry. His brother didn't need to know that, though. He caught a glimpse of something yellow, and knew it was Tuffy, no doubt sniffing out Floyd.

Zane lifted his right hand and pointed that direction. "Quit hiding behind that tree and come out here."

"Why should I?" Floyd hollered.

"Because if you don't, I'm gonna let that dog tear your throat out. Now get out here and quit skulking around like the yella-bellied coward you are."

Floyd didn't need to know the dog wouldn't bite him, let alone rip into him. Tuffy was about as gentle as they came. Regardless, Zane held onto his bravado, even though his arm stung like the dickens. At least the blood wasn't gushing from the graze. The trickle had even slowed a little.

A figured walked from behind a tree and started his way. Zane rode toward him and whistled once to the dog. Tuffy bounded over to him, panting and wagging his tail.

"Good boy, Tuffy. You're a good boy," Zane said, grinning down at the dog.

"Got yerself a dog, a horse, yer old clothes, and a place to live. Yer hard to keep down, Two-Bit. I'll hand ya that," Floyd said, coming to a stop a dozen yards away. "Thought ya were blind. How'd ya get past that obstacle?"

"A miracle," Zane said. He rode over to his brother, closing the distance. He wanted to be able to see Floyd's face when he imparted an important tidbit of news. He observed his brother, wondering what he'd been doing the last month. Floyd looked horrible, like he'd barely eaten or slept. He smelled like he hadn't had a bath since the last time he'd spoken to him.

"What happened to you?" Zane asked, shifting slightly to get a better look at his brother.

"Being on the run isn't as easy as you might think," Floyd said, leaning against his rifle.

Zane wondered if the dunce would accidentally shoot his arm off or blow a hole through his head. With Floyd, either outcome was a distinct possibility.

"That's a choice you made, like choosing to have a slimy, scum-sucking quack try to kill me. Honestly, Floyd? I thought you were better than that."

"Spit out what ya want to say or I'll shoot ya right now." Floyd started to lift the rifle.

Zane knew his brother wouldn't shoot him, at least not face to face. He might shoot him in the back, but not when he was watching him.

"What do ya want to tell me?" Floyd asked in a whiny tone that set Zane's teeth on edge.

"Put that gun back down." Zane ordered.

When Floyd complied, he gave him a long, studying glance that made his brother squirm.

"What I wanted to tell you is that I had a will drawn up and sent to Dad's attorney. A copy of it is also with my military information. The will says if I die, my half of the ranch goes jointly to Rock and his wife. So you can shoot me if you want, but the ranch still won't be yours. And if you kill them, too, it's going to look mighty suspicious. In fact, we let the local sheriff know to keep an eye out for you and dad's attorney will turn you in if he hears I've died."

The color drained from Floyd's face. The man looked deflated and defeated. A string of curses that would have made the most seasoned sailor blush rolled out of his brother's mouth until Zane scowled at him.

"Enough," Zane said authoritatively. He'd always felt like the older brother, the responsible brother, when he was growing up, and nothing had changed. Floyd was a sniveling idiot who'd never learned a single useful lesson.

"The way I see it, you have three options, Floyd. The first option is to go on a killing spree that I guarantee will land you in jail and the ranch still won't be yours. The second option is to buy me out. I'll sell you my half of the ranch at a rock-bottom price just to be rid of you. The third option is to sell your half of the ranch to me. Since I know how far you are in debt, that you have no hands to do the work, cattle-rustlers pilfering the herd a few head at a time, and the place has gone to wrack and ruin, I figure it's not worth much." Zane quoted a number so low it set Floyd into cussing again.

Zane tossed him an impatient glare. "What's it gonna be, Floyd? You gonna sell it or buy, because killing isn't an option."

"Even if I spend the rest of my life rottin' in a filthy jail cell, it might be worth it just to shoot that smirk off yer face." Floyd glowered at him then sighed, resigned. "I'll buy your half of the ranch. You'll sign the deed and I'll never have to see you again?"

Zane nodded. "I'll sign the deed and you'll never see me again, on two conditions."

"And they are?" Floyd asked, clearly annoyed.

"You'll never, ever come looking for me again. I don't care what kind of notice the military sends you, or what kind of catastrophe has happened. I don't ever want to see your face again, unless you're truly sorry for what you've done and are ready to make amends."

"That ain't ever gonna happen, Two-Bit. Ya'd be cold in the ground if things had gone the way I planned."

Zane ignored the comment and continued. "The second condition is simply that when you decide to sell the ranch, which I'm certain you will, at least find someone to buy it who'll appreciate all the blood, sweat and tears our family poured into making it successful. Mama and Daddy are buried there, after all."

Floyd started to say something, pressed his thin lips together, and nodded once. "I'll head back to Texas today. I'll have to sell some things to get yer money together. Ya should have it within a few weeks."

"As soon as I do, I'll sign the deed and send it to Dad's attorney. Fair enough?"

Floyd nodded. "Fair enough."

Zane leaned over and held out his hand. "Give me the rifle before you hurt someone or, more likely, yourself with it."

Floyd's gaze narrowed, but he handed Zane the gun.

Zane removed the remaining shells from the chamber and tucked them in his pocket. "And the pistol." He waggled his fingers at his brother.

With a huff of irritation, Floyd handed him a pistol he had tucked in the back waistband of his pants. "How'd you even know that was there?"

Zane smirked. "Because I know you, Floyd. Now get out of here."

"Can I get a ride into town?"

"No, you can't. You got yourself out here and you can get yourself back. Go." Zane kept an impassive expression on his face as Floyd tossed one last sneer his way and stomped out to the road then started walking toward the main road that would take him into town.

Zane watched until Floyd's blurry form disappeared in the distance before he started riding toward the house. Tuffy trotted along beside him. Zane wondered if the dog would like to learn to ride on the saddle with him. He might train him to jump up there for fun.

They were almost back to the house when he heard Rock calling for him.

"Come on, Big Red," he said, urging the horse into a gallop. He rode down the path and almost over Rock before he tugged on the reins and pulled the horse to stop. "Are you trying to get your dang self killed?"

Rock stared at him. "I could ask you the same question. You think it's a good idea for you to be riding when you can't see in the distance?" His friend noticed the guns he carried and the blood from his wound. "Why are you armed to the teeth and dripping blood all down your arm?"

"Floyd paid a social call," Zane said, riding the horse over to the barn.

Before he could respond, Miko and Billie raced out of the house, running toward them.

"You've been shot! What on earth happened?" Billie asked, placing a hand on his leg as he stopped in front of the barn.

He handed Rock the rifle and pistol, and then swung out of the saddle, spurs jingling. With a rakish grin, he tipped his hat back and turned to Billie. "My brother dropped in for a visit."

Billie grabbed the rifle from Rock and looked at Zane. "Where is he? I'll return the favor."

Zane laughed and took the gun away from her. "He won't be coming back. He promised to stay in Texas from now on." He handed the gun to Rock again and pulled Billie into his arms. Despite Rock and Miko's presence, the fact his arm burned like Lucifer had licked it with his fiery tongue, and the lightheaded state that threatened to bring him to his knees, he lifted Billie off her feet and kissed her the way he'd wanted to kiss her since the moment he'd left back in May.

"Zane, your arm. We need to go inside so I can take a look at it," Billie said when he finally let her up for air. "You shouldn't…"

"Wait another second to kiss you again, Billie, girl. I heartily agree." He planted another sizzling kiss on her lips while Rock laughed and Miko led Big Red into the barn.

"I sure do love you, beautiful Billie," he whispered in her ear, then kissed her once again.

✦✦★ *Chapter Twenty-Six* ★✦✦

Since the day Zane had climbed into her room when she was sick, something had changed in Billie's relationship with Miss Burwell. The woman had been softer, kinder, and far less quick to judge. In fact, Miss Burwell confided she'd known Zane had climbed in Billie's window back in May, too.

"Why do you think I stood out in the yard until he left, Billie? I didn't want the lovesick fool to break his neck climbing down the tree in the dark."

Billie had laughed and given Miss Burwell a hug, thanking her for not kicking her out even when she'd broken the rules.

"Well, it doesn't count because you didn't know he was going to do such an idiotic, entirely romantic thing as climb in your window — twice." Miss Burwell had clasped her hands beneath her chin and sighed dreamily. "Oh, how marvelous it must be for a man like your Captain West to pursue you, to be determined to win your heart. You are a very fortunate young lady, Billie."

"Yes, ma'am, I am."

With her heart warm and full, Billie thought of how Miss Burwell had become like a grandmother to her recently. When Billie stopped looking at her as a nosy, annoying burden, she realized Miss Burwell was really just lonesome and needed to feel useful and appreciated. Wasn't that what everyone needed and deserved?

Hastily tugging on the beautiful burgundy sweater Miss Burwell had given her for her birthday, Billie settled a dark wool hat edged in burgundy velvet on her curls, and picked up the bamboo handbag Zane had sent to her for her birthday.

In a rush to get out the door before Zane arrived to pick her up, she clattered down the stairs and nearly ran into Miss Burwell.

"Are you off to spend the day with Captain West?" Miss Burwell asked. She gave Billie a pleased look as she noticed she wore the sweater she'd made.

"Yes, ma'am," Billie said, smiling at the woman. "It's such a lovely day. He mentioned something about a picnic."

"Won't that be wonderful, dear? It should be quite spectacular with the leaves all changing colors, and the afternoons still warm. I don't know when I've seen such a mild October."

"It has been an unusual autumn," Billie said, thinking that statement applied to far more than the weather. So much had happened since the day Zane had ridden up to the yard at Rock and Miko's place, toting guns and bleeding from a wound his brother inflicted.

Billie had been so enthralled with the way Zane looked in his hat, boots, and spurs, she could hardly think straight. After he'd kissed her senseless, not once, but multiple times, she'd barely been able to cleanse the wound and treat it.

She thought of the many moments they'd spent together since then. Zane had been teaching her to ride. She'd learned to drive a car. And they'd grown unbelievably close as their love gained a depth and richness that seemed impossible to fathom or describe.

Together, they'd shared their dreams and made plans for the future.

As much as she hated the idea, Zane would return to duty after Christmas. He'd be stationed at Pendleton Air Field where he would train new pilots. While she wanted him to stay by her side and never leave, she understood his need to serve his country. At least he'd be close enough to visit when he had a long weekend off.

She'd made peace with the fact he was a soldier. Zane would never willingly walk away from what he saw as his duty, especially not in the midst of a war. All she could do was love him, support him, and never stop praying for him.

However, in the past weeks, with his return to duty looming ahead of them, she'd expected him to propose, but he hadn't. It was as though he hesitated to ask her to commit to a soldier, knowing how she'd fought against it when they'd first met.

But those days were behind her. She loved Zane completely and that meant loving him as a soldier, too, not just when it was convenient or easy.

Yet, she found Zane so easy to love, with his teasing, dimpled grins and fun-loving manner. Zane was funny, gentle and kind, but also a fierce protector when she needed one. And he was handsome. So incredibly good-looking in a rugged, heart-melting way. As snappy as he looked in his uniform, Billie best liked seeing him in his jeans and boots with his Stetson tipped back on his head as he rode one of the horses around Rock and Miko's farm.

She could get lost in his eyes and those kissable lips of his were often in her thoughts. The boys in room seven had teased her about daydreaming of him more than a few times in recent weeks. In truth, Billie had been trying to think of a way to take some of the men out to the farm. The outing would do them good along with the fresh air. But then she worried about how they would react to Miko and changed her mind.

Poor Miko. She and Rock had finally received a letter from her parents letting them know they were in an internment camp near Jerome, Idaho. Billie had to find a map to see where it was located. Weekly, Miko and Rock sent boxes of food and supplies to her family. Zane and Billie had asked for names of other families that could use help and sent boxes to them, hoping it would make a difference.

Billie was so proud of how far Zane had come, both mentally and physically. He still wore his sunglasses outside and perhaps he always would, but he could see well enough to drive a car, and that had given him such a feeling of freedom. Doctor Ridley had sent Zane to an eye specialist who ordered prescription glasses for Zane. Billie hoped when they arrived, they'd help him see distances with greater clarity.

When she'd first met Zane back in May, she couldn't imagine how much her life would change because of him. But it had. Her life was far richer and fuller, filled with such unconditional love. Just thinking about Zane made her smile.

The only cloud in her sky was the uncertainty of their future. Billie was coming to understand, though, that life was uncertain and no one could predict what tomorrow might bring. All they had was today, this moment, and she was learning to fully live in it and enjoy it while she could.

And that's what she intended to do with Zane today on their picnic. Enjoy each moment as it came and not worry about tomorrow.

Billie opened the door and she and Miss Burwell stepped outside onto the porch. They watched as Zane pulled up and parked out front in a convertible with gleaming chrome.

"What a gorgeous car," Miss Burwell said. "That color almost matches your sweater."

Billie glanced down at her sweater then gave her landlady a warm hug. "It does. Thank you, again, for making it for me. I love it."

"I'm glad, dear. Now, go have a splendid day with your young man." Miss Burwell gave her a little nudge forward as Zane ran around the car and jogged up the walk.

"Howdy, Miss Burwell. How are you?" he asked politely.

"Excellent, Captain West. And yourself?"

"Fit as a fiddle," he said, giving her a grin as he held out his arm to Billie. "Ready to skedaddle,

Billie, girl?"

"I believe I am, Zane."

Zane tipped his hat to Miss Burwell then escorted Billie out to the car, settling her on the passenger side of the seat before he hurried around and slid behind the wheel. He waved once at Miss Burwell before turning around and heading up the street.

Billie was glad she'd used an extra pin to hold on her hat as the wind blew around them. The air was crisp and fresh, but not too cool — perfect for an incredible autumn day.

She turned her head and studied Zane. He looked particularly handsome in a pale blue shirt that matched his eyes and his cowboy hat on his head.

"Hiya, doll," he said, stopping at a stop sign and leaning over to kiss her cheek. "You look amazing, as always. Is that a new sweater?"

"Miss Burwell made it for my birthday," she said rubbing the soft yarn along the cuff of her sleeve.

"I noticed you've got your birthday bag I sent." He gave her a rascally grin. "And you've got your birthday suit. Don't suppose you'd show it off to me later, would you?"

"Zane West! What a thing to say! You very well know it's just not proper," she fussed at him, although she was secretly amused. "And no, I won't be showing it off to you later. What has gotten into you today?"

"A fantastic autumn day with a gorgeous girl, I suppose," he said, smiling at her.

Billie ran her hand over the smooth leather seat between them. "How'd you talk Miko into letting you borrow her car?"

"She offered to let me take it when I told her my plans for the day."

"That was kind of her. How's she doing?" Billie asked.

"As well as she can. It's been rough on her knowing her family is stuck in the internment camp and no one can say for how long. She got a letter from her sister, letting her know where they were relocated and that they're doing as well as they can. I just feel so bad for them all." Zane sighed. "I couldn't have been more wrong, Billie. Those people are just like us. Patriotic. Good people. American people. They've lost so much for no good reason."

She nodded. "It's a tragedy, for certain."

Zane's hand settled over hers and he brought it to his lips. "Let's not think of unhappy things today. We'll pretend, just for today, there's no war. No sadness. Nothing but glorious sunshine and good food."

"Good food?" She glanced behind her but the backseat was empty. "Where's this good food of which you speak?"

Zane chuckled. "Patience, beautiful Billie. Patience."

The banter between them was light and playful as Zane drove out toward Rock and Miko's place. He told her about going to visit Mrs. Wilkerson and her granddaughter, the women who'd given him a ride to the hospital on the day he'd met Billie.

She smiled as he described playing with Mrs. Matthews' baby boy. Much to her surprise, he didn't slow down and turn to go to Rock and Miko's place, but drove past the Phillips' place then turned onto a side road.

"Where are you going, Zane?" Billie asked, curious when he turned off the road and pulled onto a lane lined with apple trees that had already been harvested. He topped the hill and Billie gasped, gaping at the farmhouse of her dreams. The one she'd always longed to have. It was as though Zane had peered into the corners of her mind and found the exact place she'd fantasized of calling her own. She recalled driving past the place when he was trying to teach her to drive, but never imagined it would feel so much like home.

"Zane?" she asked again, excited yet confused by his continued silence.

He kissed her fingers then parked the car in front of the house. The house she'd seen hundreds of times when she'd closed her eyes and envisioned the place she hoped to one day call home. A welcoming porch, surrounded by fall flowers, looked exactly as she knew it would.

When Tuffy loped around the corner of the house and barked in greeting, she laughed and hopped out of the car, bending over to pet the dog.

"What are we doing here?" She looked up at Zane as he stepped beside her and wrapped an arm around her shoulders.

He grinned and nudged her away from the house. "I told you. Having a picnic."

Together, they strolled past a barn, corral, and

several outbuildings, following a path strewn with leaves from the apple trees. They walked up a gently sloping hill. At the top, someone had left a faded quilt with a picnic basket holding down one corner. Tuffy raced around them, chasing leaves as they drifted from the trees.

"Oh, Zane," Billie turned and gazed at the view below them — at the house and barn, the trees in the distance, and the hope and possibilities bubbling around her. "It's perfect!"

"What's perfect? The place? The picnic? An afternoon with a handsome and dashing cowboy soldier who adores you?"

"All of it," she said with a laugh, throwing her arms around him and giving him a tight hug.

"Settle down there, Billie, girl. Let's eat our lunch, then you can flit around like a hummingbird full of fermented flowers if you want."

"I'm not a drunken bird, I'll have you know," she said, taking the hand he offered and sitting on the blanket.

"Oh, I'm well aware of what you are, Billie Brighton, but before I let that distract me, let's eat." He opened the picnic basket and removed a feast.

"Did Miko make this?" Billie asked as she bit into a piece of crispy fried chicken.

"She did make the food and Rock brought it out here for me," Zane said, taking another piece of chicken. He tossed a piece of meat to the dog. "I assume Tuffy followed him over."

When they'd eaten the delicious meal, Billie removed her hat and leaned back, letting the sun warm her face. "It's so peaceful here and the air smells so good. Like apples and autumn and home."

"What does home smell like?" Zane asked, haphazardly stuffing the leftovers back in the basket then scooting close to her.

She turned her face toward his and smiled. "You."

Zane made a sound low in his throat, something between a groan and a growl. In a blink, his arms were around her and he was kissing her so passionately, so thoroughly, Billie could think of nothing beyond how much she loved him, needed him, cherished him.

"I love you, Zane," she whispered, pressing her face against his neck and breathing in his scent, letting it fill her nose and heart. This was the smell of home. Zane. Purely Zane.

"I love you, too, more than I ever dreamed I'd love anyone." Zane hugged her tightly before he hopped to his feet and pulled her up with him.

Hand in hand, they walked along the ridge of the hill and he pointed to the house below. "This is the place where Petey's friend Ryatt lived before his folks died. Come to find out Ryatt's aunt is married to Klayne Campbell."

"Really?" Billie asked, surprised by the news. "How about that?"

Zane nodded and moved behind her, wrapping his arms around her waist and pulling her back against him. "Mrs. Campbell wants to sell this place and gave me a price I can afford. What do you think, Billie? Is this the farm you always dreamed of? The place you pictured as your home?"

She turned to him, tears in her eyes, and smiled. "Truthfully, Zane, it's exactly how I pictured the home of my dreams, but I realized something today. The home I've always wanted isn't a building. It isn't a place." She reached up and bracketed his face with her hands. "It's you. You're the dream of my heart, Zane West. You're what I've spent my lifetime longing for. Home is the love I hold in my heart for you. The love you've given me in return."

Zane picked her up and kissed her tenderly, yet with an urgency that she completely understood. "I love you so much, Billie, and if you think you could make this place into our little haven against the world, it's ours."

"Ours?" she asked, leaning back to better look at him.

"Oh, take the deuce, but I'm about bungling this badly," he said, setting her back on her feet. He removed his sunglasses, took something from his pocket and dropped to one knee. "Billie Adaleen Brighton, I fell in love with you the first time I saw you at the hospital and if I live to be a hundred, I'll love you still. In fact, I predict our love will grow and deepen each day we're together. I can't picture my future without you in it, by my side. I know things aren't gonna be easy with the war and our responsibilities, but would you do me the great honor of marrying me? Would you be my bride and make me the happiest man who ever lived?"

"Of course I'll marry you," she said, not waiting for him to stand. She threw her arms around him and they tumbled to the soft grass on the hilltop.

Zane laughed and rolled over, leaning on one elbow above her. He took her left hand in his and slipped a silver band adorned with emeralds and pearls onto her ring finger. "The ring belonged to my grandma. It just seemed perfect for you, with those beautiful green eyes of yours." He kissed her again, reverently, softly, with a promise for the future.

His forehead touched hers and he kissed her nose. "I do love you so, Billie, girl, with all my heart."

"And I love you, Zane. With all my love today, and with all my tomorrows."

*** ★ *Epilogue* ★ ***

April 1946

"The apple trees are sure full of blooms this year," Zane said as he and Billie strolled through their orchard on a warm spring day.

Billie squeezed his arm and tipped her face up to the sweet, pink blossoms overhead. "I love how pretty the orchard looks. This is the first time since you bought the place that we've been able to watch the orchard come to life after winter."

"But it won't be the last. By next year, we'll have a herd of fat cattle grazing in the pasture and a few more horses to go with the two already in the barn." He smiled at her. "I'm glad we purchased the farm when I proposed to you. Even if we rented it out these last few years, it sure gave me something to look forward to coming home to, besides you."

Billie scowled at him. "I should hope I made the list of things you wanted to come home to, Zane West. Why else did you talk me into marrying you a week after you proposed?"

Zane laughed and swung her into his arms, lifting her so her mouth lingered just inches from his. "I talked you into marrying me on that fine

October afternoon because I couldn't stand to live another day without you as my wife, Billie, girl. Don't you know by now how much I love you?"

"I do, cowboy, but I don't mind if you want to tell me again. A wife likes to hear these things once in a great while." She offered him a coy smile as she removed his cowboy hat and settled it on her head. Her fingers toyed with the thick hair at the back of his neck.

"Billie, I swear, some days I ought to just paint your back porch red. There probably isn't a woman alive who gets told 'I love you' more times a day than you do."

She giggled and he gave her a quick kiss, then tossed her over his shoulder, drawing out a squeal when he playfully swatted her bottom.

"Zane, you stop that right now!" she protested, smacking his jean-clad backside with his dusty Stetson as she dangled across his shoulder like a sack of feed.

He shifted, taking her in his arms like a new bride, and walked beneath the trees, lavishing kisses on her with each step. When he reached the top of the hill where they could look down on the house and barn, he stopped and kissed her so thoroughly Billie's toes tingled.

"Now that's what I mean by telling me how much you care," she whispered against his lips.

Zane pulled back, his smoldering blue gaze fusing to hers. "I do love you, beautiful Billie, more than anything in the world. I'm just so grateful we can put all the trials and tribulations of the war behind us and focus on building a wonderful life together."

"Together. I love the sound of that, Zane." She kissed the dimple in his right cheek then trailed kisses along his jaw to his ear. "Know what else I love?" she asked on a whisper.

"I have an idea, but tell me anyway."

"You, Zane. I love you with all my heart."

His lips captured hers in a sizzling kiss. Even after three and a half years of marriage, albeit most of it spent apart, a look from Zane could make her heart race and his kisses could make her melt faster than ice cream left in the summer sun.

Billie thought of the long, hard days she worked at the hospital while Zane was stationed in Pendleton. They were blessed, compared to many couples who spent years apart during the war. Zane managed to come home two or three times a year, and she went to Pendleton several times. Once, she took along Petey Phillips so he could visit his friend Ryatt on the ranch where he lived with Klayne and Delaney Campbell. Through Zane's time in Pendleton, they'd both become good friends with the couple. Zane had spent many happy hours at Sage Hills Ranch riding and roping, and enjoying the occasional home-cooked meal.

Zane hadn't returned to the warfront, but he'd done his part, training new pilots and developing ideas to help them fly and fight more effectively. Although his eyesight never fully returned, he managed well with glasses and a positive attitude.

The months and distance that separated them only deepened her love for Zane. Now that he was home to stay, she planned to be beside him each and every day.

"There are two things I need to tell you," she said, pulling back when he leaned in for another kiss.

He gave her a boyish, pouting look that threatened to throw her off track, but she continued. "Behave, husband of mine, for a minute or two."

"Go ahead. What do I need to know?" he asked, carrying her beneath the shade of a big oak tree. He sat down with her settled across his lap. Tuffy, their ever-faithful dog, ran over and plopped down beside them, tongue lolling out the side of his mouth and tail fanning the grass.

Billie grinned at the canine then looked back at her handsome, wonderful husband. "The first thing is that I spoke to Doctor Ridley and let him know he'll need to find a replacement for me beginning in June. I figured six weeks should provide ample time for him to find someone to do my job."

"I know you love nursing, Billie. You don't have to give it up if you don't want to," Zane said, taking his hat from her and tossing it on the grass by the dog. He ran a hand through her golden curls and smiled at her. "You know I'd love it if you were here all the time, but if you want to keep working, I'll somehow survive."

"That's a half-hearted encouragement if I ever heard one." Her tone held a hint of amusement as she scowled at him. Unable to hold back, she broke into a smile. "But I'm glad to know you miss me when I'm at work. However, it's time for me to quit and stay home, with you."

"I'm mighty glad to hear that, Billie, girl."

Zane nuzzled her neck.

She pushed back and gave him a stern look. "Don't go distracting me until I tell you the next part."

"Go on," he said, picking up her hand and pressing a trail of hot kisses across her palm and wrist, creating a molten fire in her midsection.

She did her best to ignore it and continued. "I have a special anniversary present planned for you this year, but I wanted to tell you about it now."

He lifted his head and gave her a curious glance. "Oh?"

"Yes. This year, you see, I'll be giving you that little cowpoke you've mentioned you'd like to have, although it could be a princess instead."

Zane whooped and the dog jumped up, barking excitedly, although the confused canine had no idea why.

"A baby? We're gonna have a baby?" Zane asked. He pressed a hand to her stomach while he rained kisses across her face. "Imagine that! I'm gonna be a daddy. Wait 'til Rock and Miko hear about it. A baby of our own!"

Billie laughed, wrapping her arms around him. "Yes, Zane, a baby of our own."

He hugged her close and pressed his cheek to hers. "I love you so much, Billie. Life with you is better than anything I've ever dreamed."

"You are, and shall always be, the dream of my heart, Zane. And now our baby will be, too. Thank you for loving me, for giving me a life far more beautiful than my dreams."

⋆⋆★ *Recipe* ★★⋆⋆

While I was writing this book, I looked through a Victory cookbook from the 1940s Captain Cavedweller's grandmother had passed along to me years ago and happened upon this recipe. Back in my teen years, when I was the unofficial cookie baker at home, I used to make a bar cookie quite similar to this that we enjoyed.

What I especially liked about this recipe were the fun little notes beside it in the cookbook. One offered tips for packing cookies to ship to soldiers. There was also a tip titled "How our boys enjoy cookies from home!" It said men serving in the military enjoy "cookies fragrant with spices, cookies rich with chocolate, nuts or fruits!" A third hint said, "service men 'go for' this rich cookie bar. Packs well, too."

I could just picture Zane and Bud enjoying this treat with a cup of coffee or a glass of milk.

Canteen Cookie Bars
½ cup butter, softened
1 ½ cups brown sugar, firmly packed
1 cup all-purpose flour, plus 2 tablespoons
1 teaspoon vanilla
2 eggs beaten
½ teaspoon baking powder
1 ½ cups sweetened shredded coconut
1 cup nuts, chopped

Preheat oven to 350 degrees F.
Cream butter. Add ½ cup of brown sugar and

mix. Stir in 1 cup of flour until blended. Grease (or coat with non-stick spray) a 7x11-inch baking pan and press mixture into the pan. Bake for 10 minutes, until set.

While it bakes, blend the remaining brown sugar with vanilla and eggs, beating until thick and foamy. Add remaining flour, baking powder, coconut and nuts, then blend. Spread over baked mixture and return to oven and bake 20 minutes.

Remove from oven and cool, then cut into bars.

✶✶★ *Author's Note* ★✶✶✶

When I wrote *Garden of Her Heart* and incorporated a feisty little nurse named Billie Brighton, one of the characters Rock met at the hospital, I knew she needed to have her own story. The dilemma was in figuring out what her story would be. Would she travel overseas in the Nurse's Corp or stay stateside at the veteran's hospital? And who would be a good match for such a strong, yet fun and delightful girl?

Then I realized another character from that book, the hero's best friend, would be perfect for Billie. I just had to figure out how a cowboy from Texas would end up meeting Billie. Finding a way to place Zane and Billie together happened to be quite fun for me. I hope it was fun for you, too, to read the story that took them to their happily-ever-after.

Zane West is a pilot, like Rock was from *Garden of Her Heart*. Except Zane is stationed in the Pacific, having survived Pearl Harbor. When I was reading through historical accounts of which military groups were stationed there, I happened upon information about the 11th Bombardment Group. Activated in Hawaii in early 1940, the bomber group became part of the Seventh Air Force after the attack on Pearl Harbor. During the dark days following Dec. 7, 1941, the 11th carried out patrol and search missions off Hawaii, flying B-17 airplanes, also known as the Flying Fortress.

Captain Cavedweller and I were fortunate enough to tour through a B-17 at the Evergreen

Aviation and Space Museum in McMinville, Oregon. It's a place I highly recommend visiting if you enjoy history, particularly history tied to aeronautics.

After crawling into the plane and seeing the tight, uncomfortable places (especially the belly gunner's turret on the bottom of the plane) these men rode in for hours and hours on end, it gave me a whole new level of admiration for what they endured. Our tour guide told us when the bombs got stuck and wouldn't drop out of the plane (which apparently happened with more frequency than you'd like to think), one of the men would jump up and down on the bombs until they dropped. My stomach flipped over just thinking about those young men stomping on the bombs, trying to shake them loose and the very real possibility of them falling thousands of feet out of the plane along with the bombs.

Anyway, in the story Zane is part of a bombardment squadron that flies B-17s. I used the 26th Bombardment Squadron, part of the 11th Bombardment Group, as inspiration for Zane's unit. Veterans of the Battle of Midway, they were transferred in July 1942 to New Hebrides.

Many of the details included about the conditions on the islands in the South Pacific came from accounts I read, right down to high-ranking officers helping with a bucket brigade of fuel during a rainstorm!

I think it's important to mention the Marston mat used in the story. The mat was first used at Camp Mackall Airfield, near Marston, North

Carolina, and got its name from the town. The mat was a simple piece of technology that provided a great contribution toward America's war efforts. In a short time, an entire airstrip or road could be in place, made entirely out of Marston mats.

The key to victory in the Pacific was the ability to build functioning airfields on newly-captured territory as quickly as possible. The Marston mat was basically perforated steel planks capable of being locked together at the edges. The perforations reduced the weight of the planks, offered improved traction for tires, and permitted drainage which was necessary in the tropical islands. The mat was generally laid over crushed rock or coral, but in a pinch, was tossed out over what was available. Reportedly, the Marston mat runway at Guadalcanal, which frequently received damage from five-hundred pound bombs dropped by the Japanese, could be repaired in less than an hour. Trucks loaded with sand and gravel were concealed near the runway along with foxholes for repair crews and premeasured packages of Marston mat. Once a bomb detonated and destroyed a section of mat, it could be removed, new gravel dumped into the crater, packed down with pneumatic hammers, and a replacement mat set, leaving behind no evidence of where it had been hit.

As I was digging through research, I happened to notice a mention of cattle rustling being a problem during the war. I'd never given it a thought, but I could see how, with meat rationed, people would turn to stealing beef and selling it through illegal means. One account said rustlers would come in, steal a dozen head of cattle, have it butchered and delivered before anyone noticed the cattle were missing.

Another tidbit of war history comes from the milkweed floss found in the plant's pods. In the early twentieth century, the typical filler for life preservers was a material called "kapok." Cultivated from the rainforests of Asia, kapok was a cottony fiber extracted from the pods of the ceiba tree. America's primary source for this material was the Dutch East Indies (present-day Indonesia).

Then, in 1937, came Japan's invasion of China, which initiated World War II in the Pacific. By the time the U.S. entered the war four years later, access to Asian kapok had been effectively cut off. A replacement for this critical material was needed to protect airmen and seamen from drowning and it was discovered milkweed floss served as a substitute fiber. Many states, and even parts of Canada, participated in a campaign to gather milkweed floss which served as a replacement for the no longer available kapok.

The slogan "Two bags save one life" summed up the main mission of collecting milkweed pods. The floss harvested from two bags of milkweed pods would fill one life jacket. Milkweed floss was also used to line flight suits.

Although most of the collection of pods took place in eastern states, I decided it was something perfect for Petey Phillips to do.

I started the story with Zane traveling on a train past a beautiful waterfall because I could just so clearly picture the way he might have looked at it with awe. Multnomah Falls is the inspiration for the waterfall. If you've never seen it and ever find yourself in Portland, it truly is gorgeous and worth the trip out of town to take a look. As for the legends Mrs. Wilkerson shared in the story, they were two I actually found when I searched online. I agree with Zane and Mrs. Wilkerson, though — I much prefer the romantic version than the sad story.

The mention of Zane and his brother finding a mammoth bone was inspired by a bone my dad found on our farm when I was quite young. He ended up with his photo in the newspaper for the discovery and that mention is a little nod to my dad that I remembered him finding that bone.

Have you ever thought about how potato chips were packaged before they came in such handy, disposable bags? I hadn't either until I wrote in the picnic scene where Zane set out bottles of Coca-Cola, sandwiches and chips. First, I had to confirm chips were not only in production then, but readily available. Then I had to figure out how they were packaged. I found several fun photos of potato chip tins from the 1940s.

The slang tossed around in the story is fun to write and largely comes from lists of slang popular back in the day. In this story, I think one of my favorites was the men teasing Zane about getting a "sugar report," also known as a letter from his girl.

While I'm on the subject of letters, I had no idea about V-mail until I began writing this story. What an innovative thing it was! People could use special forms, mail a letter and that letter would then be photographed and the canisters sent to the appropriate areas where the film was developed, printed and delivered — all in a few short weeks.

When I was trying to decide if Billie would remain at the veteran's hospital or join the Nurse's Corp, I have to tell you… some of the stories I read about the nurses who served during World War II just filled me with so much admiration for what these women did. Many, many of them went far and above the call of duty in their service to their country and the soldiers in their care.

One day, while I was looking through images of Japanese internment camps, I happened upon a photo of a little boy sitting on the ground, a comic book beneath his legs and an identification tag attached to his shirt. Another image showed a little girl proudly waving a little American flag. Talk about a lump in your throat. I combined the two images into one for the purposes of the story, but the raw emotion of what those children endured is incredibly real.

I couldn't write this story without somehow incorporating a little about the characters from _Home of Her Heart_ in it, so it worked well to share about Klayne's time spent in the hospital recuperating under Billie's care. In _Home of Her Heart_, that part of the story is mostly bypassed, so it was good to bring that back around to show Klayne from Billie's perspective — bushy beard, wild hair and all! Can't you just picture Zane hanging out at Sage Hills Ranch, riding and chasing cattle when he had a day off from his work at the airfield? And I loved being able to give Petey a visit to see Ryatt and the ranch.

As always, dear reader, I so appreciate you going on this adventure with me. I hope you've enjoyed another journey back to the days of World War II and reading about the good hearts that helped win the war.

Thank you for reading ***Dream of Her Heart***. I hope you enjoyed Zane and Billie's story. I'd be so appreciative if you'd share a *review* so other readers might discover the heart and history shared in this series. Even a line or two is appreciated more than you can know.

Read the rest of the books in the
Hearts of the War series today!

Also, if you haven't yet signed up for my newsletter, won't you consider subscribing? I send it out a few times a month, when I have new releases, sales, or news of freebies to share. Each month, you can enter a contest, get a new recipe to try, and discover news about upcoming events. When you sign up, you'll receive a free short and sweet historical romance. Don't wait. Sign up today!

And if newsletters aren't your thing, please follow me on BookBub. You'll receive notifications on pre-orders, new releases, and sale books!

About the Author

Hopeless romantic Shanna Hatfield spent ten years as a newspaper journalist before moving into the field of marketing and public relations. Sharing the romantic stories she dreams up in her head is a perfect outlet for her love of writing, reading, and creativity. She and her husband, lovingly referred to as Captain Cavedweller, reside in the Pacific Northwest.

Shanna loves to hear from readers.
Connect with her online:
Blog: shannahatfield.com
Facebook: Shanna Hatfield's Page
Shanna Hatfield's Hopeless Romantics Group
Pinterest: Shanna Hatfield
Email: shanna@shannahatfield.com
Check out the *Dream of Her Heart* Pinterest board to see the images that helped inspire the story!

89793915R00234

Made in the USA
San Bernardino, CA
01 October 2018